T0149329

TWO-FINGERS and the WHITE GUY

The Search Continues

Charles Still Waters

authorHOUSE®

AuthorHouse™
1663 Liberty Drive
Bloomington, IN 47403
www.authorhouse.com
Phone: 1 (800) 839-8640

Published by AuthorHouse 05/06/2016

ISBN: 978-1-5049-8587-1 (sc)
ISBN: 978-1-5246-0055-6 (hc)
ISBN: 978-1-5049-8588-8 (e)

Library of Congress Control Number: 2016904473

Print information available on the last page.

This book is printed on acid-free paper.

I am dedicating this book to all my Blackfeet friends that are dead and buried and to those who are still standing. This book is intended to honor all the Blackfeet who have overcome the ravages of the Federal Government and its Indian Policy. To the living and the dead, I respect your courage and strength and thank you for your friendship. As a young boy growing up on the Rez in the 1960's and 1970's, I witnessed and experienced things that have had a profound effect on me and this book is intended to give thanks.

My sense of humor is a direct result of all of our times together, I have never met a group of people that laugh more and I thank you for the laughter. We live in a time where people are not laughing and we must bring humor back into our lives and quit being so serious about things we have no control over.

Since we have become a nation of disclaimers here is a disclaimer for you:

"This is a work of fiction; names, characters, places and incidents are products of my imagination and any resemblance to actual events, or persons living or dead, is entirely coincidental and if that is not good enough for you, sue me."

"I woke up one morning and realized the whole thing was just a figment of my imagination."

White Guy

Preface

The Blackfeet Indians reigned supreme over the Northern Plains for centuries, they were referred to as the, "Lords of the Plains." They were the strongest, meanest and the most feared Tribe in a land filled with mean and strong Indian Tribes. Their traditional enemies feared them more than the Grizzly Bear and the Mountain Lion. They were the baddest of the bad. In short, the Blackfeet were Warriors and masters of their own destiny long before there was a United States of America.

The name "Blackfeet" originated from the distinctive black color of their moccasins; moccasins that turned black from dancing in the ashes of campfires. They are not naturally, "black footed."

At one time, the Blackfeet domain included parts of the areas now known as Montana, North Dakota, Minnesota, Alberta, Saskatchewan, Manitoba and Ontario. It stretched from the Great Lakes all the way west to the Rocky Mountains.

The Blackfeet were nomadic meat eaters who traveled in search of game. They ate a lot of buffalo, deer and elk meat. Before they had guns and horses, the Blackfeet would hunt on foot with bows and arrows. They also ate berries and vegetables and would only eat fish as a last resort.

The Blackfeet Nation was made up of three large distinct bands: the Northern Piegan, the Kainah and the Southern Piegan. During the summer, the Blackfeet lived together in large Tribal camps. It was during this season that they hunted buffalo and engaged in traditional dances and other ceremonial endeavors. Competition was fierce among the bands to see who was the strongest, fastest and smartest. Contests of manhood were engaged in to determine who was going to lead and who was going to follow. Leaders were chosen based on what they could do for the community at large and any leader that did not deliver on community needs was swiftly replaced and banished from the Tribe.

When the bands congregated in the summer, they formed distinct camps which were separated by a stream or some other natural boundary. When the Southern Piegan, Blood, and Northern Piegan joined together for ceremonial purposes, each band camped in a circle. During late fall or early winter, they would go their separate ways and forage for food in traditional hunting areas. Generally, they separated into smaller bands of between 10 and 20 lodges and each band had its own Chief.

Religion played an important role in their lives. The religious life of the Blackfeet centered on medicine bundles that were individually owned and originated from an encounter with a supernatural spirit. These encounters took the form of dreams or visions sought in a vision quest. A young Blackfeet Indian brave, with the help of a Medicine Man, would go to some lonely place far away from the Tribe and fast until he had a vision.

Bundles were symbols of their religious beliefs. Symbolism is important in all religions and the Blackfeet drew strength from the different rituals they performed just as modern religions draw strength from their symbols and rituals. Blackfeet believe in circles; what goes around, comes around, so to speak. The harmony of spirit and the continuity of the Universe was their major concern. They did not believe any person owned land. Rather, land was to be used by everyone and taken care of by everybody. Wealth came in the form of great deeds accomplished, not in how many possessions they owned. Their lives were centered on community needs, not individual needs.

Around the 1600's, the French began to move deeper into the Great Lakes region. Shortly after that, the Blackfeet began to migrate westward, eventually settling in the area now known as Northern Montana and Southern Alberta.

For years the Blackfeet tried to avoid contact with the White man. In fact, they did not trade with them until 1831. Shortly thereafter, in 1837, a small pox epidemic broke out and 6,000 Blackfeet, over two-thirds of the total population, were wiped out. In 1855, even though the Blackfeet were never conquered in battle, they agreed to a peace treaty that guaranteed them much of their traditional land. In less than five years, that treaty was broken when White settlers began to enter their territory. In 1865, fighting broke out among the White settlers and the

Blackfeet. In 1874, without consulting the Blackfeet, Congress moved their reservation boundaries north to the Birch Creek-Marias River line. This resulted in the Blackfeet losing most of their best land. Land that was sacred and holy; land that was filled with trees, lakes, streams, game and a variety of other natural resources.

Even with the loss of their best land, the Blackfeet were able to live without the assistance of the Federal Government. That changed in the Starvation Winter of 1883-1884. That was the winter the buffalo herds disappeared and over 600 Blackfeet starved to death. After that, the Blackfeet became dependent on government rations.

In 1896, the Blackfeet, desperate for food, sold what is now Glacier National Park for one million five hundred thousand dollars.

The Blackfeet have struggled to survive for years. Throughout the 1900's, they lived through several Federal policy changes. Policies made by people from outside the Reservation, people who really did not understand the Blackfeet and their needs. In order to survive, the Blackfeet had to assimilate into White culture and forget about their own.

Historically, the Blackfeet were once a proud people. They may still have pride, but it is masked behind the realities of Reservation life; a life filled with drug and alcohol abuse, abject poverty and domestic violence.

The once mighty and feared Blackfeet, the Southern Piegan, now scratch out a living on wind swept, barren reservation land; land with boundaries. Their reservation has been reduced to 1.5 million acres of land, land nobody else wanted. The Reservation lies in North Central Montana and it's boundaries run east to Cut Bank Creek, west to Glacier National Park, north to Alberta and south to the Birch Creek-Marias River line.

The Tribal headquarters of their reservation is a town called Browning. Browning lies in the shadows of the Rocky Mountains which the Blackfeet call, "The backbone of the world." Browning, Montana, the place of broken dreams and unhappy endings.

Chapter 1

First of all, you have to be out of your mind to be a writer. No sane person would sit in a room all by themselves and write something that few people will ever read, you have to be certifiably and absolutely nuts. I have tried to explain this to Two-Fingers sister, my wife, for weeks. She doesn't listen and insists I tell his story, she says it will be therapeutic for me, as if anything could help ease the pain.

She finally cut me off from having sex with her until I write his story and that has become a problem for me. I like sex, I really do. Since I am not having any sex, I find myself watching way too much television, nothing better to do I suppose. I was watching this program the other night and this commercial came on for a sexual dysfunction drug and it said that if you take this magic pill and after three hours you still have an erection you should call your doctor. Are you kidding me? He is the last person I would call. If I had an erection for three hours I would call a television station, a radio station, my neighbors, my friends and anybody else who would listen to me. I would insist on a parade down main street where I stand on a float proudly displaying my erection. Three hours? Who is shitting who here? I am 62 years of age and my entire sex life does not add up to three hours. You know, 15 seconds here, 30 seconds there, it all adds up but I'm not sure it adds up to three hours.

Well, I digress. See what happens when your old lady cuts you off? You go out of your mind, that's what. Since I am now crazy, no thanks to my wife, I just as well tell you about my best friend and my wife's brother, Two-Fingers. But just remember, I am not a professional writer, I am just a guy that needs to get laid. Besides, the Blackfeet revere him and the young Blackfeet want to know all about him and I guess that means something.

Two-Fingers has been gone for several months now and there is not a day that goes by that someone doesn't ask me about him, his people have never forgotten him. His legend has grown with each passing day, few people have ever had this big of impact on an entire Tribe.

Two-Fingers and I grew up together and we were best friends from the day we first met and I knew him very well. I suppose, that is why I am always asked about him. I do not mind talking about him and answering their questions but I sense they want more, something in writing. As time goes on, I fear my memory will begin to fade and I will not be able to tell the story accurately, that is why I am writing it all down now. That and the fact that I need some sex.

It is difficult for me to write about him because doing so brings back a lot of memories that are best left hidden away. But, I am going to tell his story anyway, I have too. Two-Fingers did everything well. He spoke well, he wrote well, he lived well and he did it all effortlessly. He deserves to have his story told and his memory kept alive. That is what I keep telling myself but we both know the real reason.

Growing up on the Rez, Two-Fingers had a front row seat to the negative impact and devastating effects of our Federal Government's failed Indian Policy, he lived underneath it. It is a policy he fought against his entire adult life because it is a flawed policy of our government's own creation. He used to laugh when politicians would visit the reservation, their visits were always as brief as possible. They would hold a news conference, shed a few tears and go back to Washington D.C. and throw a little money at the "Indian" problem.

In the 1960's, politicians were not satisfied in just ruining the Indian way of life, they took their destruction nationwide when they created the welfare system we see today. These welfare programs have made an entirely different group of people dependent. The Federal Government has created a dependency problem and they are either too blind to see it or they just don't care. Two-Fingers always suspected the latter and he spent most of his life fighting against it, he was brave that way.

He strongly believed that Federal Government dependency is an abomination and when you believe in something that strongly you are bound to make enemies. There are those that profit from such arrangements and they are always looking to protect their interests, not the interests of the people they claim they are protecting; promoting dependency is all part of their evil game.

Nobody takes responsibility at the highest level of our government, they always blame the other guy. When the politicians go to the slum areas that they helped create, they shed a few tears, make a speech, have a photo op and then they go home and throw money at the problem; they are never seen again until the next election cycle. Two-Fingers knew that the chains of dependency had to be broken on the Rez and the rest of America. His enemies made sure his voice of reason was forever silenced.

Two-Fingers knew one thing to be fact, breaking the chain of Federal Government dependency would help his people break the chains of alcoholism, drug abuse, domestic violence and poverty; abject poverty that decimates a person's pride and self importance. Two-Fingers knew that every man, woman and child had to have a purpose in life. The reliance on an all powerful government blinds people who are dependent, Two-Fingers preached this for years and was making great changes right up to the day he disappeared.

At the very peak of his powers he was taken from us. He told me many things during our time together but the things that stick in my mind the most were his insistence on freedom and liberty for all. He knew that dependency is bad in principal and in its effect. It destroys character and saps strength by encouraging greed and weakness, it destroys individualism and self worth and it kills the desire to be the best you can be. Ultimately, it destroys compassion, charity and self respect. It was this war on dependency that finally did him in, they got him. He was starting to be heard and they needed him silenced. He knew that the chains of dependency had to be broken, not only for the person dependent but for the nation at large. No nation can survive when half of the people are dependent on the government.

In the olden days, Indians were Warriors who never depended on anyone, they were free. Look no further than an Indian reservation to see the harmful effects of what a hundred and fifty years of government dependency will do to a once proud and independent people. No government can ever give you drive, ambition or a desire for self reliance. But, they can certainly take these things away.

Two-Fingers knew that all people were not racists. Instead, he believed that governments promoted racism to help divide and conquer the electorate. If there wasn't a crisis, they would create one. If you are a bad person, changing your skin color is not going to change that. Two-Fingers knew that there were enablers that promoted racism and made fortunes doing so. These enablers could care less about the plight of any minority, their welfare policies have been in effect for decades and things are worse now than at any time in the history of The United States of America. By the way, The United States of America is no longer united, the political party's hate each other. That's right, Republicans hate Democrats and Democrats hate Republicans. They blame the other party for the plight of the nation and they point fingers and make excuses.

Two-Fingers was a great leader because he took responsibility for his actions and expected those around him to do the same. He lived by this motto: "Do the right thing because it is the right thing to do." If we do not know the difference between right and wrong, we are all doomed. He always said that we need to get our act together because our enemies are at our doorstep. Life, liberty and freedom, no other country gives you that. Once it is gone, it will never return. Remember this, the best way to destroy democracy is to bankrupt it. We are up to our neck in debt and we are morally bankrupt. That is what he talked about and that is what he believed and I am going to try to tell you all about him. Perhaps then all of you will take up his cause and make him proud.

To tell you an accurate and detailed story, I will have to tell you a little bit about the time we spent together and the environment in which we grew up in, I will tell the story as clearly as I can and I hope I do his story justice. I will share stories and conversations we had and let you make up your own mind. I need to warn you up front that life on the Rez is edgy, really edgy. His story will not sugar coat things, his story will be real. The books I have read on modern Indian life on the Rez are all fantasies, Indians are portrayed as little boy scouts and girl scouts. That is not the case and this book will be real and it will be edgy. Just remember, you have been warned.

To tell his story effectively, you will need to know about Blackfeet history and language. For example, I have been asked many, many times what aenet means. Aenet is Blackfeet slang and it is interchangeable in the sense that it can be used as a statement or a question. The Blackfeet are very demonstrative in their communicating, they use their hands a lot and when there is a group of Blackfeet sitting around talking they are constantly feeding off what someone else has just said and they keep the conversation going, perpetual motion; no pregnant pauses on the Rez; plenty of pregnancies, just no pregnant pauses. Here are examples to illustrate my point.

Indian guy says to an Indian girl, "You sure look good today, aenet." She responds, "Gee you're pissy, aenet. I bet you just want to get into my pants, aenet."

Group of Blackfeet sitting around a campfire talking and one of the Blackfeet tells a story and when he finishes, the other Blackfeet nod their heads in agreement and in unison they say, "aenet."

I have never seen the word aenet written out or explained so I am taking literary license in my explanation and spelling. It sounds like I have written it and it is used extensively on the Rez. The Blackfeet have a number of words and phrases I have only heard on the Rez. If you ever go to Browning, just say aenet a lot and you will be welcomed with open arms.

By the way, Two-Fingers always said that if America is unable or unwilling to break the chains of dependency, it will become one big reservation, dependent and hopeless. If you don't believe that, you haven't been to our inner cities lately.

In the olden days, Blackfeet women would maim themselves when one of their loved ones were killed. They would cut off fingers or slit their wrists and then moan and wail their lives away. As I sit here writing Two-Fingers story, I am surrounded by moans and wailing. It seems like the entire Rez is moaning and wailing. To be missed so much that people would react this way never ceases to amaze to me.

Chapter 2

By the way, my name is Tony Church and I am a white guy. Even though we claim to be a color blind society, I think you should know that. I am not going to bore you to death with my early childhood. However, you should probably know a little about the events leading up to my white family moving to an Indian reservation.

Robert "Bud" Church and Ruby Fitzgerald Church, my mother and father, grew up in Cherry Hills, New Jersey. Mom's parents were florists who had a store in Cherry Hills and a farm nearby. They sold flowers around the entire area but mostly in Philadelphia, Pennsylvania. Dad's parents owned a bar in downtown Cherry Hill.

Mom and dad met, fell in love and married shortly after dad was discharged from the Army after World War II. I have an older brother, Stan.

Not to dwell on this stuff too much, my family and all, but you should probably know that Bud, my father, is more sophisticated and worldly than mom. Mom never lived too far from her parents. Not only did dad see a lot of the world while he served in World War II, but when he was fifteen, he ran away from home and moved to Lander, Wyoming where he made a living working on a ranch. The old man loved the west, he learned to ride and rope and eventually became quite a sensation on the rodeo circuit. He has a buddy from Cut Bank, Montana. Cut Bank is 35 miles east of Browning, just off the reservation. His buddy's name is Charles "Charley" Owen. Charlie's dad, Bob, is a big time rancher, who, as luck would have it, own's the land where the largest deposit of oil in the entire state is situated.

Evidently, Charley and dad met in Cheyenne, Wyoming back in 1936. Nowadays, Cheyenne is famous for its Frontier Days Rodeo and Celebration. Back then, it was just another rodeo. Dad won $200.00 the week they met coming in first in bareback riding and second in the saddle bronc event. Charley didn't do much that week except help dad spend the $200.00 on a cheap Ford pickup and lots of beer. You probably don't care about any of this stuff and want me to get to the part about Two-Fingers, and I will, but I had to listen to this stuff daily as a kid and I thought you should get a small taste.

Charley and the old man remained friends over the years. After the war, they reunited in New York City, New York. Dad served in the Army and was wounded by some shrapnel from an explosion while he was serving in Sicily. His left foot and both knees were badly damaged. As a result, dad spent the rest of the war in various hospitals in Sicily, Italy and then stateside in New York. Dad has never really talked about the war, most veterans of World War II don't. It must have been hell on them. Mom said dad will always carry the scars of war with him, our greatest generation is scarred.

Charley had a tough time of it too. He joined the Marines and saw a lot of action fighting the Japanese in New Guinea, New Britain, Peleliu and Okinawa. Mom said whenever Charley and dad hook up, they always start to talk about the "good old days" before the war, always a story and always plenty of beer.

While recuperating stateside in New York, dad met mom. Mom was a nurse's aide who cared for a number of the returning soldiers that had been wounded overseas. She fell in love with dad almost immediately, she admired his strength and courage. There was also a bit of rogue in dad that especially appealed to her. Dad noticed how caring and loving mom is and he vowed to win her over. Mom was very beautiful and extremely popular with all the wounded men, but she only had eyes for dad and when he proposed, she let him think it was his idea.

These are the kinds of thing I remember as a young kid, nice things. I also remember that my dad killed my pet parrot. Dad was a chain smoker and he smoked like crazy at the time. Well, at least he did until he killed my bird. Barney, my bird, liked to perch himself on my dad's shoulder when he was out of his cage. Well, one day he was sitting there on dad's shoulder and dad was smoking cigarettes and drinking Schlitz beer like crazy when, all of a sudden, Barney dropped to the floor. I jumped up from the table and held Barney in my little hands as he gasped for air and his little eyes fluttered a bit before he stopped moving. Mom said he chocked to death from all the smoke.

You have bad memories as a kid too, not everything can be sunshine and crackers. You probably did not want to hear that story either but I just wanted to get it off my chest. The good news is dad decided then and there to quit smoking.

Anyway, mom always said her happiest years were after the war when dad and her were married and they settled down and started a life together. She loved living in Cherry Hills, it was home. Dad, on the other hand, could never get adjusted to "big city life" as he referred to it. Cherry Hills is really not a big place, dad just yearned for more freedom and the wide open spaces of the west. Over the years, dad tried to make the best of it and he bought his father's bar and ran it as well as he could. But, he was unhappy and before long he was spending more and more time on the customer side of the bar. His physical and mental war injuries took a long time to heal and the alcohol he consumed helped with the pain. When dad's parents died in a car accident, he sold the bar and convinced Mom that Cut Bank, Montana was the place for us. A new start, a new beginning. Mom, against her better judgment, supported dad's decision.

By that time, I was finishing the seventh grade and Stan was finishing his junior year in high school. Stan and I pleaded with our parents not to move. Dad insisted it would be fun and a great adventure, it would make men of us he said. He was certain we needed to get out to the wild open spaces of Montana. I remember Mom consoling us the best she could.

So, on June 26, 1966, we loaded all of our worldly possessions into and onto our '57 Chevy two door sedan and started off to Montana. Dad drove the entire 2,622 miles in three days. He only stopped when it was absolutely necessary which meant only when he needed to get gas or groceries. Peeing was a luxury, the man had a bladder the size of Ohio and he thought everybody else did, dad was on a mission.

Mom made bologna sandwiches in the front seat and Stan and I held our pee as mile after lonesome mile passed us by. The really weird thing was we all slept in the car during this trip west, no fancy motels for us. In the back seat, Stan and I slept all crunched up in knots with our cheeks pressed to the windows. Stan was a big dude and when he stretched out he took up the whole back seat, I was constantly fighting for space. Dad's tactics paid off, after a thousand miles we were too worn out and exhausted to continue to fight the move. With each passing mile, dad grew stronger and stronger while the rest of us got weaker and weaker. I don't think the old man slept more than six hours the whole trip. I only mention this trip because I hope some of you can relate, if my old man is the only father that refused to stop the car and let his kids pee, I am really going to be upset.

I remember when we reached the city limits of Cut Bank, there was this big green sign with black paint that said, "Welcome to Cut Bank population 3,367." I was never so happy to see a sign in my life. I normally didn't get that excited over a sign, but it made me happy. Not only because we were in Cut Bank, I was also happy because I finally got to piss. As soon as dad stopped to get gas at a Texaco station, mom, Stan and I sprinted to the restrooms. It's little things like that that make life worth living. When I got done peeing, I walked around the station to stretch my legs and as I walked by the gas pump, I overheard my dad asking the attendant for directions to the Owen Ranch. "Owen spread, can't miss it. Go back down this road about a mile and you will come to a big old oil refinery-they own it." The attendant said as he pointed in the direction we had just come from. "Now, to get to their ranch, you take a left just before the refinery and stay on that road for about five miles. That is all their land. At the end of the road you will see their place, can't miss it." The attendant said as he finished filling up the tank. It was really nice hearing another person's voice.

After paying for the gas and getting everybody loaded back into the car, dad drove back the way we came and we soon turned onto the road leading to the Owen Ranch. We were amazed at how many oil wells there were; each one pumping at a slow, methodical pace. There were hundreds of Black Angus cattle grazing between the derricks and dozens of horses running wild on the wide open prairie.

As we drove down the road, we eventually passed under a large cast iron ornamental sign that said, "Owen Ranch." Before long, we were parked in the front yard looking up at a huge colonial style mansion, the place was massive. White columns on the porch reached skyward;

the porch was huge and it had white railing that seemed to run on for ever. When you are young, everything seems big. It is one of those great houses that your parents don't have to tell you to behave in, you just instinctively knew not to start rough housing in a place like that.

I remember us all stretching and staring at the house and this huge barn in the distance. Soon, a big cowboy came running out of the barn headed in our direction. I had never seen Charley before but I figured this must be him. As it turned out, Charley was in the barn tending to one of his prize Black Angus bulls when he saw us drive up. He shook my dad's hand for what seemed to be about five minutes before he introduced himself to Stan and me. After the introductions were made, Charley led us up the steps of his mansion and opened the door and let us in, he was really a gracious guy. Humble, unassuming with cow shit all over his boots.

When he opened up the front door to let us in, I couldn't help whistling. The place was huge. The floor was made of Marble and there was a spiral staircase that ran from the foyer to the second floor, it looked just like that staircase in "Gone with the Wind." I remember us gawking at the place when Charley's dad, Bob and his wife Juanita came busting in. They were arguing about something and they didn't spend much time chit chatting. Soon, they both stormed off in opposite directions. I will never forget the first time I saw that ranch or the first time I saw Juanita, she was far more impressive than the house.

Over the course of our week's stay, I got to know Juanita pretty well. She had an old jeep she used to take me riding in, we explored the whole ranch and talked. She talked to me a lot and I just stared at her and nodded. She really wasn't that much older than me, maybe ten years or so. She was twenty years younger than Charley and was reminded of that daily by her father-in-law Bob. She said Bob told her she was a gold digger that only married Charley for his money. I never figured out why she told me all this personal stuff, maybe it was because I just listened and kept quiet. It was the first time any women, other than my mom and my grandmothers, ever really talked to me, we enjoyed each others company. She even took me horseback riding and fishing. She was probably the most beautiful women I had ever seen up to that point in my life. I stared at her a lot and she never seemed to notice, she just kept talking away. Her mother and father lived and worked on the ranch and had for years. Helen and Ivan Bear Medicine are their names and they are both full blooded Blackfeet. Juanita was born on the ranch in a cabin that Ivan and Helen lived in. They had one other child, a boy by the name of Phillip who died in a car wreck a year before she left the ranch and moved to Los Angeles. She said I reminded her of her brother and for some reason she took a liking to me.

When she moved to California, She got work as an extra in Hollywood because they were always needing authentic looking Indians for all the Westerns, she was authentic all right. A beautiful woman who wanted children so she eventually moved out of Los Angeles and returned to the ranch. She and Charley fell in love after she returned and were married about three years by the time we showed up.

Anyway, after spending a week on the ranch looking at her and all the other scenery, I no longer missed New Jersey. Stan seemed to be adjusting to the place too. He borrowed the Chevy every night and went to Cut Bank until the wee hours of every morning we were there and nobody said anything to him about that.

It wasn't long before dad found us an apartment to rent in Cut Bank. Charley wanted dad to stay on and work at the ranch, Stan and I both thought that was a great idea but dad had other ideas; he wanted to own and operate a gas station, that was his dream he said. He loved working on cars and he figured he could make a good living at the right location.

So, we settled into life in Cut Bank and I started the eight grade and Stan started his senior year at Cut Bank High. Stan was a very good athlete and he was the star of the football team. Before long, dad found his gas station, it was a Chevron station that was open twenty-four hours a day, a real money maker. There was only one hitch, it was located on the Blackfeet Indian Reservation in Browning, Montana.

I remember mom and dad having arguments over that decision. Dad always won the arguments, he had a way of wearing you down. "Bud, did you say, an Indian reservation?" I remember my mom asking with this look of horror on her face. "That's right Honey and it is a great bargain. The current owners are really motivated to sell." Dad laid it on thick. "I would be too, Bud. We can not raise our boys on an Indian reservation. What are the schools like? Stan is at the age where he is looking at girls all the time. Do you want him marrying an Indian girl? What about Tony? He is just a baby. There is no way in hell I'm moving our children onto an Indian reservation, no way." For a brief, shining moment I thought mom was finally going to win an argument.

That was in November of 1966. By December, we had taken up residency in Browning, Montana headquarters of the Blackfeet Indian Reservation.

Our Chevron station had an attached three bedroom living area and a four unit motel. It did not take us too long to settle in, we all pitched in and worked hard at our new business and business was good. The only businesses that did better were the liquor stores and the funeral homes.

Chapter 3

Here are my first impressions of Browning: It certainly isn't the end of the world but you can see it from there. Back then, it was a hard town, visually and geologically hard. Rocks and boulders of various sizes jutted up out of the ground everywhere I looked and there were a few paved streets but most of the roads were either gravel or dirt. In the spring the roads were mud puddles and in the summer, after the mud dried, dust filled the air. In the winter, snow was everywhere. The snow would get so deep entire houses were covered over and snow tunnels were dug from the street to the front door and remained there until early spring. The Blackfeet were constantly shoveling themselves out. As a consequence, school was routinely cancelled. This is a fact, Browning is one of the coldest towns in America. Violently cold winters and the summers are unbearably hot. The wind seldom stops blowing, that is one reason there isn't a tree in Browning. There are a few lawns but not as many as you would think, if a guy had a lawn care service in Browning he would starve to death.

The few lawns that exist on the Rez are those up at the Government Square, it is literally a square section of land. In the center of the square is a large field of mowed grass. They actually mow the grass and bail it, that is how big this field is. Around the perimeter of the square is where you will find the Federal Government employees' houses. They are set out in perfect rows, well kept and with lawns. The houses are temporary housing provided to the Federal Government employees who are doing their time until they figure out a way to get transferred. The Government Square is also where the Bureau of Indian Affairs(BIA) offices are. Behind the BIA complex is the local jail, tribally owned and operated. Not far from the jail is a large warehouse where the commodities are stored.

Every Saturday morning, commodities were distributed to all enrolled members of the Blackfeet Tribe. You must be an enrolled member to receive commodities, health care and government payments.

Saturday mornings were highly anticipated, cars and trucks lined the street leading to the warehouse where hungry families waited patiently to receive their allotment of powered milk, pinto beans, canned chopped meat, bread and commodity cheese. The commodity cheese came in five pound packages and was considered a delicacy, it was highly sought after. The winos would sell their cheese for money to buy Muscatel wine. Wine and cheese was a big deal on the Rez. Well, the wine was, the cheese was just an after thought when the wine kicked in.

The Government Square is discretely separate from Browning. It even has a cattle guard you have to cross before you can enter, perhaps a futile attempt at keeping the Indians out so the white people can live their lives separately. The horror of it all, they have to send their children to the Browning public schools. Too bad, integration has arrived.

Catholicism is the dominant religion on the Rez, all good Indians are Catholic. The Catholic Church is also the biggest Church on the Rez, it is a large two story rock building that has a separate rectory for the nuns and the priests. It sits in the center of Browning not far from main street. There is a Mormon church on the Rez near Moccasin Flats, but it is small and sparsely attended. The Mormons are always trying to recruit the Blackfeet but are largely unsuccessful. Over the years, the Blackfeet have been asked to give up their ancestral religious beliefs and assimilate into White Society and they have largely done so; the Blackfeet are always being asked to give up something.

Like most towns, main street is where the majority of the businesses are located. These businesses rely heavily on the summer tourist trade and being close to Glacier National Park helps business. Tourists stop to get gas, spend the night, eat and take a few pictures. Most of the businesses back then were owned and operated by white people. There was a large Standard stucco gas station that was built to look like a giant Teepee, it was painted red, white and blue. That place always drew large crowds of picture takers because everybody wanted their picture taken in front of a huge red, white and blue stucco Teepee, everybody.

On the highway to Glacier National Park were two really nice museums, the Museum of The Plains Indians and Bob Scriver's Art

Museum. Bob was a local celebrity who once appeared on the show, "What's My Line." He became nationally known for his bronze sculptures. Across the street from his museum is the Junction Drive In, it's not like I am trying to promote the Junction or anything, but they really do put out a nice cheeseburger.

The neighborhoods that surrounded the businesses were made up of a variety of housing types. Remember, this is the Rez and there are no zoning laws. Trailer houses were scattered among the brick and mortar residences and yards were filled with broken down cars and half dressed children.

Packs of dogs ran wild all over town, there used to be a lot of cats running around until someone opened up a Chinese food restaurant. The alleys were filled with winos seeking shelter and a safe place to drink. Streets were bumpy and rough regardless of the time of year and ditches were filled with whiskey bottles, wine bottles, beer bottles, beer cans and pop bottles. Garbage would blow down the streets before becoming permanently attached to the barbed wire fences. Like I said earlier, Browning was a hard place. Browning was always just one step behind the rest of society, close but yet so far away. For example, there were plenty of handicaps on the Rez, just no handicap parking.

Anyway, I know you want to hear about Two-Fingers and what made him tick and how he became a great man and everything and I am almost there, really I am. It's just that everybody should know about Browning because this is where he spent most of his life. Besides, everybody should be warned about Browning too, I wish someone had warned me. Wouldn't you want to be warned if you were getting near quicksand or if you were about to walk off of a cliff? I would want to know. Browning, a place where you could fall and never be seen again.

Chapter 4

I remember the date and everything else regarding my first day of school in Browning, it was January 5, 1967. Browning Junior High School was not far from home so I decided to walk to school. Of course, my mother would have none of that and she insisted on driving me. I could tell she was nervous, her youngest son was headed off into the vast unknown. I am sure she was worried and wanted to protect me but there are just certain things a parent can not save you from and one of those things is your first day at a strange school, that was the real reason I was determined to walk. The last thing I wanted was my mother dropping me off at school and having the Blackfeet tease me about it. No way, I stood my ground and I finally won the argument. Mom always had a hell of a time winning arguments.

I walked the half mile to school without anything bad happening. I just remember it was bone chillingly cold and windy so I walked as fast as I could to keep warm. I got to school in one piece and was standing at the front door of the school when, all of a sudden, six or seven hard packed snowballs came cascading down on me. Luckily, I was not too badly hurt. The natives were obviously a little restless and I learned three valuable lessons from that experience: the Blackfeet have very strong arms, excellent aim and they show up when you least expect them.

I was never sure why Mr. Howard Blackstone, the principal, was standing in the front lobby waiting to greet me, unusual to see a white student I guess. "Are you OK? Don't pay any attention to them, that's just Indian lovin." Mr. Blackstone said, with this big, shit eating grin spread across his face.

"I'll show you to your room." He said as he walked down the hall with me following closely. "Your eighth grade teacher is Miss Ash and she is very nice, a recent graduate of Montana State University down in Bozeman." Miss Ash, as it turned out, was a beautiful young white woman. Looking at her took some of the sting out of my injuries, some.

"Tony, you will be sitting up here in the front row." Miss Ash said as she pointed to a small desk not too far from her.

I remember sitting down at my new desk and being immediately drawn to the intricate carvings etched onto the surface area of the desk. As I examined it closely, I was amazed to see an entire crime scene portrayed in perfect detail. Then, upon closer inspection, I realized that the crime scene was actually a group of men and women engaging in, what appeared to be, a group sex thing. Another lesson: the Blackfeet are artistic.

Miss Ash was going over a few things with me when, all of a sudden, the bell rang and the classroom door swung open and in rushed a mob of laughing, yelling Blackfeet. Finally, after everyone settled into their seats, I stood and walked towards the coat room, I had to hang up my coat. I was about halfway there when I was tripped by this long leg that appeared out of nowhere. I remember falling hard and kind of bouncing across the floor and after I stopped bouncing, I jumped up and took a swing at the boy who tripped me. Unfortunately, I missed but the other boy didn't. He smacked me on the chin and down I went for the second time in less than 30 seconds. I was laying in the middle of the room surrounded by a mob of laughing, jeering Indians when Miss Ash helped me to my feet and asked me what had happened. I told her nothing happened, I had just slipped on some snow. I hate lying, I really do.

Later that morning, I felt a slight tap on my shoulder and as I slowly turned around I discovered this pretty little Indian girl sitting directly behind me. I quickly found out she was not flirting with me, she was just passing me a note from the guy that had tripped me. I took my time opening it and then I read it very slowly and carefully. It said, "White Guy, I will see you down behind Vic's Grocery after school." It was signed, Ronnie Joe Stabs-in-the-Back. I learned later that Ronnie Joe was THE class bully in a room full of class bullies. Evidently, this was Ronnie Joe's second attempt at passing the eighth grade and he was proud of it. He liked being the biggest kid in class, it helped his confidence. After I read the note, I tore it up and glanced at the author. Ronnie, all puffed up and feeling good about himself, was staring back at me. I wasn't sure, but I figured we weren't going to the grocery store to buy candy.

For the rest of the school day, I found it very hard to concentrate, I constantly looked at the clock. When the bell rang, signaling the end of the school day, everybody jumped up and ran to get their coats. Everybody except me, I just sat at my desk and stared at the clock. After a few minutes, I stood up and retrieved my coat. Miss Ash was cleaning the blackboard when I decided to ask her a question, "Miss Ash, where is Vic's Grocery?" She just smiled and gave me directions. As it turned out, Vic's was the designated battlefield and everybody knew about it. It was close to school, yet off school property. Miss Ash seemed to know all about the place too.

She sat me down and gave me some of the best advice I have ever been given. She said she understood I was probably scared but she said I had to go. If I ran away I would be running for the rest of my time on the Rez, the worst thing I could do was run she said. She explained to me in no uncertain terms that the Blackfeet hate cowards. On the other hand, they reward bravery and if I ran they would never let me stop running. Instinctively, I knew she was right. I was scared to death but I knew I had to go, I had to. So, I thanked her and quickly made my way to Vic's.

As I approached the alley behind Vic's, I became increasingly aware of the roar of the crowd, I was amazed at how many people had shown up. Kids of all ages were lined up on both sides of the alley and they were yelling, laughing and pointing at me. I saw the movie Spartacus when I was younger and I was getting the same gut wrenching type of feeling they must have felt when they were being thrown to the lions. At least I imagined their guts were wrenching, mine did.

In the middle of the crowd stood Ronnie Joe Stabs-in-the-Back, all puffed up and looking mean. As I approached him, Ronnie Joe began to slowly take his coat off. I began to take my coat off when the same girl that passed me the note in class came up to me and volunteered to hold my coat. That act of kindness really seemed to piss off Ronnie Joe. He yelled, "I'm going to give you a bloody stick in the mud, White Guy!!" I rightfully figured it was fight time.

Ronnie Joe advanced quickly and threw a right hand that caught me squarely on the jaw and down I went. Much to my surprise, I wasn't hurt too badly, must have been the adrenaline. Ronnie Joe rushed me again and knocked me to the ground as I tried to get to my feet. He stood over the top of me and kicked the crap out of me with his heavy, pointed cowboy boots. He was really putting the boots to me when he suddenly slipped and fell down. I rolled away from him and quickly got to my feet. As he started to get up, I swung as hard as I could and ended up hitting Ronnie Joe square on the top of his head. Man, did that hurt, I thought I had broken my hand. Another lesson: the Blackfeet are hard headed.

The blow to his head must have really hurt Ronnie Joe because he laid on his back withering in pain. While Ronnie Joe was laying there, one of Ronnie Joe's friends copped a sneaker on me. In Indian terminology, copping a sneaker means that you are hit by some chickenshit when you are not looking. When I was hit, I did not go down. Instead, I spun around and grabbed the other kid and we both tumbled to the ground. While we were wrestling and hitting each other, Ronnie Joe staggered to his feet and started putting the boots to me again. I was covering my head and peeking up at Ronnie Joe when all of a sudden, like a flash, Ronnie Joe was flattened by a tackle that would have made Jim Thorpe proud. The speed and force of the impact was enough to send Ronnie Joe flying through the air. Ronnie Joe landed hard against the back wall of Vic's Grocery and slowly slid to the ground, he was finished for the day.

I slowly got to my feet when the guy I was wrestling with finally let go. We both stood there staring at the guy who knocked Ronnie Joe flat, the crowd looked too as they nodded their heads in approval.

The tackler turned to the crowd and said, "Its time to go home now, we can beat up the white guy again tomorrow - I'll bring the popcorn." The crowd laughed and slowly dispersed. The cute little girl that held my coat dropped it at my feet and said, "You are not much of a fighter but you sure can roll, aenet." She giggled as she walked away. "Who is that girl?" I asked the tackler. "Her name is Vicki Eagle

Feathers and I think she likes you." "Really, what makes you think so?" "She gave you your coat back."

That was the first time I met Two-Fingers and we have been friends ever since. Turns out he hated Ronnie Joe because he was always picking on people smaller than him. He said he was okay with me getting beat up as long as it was a fair fight but when the other guy jumped in, he decided to help. I was thankful he did, not too many people risk helping a stranger. He made light of it, but it was a big deal to me.

We spent a few minutes in the alley talking as the crowd continued to thin out. After awhile, we introduced ourselves to each other. He told me everybody called him Two-Fingers but his real name was Donny R. Schwartz and he had missed school that day because he had been helping his dad do a few chores. As it turned out, we were approximately the same age and in the same class. As I was telling him my name, I couldn't help but notice his hand and I finally had to ask him about it. "I was born that way. My mom says I was so anxious to get into the real world I didn't hang around long enough for her to finish her work. I told her she starved me when I was an infant and I ended up gnawing off the other three fingers to survive." That made me laugh, "Well, at least you've kept your sense of humor." "On the Rez, that's about all they let you keep." Two-Fingers said as he turned and walked down the alley. "Hey, wait a second, I'll walk with you." "Ok, White Guy, but you better hurry, I have things to do."

We walked in silence before I asked, "Why did you call me "White Guy" instead of Tony?" "Almost everybody, sooner or later, has a nickname on the Rez, everybody. You, whether you like it or not, are the "White Guy." "Would you like to come over to my place, it's not far from here?" I asked. "You got Koolaid?" "Yeah, and we have a pop machine filled with pop. My dad bought the Chevron station." "I know." Two-Fingers said. "On the Rez, everybody knows everything about the other guy's business. You can't fart on the Rez without everybody knowing what it smells like."

That made me laugh too. I found myself sneaking peeks at this strange looking Indian as we walked, Two-Fingers was about my size but he acted bigger somehow. He walked with an air of confidence and he handled himself as if he was normal, normal physically.

As we approached our Chevron station, I asked Two-Fingers, "Do you have any brothers or sisters?" "I have two older sisters." "I have an older brother named Stan." Two-Fingers just nodded his head and kept on walking.

Dad was pumping gas when we arrived at the station. He looked up from what he was doing and meekly waved and stared at us as we entered the front door of our station. After we each grabbed a pop, we entered the kitchen where mom was frosting a cake. "Hello Tony, how was your first day at school?" Mom asked with a look of relief on her face. "It was OK, at least nobody died." I introduced Two-Fingers to my mother and he politely shook her hand.

Mom said, "It is nice to meet you, Donny." I noticed mom conspicuously staring at Two-Fingers left hand before she asked, "Oh my, what happened to your poor hand?" "Well, when I was just a baby, my parents left me at home alone with my two older sisters. They were busy watching Captain Kangaroo on TV when a wild dog broke into our Teepee and chewed off my fingers." Two-Fingers said straight faced.

Over the course of our lifelong friendship, I never knew Two-Fingers to give the same answer twice when he was asked, "What happened to your hand?" Over the years I grew to understand that Two-Fingers made up these stories as a defense mechanism. Lesson: Fiction is less painful than fact, especially on the Rez.

My mom looked heartbroken by his answer but she continued to stare at his hand, "You had better sit down here and have some German Chocolate cake, I just took it out of the oven." Mom served up two large helpings and we devoured it like we hadn't eaten in a week. After his second helping, Two-Fingers said, "Mrs. Church, this is almost as good as my mom's fry bread."

"Thank you Donny, I will send some home with you. Just make sure you keep it away from any wild animals you might run into on your way home."

Well, there you have it, that was the day we met. Looking back, I am reminded of Two-Fingers strength and his determination to stand up for the little guy, me. He faced down all the Blackfeet in the circle that day and protected me, he risked a lot and gained little. Over the years, he risked a lot more defending what he believed was right and he always had a clear vision of what was right and wrong. Most people do I suppose, the difference is he always stuck his neck out to defend what he believed in and that virtue kind of rubbed off on me. He came by it naturally, me I had to have it pounded into my head more than once. For example, we never looked at each other as white or Indian, race was never an issue with him or me. Other people get caught up in that type of thing but we never did. I always thought he was weird looking but my opinion of him never had anything to do with race. Later on in our lives, Two-Fingers came to the conclusion that people were essentially good and that governments were bad, governments make race an issue because they want to separate and polarize people for their own political gain, it took me a long time to come to that conclusion but I finally got there.

Chapter 5

That night, a blizzard moved in across the Northern Rockies of Montana and two feet of snow fell in less than eight hours, the temperature dropped to ten below and a strong, cold wind piled the snow high over the roads and driving was virtually impossible.

I came to learn that Montana was known for its hard winters and Browning is the coldest place in Montana. As I said earlier, Browning does not have a tree in the entire town, the wind and cold see to that. Changes in weather occur rapidly on the Rez and when it gets really bad, school is usually cancelled.

That's what happened the next morning. Around 11 a.m., a chinook wind miraculously appeared and suddenly the temperature began to rise drastically, I learned to love chinook winds. At about 11:10 a.m., Two-Fingers showed up at the station.

I was inside stocking the cooler with soda pop when he said, “White Guy, let's go sledding.” Two-Fingers never really asked a question. Instead, he made statements. He figured everybody was looking for a good time and it began when he showed up, he was right about that.

So, I grabbed my coat, gloves, scarf, ear muffs and looked around frantically for the electric hand warmers I received as a Christmas present when Two-Fingers, with this real demeaning look on his face said, “Pussy.” He held his arms out as if to say, “I have no gloves, no scarf and my coat is not even zipped up.” I slowly put down my gloves, scarf and ear muffs and followed him out the door. “Where we going?” I asked. “There is a hill about a half a mile west of town that is great for sledding, get on the toboggan and I will give you a ride.”

I saw no reason to argue the point with him so I happily jumped on the toboggan. Two-Fingers gave the toboggan a mighty pull and soon we were cruising down the highway. Two-Fingers pulled harder as we slowly climbed a small hill. When we reached the top of the hill, Two-Fingers jumped on the toboggan and rode it down the hill until it stopped. This maneuver was repeated over and over again until we reached the sledding area known as, "Racine Ranch."

Evidently, Old Man Racine liked seeing his hill filled with sledders. He always had a fire going in a big fifty gallon oil barrel, he would sit there and warm himself as he watched the sledders rush down the hill. The hill is very steep and at its base there is a small lake about three hundred yards wide and long. The surface of the lake was three feet of solid ice, at least.

We arrived at the top of the hill slightly out of breath. I remember standing there and looking around, it was a beautiful clear day. The sky was a deep royal blue color with only a few clouds hanging over the Rocky Mountains.

When I looked down the hill, I was amazed to see groups of sledders bouncing off a small snow drift and going airborne, they all landed on the icy surface of the lake at break neck speed. Once a sled hit the ice on the lake, it shifted into a higher gear and raced out of control until it slammed into a snow bank on the far side of the lake. Bodies flew in all directions and, much to my surprise, all the passengers lived. In fact, they all laughed hysterically and started back up the hill for another run.

Two-Fingers was sitting on the toboggan when he looked at me and, without saying a word, nodded to the spot behind him. I figured it was a good day to die and jumped on. We tucked our legs in and started down the hill hell bent for leather. About halfway down the hill, a couple of braves tried to jump onto the toboggan, they missed badly and ran into each other.

We flew down the hill as we headed towards the biggest snow drift on the hill. Just as we reached Mach speed, we hit the drift and went airborne, higher and higher we went as we flew onward. No kidding, I looked down and birds were flying below us. Then I looked over my left shoulder and I saw Old Man Racine slowly rising from his seat with a look of terror on his face. Well, it was either terror or delight, at that altitude, I wasn't sure. It seemed like a lifetime before we landed and when we did, we hit hard, real hard. The toboggan made a loud cracking sound and instead of going straight, it began to spin around and around. I held onto Two-Fingers with all my strength and noticed that we were no longer on the toboggan. Instead, we were bouncing along the icy surface of the lake headed towards a group of sledders who were trying desperately to get out of our way. Too late, we slammed into them and they went down like pins at a bowling alley. Two-Fingers, shaken but not rattled, jumped up and said, "That was a strike, aenet."

Two-Fingers always had a way of defusing the situation, either with his fist or with his tongue. Over the years, I would grow to appreciate that-but never more than at that moment.

"You are fucking crazy Two-Fingers, you could have killed us all!!" Screamed Buzzy Still Smoking, as he brushed himself off. "What's with you?" Yelled Chubby Skunk Cap. "Don't you know that riding with a white guy is hazardous to your health!!" "Crack you, Chubby!" Two-Fingers replied. "Bone you, Two-Fingers." That was the best Chubby could come up with. Just then, another sled slammed into Chubby and Buzzy and took them out at the knees, the Blackfeet Health Service was very busy that day.

We were gathering up the splintered wood that was once Two-Fingers toboggan when Old Man Racine suddenly appeared. "Donny R., you sure know how to make friends, aenet. Who is this pale looking bird you got with you?" Old Man Racine asked. "His name is Tony Church and his parents own the Chevron station." "Aenet. I am heading into town and suppose you two could use a ride, I'll drop you off." Old Man Racine said as he continued to stare at me. "OK, but I want to pay you. How about some firewood?" Two-Fingers asked as he pointed towards the remains of the toboggan. Old Man Racine nodded his head and said, "Okaynockee." Old Man Racine always had a way with words.

Old Man Racine dropped us off in front of Two-Fingers place. His parents owned an apartment house and a curio shop right on main street in Browning. Not much of a money maker but plenty of work. Over the years, I became very close to his family, very close. They are great people and I learned a lot from them.

Back then, Two-Fingers father, Maximillian "Max" Schwartz, was a tall, dark and handsome man who inherited the best traits from his German father and Blackfeet mother. Max is a half breed on a reservation that is quickly becoming a place of diminished blood lines. Raised on a ranch not far from town, Max was never comfortable in the white world and prior to marrying his wife, Pam, he wasn't that comfortable on the Rez either. He adjusted pretty well and is no longer the loner he once was.

Pam Spotted Eagle Schwartz is a beautiful woman with high cheekbones and piercing dark eyes. She is a full-blooded Blackfeet woman who traces her lineage back to the great Chief Two Guns White Calf. She is one of the most educated Blackfeet on the Rez. She went to high school at an Indian boarding school in South Dakota and after graduating, she went to Carlisle College in Pennsylvania. Pam spent a lot of time in the white world learning their values at the expense of her own. She sat aside her traditional beliefs and tried to raise her children to be good little apples, red on the outside and white on the inside.

The Schwartz's have three children: Donny R. the youngest, Cindy Ann is the oldest and Paula is the middle child.

Cindy Ann is a little beyond beautiful, seriously. She was in her senior year at Browning High School when I first met her and she was a cheerleader who was extremely athletic, in a very feminine way.

Paula was a sophomore and very pretty in her own right. But back then, she was a tomboy. If we ever needed to have someone on our side in a fight, we called on Paula. She and Donny R. are extremely close and she did not allow Donny R. to pull any of his crap on her and he respected her for that. She was always very protective of her "little" brother.

The family was seated in their front room when Donny R. and I entered their large, tastefully decorated apartment. Introductions were quickly made and I instantly felt welcome, their greetings were warm and inviting. I could tell right away they were good people.

"Donny R., how was your day of sledding?" Max asked. "Great Pop, except Tony broke the toboggan." "He what-how did he do that?" Pam asked. "Let's just say he was a little careless on the hill, you know, new kid in town and all. I will help him pay for it by doing some extra chores around here-Tony will pitch in too."

I remember standing there in silence not wanting to get in the way of Two-Fingers story. I figured he knew how to handle these types of things, he seemed to have had a lot of practice.

"You sure he's the one that broke it, Donny R.?" Cindy Ann asked with a look of disbelief on her face. "He already feels bad about it Cindy Ann, let's not make him feel any worse, OK?" Two-Fingers said. "Yeah, right Donny R." Cindy Ann said. "What's for dinner?" Donny R. asked, successfully changing the subject. Later, after dinner, I asked Two-Fingers why he blamed the broken toboggan on me. "Simple, now you and I have an excuse to hang out together. We can do a few chores here and there and have a lot of fun in between."

Later that night, as I walked home, I tried to figure out why we needed an excuse to hang out together, must be a color barrier type of thing. Indian kid didn't want to look bad, especially in front of his parents, if the friendship didn't work out. Made sense, I guess. Two-Fingers may have been feeling the heat from his Indian buddies and maybe his family too for befriending a white guy. Who knows? The subject never came up again.

Chapter 6

There was some serious limping going on at school the next day, Two-Fingers and I kept low and moved fast until school was out. After school, we decided to do some "hooking." Well, actually, Two-Fingers decided we would do some hooking. In the winter, hooking is a popular and dangerous pastime on the Rez. The idea is to grab onto a moving vehicle and let it pull you on an icy street. Paved streets worked the best, graveled roads were hazardous to your health, hit some gravel and you will end up on your ass.

Two-Fingers perfected a one handed grab and pull-he had little choice in the matter. Being new to the game, I was less proficient. However, after about an hour of hooking, I finally got the hang of it.

Just before dark, a group of kids in a Volkswagen bug pulled up to a stop sign near us and as the bug began to pull away, we ran over and grabbed onto the thin metal rear bumper. The driver immediately saw what was happening through his rear view mirror and gunned the motor. This caused the bug to begin spinning in circles in the middle of the icy road, Two-Fingers let go and was thrown into a deep snow drift. Not me. I hung on for dear life until my feet slipped out from underneath me and down I went, right in front of the bug. I was trying desperately to get out of the way of the bug by rolling on the ground but I couldn't escape the impact, the bug ran over my right arm with one of its front tires. Fortunately, the major weight was in the rear of the vehicle and I avoided any lasting injuries. The bug sped away and Two-Fingers ran over to help inspect the damage. "Wow, that was wild." That was the best the glib, fast talking Two-Fingers could come up with.

So, I stood in the middle of the street flexing the muscles in my right arm and was totally amazed it still worked, no broken bones. "I better head home." I said as I started my walk to our gas station. After a few steps in that direction, I turned around and watched Two-Fingers disappear into the night. I remember thinking that if I lived through the weekend it would be a miracle, I shook my head and figured my odds were pretty good since it was already Friday night.

In addition to working at our station and doing chores around the house, my father thought it would be a great idea for me to get a paper route too. It seems he had one when he was a kid and he liked the idea of me keeping as busy as possible. He worked out a deal where I would deliver this paper from Cut Bank called the Western Breeze. I only had to deliver it on Saturdays and Tuesdays because it was only printed twice a week. The Blackfeet liked it because it had the show times for movies in Cut Bank and good coverage of the local sports teams. Anyway, it cost me a penny and it had a price of three cents on the cover. Everybody paid more than three cents because tipping was common. My route consisted of all the local businesses and a few select older people, mostly widows. Glasses of something good to drink and cookies were just a few of the perks. After initially rejecting the idea, I found that I really liked delivering the paper because of the great exercise and the fact that I ended up meeting virtually everybody in town. Plus, I made about $10.00 a week and back then that was pretty good money. I had to walk to the post office to pick up my bundle of papers and on the way there, I would occasionally swing by Two-Fingers house and talk him into going with me. If he was finished with his chores he would go. If not, I would deliver the papers by myself.

It was the Saturday morning after I had been ran over by the bug and as usual it was cold and wintery in Browning. Two-Fingers and I were merrily selling papers and talking about what we were going to be doing that night when all of a sudden, loud barking filled the air. It wasn't really barking, it was more like blood curdling howls and as we turned the corner next to the movie theater, we saw a pack of dogs surrounding a big Saint Bernard. Two dogs were already down and blood was pouring out of their bodies so fast there was no way they were going to survive. Dark, red blood glistened in the white snow. "That's Old McGraw, he's the meanest, toughest dog in town. He killed my dog two years ago, he is fearless. He's been known to fight off packs of dogs without getting a scratch, watch him." Two-Fingers said.

I remember standing there watching this and being mesmerized by the speed and accuracy of Old McGraw's attacks. One by one he ravaged the entire pack of dogs. He threw them down and went directly for their throats, absolutely no mercy. The dogs attacked from all angles and Old McGraw out maneuvered them every time. Finally, the last remaining dog ran off whimpering. I counted four dogs laying in the blood stained snow, dead or dying.

"Someday I am going to kill that dog." Two-Fingers said. "Why doesn't somebody do something about him?" I asked. "Because he belongs to the Mayor. The Mayor says we can't afford a dog catcher and Old McGraw provides a valuable service. That may be true to some extent, only problem is Old McGraw kills the good and the bad." "Does he attack humans?" I asked. "Not that I know of, nobody goes around the vicious bastard to find out. Let this be a lesson to you White Guy and avoid him at all costs, that's what I do."

After we delivered the papers, we were standing near main street counting the money when we were confronted by a small group of Indian boys. At the head of the group was Kenny Stabs-in-the-Back, Ronnie Joe's older brother. Ronnie Joe was there too, along with two of his cousins, Babe and Smiley Black Weasel.

"What you doing with all my money?" Kenny asked. "Gee, what a coincidence, I just saw Old McGraw and I was wondering what's that Kenny up to?" Two-Fingers was talking and that was a good sign. "What's that supposed to mean?" Kenny was big and fast, he just wasn't too quick. "You know, you and McGraw are always picking on someone smaller than yourselves. Don't you ever get tired of that, Kenny?" "No, now give me that money or I am going to bust you up." Kenny said as his gang began to close in.

Just then, a pickup pulled up and out of the passenger side stepped Paula, Kenny and his gang scattered. It turns out that Paula had dog slapped Kenny on a number of occasions. "Sister Girl, how about a ride home?" Two-Fingers asked. "Sure, jump in the back." Paula said.

On the way back to Two-Fingers home, we continued our discussion on what we were going to do that night. Not too many options on a

Saturday night in the big city. Actually, there was only one real option that was legal, we were going to the movies.

Browning has one theater and you know it's a theater because the sign out front of it says so. The owner, Mr. Boswell, was one of the few rich men in town and he got that way by not spending any of his profits on furniture or decorations. There wasn't any real lobby in the theatre; no place to buy candy, popcorn or anything like that. Those purchases were made at one of the two drugstores nearby and soda pop and sunflower seeds were the snacks of choice for the younger crowd. Hard drinks were the preference for a surprisingly large number of the theater going public and things tended to get a little rowdy about halfway through a film, no matter how good it was. If it was really bad, bottles of varying sizes and shapes were routinely thrown around the place.

The first five rows at the front of the theatre consisted of hardwood benches and that was where the real young kids were supposed to sit. The back rows of seats were actual seats with backs, but no cushions, the cushions were destroyed years ago and never replaced. Going to the bathroom was always an adventure, the holes in the doors and walls made privacy a luxury. Each bathroom, the Men and Women's, housed a single toilet; no toilet paper of any kind, just a toilet. The theater going crowd generally used other facilities before going to the movies or they held it. I truly believe that is why the Blackfeet have an abnormally high rate of kidney failure, it's the theater's fault.

The crowd was unusually large that night, it was a John Wayne movie. John Wayne was always a big draw, he always killed all the Indians but unlike other Westerns, he made you feel good about it. Always some other Tribe dying off anyway, never the Blackfeet. The Sioux, Crow, Apaches and a bunch of other Tribes getting killed, but not the Blackfeet.

Two-Fingers and I were up near the front of the ticket line and the two bit admission price was burning a hole in our pockets. When it was our turn, Two-Fingers pulled out four bits and said, "Two for the balcony and keep the change." "You are a real funny guy aren't you, Donny R.? Keep cracking wise and you will be going to the back of the line." Mr. Boswell said as he reluctantly handed over two tickets. Mr. Boswell was like all the other white merchants in town, no sense of humor. Two-Fingers snapped off a nice salute and turned and marched into the theater, I followed closely.

We made our way down to the front of the theater. Two-Fingers was still leading the way and he walked real slow, he surveyed the scene. He held his head high and pranced down the aisle, he checked out some girls in the corner that were checking him out too. Suddenly, he made his move. He sat down next to a girl by the name of Veronica Comes At Night. Next to her sat Vicki Eagle Feathers. "Move over Cousin and make room for this poor white guy I found wandering around in the bathroom."

The girls giggled and Vicki slid over one seat and nodded towards the seat next to her. There the four of us sat, Two-Fingers next to the wall, Veronica, Vicki and me next to the aisle, it was very cozy.

We sat there watching a Woody Woodpecker cartoon and it proved to be very popular. Catcalls and laughter erupted when someone in the back yelled, "Woody's got a wooden pecker just like old man Boswell!!" "You ought to know, aenet!!" Someone else yelled.

The crowd finally settled down when the movie began. I glanced over at Two-Fingers who had his arm around Veronica and a smile on his face. Two-Fingers glanced back at me and nodded his head towards Vicki. I wasn't exactly sure what he wanted me to do. Vicki noticed Two-Fingers gesture and whispered in my ear, "He wants you to put your arm around me." I hesitated briefly before raising my left arm and slowly placing it on Vicki's shoulders. I kept my eyes glued to the screen because I was not brave enough to look at her. Vicki slowly moved towards me and snuggled up real close. At first I thought she must be cold, I was not sure how that was possible because I was sweating bullets. Bullets, arrows, Vicki and John Wayne all in the same night, if I could only take a piss.

After the movie, Two-Fingers and I went outside to find a place to relieve ourselves, no way in hell we were going to use the theater's toilet. Besides, there was a really long line. We walked to the alley behind the theater and found an unoccupied spot and quickly took care of business. To successfully piss in a cold, windy Montana night took a degree of practice that I could ill afford, I had to go bad. So I learned the hard way: Never piss out in the open because the wind is very unforgiving. I'll tell you the truth, I wiped a lot of piss off my boots growing up in Browning.

Just as we finished, the siren that was attached to the water tower blasted it's warning, it was ten o'clock and the curfew was in effect and all the minors had to get off the streets or they would end up spending the night in jail, curfew on the Rez was serious business. Of course, the young Blackfeet made a game out of avoiding arrest. They would dodge out in front of the Tribal police cars and then sprint off into an open field where they couldn't be easily followed. This would go on for hours and eventually, the police would just give up. Besides, they were kept busy with all the barroom brawls, car wrecks, domestic violence calls and any number of other unlawful and dangerous acts. On the weekends, the jail and the hospital were standing room only.

Chapter 7

On the Rez, school was the only place that had any semblance of order. To keep it that way, discipline was meted out with a vengeance and absolutely no consideration was given to any potential psychological damage. On the Rez, nobody knew what psychology was. Punishment was swift and harsh, no appeals. There was a kind of beauty to it, as long as you weren't the person on the receiving end.

Back then, it really wasn't the teachers I worried about, I worried about the students. I generally put in my time and never went out of my way to cause a problem and Two-Fingers was the same way. My routine was pretty simple, get to class and hang up my coat, take my seat and do not talk unless spoken to. It seemed to work, I am still alive and I only have minimal scarring.

At recess one day, Two-Fingers and I met at the playground and began a friendly game of lagging. In lagging, coins are tossed up against a wall from a distance of about fifteen feet. Closest to the wall wins, simple enough. We were lagging for quarters and that was big money. Especially, when most of the kids had absolutely no money. On that day, Ronnie Joe had to get in, he had four quarters and he couldn't wait to take all of our money. After all, he was the best lagger in town and I normally lost every time I played that stupid game. But, for some reason, I couldn't be beat. I took him out in four straight tosses and that was more than Ronnie Joe could stand. He grabbed the money away from me and pushed me to the ground and before anyone could intervene, I jumped up and tackled Ronnie Joe. Ronnie Joe threw me off of him and we both jumped to our feet. I struck first with a punch that connected squarely on his jaw. Ronnie Joe staggered, but he did not go down. Instead, he charged me and knocked me to the ground again. We were engaged in serious hand-to-hand combat and didn't see Mr. Blackstone approach, he moved in quickly and broke up the fight.

"Who started this? It doesn't matter." Mr. Blackstone said, not waiting for an answer. He yelled for a teacher/assistant football coach by the name of Mr. Anderson to lend him a hand. Mr. Anderson walked over and grabbed us by our collars. "Hold them here, I need to get something from my office." Mr. Blackstone said as he walked to the school. He quickly returned with the weapon of mass destruction; a long, thick paddle with one inch holes drilled into the center of the flat end. He was holding the paddle so tightly his veins were popping out of his hand. "You know the drill, Ronnie Joe, assume the position." Mr. Blackstone said.

Ronnie Joe bent over at his waist and grabbed his ankles and Mr. Blackstone, breathing hard, proceeded to give Ronnie Joe ten of the most vicious whacks on the ass imaginable, I actually felt sorry for him. Then it was my turn and Mr. Blackstone didn't show any favoritism, I received the same number of whacks. In fact, on whack number ten, the force of the blow was so powerful, the paddle broke off at the base of the handle. Too late, the job was complete. It hurt so bad I had to fight back tears. I looked over at Ronnie Joe and it appeared that he was doing the same. However, within seconds Ronnie Joe's face took on its familiar look of defiance, a look honed from years of such abuse.

I remember Two-Fingers argued with Mr. Blackstone and Mr. Anderson about us getting paddled so hard. He called them chickenshit and all kinds of names, I thought he was going to take a swing at them, I really did. They finally drug him off to the detention center where he stayed the rest of the day.

One thing about it, the rest of the school year was very peaceful. No more fights, at least not on school property.

Chapter 8

Spring finally made its appearance a few days after the school yard incident. It was April and the sun came out and it was actually nice and warm for a change. Two-Fingers and I both had cabin fever and were set on having an adventure, it was time to play hooky from school.

We decided to hitchhike up to East Glacier, it was a great day for a road trip. East Glacier is thirteen miles to the west of Browning and is the east entrance to Glacier National Park, we decided to check it out before all the tourists started to show up.

We walked past the Junction Drive In and we were totally oblivious to the traffic, walking felt good. We walked along the highway throwing rocks at the beer bottles, wine bottles, whiskey bottles; anything with glass. Occasionally we found a gopher to throw at but mainly, it was glass.

Before we realized it, we had walked all the way out to Old Man Racine's place. The ice on the lake was as hard and as thick as ever, or so I thought. We were making a game out of racing along the edge of the lake and sliding on the soles of our shoes and I was getting farther and farther away from shore. Two-Fingers was behind me saying something to me and as I stopped to listen, the ice began to crack before it suddenly gave way. Down I went into the murky, freezing water.

As I began to sink away, I was overwhelmed with a feeling of helplessness. I tried desperately to pull myself out of the deathtrap and had no luck in doing so, the ice kept breaking away every time I reached the surface. I was deep underwater and freezing when I panicked big time. I finally surfaced and desperately tried to grab onto the edge of the ice and pull myself out of the water. When I did, the ice gave way and down I went again and I just kept thinking it is too nice a day to die.

I was running out of strength but I kept looking for ice solid enough to hold me, only a few minutes had passed but it seemed like hours. My hands grew numb and my teeth were chattering, I couldn't get them to stop chattering. Suddenly, I went down deep into the lake for a third time and I remember being totally submerged and looking up at the hole in the ice and seeing the clear blue sky, what a beautiful day.

Then, I saw the Levi jacket that Two-Fingers always wore floating towards me and I reached for it as I slowly rose to the surface of the lake once again. When my head cleared the water, I began to choke up water and what appeared to be a small minnow. There on the ice was Two-Fingers, sprawled out on his belly and slowly pulling me out of the hole, he kept dragging me to safety. I was belching and puking up lake water and trying desperately to catch my breath but I would not let go of that jacket and he kept pulling me across the ice until there was solid ground under us. I felt like a beached whale gasping for air, my teeth chattered like crazy and I had lost all feeling in my hands and legs but I was alive, Two-Fingers had crawled out on thin ice and saved my life.

Two-Fingers finally was able to stand me up and then we walked over to Old Man Racine's fire barrel and made a fire. Actually, Two-Fingers made the fire, I just sat on the ground and coughed up water.

Soon, the fire was nice and toasty and I began to feel almost normal after an hour or so. Two-Fingers kept throwing wood in the barrel and the flames kept getting higher and higher and ashes floated in the air before falling on my wet clothes and dissolving.

To my knowledge, Two-Fingers never mentioned this incident to anyone. He was never one to brag about things like saving my life, we both knew he had and that was enough. I don't know too many people that are willing to save another person's life when it puts their life in danger. Maybe my family would but they have never been put to the test, Two-Fingers was put to the test and he did not hesitate. I would like to think I am that courageous but I am not sure. Hopefully, I will never be tested but if I am, I hope I am as brave as Two-Fingers.

Our friendship was enriched that day, bonds were strengthened and from that day forward, Two-Fingers and I were even more inseparable.

Chapter 9

It was a couple of months after my near drowning that school was adjourned for the summer. There weren't any celebrations on the Rez when school was dismissed; no trips to the ice cream parlor, no sleepovers and certainly no parades. There were just a bunch of kids trying to get home safely before they were ran over by some drunk driver.

I remember my brother Stan was especially glad to get out of school, he had graduated and was looking forward to summer. I really hadn't seen much of Stan during his senior year, he was too busy fighting his own battles. Big and powerful, Stan never took any crap from anybody. He was a good athlete who found pleasure in playing sports with and against the Blackfeet. The Blackfeet are very good basketball players, very good.

He had a date with Two-Fingers sister Paula the Saturday night after graduation and he was very exited about that. I remember when Stan picked her up at the Schwartz's place in the 57' Chevy. He was all cleaned up and smelling good, the smell of Old Spice hung in the air as he walked up the steps leading to their apartment building. Two-Fingers, who was sitting out on the porch with me, yelled out, "Don't try anything with my sister Stan or I'll have to kick your ass." Stan continued walking up the steps and briefly glanced at Two-Fingers and said, "Yeah, I'll keep that in mind." "You better." Two-Fingers said seriously. Stan looked over at me and all I could do was shrug my shoulders and grin, Two-Fingers always had to have the last word.

While Stan was inside picking up Paula, Two-Fingers and I sat outside and surveyed the scene. There was a lot going on in Browning that night, I swear you could almost hear hearts breaking.

To me, it seemed like Stan was in the Schwartz's place for a longtime. Finally, he and Paula made their escape and as Stan held the car door open for her, she glanced up at Two-Fingers and smiled. I remember staring at her, it was the first time I had ever seen Paula wearing a dress and her nylons seemed to run on forever. Her perfume was so powerful it banished the Old Spice smell to the hell it deserved. Her jet black hair was pulled back, accentuating her high cheekbones and the only makeup she had on was just a touch of lipstick, red lipstick. She was stunning. Stan stood there patiently holding the car door for her and as she slid across the front seat I was able to briefly glimpse the top of her nylon stockings and that was when I fell off the porch and chipped my tooth.

As Stan and Paula prepared to leave, Two-Fingers yelled, "Don't forget what I told you, Stan." "Ok, little man, I won't forget." Stan smiled and then gave us both the finger.

The '57 Chevy took off in a cloud of dust with Fats Domino blaring on the radio, "Blue Monday, Oh how I love Blue Monday..." "Little man, who the hell was he calling little man?" Two-Fingers asked as he stood up and shook his hand in an act of defiance. "Hey, he's gone, you don't have to get the last word in with me." I said as I climbed back up the steps.

Not long after Paula and Stan left, a group of Blackfeet in a yellow Volkswagen van pulled up to where we were sitting and asked us if we would like to go to a party out at Cut Bank Creek. We did not hesitate and quickly jumped into the van, I remember getting squished in the back seat as more and more Blackfeet piled in. The van traveled the five miles to Cut Bank Creek with a load of underaged, slightly intoxicated Blackfeet and a white guy.

Cut Bank Creek is a perfect place for partying. There are a lot of great party places on the Rez but Cut Bank Creek is just the best place, especially on a warm summer night. High, rocky cliffs surround the area. The creek was full from the spring runoff and there was plenty of wood for the fire and plenty of beer too. Three kegs of beer were set up and flowing liberally by the time Two-Fingers and I arrived. Stan and Paula were there but they did not pay attention to either one of us, they were in deep, meaningful conversation.

Cindy Ann, Two-Fingers oldest sister, was there too. Cindy Ann was accompanied by the captain of the basketball team, "Stogie Man." Stogie Man smoked Camels since he was about ten years old, hence the name. Stogie Man was a great basketball player but by the fourth quarter he always seemed to run out of gas but that didn't stop Montana State University from offering him a full ride scholarship on the condition he quit smoking, everybody was keeping their fingers crossed. Stogie Man and Cindy Ann were planning on getting married before they left for college.

Soon after arriving, most of the girls got together and started talking about how well they looked and the guys just kept drinking and telling stories on each other, it was all quite civilized really. But then again, it was early.

Two of the things I like most about Montana are the long summer days and the fantastic sunsets. That night, Two-Fingers and I talked a couple of our girl classmates into going for a little walk. Before going, we each filled our cups with beer and walked to the top of the cliff to watch the sunset. The sunset was exceptional that night, orange and red streaks dominated the sky. There were no clouds or wind, it was a beautiful evening.

From our vantage point, we were able to see the party scene below, the city lights of Browning and the sunset. Off in the distance, we noticed a car zig-zagging sown the highway at a dangerously high speed. As is got closer, Two-Fingers said, "That must be John Hoyt." His nickname was A.J. because he loved fast cars, A.J. Hoyt. He never finished high school, he dropped out when he was about fifteen or so and his dad owned the "wrecked car graveyard" and towing business south of Browning. They say he is the best mechanic in Montana, he is so small and greasy he can fit into places nobody else can. My dad said they did't even own a jack! No need, A.J. just slid under the car and fixed the problem.

Sure enough, it was A.J. in his souped up '62 Ford Fairlane. He was downing a beer when we returned to the party. "Yeah, I just got back from towing some dumb ass tourist into town. The stupid bastard blew a rod, I bet he hasn't changed his oil in five years!!" "He should have used Quaker State, aenet, A.J.!!" Somebody yelled.

A.J.'s life was cars and he just hated to see one get hurt. To him, it was down right sacrilegious. Of course, he didn't mind racing them.

"How about a race? Who owns that '57 Chevy I saw parked over there?" A.J. asked as he pointed towards the highway. "That's mine, well it belongs to my folks but I am driving it." Stan said. "What do you say we get it on then?" A. J. asked before gulping down another beer.

The crowd roared its approval, Paula shook her head no and Stan pondered the idea as he sipped his beer. "All right, let's go." Stan said as he turned and walked to his car. When he arrived at the car, he stopped Paula from getting in and said, "Listen, this could be a little dangerous, you better stay here and wait for me." "No way, this is still our date and I am not leaving you alone. Besides, you may need a copilot."

So, they both jumped into the car and drove onto the highway facing Browning. Stogie Man lined them up side by side, a nice long straightaway beckoned them. Stogie Man had his letter jacket off and was waving it over his head when he suddenly dropped it to the ground. Stan and A.J. peeled rubber and took off in a cloud of smoke, a bunch of us jumped into the Volkswagen van and followed. Stan was in the inside lane and A.J. was straddling the center lane. They were picking up speed and it looked like A.J. was slightly ahead when, all of a sudden, a horse jumped out of the tall grass along the highway. Stan tried to avoid it but his car hit the horse square in the head. The windshield had a hole in the passenger side the size of, well the size of a horse's head and glass flew everywhere. The van full of spectators pulled over to get a good look at things, Paula stood there laughing her head off and Stan looked like he was trying desperately not to piss himself. Luckily, the only thing damaged was the windshield, no dents just a broken windshield. The horse was laying in a ditch and it didn't look so good and nobody checked to see if it was still breathing.

Well, we all decided to go back to the party and drink up the rest of the beer, everybody's blood was pumping pretty good and the night was still young. I had never seen Stan drink that much before, he really got tuned up. Come to think about it, we all got pretty loose. After all the beer was gone, the party slowly wound down and I asked Stan and Paula for a ride and they both agreed that would be a good idea. I am not sure where Two-Fingers ended up but I knew I needed to get some sleep, I was stumbling down drunk. Stan dropped Paula off at her house and gave her a quick goodbye kiss and as we drove home he asked me what he should say about the windshield. I said he should come clean and tell the folks exactly what happened.

Well, Stan was pretty looped and not thinking too clearly and when he parked the Chevy behind our gas station, he spotted a rock about the same size as the hole in the windshield. His alcohol drenched brain must have been working overtime because he placed the rock on the front passenger seat and then he stood back and looked at it for awhile. Then he adjusted it a little bit before shutting the door very quietly and then we both stumbled off to bed; great idea, the perfect crime.

The next morning, mom screamed like crazy and it woke me from my alcohol induced coma. "Some little neighborhood kid has broken our windshield!!" She repeated this about ten times, each time was a little louder than the last. Dad finally heard her and ran to her rescue, I was looking at both of them through by bedroom window and thinking to myself, "Oh, shit."

"What the hell happened here?" Dad yelled. "Some little neighborhood kid broke our windshield." She said for the eleventh time. "I am going to kill the bastard." Less than a year on the Rez and she was already losing it. "Now, now, Ruby, settle down." Dad said as he inspected the damage.

It was about that time that Stan stumbled out the back door of our living quarters looking like death warmed over, he was still dressed from the night before but his hair was standing on end. He tried to pull his left boot on as he hopped across the gravel parking lot on one leg. Mom was convinced some kid had broken the windshield and she was telling Stan all about it and Stan stood there listening politely when his conscience finally got the better of him. After mom paused to take a breath, Stan interrupted her and blurted out what had really happened.

"Well, your ass is grounded and you are paying to have this fixed." Dad said as the bright crimson red faded from his face, dad had started counting to ten in those types of situations and it really helped matters. "How could you, Stan?" Was all mom said before handing Stan the keys and walking away.

By this time, I was dressed and standing next to him. I said to him, "Man, you really fucked up." He hit me in the arm so hard I can still feel the pain to this day. Anyway, Stan and I got back in the Chevy and we drove out to the Hoyts, they must have a windshield he can buy. As we approached the Hoyt's, we were amazed at what we saw, you can never fully appreciate a junk yard until you see it up close and in the light of day. Acre after acre of old, wrecked cars greeted us. Thousands of cars were there, stacks of cars rising to the sky. License plates from all over the country were attached to these once proud vehicles that now laid stripped and abandoned.

Stan parked outside of what appeared to be the office and we slowly walked towards the entrance. He quietly opened the front door and there stood Mr. Hoyt staring back at us. Mr. Hoyt was a huge man who was covered by grease from head to toe and the only thing he had on was a pair of bib overalls, no shoes. The fat from his hairy chest spilled over the top of the overalls and gave the appearance of two little pigs feeding on a bale of hay.

"What can I do you for?" Evidently, Mr. Hoyt used this standard greeting with everyone. Seemed to work, he had several cool looking awards from the local Chamber of Commerce hanging on the wall. "Yeah, hello. I am looking for A.J." Stan figured he could get a better deal from his partner in crime. "Haven't seen him, he has been gone all night. Must have found a woman, aenet." Mr. Hoyt must have been dreaming.

It was right around that time that there was this loud noise outside his office. The three of us turned and looked out the large picture window and noticed A.J. pulling into the driveway. Well, "pulled into" is not quite accurate. He kind of wobbled in, his beautiful '62 Ford Fairlane wobbled. The tires were pointing out in all directions, steam gushed from the radiator, the grill was gone and the front bumper was pushed over the hood, the car literally wobbled. The three of us ran outside as the Ford came to a sudden stop.

"What the hell happened to your car?" Stan asked. "Well, last night, after you left, someone pulled out some whiskey." A.J. said as he glanced up at his dad. "Well, the party was still going strong around five a.m. and we all wanted some beer." A.J. took another look at his dad. "Well, I got elected to run in to the bootleggers to pick up some more beer." A.J. stared at the ground and didn't look at anyone. "A couple of other guys and gals decided to go with me. So, we all jumped in the Ford and headed into town. I was going pretty fast when, all of a sudden, I hit something. Well, the impact was so severe it caused me to come to a complete stop. I was not sure what I'd hit, so I threw the car into reverse and backed up. Pretty soon, I ran back over the top of whatever it was that I hit." A.J. appeared to be tearing up. "Well, it turns out we were sitting on top of a horse, high centered. I was stuck and I mean stuck. So, a couple of the guys got out and started to push me off of the top of this horse. I tried reversing for awhile and then I tried to go forward for awhile. We were rocking pretty good and I had it floored when all of a sudden, the car shot off that horse like a rocket and straight into the ditch we went, the only thing that stopped us was this big pine tree." A.J. was visibly sobbing. "You know that horse you hit last night, Stan? You must have just knocked it unconscious because it came to and staggered onto the highway about the time I was heading to town on the beer run. Evidently, it was standing there as I came down the road. I evidently took my eyes off the road for a split second before I hit it."

"Evidently." was all old man Hoyt had to say before he turned and walked back into his office. "You know the really bad thing about this, Stan?"

"You mean it gets worse?" Stan asked. "I am afraid so, this is open range country. That means if an animal is killed, the killer has to pay for it." A.J. was laying on the ground, too weak to cry. "Well, pull yourself together, I have some business for you-I need to replace a windshield. By the way, I'll have to charge it." I could tell Stan was suddenly feeling better about himself.

I would like to tell you that this story is unique but it is not. Things like that happened all the time on the Rez. Over the years, every time Two-Fingers and I witnessed things like this, he would always look at me and say, "Alcohol related."

Chapter 10

At the risk of overstating the obvious, alcoholism is a very bad thing. Alcoholics, no matter where they are, are on their very own reservations; heartache and despair are their boundaries. Being an alcoholic on the Rez is very, very bad but at least there is a lot of company. Eventually, the path is lonely no matter who is along for the ride. Two-Fingers and I witnessed this first hand and as teenagers we were constantly surrounded by drinking, it was as common as breathing. We started young and it took us both a long time to shake the habit. Alcohol devastates lives and after years of drinking it takes tremendous will power to quit. To quit, you have to find the power within yourself, nobody else can do it for you. There are a lot of good people struggling to get sober. Drinking was a fun thing to do when we were young but as we grew older it became a full-time, tedious job.

Two-Fingers and I were always able to get an adult to buy us booze. His sisters boyfriends got us booze a lot of times and if they weren't around we could always find a wino to get us whatever we wanted. It cost a little bit more money to have the winos buy it, but that was okay. We liked to drink and raise hell, it was our number one pastime. You can warn somebody about the evil effects of alcohol but that advice, like most advice, usually falls on deaf ears. People have to learn the hard way. But, if you have fallen and are able to find the strength to quit it puts the world into a whole new light.

Two-Fingers and I turned out to be good, upstanding citizens and all but when we were kids, we were wild. I just want you to know that because I am not going to sugar coat our youth. Everybody is shaped by their life's experiences and they either turn out good or they turn out bad. Two-Fingers turned out good and I am not really sure why. All you people that are asking me about him need to know some of the nitty gritty and here is an incident that sticks in my mind and it probably affected Two-Fingers as well.

Two-Fingers parents apartment building sat right across the street from the Businessmen's Club. Now, the Businessmen's Club is probably the swankiest bar in town but it still didn't have any windows, plenty of booze just no windows. Anyway, Two-Fingers and I were sitting there one summer night bored out of our minds watching the traffic go by when all of a sudden Two-Fingers perked up and said, "Hey, there goes Mike "Bandit" Bird Rattler walking into the Businessmen's Club. He will buy us some booze. How much money do you have on you?" Two-Fingers asked.

I remember reaching into my pocket and pulling out a wrinkled one dollar bill, one stinking dollar was all I had left from my paper route money and the money I made working at our gas station. One dollar, we spent money like we were rich. Two-Fingers had a dollar too so that gave us enough to buy a mickey of Seagrams whiskey.

We were sitting there patiently waiting for the Bandit to come out of the club when I asked Two-Fingers why is he called "Bandit?" Two-Fingers said it was because he had only one arm, his right arm was missing. Evidently, he was in a very bad car wreck and his arm was cut off and he was called "Bandit" after the slot machines down in Las Vegas. You know, "the one-armed bandits." He wore a fake arm that was made out of rubber and Two-Fingers said it looked stupid and didn't work at all, the Bandit still insisted on wearing it. See how bored you are with this story? That is how bored we were that night.

Anyway, Bandit stayed inside the Businessman's Club for a long time and we waited for him. It was a Thursday night and nobody else was around, so we waited. We were about to give up on him when the front door to the Club suddenly opened and out walked the Bandit, staggering.

Two-Fingers and I jumped up and ran across the street and caught up to Bandit before he got too far away. "Hey, Bandit." Two-Fingers whispered as we approached. Bandit, startled, slowly turned around and faced us. "Oh, it's you Two-Fingers, I thought it might be one of those damn winos trying to get my booze." He slowly removed a small bottle of whiskey from his back pocket and took a long drink. After he emptied the bottle, he threw it up against the wall of the Club and it shattered into a hundred little pieces. "Bandit, I need you to get me a mickey of Seagrams. I have two dollars, will that be enough?" "Yeah, that's plenty-I suppose the rest is my tip aenet, Two-Fingers?" "Sure, why not. We will wait for you out here." Two-Fingers placed the money in Bandit's left hand and Bandit staggered back inside the Businessmen's Club.

We were waiting in the shadows of the Club and our hearts were beating like war drums. Not only were we worried about the Bandit returning, but curfew was in effect and we were concerned the Tribal police might find us.

Finally Bandit reappeared and instead of walking towards us, he turned and walked quickly across the street and down the alley behind Two-Fingers place. We ran after the damn thief and just about got hit by a truck as we crossed the road. Bandit did not have any problems with his legs, he had both of them and he was moving fast. We started jogging after him and we were still losing ground.

My adrenaline started pumping and I was excited to give chase, so I sprinted off into the night as fast as I could leaving Two-Fingers behind. I quickly closed the gap between us and I noticed he was holding a paper sack firmly against his body with his fake arm. We were running side by side down one of the few lighted streets in Browning when I reached over and yanked on the paper sack which caused the rubber arm to come loose. There I was, running down the street looking down at his rubber, yellow fake arm and desperately trying to remove the sack from it. Finally, I got the arm separated from the whiskey and I tossed it straight up into the air. I stopped running long enough to watch the rubber arm bounce and tumble down the road Bandit stopped running too and slowly turned around to retrieve his fake arm. Just then, Two-Fingers ran over to the fake arm and kicked it as hard as he could and the arm flew end over end and landed in Mr. Boswell's front yard. Two-Fingers and I were standing in the middle of the street watching Bandit climbing over Mr. Boswell's picket fence when the Tribal police came flying by before coming to a screeching halt when they saw the Bandit straddling the fence. They quickly jumped out of the patrol car and ran over and grabbed the Bandit as he tried to retrieve his arm out of Mr. Boswell's front yard, the Bandit would have none of it. He started kicking and screaming at the top of his lungs, "My arm, I need my arm. My arm is in the yard!!" The cops finally got him under control and threw him in the back seat of the patrol car and locked all the doors. As they drove off, Two-Fingers said, "Well, now you know the real reason they call him the Bandit."

Later that night, after all the whiskey was drank, we played hide and seek with the Tribal police because the whiskey made us fast and fearless. We darted out in front of the patrol car and then ran off when they gave chase. Firewater makes you do crazy things, just saying.

Chapter 11

The next day, Friday, July 29, 1967 was the first day of the North American Indian Days PowWow celebration which is held annually in Browning. The celebration is nonstop for ten days and Tribes from all over Canada and the U.S. descend upon Browning to join in the festivities.

Each year, the celebration kicks off with a big parade and Indians of all ages join in the act. Indian regalia, unlike anything I had ever seen, was on display virtually everywhere. Beautifully decorated horses pranced up and down main street ridden by riders in full headdress and buckskin. Convertibles, with their tops down, displayed the beautiful Indian girls who were vying for "Miss North American Indian Princess." It is the Blackfeet's favorite time of year.

Two-Fingers and I were on the front porch taking it all in and nursing a monster of a hangover, we ended up partying with some classmates after the cops quit chasing us. Anyway, I had already thrown up twice and Two-Fingers looked a little green around the gills. Of course, he did not admit he was feeling poorly, not his style.

Float after float passed by and tourists filled the streets and were busily taking pictures. The sun was high in the sky and it was downright hot. We noticed Kenny and Ronnie Joe Stabs-in-the-Back walking down the street with their cousins, Babe and Smiley Black Weasel. They were all dressed up in their best Levi jeans and cowboy shirts, their boots were shined, their hair was slicked back and they all reeked of Old Spice. They stopped right in front of us and watched the parade go by. Before long, the float carrying the reigning "Miss North America Indian Princess," Miss Cindy Ann Schwartz pulled into view. "They have to get rid of her because she is no longer a maiden, aenet." Kenny was yelling at the top of his voice. "Stogie Man saw to that, aenet Kenny!!" Said Ronnie Joe. "Yeah, shit I hear they got to get married, aenet." Babe Black Weasel yelled. "I'd marry her too if she let me have some of that." Smiley Black Weasel yelled at the top of his voice.

After hearing all that, Two-Fingers was no longer green-he had turned a bright red. He slowly walked over to the fence and motioned for the gang to come closer and they did so gladly. Kenny approached and began to roll up the sleeves of his cowboy shirt. Ronnie Joe was glaring at me and the Black Weasel boys were lined up in between the Stabs-in-the-Backs and all of them were leaning over the fence.

Two-Fingers, filled with rage, began to vomit. He blew huge chunks of puke at the boys, stream after stream of vomit spewed from his mouth and splattered all over their fancy clothes and boots. Their hair was no longer slicked back. Instead, it hung down below their eyes and slimy bile dripped off them. At that point, I was unable to control myself so I joined in on the attack and all the remaining fluid in my body spilled out over my lips and onto Ronnie Joe.

Soon, A large crowd of tourists gathered and started taking pictures at a feverish pace. Kenny and his gang were desperately trying to climb over the fence but they were unable to gain the necessary footing, the sidewalk was as slick as their hair and bodies. I could see the look of hate in their eyes, they seemed to be in a trance fueled by this hatred. Suddenly, they quit trying to get over the fence when they became aware of the crowd, it had grown in size and was very loud and pushy. The gang could not stand the vomit, but they hated the laughter even more so they gave up and sulked off. I had a gut feeling that the next time we met all hell was going to break loose.

That night, Two-Fingers and I went to the fairgrounds to watch some more Indian festivities. The fairground was filled with hundreds of Teepees. Tents were plentiful too, but the primary lodging were Teepees. A number of Two-Fingers relatives were busy setting up their Teepees so there was plenty of places to stay. Even if there were no blood relatives with Teepees, during Indian Days all Indians are related and finding a place to sleep or something to eat was never an issue. There were concession stands selling Indian tacos, ice slushes, corn dogs, hot dogs, hamburgers, buffalo burgers and cotton candy. Plus, each campsite would soon have something cooking. No carnival rides allowed, nothing mechanical. Indian Days are all about the traditions of the past which includes a lot of dancing, stick games and singing; several days of just being Indian.

I ate my first Indian taco at that celebration and haven't turned back since. Indian tacos are made up of fry bread and pinto beans, easy to make and very tasty. The key is the fry bread which is made of bread dough deep fried in grease, add some pinto beans to the fry bread and you have Indian tacos. Commodity beans of course, Browning was never short of commodities and when you subsist on commodities you have to be creative in planning your menu and Indian tacos are a result of that creativity. Two-Fingers and I gorged ourselves on Indian tacos and pop, we needed to replace all the fluids we spewed on the gang.

After we ate, we walked around the Encampment taking in all the sights and sounds, we walked slow and easy. We walked over to the rodeo arena to see what was going on. Dad and Charley were there and they were getting ready to compete in the team calf roping event so we stopped to watch them take their turn. The whole idea behind team calf roping is to see which team can lasso a calf around its head and turn it so the other team member can lasso the hind legs, the team with the best time wins. Dad and Charley hadn't practiced much and they were both pretty rusty.

Dad and Charley were behind the barrier and so was the calf when their names were announced over the public address system. The calf was let loose and dad and Charley sprang into action, dad was the header and Charley was going after the hind legs. Dad did his part and was able to lasso the head and turn the calf in the right direction but Charley missed and the crowd let out a collective sigh. I thought, "oh shit, the old man is going to be pissed tonight."

Later that evening, we ran into a couple of pretty blonds about our age and it turned out they were sisters. We literally ran into them, we were looking around and not paying attention to where we were going and we nearly knocked them over. They were drinking pop and it spilled all over the place. We apologized and offered to buy them more pop and to my surprise they said okay. They both stared at Two-Fingers and looked away when they noticed his hand. They introduced themselves and told us how exciting it was to be at an Indian celebration. Their names were Samantha and Lisa and after some small talk, they asked us if we would show them around and we quickly agreed, girls who actually wanted to be around us surprised us both.

As nighttime approached, the Encampment seemed to take on a solemn, peaceful mood following the festivities of the day. Serenity was an unusual thing on the Rez, but that night was very serene. Campfires full of wood roared to life, watching flames in a campfire is a truly relaxing experience. Children darted in and out of the many hiding places playing Cowboys and Indians and the Indians were having a very good night; no additional lands lost and very few casualties.

Large canvas tents were filled with blackjack players, mainly old women with a tight grip on the cards and an even tighter grip on their money. Men were playing their stick games at a feverish pace. The "bones" were hidden and wagers were placed on who had the "bones?" Piles of money laid at their feet and things began to take on a serious tone. Who has the "bones"? Stick games, poker, blackjack-you got it, they will bet on it, the Blackfeet love to gamble. We walked and walked and took it all in.

As I reflect back on that night, I realize now how important Indian celebrations like these are to the Blackfeet. For a very brief time, they are once again free and they share their innermost beliefs during these celebrations. In current vernacular, they let it all hang out. They were happy to display parts of their culture and the tourists were enamored with their story telling and their hospitality. Young and old, rich and poor, white and red, all mingled together and shared time without concern for their station in life. The essence of these celebrations are absorbed into the very souls of those willing to embrace the beauty of it all, worries were swept away and the rejuvenation of the spirit took center stage. The Blackfeet were the stars on that night. I have often thought, was this the way it was before the White Man? Was life this beautiful in the days before the credit card and the house payment? Was life ever going to be this good again? Freedom, what an elusive commodity. Commodities, handouts by the rich to the poor to help ease their conscience, received by the down trodden and never appreciated because it was not earned. Reservation life is a misery because there is a lack of self worth. White Society's idea of achievement and the Indian way of looking at things are at complete opposites of the spectrum. Human frustration is directly related to the chasing of trinkets. Hell, even the Indians on Long Island gave up their land and souls for $26 dollars worth of trinkets, why not? Humanity is giving up a lot more for a lot less, we are losing individual freedoms daily and very few people seem to care. Anyway, I became a lot more "Indian" after that night.

Teepee crawling is the Blackfeet's version of musical chairs-without the chairs. The Blackfeet are not certain when Teepee crawling first took hold in the Blackfeet culture, they are just glad that it did. Something about a Teepee that causes the Blackfeet to get horny, no wonder they are always camping.

The key to Teepee crawling is to know whose Teepee you are crawling into. Pick the wrong Teepee and you can get your ass whipped, or shot. Always try to find a willing, unattached person and hope like hell you do not get trampled. Sex on the Rez, always an adventure.

"Have you girls ever been inside a real warriors Teepee?" Two-Fingers asked as he pulled back the flap of his parents Teepee. "Third one this month." Samantha said as she lowered her head and entered. Lisa giggled and followed her in. "Nice to see you white girls have a good sense of humor." Two-Fingers replied. "Who says I am kidding?" Samantha said as she leaned over and gave Two-Fingers a kiss on the lips. Two-Fingers seemed to be momentarily caught off guard but quickly figured it out. Samantha was breathing hard and I was concerned she may have emphysema. One of my grandmothers had emphysema and died as a result of it, just saying. Lisa turned her eyes away and quickly stepped outside. I followed after her when Two-Fingers asked, "Hey, White Guy, why don't you go get yourself a corn dog?"

"Samantha has always been boy crazy." Lisa said as we walked to the nearest corn dog stand. We were standing there enjoying our corn dogs and pop when Kenny and Ronnie Joe Stabs-in-the-Back suddenly appeared with their groupies, Babe and Smiley Black Weasel. "Hey, White Guy, what are you doing with my girlfriend?" Ronnie Joe yelled at the top of his lungs.

Never fails, you add a pretty girl into an already volatile situation and bad things are going to happen, dip shits who think they are tough are always trying to impress females. They always have to try to make themselves look good in their eyes when the truth of the matter is women think they are even bigger dip shits for always fighting and carrying on.

Ronnie Joe walked over to Lisa and took a bite out of her corn dog. Lisa stared at him for a moment before she threw her pop on him and kicked him in the knee, Ronnie Joe retaliated by hitting me squarely in the chest right above my heart. I was temporarily knocked out of wind and fell to the ground in agony. Kenny, Babe and Smiley quickly stepped in and took turns kicking me in the head with their puke stained boots, nobody stepped in to break up the fight. Evidently, Lisa ran off to find Two-Fingers when I was attacked. I was laying on the ground in a state of semi-consciousness as they continued to put the boots to me. I vaguely remember Two-Fingers showing up with a rock in his hand and he jumped into the fight and started using it. He hit Kenny squarely in the eye and Kenny shrieked in pain and fell to the ground next to me, he was desperately holding onto his face. Two-Fingers turned on Ronnie Joe and threw the rock at him with all his strength. The rock hit him in the face and tore a hole in his cheekbone and blood flew everywhere. Ronnie Joe, Babe and Smiley turned and ran away.

Two-Fingers leaned over me and I was having a hard time hearing what he was saying, blood flowed from my mouth and my left ear. He helped me to my feet as a couple of Tribal policemen made their way through the crowd.

"What the hell is going on here? Fighting over weenies?" Smiley Heavy Runner asked. Smiley is known as the smart ass of smart asses on the Rez, nobody ever called him that to his face because he is always armed and dangerous.

Corn dog man wasn't compelled to stop the attack but he was eager to tell the cops all about it, but they were not listening. They seemed more concerned with getting things straightened out so they could return to the stick games.

They walked over to where Kenny was and tried to pick him up from the fetal position he was lying in, his hands covered his face. Kenny was bleeding profusely and was starting to black out. Officer Smiley removed his hands from his face and seemed startled by what he saw, Kenny's eye was gouged out of the socket and it was swinging precariously from side to side.

Officer Smiley, suddenly sensing the gravity of the situation, asked, "Who did this?" Two-Fingers was holding onto me so I didn't fall over when he explained what happened. The other officer, Sassy Mad Plume, took a closer look at me and decided it was time to send for an ambulance. Officer Sassy used his radio and made a call to the Blackfeet Health Center and in about five minutes an ambulance arrived. "That was quick, aenet." Sassy said to the driver as he stepped out of the ambulance. "Yeah, I was parked over by the rodeo grounds waiting for customers." The driver said as he pulled out a couple of stretchers.

Without any further fanfare, they loaded Kenny and I onto stretchers and put us in the back of the ambulance together. As they began to close the rear doors, Two-Fingers jumped in and rode with me all the way to Cut Bank. Kenny was dropped off at the Blackfeet Health Center, no whites allowed.

After two weeks in the White Man's Hospital in Cut Bank, I was finally released. They treated me for several injuries but the most serious and lasting was the injury to my left ear. I have permanently lost hearing in that ear, not too bad considering Kenny Stabs-in-the-Back lost his left eye.

On the drive home from the hospital, mom, dad and Stan were real quiet. Mom was visibly upset with the old man for moving us to the Rez and she wouldn't let it go. Stan told me he had been in three separate fights with relatives of the gang and wanted more. I was just glad to be out of the hospital and when I asked them where Two-Fingers was they told me he had been sent off to an Indian boarding school in South Dakota. When I asked them why, mom said she spoke to Pam about it and Pam thought it was the safest place for her son. Evidently, the Stabs-in the-Back's sought revenge for the loss of their son's eye. Pam thought it was best to have him someplace safe until things cooled down. Pam was educated at an Indian boarding school and she thought Two-Fingers could use some guidance. She told mom both of us had been pretty wild all summer and that the change would do him good. I am not sure what hurt the most, my losing hearing in my ear or my best friend leaving for who knows how long. For the first time since all this happened, I felt like crying.

Chapter 12

Years later, when we finally met up again, Two-Fingers told me all about how he felt leaving town and what he thought about boarding school. As it turned out, crying was the last thing on Two-Finger's mind as he traveled on the Great Northern train from Browning to Pierre, South Dakota. He was angry, confused and disillusioned. Being uprooted from his friends and family was the worst punishment imaginable. He heard his parents explanation and knew they meant well. Yet, his anger was unrelenting. He was headed to a strange town, strange school and he got lonelier and lonelier with each passing mile. Still, tears were the last thing on his mind.

The Pierre Boarding School was one of over a hundred boarding schools for Indian children established since 1905. Initially, boarding schools were important instruments used by the Federal Government to assimilate young Indian boys and girls into White Society. The intent was to throw away Indian culture, values and identities and replace them with non-Indian beliefs. Pam, Two-Fingers mother, along with many of her generation and the generations dating back to the turn of the century, were assimilated in this manner. Uprooted from friends and family and sent off to an all Indian school where they were taught the white way of doing things by white teachers and disciplined by white teachers. They spent the school year at the boarding schools and then they returned home for the summer. They lived in the Indian world for three months and then they were shipped back to the boarding schools On the train trip to and from these schools the white side of you passed the Indian side of you and they wonder why they are confused as to who the hell they are? In the late 1960's, Sociologists and other learned professionals began to understand that this was a very harmful practice and attempts were made to make the Indians more aware and respectful of their "Indianness." Too late, generations of Indians were lost to this problem and only a few have survived without any lasting emotional damage, Pam was one of the lucky ones. Two-Fingers survived it all too but he never thought luck had much to do with it. Over the years, he talked to me so much about his time there, I began to think I went with him. The few letters he wrote were filled with what he did and what he thought of boarding schools. From what he could tell, boarding schools were a lot like prisons in that some were better than others but, all things considered, they were all bad. Boarding schools in the 1960's were little more than detention centers for the troubled and the troubling. Two-Fingers was neither, but he was the only one at school who knew that.

I still laugh every time I think of what Two-Fingers said about his first encounter with the boss of the boarding school, Mr. John Wiseman. Mr. Wiseman was the headmaster at the Pierre Boarding School and he had been in that position for 28 years by the time Two-Fingers showed up. Evidently, he reminded all the Indians of this every day. He never became emotional over the Indian's plight. He remained aloof and isolated from their emotional needs. He believed in the old teaching methods; Indians needed to enter the white world at all costs. He provided them with the essentials of life: food, shelter and clothing with a large dose of discipline added in for good measure. All new students reported to Mr. Wiseman upon their arrival at the school.

Two-Fingers said he sat nervously in the area outside of Mr. Wiseman's office and fidgeted with his shirt collar but he still remained cool, so he said. He softly whistled while he waited and was about to get up and leave when suddenly the door to Mr. Wiseman's office opened and out walked Mr. Wiseman. It had to be him, Two-Fingers thought, nobody else in the place could be that arrogant. Mr. Wiseman walked up to Two-Fingers and asked him why he was whistling. Two-Fingers just shrugged his shoulders and didn't say a word.

"There will be no whistling at the Pierre Boarding School." Mr. Wiseman said as he led Two-Fingers into his office. He closed the door behind them and then the interrogation began. "What is your name young man?" "Donny R. Schwartz." Two-Fingers replied "Are you German?" Mr Wiseman asked. "Blackfeet." Two-Fingers told me he was so close to him he could smell his breath. "We do not get a lot of Blackfeet here. Mainly Sioux, Crow, Arapaho and Northern Cheyenne.

What happened to your hand?" Mr. Wiseman asked when he noticed Two-Fingers deformed left hand. "I was trimming my finger nails and I got carried away." According to Two-Fingers, Mr. Wiseman's face turned a bright red and he was unable to speak for a good minute or so and when he finally spoke all he could say was, "Is that so? Well, Donny..." Mr. Wiseman said before Two-Fingers interrupted him. "My friends call me Two-Fingers." "I see. Well, Donny, as I was saying, you and I will get along fine as long as you study hard and follow the rules. I am firm but I believe I am fair. You have been assigned to building E-5 where you will find a bed and a place to clean up. E-5 is that building over there." Mr. Wiseman said as he pointed to a large quonset hut across the street from his office. "You need to take your things over there and check in with Mr. Franklin Edwards, he is in charge of that building. You may go now and remember what I said about following the rules and we will get along fine."

Two-Fingers said they had a list of rules longer than his arm. Initially, he tried to be a good little apple and follow them to the letter but that didn't last long. Soon, he took charge of the place and life took on a whole knew meaning for him. He developed a keen sense of self empowerment when he found he had power over the other inhabitants. He was brave and stood up for them and did not take any crap from the power structure, he said he wore them down and eventually won them over. He grew to like the place and it was almost three years before he returned to Browning. In an act of defiance against his parents, he did not go home during the summers. He got a job working for a veterinarian and loved it, he liked working with the animals and he was treated well by the vet. He learned a lot about life off the Rez and instead of coming home for the summers, he stayed at the vet's place and was taken in as if he was family. The vet and his wife did not have children and they spoiled Two-Fingers rotten.

Chapter 13

After Two-Fingers left Browning for boarding school, life took on an even more surrealistic tone for me. Physically, other than the occasional headaches and not being able to hear too good, I was fine. I kept busy with my paper route and worked at the gas station and pretty much kept to myself. Then one day, Max stopped in for gas and invited us all to Stogie Man and Cindy Ann's wedding. It was scheduled for the week before school started and it was taking place even though Two-Fingers would not be attending. I found myself really looking forward to the wedding.

The morning of the wedding was dreary and overcast but by wedding time it had warmed up considerably. Father Ian Kelly was the new priest in town and he was presiding over the ceremony. As I stated earlier, all good Blackfeet are Catholics and Cindy Ann and Stogie Man were no exceptions. Father Ian had recently been ordained and Browning was his first assignment, he was serious about spreading the "Word." The older Tribal members still clung to their ancestral rituals and beliefs but the years of assimilation took a toll on the younger generation, it was a traditional Catholic ceremony.

Evidently, Cindy Ann raised holy hell about Two-Fingers not being able to attend her wedding. She and Paula pleaded their case but were unable to change Pam's mind. Two-Fingers had only been gone a few weeks and Pam was still concerned for the safety of her only son and believed boarding school was the safest place for him. Cindy Ann begrudgingly accepted the decision but it never, ever sat well with her.

The wedding was well attended by friends and family, the small Catholic Church was filled to capacity. The ceremony lasted a little too long for a hot August day and the guests and participants perspired like crazy, not a lot of air conditioning on the Rez. Finally, the ceremony was officially over and everybody left for the reception at the American Legion Hall.

The American Legion Hall is one of several bars in Browning. It is on the east side of town directly across from the newly opened, "War Bonnet Lounge and Motel." Browning bars are a lot like its theater, no frills. The American Legion Hall was selected because it has a big dance area and plenty of seating. The other bars in town, The War Bonnet, Paradise Bar, Oasis Bar, Aubert's and the Businessmen's Club were all rejected because of their limited seating capacity.

For years, Browning and the other towns on the Rez were "dry." No alcohol was allowed because Indians have a drinking problem and White Society was going to help them with this problem by not allowing the lawful sale of alcohol anywhere on the Rez. This decision worked on the Rez about as well as Prohibition worked in White Society. Bootleggers sprang up all over the place and car wrecks caused from "runs" to towns just off the Rez occurred on a daily basis. Deaths mounted at an astounding pace until the powers that be decided to allow the sale of alcohol on the Rez. This did not stop the carnage, it just isolated it to the Rez. Bootleggers were still plentiful, they attracted the after hours crowd.

The American Legion was one of the first bar's built on the Rez after the sale of alcohol was allowed and it was built as a place for all Veterans of War and their families to come and drink. Well, everybody is related on the Rez so the doors were virtually wide open from day one. The Blackfeet have a long and distinguished record of serving in foreign wars, as do all Indian Tribes. However, there are more Blackfeet casualties at the Legion on a good weekend than there were in all of World War II. I went there that night and watched as my folks got sloppy drunk and all sentimental as the night wore on. I think they were trying to make up for being so mean to each other for the last few weeks. I had a great time that night watching all the craziness.

"What does it take to get a gawd damn drink in this place." Yelled Juanita Bear Medicine Owen as she bellied up to the bar. "I'm so thirsty I could spit dust." She desperately tried to hike herself up onto a bar stool. "Shit, get everybody at the bar one on me." She said as she reached into her purse and pulled out a wad of cash. I hadn't seen her since the time we stayed at her ranch and she was shit faced and loud.

Onlookers quickly rushed to the counter and placed their orders; no beer tonight, mixed drinks only.

Charley Owen and dad were seated at the end of the bar and they both were staring at Juanita as she downed drink after drink. I overheard Charley say, "Juanita found out last week that she couldn't have any children."

"I am sorry to hear that, Charley." The old man said. I felt bad about it too but I tended my business and didn't say a word, I just sat there sipping on my pop.

Just about then, Too Slim Mountain Chief rode into the Legion on his horse. He was just able to squeeze his horse inside the door with him on it, he bent down real low and held onto his cowboy hat to make it through the entrance, but he made it. Too Slim was Stogie Man's best man and he looked like he had been celebrating for a week. He slowly paraded around the bar on his horse greeting friends and family, he even took off his hat and waved to the crowd. The bartender screamed at him to get his damn horse out of there and the crowd laughed and yelled their approval until the horse lifted his tail and shit all over the dance floor, that was when Too Slim quickly departed the scene. Someone showed up with a shovel and quickly cleaned up the steaming pile of horse shit and someone in the back of the hall yelled, "That was a shitty thing to do, Too Slim." The place erupted in laughter.

By then, beer, wine and whiskey was flowing liberally and the place was becoming very liquid. The band started to play, "Louie, Louie" and the dance floor quickly filled with dancers, the party had officially began.

What happened next is Browning folklore. To this day, before the Blackfeet are allowed to graduate high school, they must memorize the details of what happened that night and recite it back to the class. Well, not really but it is quite a story and like most stories on the Rez, details have been added over time to enhance the telling of it.

Anyway, Too Slim was disappointed that the crowd did not appreciate his horse so he decided to take the horse to his uncle's pasture and let it loose for the night. Before riding off, he leaned down from his saddle and accepted a bottle of wine that was being offered.

He was taking a long drink when he suddenly spurred his horse and down the street they went. Too Slim was riding hard and drinking his wine as he galloped onto the front yard of his uncle's place. He quickly unsaddled his horse and put it in the pasture, then he tossed the saddle and bridle off to the side and began his walk back to the party.

It just so happens that directly across the street from his uncle's driveway is Browning's lone fire station. As he walked by the station, Too Slim noticed the fire engine was sitting outside all by it's lonesome. After thinking the situation over for a good 2 seconds, he decided to take Browning's only fire engine for a little ride. Too Slim tried to scale the tall chain link fence that surrounded the fire station but he kept getting to the top and falling off. After falling for the third time, Too Slim walked around to the front of the building and was surprised to find the front gate wide open. When he climbed into the cab, he was equally surprised to find the engine had the keys in it. Why not, who the hell would steal a fire engine, right?

According to Too Slim, the next thing he knew, he was sitting on top of the fire engine in the parking lot of the Legion Hall when Stogie Man came weaving out of the building holding onto a bottle of whiskey. He and Cindy Ann went home to change out of their wedding clothes and had missed an hour or so of their party, he had been making up for lost time.

"What you got there, Too Slim?" Stogie Man asked as he tried to focus on the fire engine. "Gawd damn, you have been married for less than a day and you have already gone stupid, aenet, Stogie Man?" Two Slim said as he climbed down from the top of the fire engine. "I'm stupid? Look who has stolen a fucking fire engine." Stogie Man said. "I didn't steal the fucking fire engine, I borrowed it." Too Slim replied. I was standing outside cooling off while all this was going on.

Just then, Paula walked out of the Legion Hall and jumped into the driver's seat of the fire engine. Before long, it was running and so were the sirens. Soon, Stan, myself, the groom, bride, bridesmaids, ushers, best man and the bartender were loaded onto the fire engine. The bartender had started drinking shortly after Too Slim had ridden in on the horse and was now three sheets to the wind and ready for a run away. Once we were all on, Paula pulled the fire engine onto the highway and off we went into the night.

Nobody knew for sure where the hell Paula was driving to but it was a beautiful night and the cool air was refreshing. Cindy Ann was on top of the fire engine wedged in between the steps of the ladder and she was dressed in Levi's and a blouse and was feeling no pain, her wedding veil hung haphazardly on the side of her head. Paula was feeling empowered as she shifted into fourth gear and drove towards the center of town. Paula had a few drinks but quickly sobered up as the adrenaline pumped through her body, Stan was seated next to her nursing a beer. The rest of the party was hanging on for dear life as the fire engine sped down main street.

The fire engine, with the sirens blaring and Paula at the wheel, picked up speed as we approached the Government Square. Paula was going at a pretty good clip when we passed the BIA buildings and headed up the hill towards the Blackfeet Health Center. At the Blackfeet Health Center parking lot, Paula made a sweeping, wide turn and gunned the engine. This caused the bartender, who was hanging on with one hand while the other hand held a whiskey bottle, to fly off the engine and skip across the gravel parking lot before coming to rest against the curb. "Well, at least he doesn't have far to go to get treatment, aenet." Too Slim said as he glanced back at his fallen comrade.

Paula, oblivious to everything but her need to drive, drove back down the hill towards town and we began to pick up speed as we flew past the Tribal Police Station. Much to everybody's surprise, nobody chased us.

Stan looked over at Paula and was convinced she was possessed. So, he slowly reached over and turned the sirens off. This caused some unrest with the rest of the wedding party but the sirens remained off as we flew through the night in the direction of East Glacier. As I briefly mentioned earlier, East Glacier is a town of about 100 permanent residents thirteen miles west of Browning. It is the east entrance of Glacier National Park and it has a big, beautiful hotel that was built by the railroad back in the early part of the twentieth century. It lies just off the reservation and has a golf course, swimming pool, beautifully landscaped grounds and a bar. Actually, East Glacier has several bars but most of them are on the reservation side of East Glacier.

Paula pulled into East Glacier and drove through the tunnel that separates Glacier National Park from the Rez and as we got closer to the hotel, the passengers started to yell for her to pull over so they could get a drink at the hotel bar. So, Paula pulled the fire engine into the parking area and we all disembarked as quickly as possible, all of us except for Cindy Ann who appeared to be permanently wedged into place. Too Slim and Stogie Man climbed back up onto the ladder to pry her loose and the rest of us walked into the hotel and moved quickly through the lobby and into the bar, the bartender had just announced last call for alcohol. They all ordered drinks and bought a couple of cases of beer and 2 fifths of whiskey for the road. The bartender was a Blackfeet and he asked if he could join the party. We all thought that was a great idea since we were now one bartender short. After the bar closed, we decided to drive back to Browning taking the long way home. The long way entailed going through the mountains over Looking Glass Pass. Looking Glass is a beautiful drive in the daylight but at night, it is just a treacherous, narrow two lane road without any guard rails.

Stogie Man was now at the wheel, it was his turn to drive. He had jumped into the driver's seat and Cindy Ann, Paula and Stan decided to join him in the cab. The rest of us found places to sit in the back of the fire engine and made ourselves as comfortable as possible. Stogie Man pulled onto the highway and drove out of town towards Looking Glass Pass and he was driving slowly when, all of a sudden, the fire engine began to stall out. Stogie Man noticed the gas gauge was on empty and quickly found a place to pull over. We came to a stop next to Upper Two Medicine Creek. Stogie Man yelled at Too Slim, "What, you couldn't steal an engine with a full tank of gas?" "Like I had a lot of choices, aenet." Too Slim replied.

It was very cold at that elevation and none of us were properly dressed so we quickly gathered up some wood and before long we had a huge fire burning, Blackfeet know how to build fires and how to put them out. We were all standing next to the fire when Stan said, "You know, I have never been involved in grand theft fire engine before. Does this happen quite a lot around here?" We all laughed, no one seemed to appreciate the gravity of the situation.

As the night wore on, Stogie Man and Cindy Ann retired to the cab of the fire engine to spend what was left of their wedding night and the rest of us stayed close to the fire and drank until the sun came up.

Browning Fire Chief, Smokey No Runner, received the call at approximately nine a.m. He was informed that the fire engine was missing and Smokey immediately suspected foul play and called the Tribal Police Station. "Hey, you seen my fire engine anywhere?" Smokey asked the dispatcher. "Gee, Smokey, I sure haven't. Of course, I haven't been looking for it either." The dispatcher said. "Well, it's missing and I sure as hell hope your house doesn't catch on fire, you smart ass." Smokey said. "If it does, just let it burn, I'd be better off living in a Teepee anyway." Smokey slammed the receiver down in disgust and was ready to re-dial when he got a call from his dispatcher. "Smokey, we just got a report that the fire engine is up on Looking Glass near Upper Two Medicine Creek-out of gas." "Aenet, who called in?" Smokey asked his dispatcher. "Max Schwartz."

Max went looking for his daughters and his new son-in-law early that morning. He had been in the back of the Legion dancing and getting a little crazy when he found out they were driving around in a stolen fire engine. The news didn't slow him up any, he kept dancing and drinking and when he finally sobered up, he went looking for us.

Evidently, he spent several hours traveling up and down all the local highways until he finally found us. "What in the hell were you thinking?" Max asked the assembled wedding party. He was spitting mad and kicking at rocks and everything else in his way. "You could have been killed or you could have killed someone and you are all probably going to prison over this." Max said. One of the bridesmaids said. "Grand theft fire engine, aenet." The wedding party tried to suppress their giggles but were unable to do so, we all started laughing hard and Max just stood there shaking his head.

Turns out none of us went to prison, Too Slim confessed to doing the dirty deed and threw himself on the mercy of the court. Since the Tribal judge was his cousin, he was given a $10 fine and that happened to be the exact amount it cost to fill up a fire engine in Browning, Montana in 1967.

Chapter 14

Subtle changes had taken place on the Rez over the summer of 1967. The war in Vietnam picked up steam and a number of Blackfeet were drafted and more were being drafted monthly, no college deferrals for the Blackfeet and no special treatment. Few Blackfeet go away to school because they do not do well when they go off to college. Usually, they get homesick and return home before one semester has been completed, that is what has happened for years. Some of the best basketball players in the state of Montana are Blackfeet. Certainly, the best long distance runners are Blackfeet. Yet, when they go away to college on full ride scholarships, they never stay gone. Evidently, college life just doesn't provide the necessary support system for Indians. There is a certain beauty in loving your friends and family so much you can't stand to be away from them for an extended period of time. Or, perhaps the pressures of White Society are more than they can handle, prejudice and racism are dreadful emotions that cause damage to the people displaying it and to those on the receiving end, no good comes of it.

Being drafted, now that is a whole different matter. If a Blackfeet is drafted, he will leave home and serve his country. No running off to Canada even though it is only a few miles away and there are plenty of Canadian relatives up there. No draft dodgers on the Rez, that is an act of cowardice that will not be tolerated. The Blackfeet are still warriors; that couldn't be pounded out of them.

The green Army bus from Helena had all too frequently arrived in Browning over the last several months to pick up the draftees and unfortunately, it arrived one day to pick up an unexpected passenger, my brother Stan. Stan planned on catching a ride down to Helena and enlisting. "What the hell do you mean you want to enlist?" Dad was physically shaking when he asked Stan that question. "It is what I want to do." Stan replied. The three of us were standing inside the station drinking coffee. Stan had told me what he wanted to do the night of the wedding, I had hoped he would change his mind. Not Stan, once he got something in his head, nobody was going to change his mind, nobody.

"Son, war is a terrible thing, and make no mistake, we are at war. Young kids are getting maimed and killed over in Vietnam and the whole thing is senseless." Dad said as he shook his head. Old soldiers appreciate the gravity of war and know there is no glamour in it. "I need to get away from here, Pop. I need to do something with my life and I do not want to go to college, I have made up my mind." Stan said as he looked dad squarely in the eyes. "What about Paula? What does she think about all this?" Dad asked. "She really doesn't understand it either, Pop. I thought you of all people would understand." Stan said as he gazed down at his boots. "Son, war is total bullshit, trust me on this." Dad was losing the battle and he knew it. "Have you told your mother?" "Not yet, I thought we would tell her together." Stan said. "Your mother has been through so much since we have moved here, this will break her heart." Dad said quietly. "You are both going to have to understand this is something I have to do. I will be fine, I probably won't even go to Vietnam." Stan said.

After mom was told what Stan planned to do, she went to her bedroom and cried all night long, we could hear her through the thin walls of our living quarters. Stan couldn't take it so he went downtown and I went to pumping gas and selling candy, dad went into the tire shop and got piss limber.

The next morning mom had a brave face on as she prepared Stan's breakfast and a sack lunch for the long trip to Helena. "You make sure you write me as often as you can, Stan." Mom said as she served Stan his ham and eggs. I was seated next to Stan and she didn't seem to see me, I figured my breakfast could wait so I just sat there sipping coffee. Dad had returned to the tire shop where he kept his beer cold.

The green Army bus was parked in the parking lot of the Bureau of Indian Affairs and Stan was already seated and waving bravely to mom, dad and me. Soon, the last of the passengers were seated and the trip to Helena began. The bus slowly pulled out of the parking lot and gathered speed as it drove down main street, we followed close behind in the '57 Chevy. The bus slowed down a bit as it passed over the cattle guards separating Government Square from the rest of town and then it continued on slowly as it passed the pool hall, the theater, the two drugstores, Oasis Bar, Faught's Clothing store, Buttries Food store and Gambles Hardware store. As the bus passed the winos seated on window ledges in the shade of the buildings offered weak salutes to the passengers as they slowly passed a brown paper bag among themselves. The bus picked up speed as it passed our Chevron Station, Vic's Grocery, Joe Show's Conoco, the Town Pump gas station, House's Construction, the War Bonnet Lounge and Motel and the American Legion Hall. The draftees were headed for their physicals and if they passed them, they would be shipped off to boot camp, Stan had no trouble passing the physical.

Chapter 15

I was very lonely when Stan and Two-Fingers left me, a lot of the joy in my life left with them. I spent a lot more time working at the station than I had previously, I worked every weekend and after school if I wasn't delivering my papers. Our four unit motel was always full regardless of the time of year, it was funny how some of the more prominent male citizens always needed a room for the weekend. I would rent them a room and when I looked out the window to see who they were with, it was never their wives. I kept all their secrets and these old guys trusted me and really appreciated my silence, I learned early on the importance of keeping secrets. What the old guys didn't know was I kept their wives secrets too.

School was fine. After the incident where I got jumped and had my ear ruined for life, the Blackfeet backed off and left me alone. In fact, they shunned the Stabs-in-the-Backs and the Black Weasels. They viewed what they did to me as an act of cowardice and only their relatives had anything to do with them. I had friends and did things but it was just different. My paper route flourished, all the older Blackfeet took care of me and bought up all the papers and I was able to put away some serious cash back then. Stan and Two-fingers wrote sparingly, I was just as bad though. Every time I wrote I would start feeling lonesome so I almost quit altogether. Staring out the windows of the station as the years passed gave me time to reflect on how much my life had changed since we moved to the Rez. I did a lot of reflecting on slow, snowy nights.

Sweeping changes took place in the United States in the late sixties. The war in Vietnam escalated and the anti-war movement took center stage and President Lyndon B. Johnson decided not to seek re-election and Richard Nixon was elected on the promise he would bring an honorable end to the war; social unrest bordering on anarchy was the order of the day, everybody seemed to be marching.

Dramatic changes took place on the Rez during this time too. It is uncertain as to whether the changes were a bi-product of the changes the nation at large was experiencing or a result of internal pressures. Whatever the reason, dramatic social changes took place.

I know this much, The Blackfeet began to challenge the status quo and Veteran's returning from Vietnam were a catalyst for the change. They saw the insanity that is war and were deeply affected by it. They saw too many of their fellow Blackfeet shipped home in body bags, the reservation cemeteries filled up at an alarming rate. The Veterans understood war was sometimes necessary, but 'Nam was an unnecessary war.

Young Blackfeet, even though they had never been more than a hundred miles from the Rez, sought change too. They became increasingly aware of the depravation that existed on the Rez and they wanted a better life. They wanted to run their own affairs without the help of the white man and local white business owners felt the pressure. Blackfeet Tribal members began operating their own businesses and that had a dramatic economic impact on all the white business owners. The Blackfeet began doing business only with other Blackfeet and white businessmen were being forced out and they were replaced with less experienced Blackfeet businessmen which caused an even greater economic backlash on the Rez because the new generation of Blackfeet businessmen were not particularly good at running their own operations. Credit was extended to their friends and relatives and in most cases, the credit was never repaid. Grants and loans from the Federal Government were needed to prop up these ailing businesses and the economic situation became worse with each passing day.

The tourist trade kept us in business because tourists stopped to get gas at well kept stations and our Chevron station was very well kept. Blackfeet ran stations were falling into disrepair and Browning, never a pretty place, rapidly lost what luster it had. Broken windows weren't replaced, peeling paint was ignored, streets were cluttered with even more abandoned cars and dogs roamed the town in packs. Changes took place and not necessarily for the better.

During this time I changed a lot too, both physically and mentally. Over the three years Two-Fingers was gone, I grew to be over six feet tall and about one hundred and eighty pounds. The one hundred and eighty pounds was a direct result of all the fry bread I was given when I delivered my papers. I exercised and worked a lot and I couldn't get under one hundred and eighty pounds. Oh how I long for the days I only weighed one hundred and eighty pounds. As soon as I get done telling Two-Fingers story, I am going to get a membership at the Blackfeet Fitness Center, I digress.

I wouldn't say I was handsome or anything back then but I did get my fair share of attention from the girls at school, I had all my teeth and everything worked except my left ear. I am not sure why I am telling you about this, nobody cares about how I looked, the Blackfeet are only interested in Two-Fingers. All I can say is he grew and matured a lot too, I could tell that by the few letters he wrote me. In all the time he was away, he only wrote me about six times and his last two letters were more serious than the previous four.

In those letters, he told me he had withstood the onslaught of change that was forced upon him and he prospered from it. Now doesn't that sound like he matured? According to him, he was very popular with the other students, staff and even Mr. Wiseman took a liking to the smart ass Blackfeet from Browning. Two-Fingers loved working for the veterinarian and was having second thoughts of leaving South Dakota for Browning and his senior year of high school.

Anyway, after being away from home for over three years, he decided to return home. He hadn't been home since that fateful day in 1967 and as I said earlier, his staying away was an act of defiance aimed at his parents and it took him a long time to get over his feeling of betrayal. His decision to stay away was made easier by his ability to adjust to boarding school life and for that he was thankful. But, he figured it was time to go home.

His parents had sent him fifty dollars for train fare and incidentals but Two-Fingers decided to save the money and hitchhike home. As it turned out, the real reason he hitchhiked was he lost all but seven dollars in a poker game the night before he left. Anyway, according to

Two-Fingers, Mr. Wiseman insisted on giving him a ride to the I-90 on-ramp which was not too far from the boarding school. Two-Fingers told me he felt bad leaving Mr. Wiseman and the school, so once they got to the on-ramp, he said goodbye quickly and walked away without looking back, it was hard to leave but there was no sense in getting all mushy about it.

He had one big suitcase and he was hauling it down the freeway when all of a sudden, a brand new 1970 Chevy El Camino went racing past him before the driver slammed on his breaks and came to a stop about fifty yards ahead of him. The driver got out of his car and stretched a little and yelled back at Two-Fingers, "You looking for a ride?"

Two-Fingers said he hesitated for a minute, he wasn't too sure he wanted to ride with the red neck, crew cut looking dude that was driving the El Camino. But he looked around and didn't see another car in sight and finally said, "Sure." When he was telling me this story, I was thinking that the red neck probably had second thoughts about offering the ride once he got a close look at Two-Fingers. His hair was three years longer and he looked a lot like an Indian.

The driver opened the lid covering the back of his El Camino and Two-Fingers squeezed his suitcase into the only space available to him, Two-Fingers noticed the El Camino was packed full of stuff, he was barely able to get his suitcase to fit.

According to Two-Fingers, they drove a long way in complete silence, they both glanced at each other occasionally but neither of them said a word. Finally, Two-Fingers broke the ice and after introductions were made, the driver, whose name was Bob Richardson, began to talk incessantly. "Yeah, I am just coming back from the Indianapolis 500 and I'm headed to Mount Rushmore. From there, I am headed home to Davenport, Washington." Two-Fingers said he just nodded his head politely as Bob rattled on. "I am headed home to run for Mayor. I am fed up with the way our country is being ran and I intend to do something about it." Two-Fingers nodded politely again as Bob continued, unabated. "Last month I resigned my commission in the Army and I have been seeing America ever since. I was in charge of unloading the planes that brought our dead boys back from 'Nam. After a couple of years of that bullshit, enough was enough. I have been to West Point and everything. I resigned my Lieutenancy and I am not looking back. Headed home, tired of this shit. By the way, Two-Fingers is it? Do you smoke?" Bob asked as he pointed at the glove box. "Yeah, sure." Two-Fingers said thinking Bob was referring to cigarettes. He opened up the glove box expecting to find a pack of smokes. Instead, he found a canister with a pipe on top of it. All right, a pipe, Two-Fingers had always wanted to smoke a pipe. He removed the pipe and began to fill it with what he believed to be tobacco. He stuffed the pipe as full as he could and fired it up with the butane lighter that was in the glove box. "Holy shit!!!" Two-Fingers exclaimed as the top of his head was blown off. He had never tasted anything like that in his life and he wasn't sure what the hell he was smoking all he knew was he wanted another puff. "Holy Shit!!!"

Soon, Two-Fingers was as loose as a goose and ready to sign that truce. He said he hit that pipe four or five times and thought his head was going to pop off every time he did it. Bob kept asking for the pipe and Two-Fingers just held on tight and laughed hysterically. "What the hell kind of tobacco is this?" Two-Fingers asked. "Tobacco, who said anything about tobacco? That there, is grade A Marijuana. Pot. Mary Jane. Dope. I thought you said you smoked?" Bob asked. "Pass me that pipe and let me show you how it's done." Bob took a big hit before exhaling a cloud of smoke.

"Yeah, I was in charge of unloading a lot of things when I was stationed in Texas. Did I mention I was stationed in Texas?" Bob asked as Two Fingers reached over and took the pipe from him. "All this pot was coming in from 'Nam on a daily basis. The men working under me were always getting stoned and trying to get me to try some, I never did. I was a true blue righteous military man and I didn't think it was right." Two-Fingers was half listening but was more interested in getting another puff. He said he fired up the pipe again and held his breath until his socks started to unravel, he really liked the shit.

"All those bodies kept coming over. I was in charge of getting them unloaded and sent home. Did I mention I was in charge?" Bob repeated himself a lot, it became all too clear to Two-Fingers that pot didn't have much of an effect on old Bob.

"Body, after body, after body kept coming in. I was starting to have nightmares about all those bodies. So, I tried drinking and that only made it worse. Then, one day I confiscated some of this pot and tried it and I still have nightmares but I am able to sleep better. Yep, since I have resigned my commission, I sleep like a baby. I am headed home to become the Mayor. Hey, how would you like to be the Police Chief?" Bob asked.

Two-Fingers took another hit on the pipe and passed it to Bob, "You know, I always wanted to be a Chief. Never thought about being a Police Chief though. Will I get to pack a gun?" Bob told him he could carry a gun but he couldn't have any bullets, just like Barney Fife on the Andy Griffith show. Two-Fingers said he was so stoned he started to lose sight in one eye.

Anyway, they continued their smoking and snappy banter all the way to Mount Rushmore. When they got there, they pulled into the parking lot below the guest center and they each took one more hit before getting out of the El Camino. As they exited, a huge cloud of smoke escaped and temporarily blocked out the sun.

Two-Fingers and Bob were standing at the observation deck when Bob decided he wanted to climb up the mountain and get inside Teddy Roosevelt's nose. Of course, the park rangers frowned on such a thing and they politely asked Two-Fingers and Bob to vacate the premises.

Somewhere along the line, Bob decided to take Two-Fingers all the way to Browning even though it was considerably out of his way. So, he drove through the night as Two-Fingers slept. Two-Fingers said he woke up fully rested, he had never slept that soundly in his life. When he woke up, it took him awhile to focus and realize that they were in Browning. Bob was driving past our station when Two-Fingers asked him to let him out. Bob pulled off the highway about twenty feet away from the station and got out and stretched.

Two-Fingers dug into his pockets and pulled out his last seven dollars and asked Bob if he could buy some of his weed. He said Bob just laughed and walked around to the back of the El Camino and opened up the lid covering the back. Two-Fingers watched him open up one of seven large ice cream canisters stuffed full of opium soaked pot. Neither one of them had anything to put the pot in so Two-Fingers asked Bob to stay there and he would go find something to put the pot in. He ran to our station and I was just finishing up my graveyard shift when he suddenly burst through the front door in a panic. Without saying hello, kiss my ass or anything, he demanded a milk carton. Without saying a word, I went into our living quarters and grabbed a Darigold one half gallon container of milk and brought it back to him. He promptly stepped outside and emptied it as he ran off.

I watched him run off all the while thinking he had lost his mind. He returned relatively soon carrying his suitcase and the milk carton. He tossed the suitcase on the ground next to me but he held onto the milk carton with both hands, it was gently cradled to his chest and all he could say was, "I'll tell you all about it later, let's go."

About that time, the old man came out of the station to relieve me and saw Two-Fingers standing there with this milk carton pressed against his chest and all he could say was, "Would you like some cereal to go along with that?" The three of us stood there and talked for awhile when Two-Fingers suddenly said he needed to get going. All the time he was talking he was trying to shield the milk cartoon from dad because it smelt like skunk piss.

So, the two of us left together and started walking in the general direction of the high school. On the way, he asked if I knew where Cindy Ann and Stogie Man were living. I said of course I did so we changed course and started walking to their place. I carried his heavy suitcase and he clutched the milk carton in both of his arms, he held on to it like it was gold.

Stogie Man and Cindy Ann were back living in Browning after their brief time away from home. They did go off to Bozeman and were excited about Stogie Man playing basketball for the Bobcats of Montana State, he had a full ride. Anyway, that was up until the first week of practice when Stogie Man blew out his left knee. After two surgeries and endless hours of rehabilitation, all he had to show for his athletic prowess was a pronounced limp and a severe drinking habit. He quit school, moved back to Browning and got a low rent house up on Moccasin Flats where he spent most of his time drinking and talking about his high school glory days.

On our walk to Moccasin Flats, which was about a mile away, we caught up on what we had been doing since we last saw each other. He was amazed at all the new duplexes scattered here and there. During his absence, the government had built a number of low rent houses in Browning. The Blackfeet called these new houses, "Easter egg" houses because, like Easter egg dye, they only come in six colors. Bright pink, red, blue, purple, green and yellow. The colors were repeated over and over again until all the houses were eventually painted. Cindy Ann and Stogie Man lived in one of the "Easter egg" houses.

When we arrived at their front door, we were greeted by Stogie Man who said, "The things you see when you ain't got a gun, aenet!!" Stogie Man opened the screen door and gave Two-Fingers a big hug, he just looked at me and nodded his head. Cindy Ann was in the kitchen cooking breakfast when she discovered who was at the front door. She turned to look at Two-Fingers as she wiped her hands on her apron, she seemed confused as to what she was witnessing. Then, in a flash, she ran over and grabbed Two-Fingers and held him tight and then she began to cry as she squeezed him even tighter. She was sobbing, shaking and cussing simultaneously. Two-Fingers softly stroked her hair and finally said, "Sister Girl, Sister Girl, you got to quit squeezing so hard or my belly button is going to pop out." Luckily, Two-Fingers had left the milk container out on their porch with his suitcase.

Cindy Ann finally let him go and then started yelling in earnest, "Why didn't you let us know you were coming home?" She asked. "Didn't you get my smoke signal?" Two-Fingers asked with a big smile on his face. "Geez you're pissy, aenet. I am glad you haven't changed." Cindy Ann said before starting to laugh.

"Have you seen mom and dad yet? Paula is going to kick your ass, little brother." Cindy Ann said as she grabbed him and put him into another bear hug. "No, I haven't seen mom and dad yet, I wanted you to get the first crack at me. Where is Paula?" "She is up in the Park fighting fire. Real bad fire up there and it is so early in the season. She should be home soon, I hear they may be getting the fire contained." Cindy Ann made another move towards Two-Fingers but he would have nothing more to do with her. "Holy shit, Cindy, give me a break, hug White Guy for awhile." Two-Fingers said.

Cindy Ann turned to me and gave me a big hug and I will be honest with you, I didn't mind one bit. In fact, when she tried to break away, I just hung onto her. "Okay, okay, that's enough White Guy. What am I going to have to do, hose you down?" Two-Fingers asked and we all started laughing.

Cindy Ann still looked good even though she had recently given birth to her second child. Stogie Man and her were the proud parents of two baby girls. "Where are my nieces? I want to see my nieces." Two-Fingers said. "They are still asleep, let me get them up for you." Cindy walked to the bedroom in the rear of the house and returned holding the new baby. Their two year old was walking next to her holding on to her pant leg with her index finger pressing against her lips. Two-Fingers started to act goofy trying to make them laugh, the baby fell back to sleep and the two year old started to cry when she discovered his deformed hand. The more he tried to make her laugh, the harder she cried. "Two-Fingers, quit scaring my girl, you ugly bastard." Stogie Man yelled from in front of the TV. "When is breakfast?"

After breakfast, Stogie Man, Cindy Ann and the two girls got into their car and drove off to the grocery store to pick up some provisions. After they left, Two-Fingers turned on their oven and located a cookie sheet. He then retrieved the milk carton from the porch and put part of the contents of the milk carton onto the cookie sheet before placing it in the oven. It took about a minute or so to dry the weed and when it was ready, he gingerly wrapped it in some tin foil, this maneuver was repeated until the last batch was put in the oven.

Then, Two-Fingers found some papers in Stogie Man's jacket and began to roll a joint. I watched intently as Two-Fingers rolled. "Where did you learn to do that so well?" "From this old cowboy in South Dakota, he owned a small ranch and the vet I worked for used to go see him all the time. He smoked Bull Durham cigarettes like there was no tomorrow and he could roll a cigarette while he was riding horseback.

No shit, he would open the Bull Durham bag with his teeth, sprinkle some tobacco in the paper, roll it up tight as can be and never spill a drop, I practiced until I was almost as good as him." Two-Fingers said.

When the joint was ready, Two-Fingers grabbed a stick match and lit it on his pant's zipper. He took a big hit and offered the joint to me. I had only smoked pot once before, so I kind of hesitated for a few seconds before taking a big hit. I started to choke and gag but I would not relinquish the joint, Two-Fingers shook his head and started to roll his own. We were both stoned out of our minds when we noticed the house was on fire. Well, not the whole house, just the oven. Two-Fingers forgot to take the last batch of dried pot out of the oven and it was smoking up the place. "Holy shit." He said as he opened the oven and sees the remaining weed on fire. He started to blow on the weed and that made things worse. Finally, he turned off the oven and grabbed a towel and removed the cookie sheet and placed it on top of the stove. The contents were going up in smoke so he bent over and started to inhale the smoke into his nose, I struggled to my feet and went over and joined in. We continued to inhale the smoke until it finally went out, at that point, we didn't know if we were on foot or on horseback. More importantly, we did not care.

The first time I ever got stoned was with Stan when he came home on one of his leaves. I'm not sure I can even call it getting stoned because we smoked this stuff he called Wyoming Yellow and the only way I got a buzz was by holding my breath for about five minutes until I fell over. I am not sure I got a buzz, I think I just got dizzy from not breathing. Anyway, the Wyoming Yellow was nothing compared to that stuff. That is probably more than you need to know but I promised I would tell what I knew about Two-Fingers in an honest and forthright way, I just know his pot was fantastic and we both really liked it.

Anyway, after smoking with Two-Fingers, I was so thirsty I could have spit dust. Luckily, Stogie Man had a six pack of Rainier beer in the refrigerator and I helped myself and gave one to Two-Fingers and we downed them in one long, glorious gulp. We were sitting there finishing off the six pack when we noticed that the house reeked of Marijuana, the place stunk. We were absolutely whacked and we knew we should do something about the smell but we just couldn't get motivated.

After awhile, we opened up a few windows and the front door, that was about as far as we got in airing the place out. Two-Fingers rolled a bunch of joints and stuck them into his coat pockets. Then, he put the remaining pot in his suitcase and hid the suitcase under Cindy Ann and Stogie Man's bed for safe keeping.

"Lets go." Two-Fingers said as he walked out the front door. I didn't bother asking him where we were going, it never did any good. For better or worse, spontaneity ruled his life. As it turned out, we went to see his parents.

Chapter 16

Two-Fingers reunion with his parents was a joyous event. They embraced and all the remaining anger inside of Two-Fingers was seemingly swept away, he held on to Pam and Max for all he was worth. I sat on their living room couch and gouged on fry bread and pop, I had the worst case of munchies I have ever had. Nobody did any crying or anything, but you could tell they were beside themselves with joy, Two-Fingers was smiling and telling stories and his parents had a hard time getting a word in edge wise.

After Two-Fingers wore down, they were finally able to talk about things that had happened during his absence. Pam cooked a big lunch and we all sat down to eat, Two-Finger was at the head of the table. "I missed everything about this place, especially your fry bread, mom." Two-Fingers said as he worked on his second helping. We sat at the kitchen table and talked nonstop for about two hours and after lunch, Two-Fingers asked to borrow the family car. "You got a driver's license?" Max asked. "Since when do you need a driver's license to drive on the Rez?" Two-Fingers asked. "The cops are really cracking down on things lately. There's been a lot of dope running around here and the drunks and pot heads are getting behind the wheel and getting into accidents, seems like someone is getting killed everyday; the highways on the Rez are littered with crosses. Last week, Joe Bird Rattler's boys were out joy riding and ran into a telephone pole and they didn't have a license and they threw them into jail. So I don't think it is a good idea. Get your license and then you can drive." Max said. "Fair enough, we are going up to East Glacier and we will hitchhike." Two-Fingers said as he reached for his Levi jacket. "Be careful, the Stabs-in-the-Backs are still around." Pam said with a look of concern on her face.

We left and walked across the street and stood in front of the Businessmen's Club for a while. The winos were in their assigned seating and they all stopped us with a request for a handout. "Geez, Rubber Joe, how much money you taking in these days? Are you paying your income taxes?" Two-Fingers asked as he handed Rubber Joe my dollar bill. "Ah hell, Two-Fingers, you know them bastards would just buy another bomb or something with it anyway." Rubber Joe said.

Before Rubber Joe began his descent into alcoholism, he was a rancher with a pretty good size spread north of town. His house started on fire one day and his two small children burned to death. Shortly thereafter, Rubber Joe lost everything to drink and has been one of the town's winos ever since. He was called Rubber Joe because he bounced around aimlessly.

"What about your Auntie, Two-Fingers? Don't forget your Auntie." Maggie Stink Pits said as she extended her hand.

Maggie really wasn't Two-Fingers aunt, Maggie doesn't have any relatives on the Rez and nobody is quite sure where she came from, it is widely believed she came from Butte, Montana. It was suspected that she was quite promiscuous when she was a young women, the Blackfeet say she sold herself professionally. The story is she used to pull quite a few tricks during the course of a day and she was never too concerned about personal hygiene. After servicing ten guys one day, Mr. Eleven came in and was going at it real hard, his head buried between her ample breasts when all of a sudden he yelled, "Holy shit Maggie, your pits stink." That is the story, the bordello must of had thin walls. Nobody knows for sure if it is true or not, nobody except Maggie, that is. "Stay there Maggie, I can smell you from here." Two-Fingers said as he handed her another one of my dollars. "No hugs." "Bless you my boy." Was all Maggie said.

We started to walk away when Two-Fingers noticed another wino passed out on the sidewalk next to the Businessmen's Club. "That is the Governor." Two-Fingers said. "When I was a kid I used to steal pennies from my old man and give them to the Governor here, he used to hang out in the alley behind our place." Two-Fingers said as he pointed across the street. "I used to sneak him out food too. He was a great athlete back in the 1930's, he told me he was selected for the Olympic's and knew Jesse Owens. He also told me his parents were killed when a train hit their truck, he never made it to the Olympic's. He used to always carry around a little case with medals in it." Two-Fingers said as he dug around inside the Governor's coat pocket looking for the case. Just then, the Governor stirred to life and started to slap at Two-Fingers hand. "Leave me alone, leave me alone." The Governor said as he struggled to his feet.

He was all blurry eyed and it took him awhile to recognize Two-Fingers but when he did he smiled and said, "Oh, it's you Donny R. I thought it was one of those damn winos trying to roll me. How are you my boy?" The Governor asked as he stepped forward and gave Two-Fingers a hug. "I am just fine, Gov. How you doing? Won any races lately?" Two-Fingers asked. "Not since I ran you into the ground last year." The Governor said proudly. "I wasn't around last year Gov, you must be thinking of someone else." Two-Fingers said. "Well, hell, why don't we try it right now." The Governor said as he assumed a sprinter's stance. "No, no, not today, I need to train a little more before I am ready for you Gov." Two-Fingers said as he gently brushed dust off of the Governor's coat. "I am sorry I disturbed you, I was going to show my friend your medals. Do you still have them?" Two-Fingers asked. "Sure I still have them but I have to hide them, the damn winos are always trying to steal them and sell them for some Muscatel. You know how it is, aenet, Donny R." The Governor said as he opened up his shirt to reveal his money belt. He looked around suspiciously and then slowly removed a little black case from its hiding place. He opened the case very gently and took out one of two medals and handed it to Two-Fingers. "I won this gold medal for the mile in 1935 down in California. I was running for my old school Carlisle back in those days. You know Carlisle don't you Donny R.? That's the school Jim Thorpe went to. I never finished school...." The Governor said as he stared off into the distance with a look of anguish on his face. "Lot of us Indian boys went to Carlisle back in those days, a lot of good runners. All we did all day long was run. Run to town, run to school, run home, run away from it all. We were always running." The Governor said as he gingerly held onto his other medal. "When did you win that medal?" Two-Fingers asked as he pointed to the other medal the Governor was clinging onto. "I won this in high school, it is for the 100 yard dash. I won a lot of races that day and it was the first time my parents were able to see me run competitively, I put on a show." The Governor smiled broadly as he once again stared off into the distance.

Two-Fingers slowly reached over and took the medal from the Governor and examined it. It was very old and the engraving on the back was mostly worn off and we both had a hard time making out what the inscription said. Finally, the sunlight hit it just right and we able to make out the words: "1930-1st place-100yd dash." "I used to have a lot of medals but I have been rolled so many times that these are the only two I have left." The Governor said as he gathered them up and returned them to their hiding place. "Donny R. I sure could use something to eat. Do you have a dollar I can borrow?" The Governor asked as he extended his hand. "Sure, Gov." Two-Fingers said as he handed him my five dollars. "I owe you this anyway from last year when you ran me into the ground, remember?" "Hell yes I remember, I had you by a good quarter of a mile, aenet, Donny R." The Governor said before he slowly turned and walked away.

After the Governor left, we looked around and realized we were the only two people left in front of the Businessmen's Club. "Well brother, I would buy you a cold one but it appears I am out of money." Two-Fingers said as he examined the entry way to the Businessmen's Club. "How you situated financially?" "I have twenty dollars left, but at the rate you are handing out my money we will be broke before we hit the Junction." I said as we walked off in that direction.

During the summer, The Junction Drive In is the hot spot in Browning, people cruising main always went past the Junction at least a dozen times a day. The Junction sits back a little ways from the main highway and this allows for plenty of parking in it's unpaved parking lot. As I stated earlier, The Junction served the best cheeseburgers in town and the coldest pop but personally, I liked it because the Junction employed the most beautiful car hops in town.

As we slowly made our way to the Junction, we were constantly being stopped by friends, acquaintances and other well wishers. People drove past us and yelled things like, "Nice to see you got out of prison in one piece, Two-Fingers." Someone said. "Been real quiet around here since you have been gone, Two-Fingers." "Two-Fingers, where is that money you owe me?" Half the town seemed to ask that question. Two-Fingers just smiled and waved to everybody, he really ate it up. He turned to me and said, "Should leave home more often, aenet." "Yeah, this is real nice but you would think one of them sum bitches would give us a ride." I said as we continued walking.

It was a particularly busy afternoon at the Junction, the parking lot was full and the air was heavy with dust from all the traffic driving in and out of the parking lot. Two-Fingers continued to take his bows while making small talk with as many of the patrons as would listen. As he moved from car to car, I went inside to get something to drink and was happy to see Vicki Eagle Feathers at the counter waiting for an order. Vicki had been working there the last couple of summers as a car hop.

"Hey, Tony, I see your friend has finally made it back. Maybe now you will quit mopping around, aenet." Vicki said as she walked out the door with her order. "Mopping, I haven't been mopping." I said as the screen door slammed shut in my face.

Two-Fingers finished campaigning and was walking towards the screen door of the Junction and just as he opened it, Vicki rushed back inside. "You are certainly welcome, ma'am." Two-Fingers said as he bowed at the waist. "Welcome, I will show you who is welcome." Vicki said as she picked up a fly swatter and swatted Two-Fingers on the arm. "You too good to let anybody know you are coming home? Most people don't give a shit Two-Fingers, but some people do." She said as she glanced over at me "I didn't know you would miss me Vicki or I would have written, honest." Two-Fingers said as he rubbed his arm. "You wish I missed you, aenet, you asshole." Vicki said as she rushed out the door with another order.

"That chick is crazy. Oh well, enough of this old home week shit, I got us a ride to East Glacier." Two-Fingers said as he opened the screen door. "Who with?" I asked as I followed him outside. "Jimmie B." Two-Fingers said as we walked down the steps of the Junction. After digesting his response, I stopped dead in my tracks. There was no way I was getting into a vehicle with Jimmy B. He was the fastest driving maniac on the Rez, he made A.J. Hoyt look like a saint. To make things worse, he had just bought a used black 1969 Chevy Super Sport with money his recently departed grandmother left him. It had a 396 cubic inch engine and a three speed manual and the entire car only weighed about ninety pounds, it was light and the thing literally flew. "Two-Fingers listen to me, you have been away a long time and don't know what you are getting into. Trust me, you do not want Jimmy B driving you anywhere." I said all this as we approached Jimmy B's car. "Who said anything about him driving? Get in the back." Jimmy B was already sitting in the front passenger seat smoking a joint. "Now, remember Two-Fingers, keep it under a hundred." Jimmy B said as ashes fell down the front of his shirt.

"Roger." Two-Fingers said as he fired up the Super Sport and put it in first gear. He quickly glanced back at me with a shit eating grin on his face and said, "Are you buckled up?" Before I could say anything, Two-Fingers put the petal to the metal and spun out of the parking lot and onto Highway 2, leaving a cloud of dust hanging over the Junction. Two-Fingers got rubber in second and then third gear as we approached a Volkswagen van from Iowa. Well, I thought if was from Iowa but we were going so fast, I wasn't certain. Jimmy B waved at the Volkswagen as we flew past it.

Two-Fingers was holding onto the steering wheel with his deformed hand and reached inside his Levi jacket with his right hand and pulled out a joint. The telephone poles along the highway passed at an alarming rate as Two-Fingers reached down and pushed in the cigarette lighter and when it popped out, he placed the hot end to the tip of the joint and then handed it back to me. "You got to learn to relax, White Guy. Haven't you ever seen Starsky and Hutch?" Two-Fingers said as he lit up a joint for himself. "Starsky and Hutch? What the hell does that mean, Starsky and Hutch?" I asked. Two-Fingers eventually slowed down once the grass took hold.

Actually, we all mellowed out quickly as we drove to East Glacier, we focused in on the sights and sounds of the Rez. Partially clothed children were playing on top of broken down cars, cars that were left in the front yards with the promise of someday being repaired, dogs ran wild, off in the distance a group of youngsters were riding horseback across the barren, windswept plains. "God, how I have missed this place." Two-Fingers said as he slipped a Jim Croce tape into the eight track tape player.

We were thirsty by the time we reached East Glacier, really thirsty. Jimmy B was selected to go into the Glacier Park Bar and grab us a case of beer. Jimmy B had just graduated from Browning High and was only eighteen but he looked thirty five, so much for clean living.

"Shit yeah, I'll go in and get us a case of Rainier, just pull up over there." Jimmy B said as he pointed to a space in front of the Glacier Park Bar. "You got any money, Two-Fingers?" Jimmy B asked as he hopped out of the back seat of his Chevy. "Let me talk to my banker." Two-Fingers then turned to me and put his hand out. I handed over my last twenty dollars and said, "Make sure you get a receipt."

Two-Fingers and I patiently waited in the car for about half an hour before we decided to go find out what was keeping Jimmy B. We walked into the bar and I was surprised at how busy it was, it was about four in the afternoon and it was already standing room only. Jimmy B stood at the counter of the bar trying to get the bartender's attention but he was busy getting quarters for a couple of pool players. We slowly eased our way through the crowd and made a place to stand next to Jimmy B and as I looked around the place, I noticed a few women from Browning having drinks with men who were not their husbands, no place to hide on the Rez. I looked over and noticed Two-Fingers staring at two pretty blondes who were making selections at the Juke Box. Things were pretty peaceful but of course, it was early.

"Hey bartender I am tired of waiting, I need a case of Rainier." Jimmy B said as he slammed my twenty onto the bar. "Don't you see I am busy down here? I will be with you in a minute." The bartender said.

Jimmy B reached into a bowl containing peanuts and grabbed a handful. He popped a couple in his mouth as the two blondes nudged their way to the bar. "You are in our spots." One of the blondes said to us.

Before Two-Fingers and I could say anything, Jimmy B, his mouth full of peanut shells, tried to talk but all he accomplished was to spit up a few peanuts shells onto the girls. Finally, he swallowed hard and the remaining peanut shells were flushed down his dry, parched throat. "Can I buy you a beer?" Jimmy B asked as he reached over to brush the shells off the girls blouses. "Keep your hands off of us and get out of our spots." The other blonde said just as the bartender arrived on the scene. "What can I get you, Bud?" The bartender asked as he wiped the bar. "Case of Rainier." Jimmy B said as the three of us watched the blondes turn and walk out the door. "Gawd damn white women think their shit don't stink, aenet." Jimmy B mumbled.

The bartender returned with a case of Rainier in cans. Since the advent of pop tops in 1963, canned beer has gained a large foothold with the alcohol drinking public on the Rez. Besides staying cooler longer, it is easier to open, trying to open a bottle of beer with a church key while you are driving is downright dangerous. Pop tops have been credited with saving a lot of lives on the Rez.

"Five dollars? What the hell you mean, five dollars? I didn't want to buy the place I just wanted a case of beer, Bud." Jimmy B said as he stuffed my change into his pocket. Every Blackfeet with a cold case of beer and change in his pocket will always get the last word.

Chapter 17

The day Two-Fingers returned from boarding school marked Paula's third full week of fire fighting. The Blackfeet are always in demand as fire fighters, they are very good at it. The Vietnam War depleted the supply of able bodied young Blackfeet men, so women were getting their first real taste of fire fighting. Besides, Paula was already an experienced fire truck driver.

Paula's crew was called in to fight a fire that broke out in the Quartz Creek area of Glacier National Park and after battling the blaze for three weeks, they had it pretty well contained. Plus, it started to rain that night in the mountains and continued doing so for two days. A hard, glorious rain fell and put out all remaining signs of fire. That meant that all the crews would be going back to Browning for days of celebration, the Blackfeet needed to put out their own fires.

They quickly gathered up all their gear and found comfortable seats on the green BIA buses. Everybody, except the driver of the bus, was soon fast asleep. Word quickly spread around town that the crews were headed back. All the bar owners were always their happiest when the fire crews came to town. Big John Fisher, the owner of the Oasis Bar, gladly extended credit because he knew once they were paid he would be cashing a lot of government checks and selling a lot of liquor. If he was not repaid in a timely fashion, he charged some serious interest. Later on, the other bars in town started to extend credit on such occasions but Big John was the first to do so and that meant his bar got first crack at the firefighters.

Two-Fingers, Jimmy B and I were coming off a three day runner when we found out Paula was down at the Oasis celebrating. Two-Fingers was fired up to see her but Jimmy B and I were both showing some serious signs of wear and tear. Jimmy B declined to go with us and I insisted we needed to get some food and check in with my parents. After arguing about it for awhile, Two-Fingers finally agreed to get something to eat. So, Jimmy B dropped us at the station so we could get some food and a little rest.

Mom and dad were glad to see us and I explained to them we could not stay long, I just needed some food and a change of clothes. Mom fixed us both a big breakfast and after we drank several cups of coffee, we suddenly caught a second wind. My folks seemed to understand and did not say anything to stop us. So, after eating, Two-Fingers and I walked the half mile down to the Oasis. It felt really good to walk and by the time we got there, we were almost sober.

The front door to the Oasis was slightly ajar when Two-Fingers threw the door open and asked, "Anybody in here killed a buffalo lately?" A hush fell over the crowd. "Me either." Two-Fingers said as he looked into the dimly lit bar. "Still a smart ass, aenet, Two-Fingers." Big John said. "Still a smart ass, always a smart ass and looking for some ass. How about a beer, Big John and get White Guy a half of one." Two-Fingers said as he looked my way. "Yeah, right. How about I just bounce your phony ass out of here, aenet." Big John said.

Just then, Paula jumped up from her bar stool and ran over to Two-Fingers who was holding his arms wide open and for a split second I thought she was going to haul off and hit him. But after slightly hesitating, she jumped into Two-Fingers arms and gave him a big hug. Two-Fingers wobbled back a little and then lost his balance completely and they both tumbled to the floor. "Holy shit Paula, you got to lay off that fry bread, aenet." Two-Fingers said as he held her in his arms. "You just need to eat more of it little brother, you are getting weak." Paula said as she reached over and pulled his long hair. "What is this all about, you gone hippie on me?" "Naw, just defying the dress code. You know the drill, cut all the Indians hair off, put them in white shirts, Levi's and boots and everything will be all right." Two-Fingers said as he helped her up. "I started to let it grow as soon as I got those white folks thinking right."

"What you crying about now, Two-Fingers?" Bitsy Running Rabbit asked as he walked over and handed Paula a Rainier. "Crying, I'll show you who will be crying." Two-Fingers said as he started to shadow box around Bitsy. Just then, Curly Big Springs snuck up behind Two-Fingers and wrapped his arms around him and lifted him up off the floor. "Say uncle or I am going to have to hurt you." Curly said as he gently shook Two-Fingers. "I always knew you had a thing for me, aenet, Curly." Two-Fingers said as he broke loose. "It's just because you are so pretty, Two-Fingers." Liquid Louie Arrowtop said as he gave Two-Fingers a beer. Two-Fingers turned his back to Big John and gulped down half the beer. "White Guy and I have been on a little runner and we need to get our juices flowing. How about getting some beer and going for a swim out at Cut Bank Creek?" Two-Fingers asked the assembled crowd.

"What a great idea, I could use a swim. What about you guys?" Paula asked her crew mates. "Swimming? I don't know about getting wet but I wouldn't mind seeing you in a swimsuit." Curly said. "Who said anything about a swimming suit?" Paula said as the whole bar emptied out. Thirty seconds later, the Oasis Bar was totally empty except for Big John and his I.O.U.'s.

Two-Fingers, Paula, Curly, Liquid Louie and I jumped into Bitsy's Volkswagen Bug and before going out to Cut Bank Creek, we made a quick stop at Stogie Man and Cindy Ann's so Two-Fingers could retrieve some of his stash.

It was a short fifteen minute drive to Cut Bank Creek but it seemed longer to the four of us stuck in the back seat of the Bug. Two-Fingers was seated behind Bitsy, I was in the middle next to Paula, who was seated on Curly's lap. "So, my little brother returns home a pot head, aenet." Paula said as she watched Two-Fingers furiously roll some joints. "Don't tell me you never smoked any dope, Paula." Two-Fingers said in his defense. "I have tried it and I do not see the big deal." Paula said. "Well, the big deal is this." Two-Fingers said as he lit a joint and handed it to her. Paula took a small puff and passed it to Curly who knew exactly what to do with it. Soon the joint made its rounds and ended up back in Paula's hands and she was suddenly less willing to give it up. The other passengers insisted on getting their turn but Paula was steadfast in her refusal. "Man, this shit is good, aenet." Is all she was able to say.

It was around noon when we arrived at Cut Bank Creek. It was a rare, hot June day and the swimming area was packed. Swimmers were diving off the cliffs into the deep, cool water. The fire crew established a nice camp in a shaded area next to the creek and put several cases of beer in the water to keep it cool. Paula climbed out of the Volkswagen and stretched out on a nice grassy area near a tree. We all followed her and were soon resting comfortably. "Sister Girl, is it time for a nap?" Two-Fingers asked a drowsy Paula. "Nope, time for a swim." Paula said as she stood and stripped off her boots, Levi's and her blouse. She walked into the water wearing only her bra and panties. "I have created a monster." Two-Fingers said as he handed out beer.

After Paula entered the water, the remaining members of the crew who were not already swimming quickly stripped down and jumped in and all these additional swimmers caused the water level to rise a good three feet. Curly retrieved a bar of soap from his backpack and swam out to where Paula was swimming. He began to slowly rub the bar of soap against her shoulders until a nice lather formed. Paula turned towards him and he continued to rub her shoulders and arms. Then, Paula slowly removed her bra and Curly began to scrub her breasts in earnest, Curly was taking his job very seriously and was extremely disappointed when Paula swam away.

"That is just not natural." Two-Fingers said as he chugged another beer. "What is not natural?" I asked. "Sis getting naked like that." Two-Fingers said as he walked to the creek to get more beer. "I think it is an absolutely beautiful thing. Why don't you fire up one of those joints of your's so we can really appreciate the beauty of it all?" "Keep your eyes in your head, White Guy." Two-Fingers said as he lit up. "Hey, if I had a sister that looked like Paula I would be proud to show her off." All Two-Fingers could say was, "Skin you, let's go for a swim."

We stripped down to our underwear and joined the crowd and soon we were swimming and diving off the cliffs, the sun was bright and it was hot out. The water rejuvenated the crew and they drank like crazy. Bitsy went into town to pick up more beer as the party shifted into overdrive. Someone built a fire and the swimmers slowly gathering around it to warm up and dry off. Two-Fingers walked over to the crowd and started passing out joints. "Yeah, I ran into this guy who had just resigned his commission from the Army. He had all this pot soaking in opium and he gave me some." Two-Fingers said as he dressed. "My cousin had some shit just like this when he came home on his last leave." Curly said as he took a hit. "Yeah, I know a lot of guys trying this stuff. I think it is good, seems to mellow them out. Not as many fights around here anymore, aenet. Even the Stabs-in-the Backs have settled down." Liquid Louie said.

A few minutes passed before Big Man Bear Claw said, "I was in 'Nam and everybody seemed to be getting high." Big Man was only about 5'8" but he was one tough SOB. He just returned from 'Nam and everybody was amazed at how gentle he had become. "Talk about mellowing, what about Big Man. He used to beat up someone everyday, aenet." Brenda "Peaches" Running Wolf said.

Big Man was still staring into the fire puffing on a joint when he said, "I just don't want to hurt anyone anymore, I saw too much of that shit in 'Nam. These young guys around here are still trying to get tough with me and I just ignore them. What's the point?" Big Man took another hit before passing the joint.

"I always knew I could kick your ass, aenet." Two Fingers said as he started to shadow box around Big Man. "Shut up." Paula said as she slapped Two-Fingers along the side of his head. "Two-Fingers, still has to get the last word in, aenet." Big Man said as he passed Two-Fingers the joint. "Keep getting smart little man and I may have to come out of retirement." Big Man said as he continued staring into the fire. Two-Fingers was about to say something when Paula reached over and hit him on the top of his head.

"So, Two-Fingers, how did you like boarding school?" Peaches asked. "Typical white horse shit. Always someone telling me what to do, where to go and what to think. They tried to make a good white boy out of me and they almost succeeded until I figured out how to play their game. When I first got down there, I had my share of fights with the other Indians. But shit, I finally realized we were all in the same boat and needed to stick together. We should have done that four hundred years ago and there wouldn't be any whites here now, aenet?" Two-Fingers looked around the campfire and gave me the finger. "Shit, don't mind me, tell us how you really feel about it." I said as I reached for the joint. "You are my brother. Besides, you will be more Indian than all of us if you do not change your evil ways." Two-Fingers said as the other Blackfeet nodded their heads.

"I saw a lot of stuff down there. The whites are so rich, that's all they care about is money. Keeping up with the Joneses, aenet. Us Indians are all poor, the Crow, Sioux, Flathead, Northern Cheyenne and all the other Tribes, we are poor. We are living off what the whites give us and then we piss it away as soon as we get it. Dependent on the government, they give us everything but hope. Money has screwed them up and it will screw us up too." Two-Fingers said as he gulped down his beer. "I know a lot of Tribes are getting educated, sending their kids off to college and shit. Some Tribes are even starting up their own four year colleges, aenet." Curly said. "Look at the Flatheads, right over there on the other side of those mountains, they are building a college to help educate their people." Big Man said as he pointed west in the direction of the Rocky Mountains.

Two-Fingers rolled more joints as night fell on the impromptu camp. Additional firewood was gathered and thrown onto the fire and the beer was consumed at a slower pace as the citizens continued to reflect on their circumstances.

"I am going to college in Missoula." Paula said matter of factly. "I decided that the first day of fire fighting." The crowd voiced their approval. "We can get government grants and shit. I say we use their guilt money and beat them at their own game. Politicians are always saying how bad they feel for us when it is their policies that have caused all of the problems, they want us to depend on them. Their Great Society will be a failure just like their Indian policy is a failure. Before they started all of their national give away welfare programs, they should have spent some time on the Rez, a blind man would have seen that type of policy doesn't work. All it does is create a society filled with people with no hope, no dreams and no motivation; I got philosophical on the fire line. I like working and I do not want to sit on my ass all day and watch cartoons. We need to go and get educated so we can take care of ourselves better, aenet." "Why don't you do that Paula and let us know how it goes." Peaches said. "Hey, I ain't no chicken shit, I will go and you can stay here and be pregnant and barefoot." Paula said as she stared at Peaches. "Don't talk to me like I am ignorant, Paula. I am not scared of you. You think you are so damn tough, aenet." Peaches said as she rolled up her sleeves. "Where has all that brotherly love gone?" Two-Fingers said as he slowly rose to his feet. "You better hurry up with those joints, the women are about ready to go on the warpath, aenet." Big Man said as he handed out more beer.

"That's what I'm saying, we are always fighting ourselves over the stupidest things, aenet." Two-Fingers said as he lit up another joint and passed it to Paula. "Look who is talking." Paula said as she puffed away on the joint.

Chapter 18

Later that summer, on July 5, 1970, Paula and her fire crew were called out to fight a fire that was burning near the Many Glacier area of Glacier National Park. It was suspected that the fire was started by someone firing off fireworks, but nobody knew for sure. What was known, was it was moving quickly and posed a serious threat to the entire Park.

The next day, the winds picked up and the fire spread at an alarming rate. The Lodge at Many Glaciers burned to the ground and the entire area was evacuated and smoke poured out of the Park and Browning was cast into virtual darkness, that was when calls went out for volunteers to help fight the runaway fire.

Max and Two-Fingers volunteered and left town immediately in a blue forest service bus loaded with Blackfeet of varying ages, the fire was serious and the professional crews needed replacements. My old man would not let me go, he said it was too dangerous and he needed help with the station, the Blackfeet that occasionally worked for us left to fight the fire.

Browning was only fifty miles from the fire but it took a couple of hours to get there, visibility was terrible. According to Two-Fingers, as the bus approached the Many Glaciers area, it was stopped by a park ranger who told the driver to empty all the contents of the bus and to get the bus the hell out of there. The fire was burning so hot that it jumped back and forth across the road, a water truck and two caterpillars had already burned to the ground.

Max quickly took charge of the volunteers and marched them up the road in a single file formation. Two-Fingers said it was so hot and smokey he almost passed out, every time he told me the story he literally turned pale.

As the volunteers approached the top of the hill, they were greeted by a group of professional fire fighters who were sitting alongside the road resting and taking nourishment, Paula was in this group. She was concerned that Max and Two-Fingers were there, they had the equipment to fight a fire but they did not have the experience. Max had fought fires when he was younger but he was too out of shape to be of any real help but he insisted on helping and Two-Fingers was going to fight alongside of him.

About that time, a jeep rolled to a stop in front of them and Two Shoes Crossguns jumped out, Two Shoes was in the unenviable position of being in charge. "Max, I am sure glad you are here, we can use all the help we can get." Two Shoes said as he walked up to Paula, Two-Fingers and Max." Evidently, he never mentioned anything about how nice it was to see Two-Fingers. "This thing is really getting out of hand. I have called for reinforcements and was told the Governor is releasing some of the National Guard to help out. The problem is, they will not be here for quite awhile so in the meantime, the Forest Service is sending in planes to douse this thing along with some smoke jumpers, they should be getting here soon." Two Shoes said as he leaned back against the jeep and tried to catch his breath. "What do you want us to do?" Max asked. "I need you to take your crew over to the north side of Swift Current Lake and start to clear brush and establish a fire line. I am going to make you the line boss and put you in charge of these volunteers." Two Shoes said as he took a long drink from his canteen.

"What a mess." Two Shoes said before continuing, "We have a camp established down by Swift Current Creek and I am going to pull Paula's crew out of here and have them go down there and rest up, they have been going at it ever since their arrival and they can use some sleep. If you can keep this thing from spreading north, we may have a chance." Two Shoes said as he spread a map out on top of the hood of the Jeep. "Swift Current Lake will stop it from spreading to the south and if the smoke jumpers and the planes do their job and keep this thing from going any further west of here, we should be in pretty good shape, I just wish we had more people." Two Shoes said as he folded up the map.

"The problem with this plan, Two Shoes, is you need more people up on that ridge." Paula said as she pointed to the north. "If we can get the northern area contained, then you are right, we will have a chance.

But, you need to send us all up there to get it done." Paula looked to Max for approval. "Paula, Two Shoes is right, your crew is tired and needs a rest, we can get up there and hold this thing until the National Guard arrives." Max said. "The National Guard my ass." Paula said as she kicked the ground. "Them boys have never been around a forest fire, they will just get in our way just like Donny R. here. Why did you let him come?" Two-Fingers said she didn't stop for an answer. "Besides, it could be days before they get here and we can't wait that long and your crew will not be enough, Dad." Paula wiped her face on the sleeve of her green forest service shirt.

Max and Two Shoes knew she was right. Hell, even Two-Fingers knew she was right and he knew nothing about fighting a fire. He told me later he wondered why he was up there too. Two Shoes walked over to talk with Curly, who was the line boss of his crew, and asked him his opinion. "If we don't get this thing contained she is going to run all the way into Canada, we got no choice." Everybody looked to the sky to watch a plane flying overhead. "We better get a move on it then. If they stop this thing spreading to the west, it will have to start going north." "Okay, lets double time it back there then. I will call to see where the hell the reinforcements are." Two Shoes said before driving off in his jeep.

Curly and Max took charge of their crews and they walked in the direction of the blaze and began to work their way to the north of it. Their crews spread out and began to cut down trees and brush in an attempt to establish a fire line. Planes to the west were dumping fire retardant on the fire and smoke jumpers were working hard to stop the spread of the fire. All the hard work seemed to be paying off until the wind shifted direction and the fire started to head north, with a vengeance.

"Curly, we need the planes to stop dropping to the west of here and concentrate on the north. Get on the radio and let Two Shoes know what the hell is going on up here." Max yelled over the roar of the flames. "We need to get these crews away from here, this thing is getting too hot, let's make a break for Kennedy Lake and establish a fire line there. We need to get further north." Two-Fingers had been fighting the fire for less than an hour and he was already worn out. "I can't get him on the radio, Max. I think the heat has melted the insides of this damn thing." Curly said as he shook the radio. "Give it to me." Max said before yanking the radio away from Curly. "Shit, this thing is deader than a door knob." Max threw the radio down the hill and into the fire. "Let's move." Max said with a look of terror on his face. "Donny R., you stay close to me."

Max, Curly and Two-Fingers were moving as quickly as possible down the fire line gathering up the members of the crews and getting them to head as far north as possible. Max was looking frantically for Paula when he saw Bitsy. "Where the hell is Paula?" Max asked as he grabbed Bitsy by the arm. "Last I seen of her, she was down over that ridge." Bitsy said as he shook his arm loose and pointed to an area off to the south.

Max and Two-Fingers ran to the top of the ridge and were unable to see anybody, the smoke was unrelenting and the heat unbearable. They both yelled Paula's name as loud as they could. No answer, their pleas were drowned out by the roar of the fire.

They continued on until they finally found Paula. She was desperately struggling to get back up the ridge, trees were on fire all around her. Max jumped over a fallen, burning tree and was within twenty feet of Paula when he noticed a big pine tree starting to fall over, it was falling directly towards Paula. Max ran down the ridge towards Paula as fast as he could with Two-Fingers right behind him. Max reached Paula and shoved her out of the way just as the pine tree fell on top of him. Paula was momentarily stunned when a burning branch from the pine tree struck her alongside her head. She tumbled to the ground and laid there in semi-consciousness. Two-Fingers was trying to pull his dad from underneath the burning pine tree when Curly and Bitsy arrived a few minutes later and started to help. Curly took out his shovel and began to pound on the tree, this caused embers to fly all over the place. Two-Fingers frantically tore burning branches away from his father. Finally, they were able to pull Max out. Max was unconscious and the whole left side of his body was one mangled mess. Two-Fingers and Bitsy were able to lift Max up and they slung him over Curly's shoulder. Curly slowly walked back up the hill and Two-Fingers helped Paula to her feet and, with Bitsy's help, they were able to get her to the top of the ridge and to safety. Max laid on the ground unconscious as the crew turned to watch a number of large pine trees crash to the ground.

Paula screamed hysterically when she realized the severity of Max's injuries. She laid down next to him and wept as Two-Fingers threw his shovel into the raging fire below.

Chapter 19

Max lost a lot of blood before he finally arrived at the Blackfeet Health Center in Browning. However, even in his weakened state, it took half the emergency room staff to hold him down when he was told his left leg had to be amputated. After being strapped down and heavily sedated, Max was wheeled into the operating room where his leg was unceremoniously chopped off; friends and family members were shocked when they heard the news.

That was not the only bad news that hit the Rez that day, mom and dad received a telegram from the War Department informing them Stan was missing in action. Upon receiving the news, mom went into shock and had to be sedated, dad closed the station so he could be by her side and I went to find Two-Fingers.

Two-Fingers was not hard to find, he was in the waiting room pacing the floor when I arrived at the Blackfeet Health Center. The other members of his immediate family were all seated with blank looks on their face, shock had sit in. "I am so sorry to hear about Max and I hope he will be all right." I did not learn the severity of his injuries until later. They sat there in silence seemingly unaware of my presence. Finally, Paula reached up and took hold of my hands. "We are glad you came, it means a lot to us." She said as she stood and brushed the hair away from my eyes. I stared at her awhile before I blurted out, "Paula, we just got word that Stan is missing in action." Without saying a word, Paula got up and ran out the front door. Two-Fingers, Pam, Cindy Ann and Stogie Man looked at me in complete silence until Stogie Man said, "What do they mean missing in action? He was supposed to be getting discharged in a couple of months." Stogie Man said as he reached for a cigarette. Pam and Cindy Ann got up and hugged me for the longest time.

"Fucking 'Nam, aenet. Fuck me." Two-Fingers said before slamming his fist into the wall. "Let's get out of here." Two-Fingers and I turned and walked out the front door and as we exited the building we noticed that business was starting to pick up, cars and trucks were being unloaded at a rapid pace and patients were heading to the check in area. Just another busy night; business as usual on the Rez.

Two-Fingers and I were putting as much distance as we could between us and the Blackfeet Health Center when Jimmy B suddenly appeared in his Chevy. "Hey, numb nuts, what's up?" Jimmy B asked as he brought his Chevy to a complete stop. "What do you mean "what's up?" Where the hell have you been?" Two-Fingers asked as he opened the passenger door. "I've been in Great Falls and just pulled into town. So, what's up?" "You ain't going to believe this shit." Two Fingers said as I jumped into the back seat. "Just drive, we'll tell you all about it." Two-Fingers sat down and slammed the door shut.

After digesting all the news Jimmy B said, "Brothers, that is some bad shit and it don't get any better, guess who got drafted?" Jimmy B said as he pulled a bottle of Seagrams from under the front seat. "Don't fucking tell me, you got drafted?" Two-Fingers let out a whistle and reached for the whiskey. "You can't go, Jimmy B. You got to go to Canada, man. You can't go." Was about all I could say as I reached for the bottle. "Lots of people going to Canada these days. Shit, Canada is less than a hundred miles from here, man. You can stay with some of our northern brothers and sisters, they will never find you up there. You know what they say, we all look alike." Two-Fingers said as he raised the whiskey bottle to his lips. "They must have never seen you Two-Fingers if they think we all look alike. Fuck man, you don't look like anything on this planet." Jimmy B said as he reached for more whiskey. "Besides, those are white's hiding up there not warriors." "Crack you, Jimmy B." Two Fingers said as he yanked the bottle out of Jimmy B's mouth. "Bone you, Two-Fingers." Jimmy B said as he gunned the engine. The sudden acceleration caused Two-Fingers to lose his grip on the Seagrams bottle and it banged against the windshield. Luckily, the bottle only caused a small crack on the passenger side of the windshield, most of the whiskey was saved.

"Ah, fuck it." Jimmy B said as he surveyed the damage. "Nothing stays new forever, aenet." "Nothing stays new forever and nobody lives forever, aenet." I mumbled from the back seat "You start crying about all the bad shit that happens on the Rez and you'll be crying all day long, my brother is probably dead and I don't know if I can handle that."

After digesting that for a minute or so, Jimmy B said, "Well, I say we get us some beer and make this my going away party." Jimmy B rolled down his window and tossed the empty Seagrams bottle towards a "Do Not Litter" sign. "When are you going in?" Two-Fingers asked. "In two weeks." With that, silence invaded our space before Two-Fingers said, "Let's head up to Moccasin Flats so I can pick up my stash, the whiskey fucked me up."

We were driving back into town when Too Slim passed us in his pickup going like a bat out of hell. Jimmy B couldn't resist the challenge so he took off after him and in no time Jimmy B was right on his tail. Jimmy B flashed his brights off and on hoping to get Too Slim to pull over. Just then, Juanita Bear Medicine Owen lifted her head up and squinted into Jimmy B's headlights. Too Slim quickly grabbed the top of her head and pushed it out of view. "Oh, fuck. Did you see who that was?" I asked as we slowed down and watched Too Slim's pickup fade from view.

We stayed out all night drinking, driving and smoking. By daybreak the next morning, we were nearly out of gas so Jimmy B instinctively went to our Chevron station. I was kinda dozing off in the back seat when I looked up and saw my old man and Charley Owen standing in front of our station.

The station still wasn't open, so I jumped out of the back seat and ran inside to turn the gas pumps on. I was standing there filling up Jimmy B's Chevy when Charley walked up to us and asked if we had seen Juanita. Evidently, she hadn't been home for awhile. I remember feeling very uncomfortable and unsure what to say when all of a sudden, Jimmy B said, "Never seen her. We were out rabbit hunting in the country and we never seen her." Dad was looking at us suspiciously when Two-Fingers said, "I am sorry about Stan, he is a good man. I hope they find him alive and well, Mr. Church." Jimmy B nodded his head in agreement. "I'm sorry about the whole damn thing." Charley said as he walked to his pickup. "You have to excuse old Charley there, he has been up all night worrying about Juanita. Lately, she has been drinking more than usual." Dad hung his head and just walked away. As he disappeared from view I said, "Let's get the hell out of here."

We drove in silence to the Blackfeet Health Center to see how Max was doing, Two-Fingers was fidgety and very apprehensive when we entered the waiting room. The waiting room was empty except for Stogie Man who was asleep in one of the chairs. "Stogie Man, wake up. Where is everybody?" Two Fingers shook him until he woke up. Stogie Man took awhile before he got his bearings. "Your dad came to early this morning and the women have been in his room ever since." Stogie Man stretched his legs out and quickly fell back to sleep.

Two-Fingers, Jimmy B and I walked down the corridor that led to the Intensive Care unit and began looking into doors trying to locate Max. After waking up half of the sick and dying, we finally found Max's room. Pam, Paula and Cindy Ann were all there standing guard and we got a decidedly cold look as we entered the room. "Nice you could show up, Donny R." Paula said. "Shit, Sis, I'm sorry but I can't take this." Two Fingers said as he paced around the room.

Max was laying in bed with tubes and wires running in and out of him, his skin was a deep yellow color and there was an empty space under his blanket where his left leg used to be. Max was sleeping, but it was a fitful sleep. Pam sat by his side holding his right hand. "My boy, there is nothing you can do here." Pam said as she weakly smiled at Donny R. "Why don't you take the girls and go get something to eat?"

Paula and Cindy Ann insisted on staying, so the three of us took the opportunity to get out of there. Before the door closed behind us, I heard Pam say, "Don't be too hard on him, he has never been able to handle these types of things."

Chapter 20

Two-Fingers was always deeply moved whenever anyone he liked was injured or killed. He always rooted for the underdog and had a real problem with unfairness and he took those things seriously, more seriously than most. It is difficult to acknowledge sensitivity in a place as insensitive as Browning because sensitivity is a foreign concept. Yet, Two-Fingers was sensitive, sensitive to the plight of others and confused as to why these injustices happened. His father's injuries had him questioning a lot of things and he began to look for answers, the first stop on this quest was the Paradise Bar where all the patrons were searching for something.

The Paradise had just opened for the day and the place was already filled to capacity, I was beginning to wonder if there was ever an empty seat at any bar on the Rez.

So, Jimmy B, Two-Fingers and I walked up to the bar and ordered a round and the bartender served us without asking any questions. The Paradise was notorious for serving just about anybody. There were only three rules at the Paradise: First, in order to get served, you must be as tall as the bar, which is four feet high. Second, you must have money; bullshit walks and money talks. Third, your head must never hit the bar. If your head hits the bar, you are taken out back and laid in the alley to sober up. There was so much booze being drank that day I concluded the alley would need to be widened to hold the overflow.

The Paradise is the filthiest bar on the Rez. In fact, it is so ugly and beat up it makes the other bars on the Rez look like piano bars. Of course, nobody goes there for the scenery or the stimulating conversation, they go there to drown their sorrows. For those who have fallen, it is an oasis.

We were working on our third boilermaker when Two-Fingers said, "Fuck me a running, I'm starting to like this place." I was chasing my last shot of whiskey with a beer when he said that and I ended up spewing the beer across the bar and onto the cracked mirror located directly behind the bartender. "If that's the case, it is time to go." I said as I slowly wiped the beer from my chin with my shirt sleeve. "Go where? Where we going to go? You go into the Paradise and there ain't no place left to go." Jimmy B said as he ordered another round. "That's pretty heavy shit there, Jimmy B. I never knew you to be such a thinker." Two-Fingers said as he glanced at the front door. "Oh shit, here comes Red Stabs-in-the-Back." Two-Fingers took a long drink of his beer before he sat it down on the bar.

Red was Kenny and Ronnie Joe's uncle and he was one mean son-of-a-bitch. "So, Two-Fingers, I hear your dad had a little bad luck." Red said as he stepped up to the bar next to me. Two-Fingers didn't say a word he just stood there nodding his head and staring into the mirror. "Well, you know, maybe now you and him can join the circus and be in one of them freak shows. You know, you could call yourselves, "Two-Fingers and the One Legged Gimp, aenet." Red said as he stared at Two-Fingers. Two-Fingers slowly turned to look at Red and said, "I have a better idea, why don't you, Dad and me start a band. We can call it, "Two-Fingers, One Leg and No Brain."

Red started to make a move towards Two-Fingers when I turned around and hit him square in the throat with my fist, I hit his ass hard. He slumped over and grabbed his throat with both hands as he gagged and choked up blood, he was making a real mess of the place. That was about the time I moved closer to him and kicked him right square in the nuts. Red fell to the floor and I stood over him yelling, "What did you say? I can't hear you, what did you say?" He slowly turned over onto his left side and curled up into a fetal position.

Nobody in the bar moved, it was deathly quiet. Two-Fingers and Jimmy B stood with their backs to the bar, ready for any action that may have come their way. They looked around to see if any of the patrons were going to join the fight and nobody seemed to give a shit, least of all the bartender. "Well now, ah, White Guy, what do you say we get out of here?" Two-Fingers asked as he waved his hand in front of my eyes, I was staring down at Red in a trance like state. That is what happens when bottled up rage comes to the surface. Hate and boiler makers will make a weak man strong, at least until he sobers up. All I could say was, "You want to go, we can go."

Jimmy B quickly ordered a case of Rainier for the road and threw five dollars on the bar. We slowly eased out the front door and climbed into the Chevy. Before driving off, Jimmy B spun a donut in the parking lot which caused gravel to fly everywhere and as he turned onto the road, he narrowly missed hitting a tourist taking pictures of the Standard station shaped like a Teepee. I think the guy was Asian, not really sure, my blood was still pumping pretty good. I think it is important to know the nationality of anybody you nearly run over, right?

We drove around the Rez for hours drinking beer and checking our rearview mirror. "Never seen a guy go down like that, went to his knees faster than a five dollar whore, aenet." Jimmy B said for a third time. Fights only last a few minutes but the retelling of them last a lifetime, especially if you think you won. Of course, on the Rez, you never really know who has won because fights last for years, the time in between the fighting is just an intermission. I know guys on the Rez who have been fighting each other for over forty years. Every time they see each other, the fight is back on.

"Looks like Too Slim is having a party." Two-Fingers said as we drove by Too Slim's house. Too Slim lived in a "Easter egg" house on Moccasin Flats not far from Stogie Man and Cindy Ann's place. Too Slim was always throwing a party so this announcement did not come as much of a surprise.

There were eight cars strategically parked in Too Slim's front yard when Jimmy B pulled his Chevy in and made it nine. We got out of the Chevy and walked right into Too Slim's house, nobody locks their doors on the Rez. It was around five p.m. and the party was well underway. In the living room, a sixteen gallon keg was tapped and the beer was flowing very liberally.

"Oki, oki, good party but no whiskey." Two Finger said as he made his grand entrance.

Over in the corner, sitting on the couch, was Stogie Man and Juanita Owen. Two-Fingers walked over to where they were sitting and asked,

"So, who is taking care of my nieces tonight?" Stogie Man staggered to his feet and said, "None of your fucking business, that's who." Just then, Too Slim rushed in from the kitchen and stood between them and said, "If you want to stay here you keep your mouth shut." Two-Fingers looked past both of them and stared at Juanita. "One word and we get after it right here." Too Slim said as he placed a hand on Two-Fingers shoulder. That's when I intervened and sat down next Juanita. "How you doing tonight, Mrs. Owen? We ran into Charley this morning and he asked us if we saw you last night. We told him we hadn't but I could've sworn we saw you in Too Slim's pickup truck, Charley seemed awfully worried." I looked up at Too Slim as the blood vanished from his face. "Listen, why don't you guys have some beer and relax." Too Slim said as he took his hand off of Two-Fingers shoulder and disappeared into the kitchen. "Relax, fuck we are relaxed, aenet. You guys are the ones that need to relax, White Guy and I have been out making the streets safe for the women and children while you guys have been hiding out up here. Jimmy B, how about a beer?" Two-Fingers said as he walked over to the keg. "You are sitting in my seat, White Guy." Stogie Man said as he stared down at me. "Why don't you run downtown and get us some whiskey, Stogie Man?" Juanita asked as she handed him a hundred dollar bill. "Tony will keep your spot warm, won't you Tony?" Juanita asked as she patted my leg. "If his spot gets any warmer the whole fucking place is going to burn down." I said as Stogie Man headed for the front door.

Juanita laughed and moved a little closer to me. "You turned out to be a handsome white boy, aenet." Before I could reply, Juanita continued talking, "You don't like me much do you, Tony?" "I like you fine. But, since you asked, you are married to my dad's best friend, remember?" Juanita was now running her hand through my hair. "Remember, how the hell could I forget? If you marry an Owen you are not allowed to forget. Well, I am forgetting him and his whole fucking family. Besides, I can't give him a baby so what the fuck difference does it make?" Juanita asked as she lit a cigarette.

Two-Fingers walked over and handed me a cup of beer. He looked over at Juanita and asked, "Sister, can I bum a smoke from you?" "You can have the whole pack if I don't have to look at your ugly face the rest of the night." Juanita said as she handed him her pack of Marlboros. "Hey, I leave, and White Guy goes with me." Two-Fingers said as he filled his Levi jacket pockets with cigarettes. "What, you two joined at the hip? I can give him something you can only dream about, aenet." Juanita said as she inspected the empty cigarette pack Two-Fingers handed back.

Two-Fingers eyes widened as he glanced at me, we both started to get a better understanding of the possibilities the opportunity presented. "Well now, is that Peaches Running Wolf I see out there in the kitchen? If you two will excuse me, I have to run along." Two-Fingers said as he exited. "Always the fucking gentleman that one, lets dance." Juanita said as she stood and extended her hand to me. I stood up and took hold of her hand when someone turned up the radio, soon the place was hopping. Juanita and I were slow dancing when Juanita whispered into my ear, "I think I am going to stay sober the rest of night." I wasn't sure what to think of that. In fact, I wasn't doing much thinking since Juanita climbed into my arms, the only thing I knew for sure was I had a hard-on a cat couldn't scratch.

Stogie Man came back with a case of Jack Daniels and the party shifted into overdrive. Cars full of people arrived and the valet service went to hell, Too Slim's front yard soon looked like a used car lot.

Juanita and I were standing in the middle of the living room when she took my hand and led me down the hallway. The crowd stopped to watch us go into the bathroom and before the bathroom door closed, I heard Two-Fingers say, "Looks like we are going to have to piss outside for awhile, watch the wind." Everybody laughed.

Juanita locked the door behind us and started to slowly undress. She took off her blouse and revealed the most beautiful breasts I had ever seen. They were large, but not too big. Her nipples were pink on a brown canvass; they were a work of art. Well, I am going to have to leave it right there. You can use your imagination as to what happened next. As I have grown older, I have learned the importance of discretion and I am going to exercise that now. Gentlemen should never talk about their sex lives and especially not their partners, Two-Fingers always talked about his partners but nobody ever believed him. Besides, my wife is a very forgiving woman but forgiveness has it's limits.

At 5 a.m. the next morning, I was startled out of a deep, deep sleep when Two-Fingers shook my shoulders and whispered, "Hey, White Guy, we got to get going." "Why? What the hell is going on?" "Peaches is pissed off, I'll explain later." Two-Fingers said as he opened the bedroom door an inch and peaked out. I dressed as quickly as possible and tried not to wake Juanita.

Two-Fingers and I were tiptoeing down the hall when, all of a sudden, Peaches jumped out of the shadows and started to cuss Two-Fingers. "Where are you going you bastard? Do you think you can just fuck me and then just leave me?" Peaches screamed at the top of her lungs. She was standing next to Two-Fingers when she reared back and hit him square in the jaw, I was surprised Two-Fingers was able to remain standing.

We turned and ran out the front door as fast as we could. As we ran, I turned around to look and I saw Peaches, half dressed, running after us. "You think you can use me and not even think twice about it." Peaches said as she picked up a rock and threw it at Two-Fingers. Luckily, it just whizzed by our heads and hit the window of one of the cars in the front yard, glass flew everywhere. Peaches started to run after us in earnest when she suddenly stopped and picked up another rock. "What do you think I am just a cheap piece of shit?" Peaches threw a strike and the rock hit Two-Fingers right in the middle of his back. "Ouch, that bitch has a better arm than Tom Seaver." Two-Fingers said as he began to run as fast as he could.

I was out in front of him running for all I was worth but Peaches kept pace and was actually starting to gain on us. Two-Fingers started to panic. "Listen, this chick is faster than I am, we need to do something." Two-Fingers said as he continued to sprint. "Why don't we split up?" I suggested. "Split up? What the fuck good would that do? That bitch wants to kill me so she ain't going to follow you." Two-Fingers said as a rock hit him in the back of the leg. "Exactly." Was all I said before running off in the opposite direction.

"Never fuck a chick from East Glacier, they all run like deers." Two-Fingers yelled as he ran down an alley and jumped over a fence. He looked over his shoulder and, much to his surprise, Peaches was hurdling the fence without breaking stride. Two-Fingers was running out of gas so he started running for his house. He ran all the way there before he was brave enough to stop and look behind him, Peaches was still in hot pursuit. Two-Fingers pushed the gate open and seemed surprised to see me sitting on the porch watching the whole thing. Two-Fingers ran past the porch to the basement door that he quickly opened and shut, he then locked the door and braced his body up against it hoping it would be enough to keep her out. He told me later that he swore his lungs were going to explode.

Peaches stopped running when she saw me sitting on the porch and she proceeded to unload on me, she called me everything but a white man. She yelled and screamed for a good five minutes when, all of a sudden, she stopped, looked around, and started walking back towards Moccasin Flats. Like a hurricane, she had blown herself out.

I calmly walked downstairs and gently tapped on the door and said, "It's safe to come out now lover boy." Two-Fingers gingerly opened the door and let me in and before closing the door, he looked around to make sure the coast was clear. "Holy shit." Two-Fingers said as he leaned over and put seven fingers on his knees and tried to catch his breath. "What was that all about? Really, what the hell was that all about?" I asked as he sat down next to me on the basement floor.

After a few minutes, Two-Fingers straightened up and walked over to an old GE refrigerator that was in the basement. He opened the refrigerator door and reached in and pulled out two quarts of Olympia beer. He tipped one quart upside down and used its cap to pop the top off of the other quart. Mission accomplished, the cap popped off with a minimal amount of foam. He put the unopened quart back into the refrigerator before taking a long pull on the Oly. He wiped the top of the bottle with his sleeve and handed it to me, I watched him do all this like he was in slow motion. I took a long, satisfying drink of the beer before I handed it back to him.

He was still rattled when he started to speak. "Well, while you were in there doing the horizontal bop with Juanita, I decided it was time for me and Peaches to get it on. Well, I took her back to Too Slim's bedroom and start working on her and believe me, I was getting nowhere fast. She let me do about anything I wanted except have sex with her. Oh no, no sex for old Two-Fingers. I was killing myself and getting hornier and hornier and this babe doesn't do anything but tease me. Finally, I wear down her resistance and I make my move. Well, by this time, I am so worked up that I am only good for three, maybe four strokes before I shoot my load." Two-Fingers said as he finished off the quart. "Well, that wasn't good enough for good old Peaches, oh no. She wanted more and said so in no uncertain terms. I told her I needed to rest awhile and have a beer or two and that's when she started calling me dirty names." Two Fingers said before opening the other quart of Oly with his teeth. "I thought I could get you and get out of there before she got dressed. That bitch is fast. You ever seen a chick run that fast? Fast runner, fast dresser and a slow comer. I don't know how much more she could stand, I gave her the best five strokes of my life." Two-Fingers said as he sat back down next to me on the floor. "I thought you said it was four strokes?" I asked as I reached for the quart. "Four, five, who knows, things were moving kind of fast, if you know what I mean." "You should have just left me, I could have used some more sleep." "Sleep, it didn't sound like you were getting any sleep, that bed was creaking all night long." Two-Fingers said with a look of admiration in his eyes. "Besides, Charley find's your ass in bed with her and you are dead."

"Can you believe the shit that has happened to us in the last twenty-four hours?" Two-Fingers asked as he stood up and drank more Oly. I stood up to take the bottle from him when it slipped from my hand and crashed to the floor, glass and beer flew everywhere. "Fuck it, I'll clean it up later. Let's go for a walk and smoke some pot." Two-Fingers said as he peeked out the basement window.

As we excited the basement I said, "Man, you are eighteen years old and you let that old women out run you, that is sad." Two-Fingers stared at me for a while and then said, "She may be older than me but she hasn't lost a step, bitch should play for the Packers."

We walked about a half mile down main street before stopping to rest on the ledge of the theater. The ledge is a prime sitting spot and it is usually inhabited by the town's winos. The ledge is a foot wide, made of brick and about twenty feet in length, it is sturdy and not too terribly uncomfortable. The best thing about the ledge is it sit's directly across the street from the Oasis Bar. If you sit on that ledge long enough eventually the whole town will pass you by and so will your life.

It was around 6 a.m. and out of the shadows the winos began to appear, one by one they stirred from their sleep. Two-Fingers recognized the Governor and waved him over. Soon the Governor, Maggie Stink Pits, and Rubber Joe were seated between Two-Fingers and me on the ledge. There were other winos milling around, but it was just the five of us that were seated.

Two-Fingers lit up a joint and handed it to the Governor who was sitting next to him, the Governor inspected the joint for awhile before taking a puff. "I haven't smoked this shit since back in the '30's. Tried some Hash when I was down in California too." The Governor said before he passed the joint to Maggie. "Thank you cousin." Maggie said before she took a big hit. "My husband got me started on Opium when I worked in Butte, smoked a lot of that stuff." Maggie passed the joint to Rubber Joe. "I never did try this shit before...what the hell, you only live once, aenet." Rubber Joe said as he wrapped his sloppy wet lips around the joint and inhaled for all he was worth. Smoke started to pour out of his nostrils and mouth before Rubber Joe finally exhaled. "Shit, I've gotten higher smoking Bull Durham tobacco." Rubber Joe then handed the sloppy wet joint to me. I took my time inspecting the soggy joint as the other members of the party stared at me anxiously. So, not wanting to disappoint, I took a big hit before handing the joint back to Rubber Joe. We sat on the ledge and smoked a couple of joints and we were totally oblivious to what was going on around us. Which, as it turned out, wasn't much that early in the morning.

"My real name is Joseph Many Guns." Rubber Joe suddenly announced. "I was raised up on a ranch north of town." Rubber

Joe pointed to the north. "Back then, things were really different, aenet. Never went to town but about twice a year, we raised cattle and pigs. Can't grow no crops in this fucking place so we ate meat and occasionally some fish, but mostly meat. Got married and had two kids, a boy and a girl." Rubber Joe took another hit and stared off into space before continuing. "Took a load of cattle down to Shelby to sell at the livestock auction one day and while I was gone our house started on fire, nobody ever told me how it happened. How could it happen?" Rubber Joe painfully asked. "My wife tried to save our kids but the place burned up too quick, she was in the hospital for several weeks, aenet." Rubber Joe handed the joint to Maggie. "My wife ran away shortly after that, I heard she went back to live with some relatives up in Canada. Shit, I don't blame her. I moved to town and have never been back myself, too many ghosts." Rubber Joe said as he stared directly at me. "Now I am Rubber Joe, aenet. Rubber Joe with no place to go." Again, Joseph Many Guns pointed to the north.

"That is a sad story, Cousin." Maggie said as she shook her head. "My real name is Margaret White Horse and I am a Cree Indian. My people come from up around Lethbridge, Alberta. I got married to a white American when I was sixteen years old, aenet. I had never been to the States before I moved to Butte when my husband got a job down in the silver mines. Good job, but my husband drank up all the money. He turned out to be a lazy, worthless bastard. He never kept a job past payday, he was drunk all the time and when he got drunk he beat me. I was pregnant and he beat me so bad I lost my baby, I never could get pregnant again." Maggie handed the joint to the Governor. "I never was no good after that and he ended up getting killed over a poker game, good riddance to the fool. I had no place to go so I went to work at a whorehouse. My heavens, Butte had a whorehouse on every corner in those days, lot of money in Butte back then. I saved my money and, after about a year, I quit whoring and got a good job cleaning rooms at a hotel. Rooms were rented out in eight hour shifts back then, Butte was so busy and space was limited. I would clean the rooms up as quickly as they emptied. One day, I was cleaning up a room on the top floor when a miner came in. He was in a hurry for his room and he wanted to know what was taking me so long. Before I could say anything, he knocked me down and raped me. When I reported him, nobody did shit about it. Once a whore, always a whore, aenet." Maggie said as she stood up and stretched her legs and anxiously looked in the direction of the Oasis Bar. "Drinking helps me to forget, aenet."

"I know why I drink, I drink to forget too... but I have been drinking for so long I can't remember exactly what it was I was trying to forget. I guess I have finally succeeded at something in my life, aenet." The Governor said philosophically. "I do know this much, everybody can find an excuse to drink. Everybody has bad stuff happening to them, drinking is a weakness and once you start down that road it takes a lot of strength to turn back. I have never been that strong, no turning back for me. Best thing to do is to avoid any bad luck, aenet. What about you my boy, why do you drink?" The Governor asked Two-Fingers.

Two-Fingers was silently pondering that question when the front door of the Oasis swung open and the day Bartender placed a brick under the door to keep it open before going back inside. Before Two-Fingers could answer the Governor's question, Maggie, Rubber Joe and the Governor stood up and walked towards the Oasis, we sat and watched them go. After they disappeared inside, we looked at each other and shrugged our shoulders. "Wow, shit. That was pretty heavy, aenet." Two-Fingers said. "Too heavy." I replied. "Why do we drink, Two-Fingers?" "Shit, you got me, all I know is I don't want to end up like them. Did you notice how quickly they got out of here when the Oasis opened?" Two-Fingers asked as he slowly shook his head.

We sat there lost in our own thoughts as Browning slowly stirred to life. "I think I am going up to visit my folks." Two-Fingers said as he pointed in the direction of the Blackfeet Health Center. "Yeah, I think I am going to go see mine." I said as I pointed in the opposite direction.

Two-Fingers and I were separated for three years. Yet, when we were reunited it was as if we had never been apart and the tragedies that struck our families further strengthened our friendship, true friendship is a rare and interesting phenomenon.

Chapter 21

Two-Fingers and I were affected by our encounter and conversation with the winos, not profoundly affected to the point of joining a bible class or converting to Hinduism but we were moved enough to slowdown on our partying and take care of business.

In fact, for a full week after the experience on the ledge, Two-Fingers and I were on our best behavior. Each day, after doing his chores, he sat with his dad at the Blackfeet Health Center. The family pulled together and Max got stronger with each passing day. I visited the hospital as frequently as I could but I was busy with family and work too.

I was at Max's bedside when Two-Fingers and his father had this conversation: "The doctor said as soon as this swelling goes down I can get fitted for a prosthesis." Max said as he patted the side of his hospital bed. "Really? Maybe I should call up Bandit Bird Rattler and find out where he shop's for parts." Two-Fingers said as he smiled at his father. "Well, if you talk to him, tell him I want a new leg, nothing used." Max said as he smiled back at Two-Fingers. "Seriously, I am probably going to be in this place for quite awhile, I need to get healed up and then I will need some extensive physical therapy and rehabilitation. I will need to learn how to walk and drive with my new leg, so it is going to take some time." Max said. "I am going to need your help and I am very glad you decided to come home. Paula and Cindy Ann are needed at the apartment house and the curios shop so you are going to have to help out as much as you can." Max said as he reached for a cup of water. "Man, these pills really get to me." Two-Fingers glanced over at me before helping him with the water. "I'm feeling kind of sleepy, Donny R., I think I will get some sleep now. You think about what I said." Max said as he leaned back against his pillow. "Hell Pop, sounds good to me, I never wanted to go to boarding school in the first place." Two-Fingers said as Max began to snore. I remember leaving the room and looking back over my shoulder as Two-Fingers gently wiped sweat from Max's forehead.

That was the same day I found out my parents were planning on moving away from Browning and back to Cherry Hills. After returning from the hospital, I was given the news. "What do you mean you want to move?" I asked dad. "Your mom and I have decided to sell and get out of here, she needs to get out of here Tony." "I thought you liked it here, Pop. You always wanted a gas station." I said knowing full well I was going to lose the argument. "One bad thing after another has happened since we moved here, your mom hates the place and I am beginning to." Dad stated defiantly. "Yeah, but I like it here. Besides, I am a senior this year and I do not want to move. What about Stan? He will want to come back here." "Tony." Dad said as he grabbed me by the shoulders. "We have to accept the possibility that Stan may not come home." "I can't accept that, Pop. I won't accept that, he has to come back." I said before slumping against the wall. Dad leaned against the pop cooler and whispered, "I hope, with all my heart, you are right. But your mother is nearing a nervous breakdown and she needs to get the hell out of here. There is a greenhouse for sale back in Cherry Hills and I am going to buy it for her if I can get this place sold." "Well, you will never get this place sold, Pop. No white family is going to move here now, not with all the militants running around. This place is changing so fast." I said as I stared out the front window of the station. "All the more reason for us to get the hell out of here." Dad stated before walking outside to wait on a customer. "I am not leaving." I said as I followed him outside. "Look, Tony, business is off, tourists are going right through town without even stopping. We either sell now and get something or wait and get nothing." Dad said as he washed the customer's windshield. "Who is going to buy the place? Nobody in town has any money." "I have been talking with Bobby Racine and he is trying to get a loan through the Tribe. Bobby is a good guy, at least he isn't drunk all the damn time." Bud said as he finished with the windshield. "If I can't get this place sold I will board it up, Charley said he would loan me the money for the greenhouse and the move. I hate to have to do that but I am running out of options." Dad said as he finished filling up the car. "Has Charley found Juanita?" I asked without making eye contact. "Oh yeah, funniest thing happened. I guess she went home a few days ago and was very remorseful about running away and all. Charley say's she has stopped drinking and has been staying at home lately. I don't know how long that will last, she is too damn young and wild. I feel sorry for Charley, he deserves better." Dad said as he handed some change back to the customer. "Did he say where she ran off to?" I asked as I looked away. "He never said and I doubt he knows where she went, exactly." Dad said before he turned and walked back to the the station.

Actually, Charley didn't want to know where Juanita ran off to, he was just glad she was home. Juanita was diagnosed with endometriosis which is the inflammation of the lining of the uterus and at the time of her diagnosis, she was told it was highly unlikely she could ever become pregnant. Charley was disappointed but Juanita was devastated. Never that self confident, she thought of herself as a failure. So, to hide from the pain, she began to drink and when she drank, she drank hard. The more she drank the less self esteem she had and the spiral downward worsened.

It was always the same after Juanita returned home; she was remorseful for awhile and then the fever hit her and off she would go again. Sometimes she was gone for only a day and sometimes, like the last time, she was gone for several days. But, she always returned home.

Chapter 22

By this time, Jimmy B was just a few days away from going into the Army. He had kept on partying since the night at Too Slim's a week before and he started to feel the effects; too much whiskey and not enough sleep. It was good to see him drive up to the station. "Fill it up, White Guy." Jimmy B said as he fell out of his Chevy. "What the hell have you been up to, Jimmy B?" I asked as we shook hands. "Been out breaking a few hearts before I go into the Army. Man, I can't believe I go in next week. Time flies when you are having fun." Jimmy B said as he pulled out a wad of cash. "Wow, where did you get all that money?" I asked. "Sold the Chevy to A.J. Hoyt for $2,000.00. He put down $500 and will give me the rest when I turn over the car." Jimmy B said as he leaned against the Chevy. "A.J. better hope you don't turn it over to him all busted up." I said as I began to fill up the tank. "Shit, A.J. would fix it better than new anyway. That reminds me, I better check the oil." "So what have you and Two-Fingers been up to? I heard through the grapevine that you both have been on the wagon." Jimmy B said as he opened the hood of the Chevy "Yeah, it's a long story, basically we both decided it was time to cool it for awhile and help out around home." I said as I handed Jimmy B an oil rag. "Well, Indian Days starts the day before I go into the Army next week and I say you boys fall off before then." Jimmy B said as he inspected the dipstick. "I say you are right. Shit, I can't believe we've lasted this long." "Well, since you are going to fall off anyway, why don't you jump in and we'll go find him?" Jimmy asked as he closed the hood. "I don't know, the old man has been acting kind of weird lately, he is talking about selling out and moving back to New Jersey." I said. "No shit, have you told Two-Fingers?" Jimmy B asked. "No, I just found out this morning." Jimmy B stared at me for awhile before saying, "You better come with me and tell Two-Fingers yourself, you do not want him finding out from someone else." "You are right, I'll go tell my dad I need to take some time off."

It didn't take us long to find Two-Fingers, he was sitting outside the Schwartz's apartment house smoking a cigarette and drinking a cup of coffee when Jimmy B and I drove up. "You seen Peaches lately?" Two-Fingers asked as we approached. "Not since you and her were making out up at Too Slim's. Why? You two thinking about running off and getting married?" Jimmy B asked as he sat down on the porch next to Two-Fingers. "Well, she used me that night and I haven't heard from her since, not one phone call." Two-Fingers said as he quickly glanced over his shoulder. "Whoa, you seem a little jumpy there partner. You don't think she is going to sneak up and start throwing rocks at you again do you?" Jimmy B asked as he began smiling. "You heard?" Two Fingers asked. "Hell yes I heard, half the town has probably heard by now." Jimmy B said as he took a drag off of Two-Fingers cigarette.

"How embarrassing." Two-Fingers said as he hung his head. "Yeah, I know. The poor girl must be embarrassed to death knowing that everybody in town knows you fucked her, aenet, Two-Fingers." Jimmy B said as he flicked the cigarette butt towards main street. "Bone you, Jimmy B," Two-Fingers said as he reached into his Levi jacket for another cigarette. Jimmy B started to laugh uncontrollably when Two-Fingers told him his version of the episode. To add effect, Two-Fingers stood and removed his T-shirt to reveal the marks on his back he received from the rock attack. "Yeah, and the fucking White Guy said we ought to split up so he is out of the line of fire." Two-Fingers said as he smiled at me. Jimmy B laughed hard and tears ran down his cheek. He finally stopped laughing long enough to blurt out, "White Guy has something he wants to tell you." I looked at him and cursed his name under my breath before telling Two Fingers the news of our moving, Two-Fingers just sat there staring at me in silence.

"Do not get pissed off, I just found out this morning." I said. "All right, I'm listening. Why don't you tell me what is going on." Two-Fingers said as he lit up another cigarette. "Man, what is it with you and these cigarettes?" I asked. "I need to do something with my hand." Two-Fingers said. "You ever think about just sitting on the mother fucker?" I asked between coughs. "Getting awful cocky since you got a piece of ass, aenet, White Guy." Two-Fingers said as he blew smoke in my direction. "Hey, If you gave Peaches a little more cocky, she wouldn't have chased your sorry ass down the street." "Crack you, White Guy." Two-Fingers said as he stood up to face me. "Bone you, Two-Fingers." I couldn't tell if he was really mad at me so I left it at that.

"I see you boys have gotten a little feisty since you been on the wagon. We better get us some beer before there is bloodshed." Jimmy B said as he walked towards his car. Two-Fingers and I followed and then we drove down to the Paradise Bar. "I'll be right back, it's on me. You girls kiss and make up while I am gone." Jimmy B jumped out of the Chevy and walked towards the Paradise, he had a spring in his step now that he was at the watering hole. "Girls, who you calling girls?" Two-Fingers said as Jimmy B disappeared inside the Paradise. "Always got to get the last word in, aenet, Two-Fingers." I asked. "You want to get it on? We can step outside right now." Two-Fingers said as he reached for the door handle. "You feeling froggy, jump." I said as I began to get out of the back seat.

Just then, Jimmy B came bouncing out of The Paradise head first, he hit the gravel and slid up against the bumper of his Chevy and in the doorway stood Red Stabs-in-the-Back and two of his buddies. "Been looking for you guys." Red said as he and his two friends walked towards the Chevy. "Oh, fuck." Two-Fingers said as he locked the passenger door and quickly slid down the bench seat and locked the driver's door.

Red stood at the driver's door yanking on the door handle and pounding on the side window. Luckily, Jimmy B left the car keys in the ignition. As Two-Fingers started the car, the other two thugs ran over to the passenger door and start yanking on the handle. Just then, Red picked up a rock from the parking lot and hit the driver's side window with it. Luckily, it did not break. Before Red was able to hit it again, Two-Fingers put the Chevy in reverse and gunned the engine, dust flew everywhere as the car traveled backwards towards main street, Red and his friends gave chase. Two-Finger quickly shifted into first gear and floored the accelerator, this caused gravel and even more dust to fly. Two-Fingers drove right at Red who momentarily froze in place before diving out of the way. Jimmy B was just getting to his feet and as the Chevy slowed, he threw himself onto the hood and grabbed the windshield wipers for support. "Go, go, go." Jimmy B yelled as Red regained his footing and threw another rock that narrowly missed the rear window. "A.J. should be pleased about that." I said as we sped out of the parking lot and onto main street, narrowly missing a family in a pickup truck. "This is the rock throwingest place I have ever seen." Two-Fingers said as he shifted into second.

Jimmy B was face down on the hood holding onto the windshield wipers with all of his strength as the Chevy roared down main street. He slowly lifted his head and made eye contact with Two-Fingers who was driving like a man possessed. Jimmy B motioned towards the side of the road with his head, his hands were still firmly attached to the windshield wipers. "What do you think he wants?" Two-Fingers asked "Looks like he wants you to pull over." I said as we narrowly missed a pack of dogs.

Just then, Two-Fingers pulled into the Junction's parking lot, slowed down slightly and then slammed on the brakes. That caused Jimmy B to lose his grip on the windshield wipers and he flew off the front of the Chevy and bounced across the graveled parking lot before coming to rest at the feet of Vicki Eagle Feathers. He laid there flat on his back looking up at Vicki when he asked, "What's a guy got to do to get a little service around here?" "You're a funny guy, aenet, Jimmy B." Vicki said as she stepped over him and went inside the Junction.

Two-Fingers and I were laughing our asses off as we walked over to help Jimmy B to his feet. Jimmy B was desperately trying to get mad but all he could do was laugh along with us. "Jimmy B, just think of it as advanced training, you will probably be doing a lot of that type of shit in the Army." Two-Fingers said as he wiped tears from his eyes.

"Can't just come here like a normal human being can you Two-Fingers? Always got to make an entrance, aenet." Vicki said as she walked up to where we were standing. "Just checking the brakes, I think she's pulling a little to the right." Two-Fingers said. "That's real clever. Tony, why do you run around with this dip shit?" Vicki asked as she looked me in the eyes. "Why are you always so angry Vicki?" I asked. "This place makes me angry. All I see is stupid shit all day long, it never changes around here. The Rez never changes, Tony." Vicki said. "Well, you need to relax. Why don't you come for a ride with us?" I asked. "You asking me for a date, Tony?" Vicki asked.

Before I could answer, Two-Fingers interrupted and said, "Maybe you can find a couple of your girlfriends to go with you." "Do you mind? I am talking to Tony." Vicki said as she stared coldly at Two-Fingers. "White Guy, we'll wait for you in the car." Jimmy B said as he led Two-Fingers away. "I am not like the rest of the girls around here, Tony. I just don't go riding with anybody." Vicki said. "Look, I am just asking you if you want to go for a ride, I am not looking to get married." Vicki was quiet for awhile before she said, "Okay, I'll go for a ride on two conditions: First, no drinking and second, you have to drive. "Making it kind of hard on me aren't you? I'll have to ask Jimmy B and Two-Fingers." I said. "Tell them I will try to get a couple of my friends to go with me, but it won't be easy." Vicki said.

"Well, it looks like we both have some convincing to do." I said as I looked in the direction of the Chevy. "You see what you can do, I get off in one hour." Vicki said as she turned and walked away.

"Well guys, here is the deal. Vicki and a couple of her girlfriends will go with us if I drive and we don't drink." I was standing at the driver's side window looking in at the two of them as they contemplated the news. "I don't mind you driving, but what is the point of them going if we can't drink?" Jimmy B asked. "Well, to paraphrase the Governor, what is the point of all this drinking? Let's stay sober and see if we can get lucky." I said as they suddenly sat up taller in their seats. "The point is, I am going into the Army in less than a week and I want to have some fun." Jimmy B said weakly. "Let's try to have some fun without drinking." I said as a tumbleweed bounced across the windswept parking lot. "Well, I will leave it up to you Two-Fingers. I guess I can use a little sleep anyway." Jimmy B said as he stretched his long arms. "Well, I am philosophically opposed to the whole thing. First of all, it is a bad deal when women start telling us what they want. Secondly, I don't know how we are going to get laid unless they are plastered." Two-Fingers said. "Well, well, well. Now we get to the core of the matter, you need to get them drunk to get laid." I said. "Hey, they need to drink me pretty." Two-Fingers said. "I don't think there is enough booze in the world to do that. Besides, she said no drinking, she didn't say anything about no fucking." That seemed to do the trick. "Really, what time does she get off?" Two-Fingers asked with renewed interest.

Vicki was able to convince two of her girlfriends, Veronica Comes at Night and Laurie Aims Back, to go along with her; it was not as hard of a sell as she thought it was going to be.

"I thought we would drive to St. Mary and go through the Park." I said when asked where we were going. Highway 89 from Browning to St. Mary is a narrow, curvy, dangerous, two lane highway. This road, more than any other road on the reservation, illustrates the dichotomy that exists between reservation life and the best White Society has to offer. On the east side of the road is the Rez with it's barren land stretching on as far as the eye can see, rocks of varying sizes jut out from the hard ground and are so numerous it looks like a rock garden. On the west side of the road, off in the distance, is Glacier National Park. Even though it was an extremely hot summer with a number of forest fires, Glacier was still a beautiful and pristine place. A forest full of trees stretched from one mountain range to another, the mountains reached high into the sky and formed a majestic panorama. All of us, perhaps for the first time, realized the stark contrast that existed between the reservation side of the road and the Park side of the road.

Two-Fingers sat in the back seat between Laurie and Veronica and was surveying the scene when he said, "Shit, I think we ought to re-examine those treaties a little more closely, I think we got screwed." "You just figuring that out, Two-Fingers?" Vicki asked. "I think everybody is just starting to figure it out, aenet." Veronica said as she snuggled up against Two-Fingers. "My grandfather told me when he was a kid his family could come up here and hunt, fish and gather berries. Now, they won't even let us do that." Vicki said as she slowly shook her head. "We were only supposed to do that as long as the sun shined and the rivers flowed or until they opened a Buttries Food Store on the Rez." Two-Fingers said. "Plus, we have commodities coming in every Saturday morning. What the hell do we need fish, meat and berries for?" Jimmy B said before continuing, "Shit, I'm getting hooked on that commodity cheese, I hope they don't take that away from us too." "Go ahead and laugh you assholes." Vicki said. "We have already lost so much we don't even know what we had." "I thought we were going to have a nice peaceful day. What's with all this political talk?" I asked. "Just like a white guy to tell us not to get too political, aenet." Two-Fingers said. "Hey, I have lived here for almost four years and I know what you are talking about. But, I don't think they are going to give you the land back." I replied as I drove slowly down the road. "How about putting some jobs on the Rez so we can work for a living?" Laurie asked. "I don't know, I know we need jobs but if the Federal Government steps in and provides them, isn't that just like giving out commodities and free housing? I mean, the more you get for nothing, the less likely you are to work for it, right?" I asked. "Damn, white guys always win the argument. No wonder we got this and they got that." Two-Fingers said as he pointed to the Park. "I am on your side, I just don't have the answers. Do you?" I asked. "I don't know if there is an answer, all I know is the young bucks are getting restless." Vicki said as she gazed out the side window. "At boarding school, all the bloods from the different Tribes were talking about joining forces and fighting all the injustice. There was a lot of talk about this new organization called the American Indian Movement and how it was going to help make things right, I never got into that. Different Tribes never get along, aenet." Two-Fingers said. "Shit, all this talking has made me hungry. Let's stop at St. Mary and pick up some bologna and bread and go have a picnic." Jimmy B said before turning on his right side and falling asleep against the passenger door. Vicki slowly reached over and placed her left hand in my right hand and we drove the rest of the way to St. Mary in silence.

After stopping in St. Mary to pick up some provisions, we proceeded to the entrance to the park. Before entering, we were told it was going to cost us $2.50 to get in. "$2.50?" Two-Fingers asked. "We didn't get that much for the whole place when you bought it." "You want in or don't you?" The uniformed park attendant asked. "Yeah, we want in."

I said as I dug the money out of my tight fitting Levi's, they got tight the minute Vicki put her hand on my thigh.

It was a short drive to the Sunrift Gorge where we parked the Chevy and after gathering up all the provisions and a couple of blankets, we hiked back into the mountains until we came to St. Mary Falls. We found a comfortable place under a big cedar tree and spread out the blankets and the girls made sandwiches while we explored the base of the falls. "Shit, that water's cold, aenet." Jimmy B said as he placed his hand in the water. "Still plenty of runoff from the Glaciers, I say we go for a swim after we eat." They both looked at me like I was crazy. "We'll freeze our nuts off." Two-Fingers said as he shook his head. "You ever hear of skinny dipping?" I said before the light came on in Two-Fingers head. "Looks like they got the fires out, aenet, Two-Fingers." Jimmy B said as he pointed to the clear blue sky. "Yep, looks like the fires are out." Two-Fingers said as he stared off into the distance.

After eating, we walked over to the lake and began skipping rocks across a calm expanse of water a hundred yards away from the falls. "Shit, don't tell me you chicks like to throw rocks." Two-Fingers said. We all laughed and before too long, we were stripped down to our underwear and jumping into the water. We alternated between swimming and warming ourselves in the sun. Vicki went down to the Chevy and came back with a bottle of suntan lotion and she asked me to put some on her as she spread out on the blanket with her eyes closed. I gently rubbed the lotion onto her beautiful, brown skin as the sun slowly disappeared behind the mountains, I began to regret the promise I made to my father about working that night. Vicki did not say anything when I told her we had to get going, She just smiled and put her clothes back on.

As we walked back to the Chevy, I overheard Two-Fingers whispering into Veronica ear, "I noticed you don't have much of an arm." "Yeah, but I can kick like a mule, so you better watch it." Veronica said as she reached for his deformed left hand. Two-Fingers seemed to be startled by this sign of affection but he allowed her to hold onto him.

It was completely dark by the time we reached St. Mary. I drove very slowly and was able to avoid all the deer, horses and cattle that occasionally ran across the highway. Jimmy B was sound asleep in the front seat as was Laurie in the back seat. Vicki was gently resting her head on my shoulder and Two-Fingers and Veronica were talking about getting together for Indian Days. "I can't believe it is already time for Indian Days, the summer has flown by this year, aenet." Veronica said to Two-Fingers. "Yeah, I am looking forward to it, I haven't been in awhile. I need to take care of a few things for my folks so I can get away, this is going to be a busy week." Two-Fingers said as we pulled onto the parking lot of the Junction. "Well, I hope you didn't mind not drinking today." Vicki said as I held the driver's door open for her. "It's still early." Two-Fingers yelled as he nudged Jimmy B awake. "Ignore him." I said before Vicki could respond to him. "Why don't we get together over Indian Days?" "Would that be like our second date?" Vicki asked. "Yeah, I guess it would be." I said as I leaned down and kissed her goodbye.

After letting the girls out, Jimmy B dropped Two-Fingers off at his home before taking me to the station. I had to work the late shift and things were pretty quiet until after the bars closed at 2 a.m. That was when the after hours crowd descended on our gas station with a vengeance, cars were gassed up and snacks were sold at a feverish pace. If you have been paying attention, you probably noticed I like to use the words, "feverish pace" a lot, just checking.

Around 3:30 a.m. that morning, things had slowed down to a crawl when Juanita suddenly appeared in her new, red half ton Chevy pickup. "What time you get off?" She asked me. "Eight or nine in the morning, why?" I asked as I cautiously approached her pickup. "I'll pick you up and we can go for a ride." She said. "No, no rides." I said as I shook my head. "Why not? You scared to be seen with me in the daylight?" Juanita asked. "Hey, look, we were both a little loaded the other night, let's just forget it ever happened." I said. "I wasn't loaded, you may have been, but I wasn't." Juanita said before taking a sip from her bottle of Southern Comfort. "I knew exactly what I was doing and don't regret it one bit. You got a conscience, Tony?" Juanita asked as she reached out and touched my cheek. "You are married to my dad's best friend. Yeah, I got a conscience." I said as I took a step back. "That didn't seem to bother you the other night." Juanita said as she turned off the engine. "Don't tell me you were too whacked, I know better. Maybe you didn't like making it with me?" Juanita asked. "I liked it, I liked it a lot." I mumbled with my head hanging down like a whipped pup. "So what's the problem? You think it is easy for me to come to you like this? Shit, I am an old married woman chasing after an eighteen year old guy. Hell, for all I know they could throw my ass in jail for seducing you." Juanita said as she raised the bottle of Southern Comfort to her full, red lips. "Yeah, so why are you doing it?" I asked. "Because I can't stop thinking about that night, can you?" Juanita asked as she leaned her head back against the seat and stared at me.

Before I was able to answer, a carload of partying Blackfeet pulled up and started demanding gas. "I am going to use your restroom, you better stick your gas hose into my pickup before people start getting the wrong idea." Juanita said as she slid out of the pickup.

After returning from the restroom Juanita said, "So, what are we going to do about it?" I was trying to avoid the question when I suddenly asked, "Where is Charley?" "He had to fly to Chicago on some business, some kind of cattle convention or something. He'll be gone for a week or so." Juanita said as she leaned against her pickup. "Look, Juanita, I..." I started to say something before Juanita interrupted me. "What is that building over there?" Juanita asked as she pointed to a building off to the side of the main station. "That's the tire shop." I said as Juanita turned and walked in that direction.

I wasn't sure if Juanita heard me because she was walking pretty fast. She stopped at the entrance of the tire shop and tried to open the door, it was locked. "You got the key, Tony?" Juanita asked as I approached. I took a quick look around before unlocking the door, Juanita quickly stepped inside and I followed. The shop was dark and musky and there was a low humming sound coming from the air compressor. After adjusting to the darkness, Juanita slowly turned around and leaned against me and before long, we were kissing and touching each other and I knew there was no turning back as I slowly shut the tire shop door.

This part of the story has very little to do with Two-Fingers. I only mention it because my wife is always aroused by this story and I can use all the help I can get. Besides, it is only human nature. There is not a guy in this world that would have turned her down, right?

Chapter 23

The much anticipated North American Indian Days PowWow celebration began the next day. Two-Fingers and I had satisfied all our family obligations and were ready to enjoy ourselves. "Yeah, Bobby Racine and dad have worked out a deal where Bobby will get some on-the-job training in case his loan comes through. He may change his mind after working a few graveyard shifts." I told Two-Fingers this as we walked towards the fairgrounds. "Anyway, I get a few days off." "Me too, my old man is so medicated he doesn't even know I am in the room half the time and mom and my sisters are tired of me being in their way all the time. So, let's party." Two-Fingers said.

The annual parade was well under way and moving down main street in the opposite direction we were walking, the fairgrounds was about a mile away and we were in no particular hurry to get there. As we walked past the front door of the Bob Scriver's Museum and Taxidermy, Two-Fingers stuck his head in and yelled, "Bob, that bear really does look like he is taking a shit, good job." We kept walking before anyone in the museum could respond. "Where do you come up with that shit?" I asked. "Right up here and there are plenty more where that came from." Two-Fingers said as he pointed to his head.

We successfully crossed the street without getting ran over and before long we were standing at the entrance of the fairgrounds. As we entered, we couldn't help but notice all the campaign booths scattered throughout the main entrance area. "Damn, look at all that stuff, the Tribal elections are still weeks away and already they are polluting the place with their bullshit. The only thing this place is missing is Huntley and Brinkley, aenet." Two-Fingers said.

The Blackfeet are governed by a Tribal Council of seven duly elected citizens, there are seven districts on the Rez and each district gets representation. Once elected, the councilmen serve two-year terms and just like in American politics, the incumbents have an advantage in the electoral process. Everybody wants to be a councilman because they get a say on who gets the best housing, who gets a job, who gets assistance and who doesn't; politics at it's finest. Being a councilman means you have money and power which can be used to get re-elected. New candidates, since they do not have power, must show they have something else to offer. There has to be a ground swell of support over some galvanizing issue and this election was more issue focused than previous elections. That year, younger voters were taking a more active role in who got elected. In the past, they left that to their elders, not anymore. The younger generation was more politically active and their awareness of the issues was at an all time high. The Blackfeet were becoming more and more dissatisfied with the status quo, change was desperately needed to shake the chains of government dependency; social unrest had arrived on the Rez.

The recent formation of the American Indian Movement(AIM) gave the younger Indians a platform from which they could advance their ideas, AIM stressed the importance of spiritual strength and the preservation of reservation land and Indian traditions. They wanted to shake up the current system as opposed to those in the system that wanted to keep things as they were, the incumbents were feeling the heat and campaigned hard to get re-elected.

"I have never seen so many young guys running for office. Shit, even Johnny Kills-at-Night is running." Two Fingers said. "I never knew he was interested in anything but screwing. He ought to hand out a campaign button that says, "Vote for me and I won't sleep with your old lady." Probably win by a landslide, aenet." "Looks like there are a lot of different Tribes this year, more than usual, aenet." I said. Two-Fingers nodded his head in agreement as we watched all the activity swirling around us, long-haired strangers in fatigue jackets and bandanas were everywhere.

Two-Fingers and I continued to walk around the Encampment taking in the sights and sounds. It was a beautiful July day and, other than the activity surrounding the campaigners, things were pretty quiet. Most of the Teepees and tents were already standing tall and the late arrivals worked hard to get their lodging in place before all the festivities officially began. Outside the Teepees, mothers were putting the finishing touches on their children's attire. Faces were painted, hair combed and styled and eagle feathers were strategically placed in preparation for the dancing.

We were standing there watching all this when we suddenly heard, "Hello, girls." We turned around and found Jimmy B approaching. "Where the hell you been, Jimmy B?" I asked. "Just dropped the Chevy off at A.J.'s and then I went over to the bank and put the rest of my money into a savings account, I should be a rich man when I get out of the Army, aenet." Jimmy B said. "Did they give you a toaster for opening up your account?" Two-Fingers asked. "Naw, nothing but a sweaty palm." Jimmy B said. "When do you have to report for duty?" Two-Fingers asked. "Tomorrow morning at 9 a.m. up at the Government Square then I get to ride the bus to Helena and later on a slow boat to 'Nam." Jimmy B said. "I still say we take your sorry ass up to Canada and get you married off to a Cree." I offered. "No way, I would rather go to the jungle and take my chances with the Vietnamese." We were standing there bullshitting when Two-Fingers looked over Jimmy B's shoulder and noticed his uncle Billy Spotted Eagle approaching. "Oh, shit. Here comes Uncle Billy."

Billy Spotted Eagle is Pam's older brother and he is the Spiritual Leader of the Blackfeet. In the olden days, he would have been known as the Holy Man and in the olden days, he would have been highly respected, even revered. But, the assimilation process that has been in effect over the last century has diminished the effect and stature of the Holy Man. Only the oldest Blackfeet remember the old ways, several generations have been lost to the white cultural experience. But, things were beginning to change and younger Indians from all over the country were yearning for a return to their roots and the Spiritual Leaders of each Tribe were regaining their stature and influence. Billy sensed the change in attitude and wanted to strike while the iron was hot, he believed this Indian Days celebration would provide a forum in which he could spread the word; there was true spiritual and social unrest taking place and the time to act was now.

I really like and respect Billy, he is one of the most honest and principled men I have ever met and Billy knew he had a daunting task ahead of him. Even in his own family there was a huge difference of opinion, Billy lived a traditional life style as opposed to his sister Pam's modern life style. Pam chose to accept the white culture and she embraced it as her own because she was influenced in doing so. Billy, on the other hand, resisted losing his heritage because his mentors taught him the value of the traditional lifestyle and he cherished it. This dichotomy existed in their family and it existed throughout the entire Rez. Spiritually and socially the Rez was a house divided, so to speak.

"Your mom said I could find you here." Billy said as he approached. "Hello, Uncle. What has brought you down from the Mountain?" Two-Fingers asked. "Well, it wasn't the cotton candy my misguided nephew." Billy said as he hugged Two-Fingers. "It is good to see you my boy." Billy said as he held Two-Fingers at arms length. "You have been away too long." He hugged Two-Fingers again before saying, "I just saw Max, what a shame." "Yeah, I know." Two-Fingers said as he shook his head. "But, it is good to see you Uncle. Do you know these two vagrants?" "Of course I know them, hello you two." Billy said. Jimmy B and I extended a warm greeting and Jimmy B, standing behind Billy, tried to get Two-Fingers attention by motioning with his head. It was obvious that Jimmy B wanted to get out of there and start partying. Two-Fingers tried to make a graceful exit and said to Billy, "I will come visit you sometime during Indian Days and we will have a nice visit, Jimmy B is going into the Army tomorrow and we need to get him a shot of penicillin." Billy laughed and said, "You can get him a shot later. I am setting up a Sweat Lodge down by the river and I am running behind schedule. There is a lot more interest in the sweat this year and I am going to need your help." "How long will it take, Uncle?" Two-Fingers asked. "If we hurry, we will be done by sundown." Billy said. Jimmy B was visibly distressed over the latest development. But, after a few minutes of discussion, he was finally persuaded to help out. During our half mile walk to the river, Jimmy B asked, "What's it take to get drunk around here?"

Sweat Lodges are associated with prayer and preparation and they are used to cleanse the body of toxins, thereby enhancing the religious experience. The sweat can last for several hours and it is enhanced by the participation of Spiritual Leaders who lead the prayers.

Billy chose the perfect spot for a Sweat Lodge, it was far enough away from the main Encampment that the participants had their privacy and still within walking distance of the Encampment. Two-Fingers, Jimmy B and I cleared a place for the Lodge while Billy unloaded wood, rope and buffalo hides from his pickup.

We dug a three foot deep pit in the sand next to the river. Next, a dome shaped structure was assembled using the wood and rope Billy brought and then everything was placed over the pit. The buffalo hides were then placed over the entire structure and after several hours of work, Billy said, "Oki, looking good. Now I need you to gather up a bunch of rocks about the size of my head." The rocks were to be heated in a large fire pit just outside the Lodge and when they are red hot, the rocks are removed from the fire and placed in a circle inside the Lodge where cold water is poured over them. The steam that is emitted causes the temperature inside the Lodge to rise dramatically.

Gathering up the rocks didn't take long, hell rocks were everywhere. After stacking the rocks outside the entrance to the lodge, we stretched out in the sand to relax when Billy said, "Beginning tomorrow, I am going to have a sweat every day of Indian Days. I want you two to come back and participate. Jimmy B, since you will be gone, I will pray for you."

Two-Fingers and I reluctantly accepted this invitation before the three of us started walking back to the main Encampment. Billy stayed behind and began putting up his Teepee. "Let's move a little faster boys, we are burning daylight." Jimmy B said as the sun began to set.

Vicki, Veronica and Laurie were sitting patiently watching the dancers perform when we snuck up on them. "Where have you been?" Laurie asked. "Been helping Billy Spotted Eagle build a Sweat Lodge down by the river." Jimmy B said. "Damn, actually got a little work out of you did he?" Vicki asked. "Worked our asses off and now its time to play, aenet." Two-Fingers said as he reached into his boot and pulled out a baggie with ten rolled joints in it. "Been saving this shit for a special occasion." He said as took a joint out and put it into his mouth.

"Hey, what are you doing? You can't smoke that here." Vicki said. "Why not?" Two-Fingers asked. "Why not? Shit, there are hundreds of people around." Vicki said. "They are going to have to find their own, I only have ten joints left." Two-Fingers said as he searched for his matches. "Hey, look, my uncle has set up a Teepee for us girls, if you behave we can go there." Vicki said. "What do you guys think, can we trust these girls?" Two-Fingers asked. "Shit, I don't know but we better do something fast because I only have about ten hours left before I leave to serve my country." Jimmy B said. "We better hurry then." Laurie said as she stood up and grabbed his hand.

Before going to the Teepee, we stopped and got a good supply of fry bread, chips, corn dogs and lots of pop; nothing but health food on the Rez. After entering the Teepee, we quickly built a fire, not for the heat but for the light.

"You girls ever smoke any pot?" Two-Fingers asked as they stared into the fire. "Sure." Veronica said. "I have tried it and I like it." Laurie says as she nodded her head. "It's the drinking we don't like, we never said we didn't like smoking." Vicki said. "Besides, what do you think our ancestors were smoking in those peace pipes?" "Damn, you girls are full of surprises aren't you?" I said as I snuggled up to Vicki. "Well, I doubt you have smoked anything like this." Two-Fingers said. "This shit will make a mouse sass a wolf."

Two-Fingers reached into the fire and grabbed a stick to light the joint. We sat in a circle around the fire and passed the joint around, oblivious to the rest of the world. After it was finished, Two-Fingers lit another. "Damn, this is some groovy shit, aenet." Vicki said as she reached for the joint. "Groovy? Damn, you are starting to sound like Sammy Davis, Jr." Laurie said. "I have never been this high before." Veronica said as she stared into the fire. "I am getting hot, is anybody else getting hot?" Vicki asked as she removed her boots. "Shit, sister girl, put those boots back on before we all suffocate." Two-Fingers said as he pinched his nose. "Crack you." Vicki said without much conviction. "I am starting to get a little hot too." Laurie said as she unbuttoned her blouse. "I don't know, I think its kind of cold in here." Jimmy B said as he threw another log on the fire. "Yeah, I'm fine. How about you Two-Fingers?" I asked. "I am actually chilly." Two-Fingers said as he puffed away on the joint.

Before the joint was finished, the girls were stripped down to their underwear and their bodies glistened from the light of the campfire. The guys were sweating profusely but Jimmy B kept throwing logs onto the fire. It was almost midnight and the girls were nearly naked as the fire grew and grew. "Let's go dance." Veronica said as she stood and walked outside. "Yeah, I need some air." Vicki said as she reached over and helped Laurie to her feet. "Well, boys, what do you think? I don't think I have ever danced without clothes." Jimmy B said as he started to strip down. "Shit, we don't want them to feel out of place." I said as I staggered to my feet and began to take off my shirt.

After stripping down to our underwear, we stepped outside into the clear, cool Montana air and it was about that time the girls started dancing around the Teepee to the beat of distant drums. We joined in and soon we were all dancing at a feverish pace, oblivious to everything but the beat. Two-Fingers began to sing Indian in a deep guttural voice. Of course, he only knew a few Blackfeet words so he repeated them over and over again as he danced around the Teepee. Soon, we were all singing the words and following him. Around and around the Teepee we danced until Two-Fingers suddenly stopped and said, "I sure as hell hope this isn't a rain dance." We all glanced up at the sky before we continued dancing, not a cloud in sight.

After dancing, we went for a walk and instead of getting dressed, each couple wrapped themselves in a blanket and slowly strolled through the Encampment. It was really late and there wasn't much going on so we just wandered around taking in the sights. Outside the Teepees, once roaring fires were now just burning embers, dogs ran through the area and only stopped when they found scraps to eat. As usual, the larger canvass tents were filled with blackjack and stick game players who played until the sun came up. Two-Fingers and Veronica walked in front of Vicki and me, Laurie and Jimmy B brought up the rear. We all stopped to take a long, cool drink from a makeshift water fountain, water never tasted so good. We turned and slowly walked back to Vicki's uncle's Teepee.

After entering the Teepee, I threw a log on the dying fire and it quickly came back to life. Each couple laid down on hastily arranged bedding and soon we were oblivious to the other members of the party. "I remember the very first time I saw you." Vicki whispered in my ear. "You mean when you held my coat before I fought Ronnie Joe Stabs-in-the Back?" I whispered back. "No, no. Well, it was that day all right. But, the very first time was when you were sitting in front of me in eighth grade trying not to act scared, I thought you were so brave." Vicki said as she snuggled up closer to me. "I wasn't brave, I was scared to death." I said as I gently stroked her hair. "Oh no, you were brave, you stayed and fought and didn't run home." Vicki said. "I have liked you ever since that very first day, Tony." Vicki leaned her head back and allowed herself to be kissed. We kissed and hugged until the sun began to come up. "I've always liked you." Vicki said before finally falling asleep in my arms.

Not long after that, everybody was awakened by Jimmy B yelling, "Holy shit!! What time is it?" Not waiting for an answer, he grabbed his clothes and started running as fast as he could towards the Government Square. "Damn, I have never seen a guy in such a hurry to get his ass shot off." Two-Fingers said before he and I got dressed and went outside the Teepee. The girls had already fallen back to sleep and we both thought it would be a good time to go get some coffee and stretch.

After getting coffee, we ran into Stogie Man and a group of his friends. As usual, they had been up all night drinking and raising hell. Stogie Man did not have to worry about being drafted since he was married and was the sole support for his family. Of course, like most of the other members of his group, he hadn't worked in months.

They mentioned that they had just seen Jimmy B running like a mad man towards the Government Square. We were sharing a bottle of wine with them when Stogie Man said, "Tough way to make a living but at least Jimmy B has a job, aenet." "Tough way to make a living? Hell, 'Nam is about dying, it ain't about living." Two Slim said as he handed the bottle of wine to Two-Fingers.

Big Man Bear Claw was in the group and he began to tell stories about his Vietnam experiences. He had told the stories on many occasions since his return from 'Nam, I supposed it helped him in some way. He spoke of the night patrols he and his unit were on and how the Vietnamese snipers picked them off one by one, how the heat was so oppressive he thought he was going to die from it and how the grunts hated their commanding officers and how they plotted their demise. He also talked about the destruction of entire villages and the cover ups that followed. Big Man had seen it all and Stogie Man and the rest of us listened quietly, only occasionally interrupting with a question. When the wine was all gone, Stogie Man said good-bye and staggered away towards home.

Later that day, Two-Fingers I were told what happened when Stogie Man finally made it home. The story was similar to stories we had heard or personally witnessed before. On the Rez, domestic abuse was all too common.

Evidently, Cindy Ann got up extra early that morning to tend to her girls, they were growing fast and were a handful. Cindy Ann was not surprised when Stogie Man hadn't come home the night before. He was not home much and when he was home, she wished he was gone. Cindy Ann, like many women on the Rez, was trapped in a bad marriage. The story was all too common; they got married too young, they had children too young and they grew old too fast. In between all of that, was domestic violence that was brought on by drinking and the drinking was brought on by a lack of self worth which was fostered by the lack of a good job, everybody needs a purpose in life. Excuses were made as to why this behavior existed and Cindy Ann had made her share of excuses even though she knew there was no excuse. Everybody knew there was no excuse, that knowledge added to the lack of self worth the abuser already experienced. Once all self worth is stripped away, no boundaries are left in place to restrain the actions of the abuser. As far as Cindy Ann was concerned, Stogie Man busted through those boundaries on that day.

"What's for lunch?" Stogie Man said as he stumbled into their kitchen. "There is some leftover chicken in the refrigerator." Cindy Ann said as she took the car keys from the kitchen counter. "Aren't you going to fix me something fresh? I don't want no fucking cold chicken, cook me a steak." Stogie Man said as he walked over and stood in front of Cindy Ann. "Steak? Shit, we haven't had a steak in here for months. I have to go over to Mom's and help out." Cindy Ann said as she placed the keys in her purse.

"You are always going home to help out, aenet. Why don't you stay here and clean this fucking pigsty." Stogie Man said as he picked the kitchen table up and threw it against the wall. Cindy Ann gathered up her two girls and ran out the front door as Stogie Man stumbled to the couch and passed out.

Cindy Ann cried all the way to her parent's apartment house. She had kept quiet as the abuse escalated but she needed to talk to someone about it and she decided to tell her mother. After putting her girls down for their morning nap, Cindy Ann sat Pam down at the kitchen table and told her about the problems she was facing at home. "Has he ever hit you?" Pam asked. "No, not yet. But, he is constantly yelling at me and belittling me. I am scared he will fly off the handle and hurt me and the girls one of these days." "Stogie Man needs to find a job and quit his drinking." Pam said. "He doesn't even look for work anymore, he has been rejected so many times he is feeling useless." Cindy Ann said. "We live on commodities and federal assistance and that makes him mad, he is feeling so inadequate." "I know. But, that is no excuse and I think the best thing to do is to have you and the girls move in here, your bedroom is big enough for all three of you." Pam said. "What will Dad say?" Cindy Ann asked. "Well, for now, we won't tell your Dad. He will get upset and he doesn't need that. Besides, he won't be able to come home for awhile and maybe Stogie Man will come to his senses by then." "Stogie Man doesn't have any sense left." Cindy Ann said. "Stogie Man doesn't have any sense?" Paula asked as she walked into the kitchen. "What's going on?" "Sister is moving back home for a while, Stogie Man and your sister are having troubles." Pam said. "Go find your brother and take him with you to their house and get Cindy Ann and the girls some clothes. If you run into Stogie ..." "Hey, I know the score, if I run into Stogie, I will slap the dog shit out of him." Paula said as she rushed towards the front door. "Don't do that Sister, he is crazy enough the way it is." Cindy Ann said. "Hell, he is probably gone or passed out anyway. Besides, Brother will be with me." Paula said as she walked out the front door.

Two-Fingers and I walked the girls to the Junction just in time for their shift, somebody had to work during Indian Days. We were walking out the front door when we noticed Paula driving up. "Get in you two, we have things to do." Two-Fingers and I got in the car and Paula filled us in on what was happening. "Aenet." Two-Fingers said after he heard the news. "I figured something was up, he's been partying like he isn't even married. I don't even know why we get married on the Rez, nobody stays at home." "Mom and dad stay at home." Paula said as she drove onto the front yard of Cindy Ann's house.

Paula parked and walked quickly towards the house, Two-Fingers and I walked as fast as we could to keep up. When we entered their house, we found Stogie Man sound asleep on the couch. Paula walked to their bedroom and began to pack for Cindy Ann and her nieces. We stayed in the living room and looked down at Stogie Man as he slept. Just before we left, Two-Fingers leaned down and grabbed Stogie Man by the shoulders and shook him awake. Stogie Man slowly opened his rummy eyes and tried to focus. Two-Fingers was holding him down when he said, "Just so you know, Cindy Ann is leaving your sorry ass and we are helping her move out." Stogie Man was shaking his head trying to get the cobwebs out when Two-Fingers added, "Don't try to get ringy with her either, Stogie Man, or I will fix you good." Stogie Man was beginning to regain consciousness when he said, "She's moving out? Good riddance and good riddance to your whole fucking family."

Just then, Paula walked into the living room with two grocery sacks full of clothing and other personal items and stared coldly at Stogie Man but didn't say a word, she just turned and walked out the front door. Two-Fingers and I were following her out when Stogie Man sat up and said, "She'll be back, aenet, Two-Fingers. The bitches always come back, don't they?" Two-Fingers stopped in the doorway and began to walk back inside when I grabbed his arm and stopped him. "It's not worth it, not now." I said. Two-Fingers considered whipping

Stogie Man's ass right then and there but figured there would be plenty of opportunity once Stogie Man sobered up, if he ever did. As we walked towards the car, we could hear Stogie Man yelling, "She'll be back, aenet, Two-Fingers, she'll be back."

Paula drove us to the fairgrounds in silence, it is the quietest I have ever seen the women. She must have been thinking about how messed up life was when she said, "I got to get away from here, I want to go to college so bad and now dad is hurt and mom needs my help, I am going crazy." "Shit Sis, go. Just go. I can help out, just go." Two-Fingers said. "I have to decide soon, registration is in a couple of weeks. If I go, I'll go to the University of Montana over in Missoula. At least I won't be too far away and I can come home on the weekends." Paula said as she drove up to the fairgrounds entrance. "Just go." Two-Fingers said as he stepped out of the car. As I was climbing out of the backseat, Paula put her hand on my arm and asked, "Any word about Stan?" All I could do was look at her and shake my head no. "Your folks must be going crazy." As she drove off I muttered, "The whole world is going crazy, aenet."

Chapter 24

Two-Fingers and I were standing under the fairground's sign as Paula drove away and as we turned and started to walk inside the campground, we noticed Kenny and Ronnie Joe Stabs-in-the-Back walking our way. It was the first time Two-Fingers had seen the brothers since he left town over three years before, he was shocked by their appearance. They both looked as if they had been sleeping in their clothes for weeks. Kenny was wearing a black patch over his left eye and his clothes were filthy, he looked like he had pissed himself. They were both falling down drunk and holding onto each other as they approached us and when Kenny looked up and recognized Two-Fingers, the blood slowly drained from his face. He looked around for a place to hide but there was no place to run. Two-Fingers walked up to them and took a closer look and quickly came to the conclusion that the last three years hadn't been kind to the Stabs-in-the-Backs. They had shrunk, visibly shrunk and Two-Fingers was now a foot taller than they were and a lot more muscular.

"You boys don't look so good, aenet." Two-Fingers said. "Hey, Two-Fingers, how you been? Haven't seen you around for awhile." Ronnie Joe said as he tried to straighten up. "How you doing, Tony?" "I am doing a lot better than you two." I said. "How come you're not as smart mouthed as you used to be?" "Ayee, no sense fighting anymore, aenet, you guys." Kenny said as he leaned against Ronnie Joe. "You guys sound like you've turned chicken shit to me. You two scared we might kick your ass?" Two-Fingers asked. "I bet you will try to get tough again when your gang shows up, aenet." "Shit yeah, we got a gang, aenet." Ronnie Joe said as he looked at Kenny. "You better leave us alone before our gang gets here." "You ain't got no fucking gang, nobody can stand being around you, aenet." I said. "Tell you what, you two get the fuck out of here and stay out of here and we won't kick your ass, get going. If we see you around here again we are going to give you exactly what you deserve. Are you listening?" Two-Fingers asked. "Don't make us tell you again." I said as I stepped in front of Ronnie Joe.

Ronnie Joe mumbled something and started to walk towards the exit with Kenny following close behind. They walked much better, scared straight I suppose. "Imagine, I used to have some respect for those assholes." I said as they scurried off. "Really? Respect, I never did, I always thought they were punks." Two-Fingers said as he started walking towards the center of the Encampment. "Well, I wouldn't exactly call it respect either..." I was saying when Two-Fingers interrupted me. "Hell, I know what you mean, you were scared shitless of them two, aenet." Two-Fingers said. "Crack you, Two-Fingers." "Bone you, White Guy." Two-Fingers said as he shadow boxed around me.

"There you are, I was hoping to find you two." Uncle Billy said as he appeared out of nowhere. "I am going to start the sweat in about an hour and there is room for two more, come on." Uncle Billy said as he walked towards the river. "Oh boy, a sweat." Two-Fingers said as he rolled his eyes.

Uncle Billy walked fast and it took us a minute or so to catch up with him. "Have you noticed all the long haired Indians around here?" Uncle Billy asked. "Yeah, we were talking about that yesterday, Uncle." Two-Fingers replied. "Lot of these young guys are with the American Indian Movement, they got some good ideas." Billy said. "I am having a sweat tomorrow with some of their spiritual leaders." "What type of ideas do they have?" I asked. "They are talking about Indian sovereignty and the re-examination of all the broken treaties." Billy said. "They are also talking about spiritualism and preserving our culture." "You think all these different Tribes are going to get along, Uncle?" Two-Fingers asked. "Shit, the Blackfeet have never had any allies." "True, our Tribe will be the last to embrace unity. I think the other Tribes already have but we have a lot of traditional enemies with good memories, aenet." Billy said. "That is why there are only Blackfeet at the sweat today."

We walked the rest of the way in silence and as we neared the camp, we stopped for a moment to enjoy the view. Billy's Teepee was standing tall against the skyline and there was a lone horse tethered to a stake in front of it. In the distance, the Rocky Mountains rose high in the sky and provided a beautiful backdrop to the entire scene. The Sweat Lodge sat next to a clear, blue stream that ran swiftly between its banks, it was truly a magnificent setting.

Standing next to the Sweat Lodge were eight Blackfeet men of varying ages and they were there to experience a spiritual as well as a physical cleansing. Nearby, three young Blackfeet boys were tending the fire and the rocks. Greetings were extended, everybody knew each other.

"Oki." Billy said to the assembled group. "Many of you have attended sweats before and to those of you who have not, here is what happens." Billy said as he looked at Two-Fingers and me. "After we undress, we will sit in a circle around the rocks and I will lead us in prayer and you will be free to add any of your own personal thoughts and prayers. Water will be poured over the rocks and it will be very hot in the Lodge. That is why the Sweat Lodge is always set up next to water, you will want to go for a swim and cool off."

Billy lifted the buffalo hide that covered the entrance to the Sweat Lodge, he bent down low and entered quickly. The rest of us went inside and soon we were naked and sitting in a circle watching the young boys bring in red hot rocks on shovels and arrange them in a circle in front of us. Once they were in place, Billy poured cold water over them as the rocks hissed and sizzled. Steam filled the air and soon the Lodge was as hot as a furnace and the only light in the place was the light escaping from the amber glowing rocks.

Billy chanted ancient Blackfeet songs and spread dry sweet grass over the rocks. When the sweet grass caught fire, he took his hand and waved at the smoke sending it in all directions inside the Lodge. He poured more cold water on the rocks and steam continued to fill the air. Billy was surrounded by sacred medicine bundles, the bundles were passed down from one generation to the other. He lifted up one of the bundles and continued his chanting and then he lowered it and picked up another, all the while he was chanting. He said a prayer to the Sun, the principal deity of the Blackfeet and all the other Blackfeet chanted.

Two-Fingers and I sat there quietly, entranced by the ritual as sweat poured down our bodies and onto the sand floor. Soon, everyone was chanting and saying prayers. Out loud, I prayed hard for the safe return of my brother and the other members chanted loudly. Two-Fingers prayed for his father and the group responded with more chanting. Each member of the group said a prayer and the chanting continued until Billy stood and walked outside. The rest of us followed and soon we were all in the stream. "This water feels good, aenet." Ivan Bear Medicine said. Ivan is a traditionalist who believes in the old ways. "It is very refreshing, aenet." Sonny Mountain Chief said.

After cooling off, Billy stepped out of the water and returned to the Sweat Lodge and the rest of the party followed.

Soon, fresh red hot rocks were brought in and the sweat continued as the Lodge grew hotter. The group began to talk in a nice, conversational tone about things they seldom talked about. "I noticed all these young Indians from all these different Tribes are in town, aenet." Tommy No Runner said. "Yeah, I noticed that too. Never seen this many Crow since we raided their camp and ran off with all their women, aenet." Joe Arrowtop said. "Aye, and I never knew there were this many Flathead that were still able to walk." Big Gun Mad Plume said. "You guys are exaggerating a little bit, don't you think?" Billy asked as he poured water on the rocks. "Of course we exaggerate. We haven't been at war with these Tribes for a hundred years and we still talk like we fought them yesterday, aenet." Ivan Bear Medicine said. "Blackfeet never forget the victories and can never remember the defeats, aenet." Glenn Still Smoking said. "These aren't just our traditional enemies in town, there are Apache, Seminole, Choctaw and a bunch of other Tribes I never even heard of, aenet." Louie Heavy Runner said. "They are all with the American Indian Movement." "Things are changing in America and on all the reservations." Billy said. "It is about time, too." "They always say there is going to be change, but there never is. We are still living off of government handouts like a bunch of refugees, aenet." Glenn Still Smoking said. "I don't know, things are different this time." Billy said. "I think the hypocrisy of fighting for freedom in Vietnam while being treated like second class citizens at home is starting to sink in on our returning Veterans and their families." "Racism has always been a problem and it always will be." Big Gun Mad Plume said. "That will always be the case if we don't stand together and fight it." Billy said as he poured the last of the water on the rocks. "Well, I don't mind them being in town as long as they don't cause any trouble." Tommy No Runner said.

Two-Fingers and I sat patiently and listened to our Elders discuss issue after issue. After awhile, we realized no immediate changes in the social order were about to take place so we excused ourselves and went outside for another swim.

"Man, I was sweating my ass off in there even before they brought the rocks in." Two-Fingers said. "Good sweat, it felt good to pray, aenet." I said before sticking my head under the water.

We were quietly relaxing in the water when, off in the distance, we saw a horseback rider galloping towards us at a break neck speed. As the rider got closer, we could hear him yelling, "I am Fred Schwartz and I am the last of the wild bunch, I am Fred Schwartz and I am the last of the wild bunch!!" Fred repeated this several times as he raced across the prairie. "Looks like your Uncle Fred made it to town, aenet, Two-Fingers." "Hide me." Two-Fingers said before he took a deep breath and disappeared under the water.

Fred's horse was at a full gallop as it approached the stream and without slowing, the horse jumped off the bank and landed belly deep in the water. Fred maneuvered his horse to dry ground and before dismounting he yelled, "I am Fred Schwartz and I am the last of the wild bunch!!" "You weren't trying to hide from your old uncle now were you, Two-Fingers?" Fred asked as a blue faced Two-Fingers resurfaced. "Get your ass up out of there and give me a hug, I haven't seen you in three years you little shit." Fred is Max's younger brother and he is, well hell, the last of the wild bunch. Fred seldom came to town but when he did, he came hard. Back then, he lived on a small ranch in a small log cabin that just recently got electricity and running water. He was tougher than nails and could ride anything that walked, when he was sober. He preferred his privacy but when he came to town, watch out.

Two-Fingers, without saying a word, stood up and slowly walked towards his uncle. "Damn son, you are naked." Fred said as he watched Two-Fingers walk his way. "What the hell are you trying to do, give the family a bad name?" Fred asked. "With all due respect Uncle, I don't think that's possible." Two Fingers said as he extended his hand. "Don't hand me that shit." Fred said as he pushed Two-Fingers hand away. "You know, I never hugged a naked guy before." "That makes two of us." Two-Fingers said as Fred put him in a bear hug. "I just came from seeing your dad. Man, he is as ornery as ever." Fred said. "He better get off that dope though, its got him so screwed up he can't think straight."

"You know my partner, Tony, don't you Uncle Fred?" Two-Fingers said. "Sure I know Tony, I gas up at their place when I get to town." Fred said. "How you doing Tony? No need to stand up." "I am doing fine Fred, how you doing?" I politely asked. "Doing great, I just ran off my old lady and am ready to have some fun." Fred said as he walked back to his horse. "I never knew you got married, congratulations. Two-Fingers said. "I'm not married, I have been living in sin, aenet." Fred said as he retrieved a fifth of Black Velvet from his saddlebags. "Over the gums and down the throat, hold on tight if you are too young to vote." Fred said before taking a long drink of the whiskey. "This is a good looking horse you got here, Uncle." Two-Fingers said as he stroked its mane. "You like it, you can have it." Fred said before taking another drink. "Really? Where the hell would I keep it?" Two-Fingers asked. "You can keep it on my ranch and ride it whenever you want to." Fred said as he raised the bottle to his lips. "I'll only charge you for the feed." "All right, I always wanted my own horse, thanks Uncle." Two-Fingers said before jumping onto the saddle. "Damn, this saddle is hot." "Better get some clothes on before you blister your ass." Fred said as he inspected the camp. "Looks like you've been to one of your Uncle Billy's sweats. If so, you need a drink more than I do." Fred said before tossing the bottle of Black Velvet up to Two-Fingers. "Over the gums and down the throat, I'm holding on tight 'cause I'm too young to vote." Two-Fingers said as he held the bottle to his lips. "Too young to vote but old enough to drink, aenet, Two-Fingers." Fred said. "What do you say you and your old uncle hang one on tonight?" "Sure, if White

Guy can come along." Two-Fingers said as he jumped off the horse. "Sounds good to me. I have my Teepee set up at the fairgrounds, I'll meet you there." Fred said as he climbed onto the saddle. "You can't miss my place, my pickup and horse trailer are out front." "We'll be along soon." Two-Fingers said before handing over the bottle of Black Velvet.

Even though the sun was beginning to set by the time Two-Fingers and I left the Sweat, we didn't have any trouble finding Fred's Teepee. Like he said, he had his pickup and horse trailer in front of it and Two-Fingers new horse was tied to the back of the horse trailer.

When we entered the Teepee, Fred was leaning back against his saddle next to a kerosene lamp. Fred looked like he was working on a second bottle of Black Velvet, he was feeling no pain. Soon, we weren't feeling any pain either, we both were hungry and dehydrated from the Sweat so the whiskey had an almost immediate effect on us. We quickly finished the bottle and Fred decided to go to town and get more whiskey, another alcohol related decision. He decided to ride Two-Fingers horse "Indian style," no fancy bridle or saddle for him. He fashioned the rope he had tied the horse up with into a makeshift bridle and once it was securely in place, he jumped on the horse and galloped off towards town. Two-Fingers and I were worn out from the day's activities and the whiskey, so we ended up falling asleep.

As it turned out, Fred, after finding more whiskey, decided to ride around town for awhile. He was heard yelling, "I am the last of the wild bunch, I am the last of the wild bunch!!" He was seen riding up and down main street drinking his whiskey and yelling when a pack of dogs spooked his horse and he ended up getting tossed to the pavement. Witnesses say Fred bounced along the road and was unable to protect his bottle of whiskey and shattered glass flew everywhere. After retrieving his horse, Fred remounted and rode back to the fairgrounds. Nobody is sure when Fred got back to his Teepee, one thing was certain, it was late. All Fred remembers was getting off the horse and tying it to the horse trailer and then crawling inside the Teepee and passing out with his boots on.

It was sometime late that night when Joe Arrowtop decided to drive home. He had spent the previous eight hours playing blackjack and he was worn out, he too felt the effects of the Sweat. Now, Joe is not a drinking man so nobody was too concerned about his driving home alone. So, after leaving the Black Jack tent, Joe jumped into his pickup and slowly drove out of the fairgrounds, it was pitch dark outside. Joe lived about five miles south of town and it didn't take him too long to get there, traffic was light. He parked his pickup and horse trailer in his front yard like always and went inside his house to get a couple of hours of sleep.

The next morning, Fred was startled out of a deep sleep and he sat straight up and looked around the Teepee. He wasn't sure what woke him, he only knew something wasn't quite right, he was all alone in the Teepee. As the story goes, Fred was sitting there looking around the Teepee trying to figure out what the hell had happened the previous night, the details were still very fuzzy. Finally, after looking around, it became obvious to him that he was not in his Teepee. During Indian Days that happens a lot. In fact, it happened to Fred several times over the years. So, he laid back down and started to replay the night's events in his head when he suddenly jumped up and rushed outside. "Where the hell is that horse?" He muttered to himself as he stood in front of the Teepee. He walked around the Encampment looking for his horse and he asked several people if they had seen his horse but nobody was able to help him. After awhile, he found his pickup and ran around the back to the horse trailer to see if his horse was tied there, no horse. "Where the hell is my horse?" He asked out loud.

About that time, Joe Arrowtop was finishing up his first cup of coffee and absentmindedly staring out his kitchen window. Suddenly, something caught his eye that caused him to focus real hard, there was a strange object tied to the back of his horse trailer. He slowly took the last sip of coffee before leaning forward to get a better look. "What the hell is that?" Joe asked before rushing outside.

Sometime that morning, I remember Fred shaking Two-Fingers awake. "Two-Fingers, wake up. I think some kids have taken your horse for a joy ride." Fred said. "What?" Two-Fingers asked. "Who cares, let me go back to sleep." "No, no. You need to go find your horse, I can't believe you have owned it for less than a day and you have already lost it." Fred said as he leaned back against his saddle and closed his eyes. "Lost it, shit Uncle, you've lost it." Two-Fingers said as he sat up and shook the cobwebs out of his head. "White Guy, get your ass up, we have to go find my horse." I was already awake, when you are white and in a Teepee, you always sleep with one eye open.

Two-Fingers and I were standing at the coffee stand when Joe Arrowtop drove up in his pickup. "You seen your uncle Fred today?" Joe asked Two-Fingers before ordering a cup of coffee. "Yeah, I've seen him, he is over in his Teepee getting some sleep." Two-Fingers said. "Did he say anything about a missing horse?" Joe asked. "Yeah, as a matter of fact he did, he lost it and he thinks some kids are riding around on it." Two-Fingers said as he leaned towards Joe. "Well, why don't you go wake him up and tell him I found it. Evidently, he mistakenly tied it to my horse trailer last night." Joe said as he sipped on his coffee. "Well, at least you found it." Two-Fingers said before lighting a cigarette. "Yeah, I found it all right, at least I found what was left of it." Joe said as took the cigarette out of Two-Fingers mouth and took a long, deep drag. Two-Fingers and I stood there looking at each other when I asked, "What do you mean, exactly?" "Well, I mean I drug the fucking horse to death last night and there ain't a whole lot of it left." Joe said before taking another drag of the cigarette. "Holy shit, the last of the wild bunch killed my horse." Two-Fingers said as we all shook our heads in disbelief. Fred, after we woke him up and told him what had happened to the horse, slowly shook his head and said, "Well, have Joe drag it back here and we'll cook up what's left of the damn thing!!" Fred then laid back down and was soon fast asleep.

Later that morning, Two-Fingers and I decided to go for a walk and get a feel for what was going on. It was Sunday and the Encampment was real quiet after the festivities of Saturday night, all the people we ran into were nursing hangovers and moving very slow so we decided to look for Vicki and Veronica.

"Damn, I can't remember which Teepee is theirs, do you remember? Two-Fingers asked. "Yeah, I think it is that one over there." I said pointing to a Teepee. "Why don't you go check it out?"

Two-Fingers pulled the flap of the Teepee open and quickly stepped inside. Within 10 second he stepped back outside and yelled, "Sorry about that Mr. Boswell, make sure you are done before the evening show starts." Two-Fingers grabbed my arm and quickly led me away. "You won't believe who old man Boswell is fucking in there." Without waiting for a response Two-Fingers said, "Maggie Stink Pits!!" "No way. Man, don't tell me that." I said as shivers ran up my spine. "That makes my skin crawl." "I know, I can't imagine anybody fucking old man Boswell." Two-Fingers said before we both started laughing. We were standing there laughing hysterically when all of a sudden Vicki poked her head out of her Teepee. "There you two are, Veronica and I have been looking all over the place for you." "Well, damn it, you found us. Get some clothes on and we'll go down to the Club Cafe for some lunch." Two-Fingers said. "I hope you got paid yesterday."

So, Two-Fingers and I waited patiently outside the Teepee and to pass the time, we decided to play chicken with Two-Fingers pocket knife. I was closing in for the kill and about to throw the knife when Two-Fingers said, "Damn it White Guy, be careful with that thing, I can't afford to lose any more parts." Before I threw the knife, Veronica and Vicki stepped out of the Teepee and into the bright sunlight. "Wow, may I say you both look gorgeous this morning." I said as I stared at Vicki with my mouth wide open. "Yeah, it was worth the wait." Two-Fingers said as he walked over and took Veronica by the hand.

I just stood there and continued staring at Vicki. Her long, black hair was tied behind her head and her face was free of makeup. Her dark eyes sparkled in the morning light and her lips were pouty. Her tight body was dressed in buckskin and she wore knee high moccasins. "Where have you been all my life?" I asked before extending my hand to her. Vicki giggled and asked, "You guys already smoking dope this morning?"

We walked slowly through the Encampment, stopping from time to time to visit with friends. The Club Cafe was back in town a half mile away and we took our time getting there. We were talking and having a great time when Two-Fingers decided to tell them about his dead horse, they were probably the only two people on the Rez who hadn't heard the story.

"Are you serious? That poor horse was drug to death?" Veronica asked with a look of shock on her face. "Yep, Uncle was a little shit faced last night and thought he was tying it up to his horse trailer." Two-Fingers said. "Can you imagine the look on Joe Arrowtop's face when he found it?" "That is absolutely criminal." Vicki said. "Your uncle ought to be ashamed of himself." "Yeah, he ought to be, but he ain't." Two-Fingers said. "Damn, I was really starting to get attached to that horse too." "Good thing you weren't attached to it last night or we would be picking up your pieces this morning." I said as we arrived at the Club Cafe.

The Club Cafe is situated on main street and is owned and operated by the Bird family, it is a popular meeting place with tolerable food. After being seated next to a window, we all scanned the menu and before we ordered, Juanita pulled up to the curb in front of the cafe in her new pickup and started to honk her horn incessantly. I looked out the window and saw Juanita motioning for me to come outside. I excused himself and walked slowly to the pickup. "I was driving to the Encampment when I saw you walk in with that girl, Tony." Juanita said as she leaned out the passenger window. "You two-timing me?" "Hey, I didn't know we were engaged." I said as I nervously looked up and down main street. "No, I guess we aren't." Juanita said as she lit a cigarette. "My father has set up a Teepee for me and I would like you to stop by tonight." "You always get right to the point, don't you Juanita?" "You didn't seem to mind the other night, Tony." Juanita said as she flicked ashes out the window. "That was the other night, I am busy tonight." I turned and walked back inside without looking back. Juanita gunned her engine and peeled out of the parking space sending dirt and gravel flying everywhere. "She want you to check her oil, Tony?" Vicki asked as she slid over and made room for me to sit down. "Something like that. Let's eat, I am starving."

I was sitting there staring out the window trying to pay attention to the conversation when I noticed Juanita park in front of the Businessmen's Club. As she entered, Johnny Kills-At-Night was trying to exit. As I mentioned earlier, Johnny was running for a seat on the Tribal Council and it looked like he had been drinking and campaigning non-stop for days. He staggered out of the Businessmen's Club and fell up against the hood of Juanita's pickup and Juanita turned around and helped him into the passenger seat. After getting Johnny seated, she walked inside and a few minutes later, she returned carrying two brown paper bags. As she backed out of her parking place, she glanced over and saw me and flipped me the bird.

Vicki was finishing her second cup of coffee and was clearly agitated over Juanita's appearance and my staring out the window. "She must think her shit don't stink, aenet." "I know it. She honked the damn horn, aenet." Veronica said. "What do you girls say to a game of pinball?" Two-Fingers asked in a vain attempt at getting them to change the subject. "Next time I see her I am going to ask her why she thinks she's better than the rest of us, aenet." Vicki said. "I think pinball is a great idea, Two-Fingers." I said as I got up and started walking to the pinball machine. Two-Fingers whispered in my ear, "Son, you got these women ready to go on the warpath." "Naw, they will get over it." I said as I placed a nickel into the slot. "Guys get over it, girls never do." Two-Fingers said as he looked over his shoulder. "You ever seen girls fight on the Rez, White Guy?" "Yeah, a couple of times. It gets pretty wicked." I said as I recalled a number of incidents where Indian girls kicked the crap out of each other, hair pulling and gouged out eyes came to mind. "Vicki is not the type though." "She is a female in love and that makes her the type, trust me." Two-Fingers said before taking his turn on the pinball machine. "Well, what is it you want me to do about it?" I asked. "There isn't anything you can do, really. I was just thinking that maybe we should stay away from Indian Days for the rest of the day and night." Two-Fingers said. "You know, let them cool down a little." "Stay away? Where the hell would we go?" "Uncle Fred has a cabin he isn't using, I say we go there." Two-Fingers said. "Shit, that ranch of his is way out by Heart Butte. How we going to get there?" I asked. "Bitsy." Two-Fingers said as he pointed out the window.

Bitsy was fighting a terrible hangover and just needed some coffee, he didn't want to hear our request. Finally, Bitsy was persuaded to give us a ride, Two-Fingers offered him a joint and five dollars. The girls were a little harder sell but eventually they came around to the idea. Soon, we were all driving towards Fred's ranch in Bitsy's Volkswagen.

"Damn, I don't know if the pot is really this good or if it's the sweat off of my feet." Two-Fingers said as he returned the baggie to his boot. "Whatever it is I wish I had a car load of it, aenet, Two-Fingers." Bitsy said. "Carload of this shit my friend and we could rule the world, aenet." Two-Fingers said as he lit another joint. "Well, I don't know about ruling the world but I bet we could be very big men in Heart Butte." Bitsy said as he accepted the joint from Two-Fingers. "You two couldn't be big men if you stood on ladders, aenet." Vicki said. "You have to excuse Sister, she got a little jealous today and she still hasn't gotten over it." Two-Fingers said as he pulled the joint from Bitsy hand and gave it to me. "Bitch." Vicki said as she stared at me. "What do you say we change the subject?" I asked as I handed the joint to Vicki. "Why do you want us to change the subject?" Vicki asked. "You got a guilty conscious or something?" "No, I...thanks a lot Two-Fingers for bringing this up." "Hey, it's a long drive and I was just trying to stimulate a little conversation." Two-Fingers said as he lit another joint. "You guys keep that one back there, Bitsy and I will share this one." We drove the rest of the way to Heart Butte in deafening silence.

Heart Butte is a small reservation town about thirty miles south of Browning. It has a small grocery/clothing store, a bar, a gas station, a school, a Catholic Church and a large cemetery; all the essentials for living and dying. Fred's ranch is located five miles west of Heart Butte at the end of a narrow dirt road.

"Damn, your uncle lives out in the boondocks, aenet, Two-Fingers." Bitsy said as he drove onto Fred's front yard. "Yeah, but it looks like he finally has electricity." Two-Fingers said as he pointed towards a freshly placed power pole. "I hope that outhouse is just for decoration." Vicki said as she rolled out of the back-seat. "Now who thinks her shit don't stink, aenet?" Two-Fingers asked as he handed Bitsy five dollars and a joint. "Remember to pick us up tomorrow, Bitsy."

We were pretty well buzzed up and glad to be out of the car. "This is a beautiful place." I commented. Fred's log cabin stretched out in front of us and across the dirt road, near a stand of birch trees, was a small corral and next to it was a barn. Down the road we drove in on, was a large, green meadow with a small creek running through it. Behind the cabin was a large stand of pine trees and off in the distance were the Rocky Mountains. "Well, girls, you go in and build a fire and White Guy and I will catch dinner." Two-Fingers said. "And don't act like you never seen a wood stove either." "Don't worry about us getting a fire built, you just worry about catching some fish." Veronica said as she walked towards the cabin. "Who said anything about fish? I was thinking of catching a Grizzly bear." Two-Fingers said as he watched her go. "You couldn't catch a cold." Vicki said as she turned and ran after Veronica.

Two-Fingers stood there with his mouth open when I said, "Finally found someone who could out talk you, I think I like her." "Never get serious about a women that talks more than me, she will ruin your life." Two-Fingers said as he walked towards the creek. He stopped at a stand of birch trees and broke off a small branch and then he took out his pocketknife and started to sharpen the tip of it. After finishing, he gave me the knife so I could do the same thing. "I propose we spear us some fish." Two-Fingers said as he put his pocket knife away. I felt compelled to ask him, "You ever speared a fish?" "Son, my people have been spearing fish for centuries." Two-Fingers said proudly. "Yeah, yeah, I know. But you personally, have you ever speared a fish?" "This will be my first time." Two-Fingers admitted as we approached the creek.

The creek was about three feet wide and just as deep. Surprisingly, there were a lot of fish swimming around and it didn't take me long before I had one speared. "Wow, look at the size of this trout." I said as I held the spear above my head. I quickly removed the fish from the spear and tossed it down on the grass where the fish flopped around before it eventually quit moving. Soon, it was joined by another and then another, I had a great time spearing fish. Two-Fingers finally speared a small one and proudly showed it to me. "Good job, that ought to make your ancestors proud, aenet, Two-Fingers." "My people never ate much fish so it is difficult for me to catch such small things." Two-Fingers said as he lit up a joint. "Buffalo, they're more my speed."

After I caught enough fish to feed all of us, I cleaned them and placed them onto my spear. Two-Fingers had only the one puny little fish and it did not take him long to clean it.

The girls were busy cleaning up the place when we entered the cabin and they were understandably impressed when they saw my fish. "My great white hunter, aenet." Vicki said as she took my fish from me. "What, you on a diet?" Veronica asked as she stared at Two-Fingers puny little fish. Two-Fingers hung his head a little before opening the refrigerator and grabbing a couple of Rainier beers. He and I walked into the living room and stood there staring at the fireplace. "You going to start a fire or should I?" I asked Two-Fingers. "Fire, my people have been building fires for centuries…" "Yeah, yeah. I know." I said as I tossed some kindling into the fireplace. Before long, I had a rip roaring fire going. Two-Fingers was looking under things for a cigarette and he eventually stumbled on to some Bull Durham and quickly rolled one up. "It is awful nice of your uncle to let us use his place, aenet." Veronica said. "Shit, he owes me, aenet, he killed my only horse." Two-Fingers said before taking a drag off his cigarette. "Besides, he doesn't know we are here."

The girls prepared a fine dinner and we ate until we were stuffed and after eating, we all retired to the living room and got comfortable in front of the fire. Two-Fingers and Veronica stretched out on the couch while Vicki and I laid on blankets next to the fireplace. Soon, they were all asleep and I was left alone with my thoughts. Vicki slept peacefully in my arms as I quietly watched her. Then, she suddenly stirred ever so slightly and opened her eyes and smiled sweetly at me before standing up and taking my hand as we walked to Fred's bedroom.

I closed the door behind us and slowly began to take Vicki's clothes off. Vicki, not moving, looked into my eyes and then reached up behind her head and unfastened the beaded barrette that held her hair in place and once it was unfastened, she shook her head and her long, shiny black hair fell over her shoulders. I picked her up off of the cold, wood floor and gently placed her on the bed. Then, I quickly undressed and laid down beside her. Vicki leaned over and gave me a long, sweet kiss and I hesitated momentarily before Vicki said, "Please Tony, please."

Late the next morning, Vicki and I were awakened by a knock on the bedroom door. "Come in." I yelled as I pulled the blankets up over Vicki's shoulders. Veronica peeked her head in and said, "Two-Fingers thinks we ought to get going soon, Bitsy hasn't shown up yet and probably won't, so we better start walking." After Veronica left, I pulled Vicki close to me and she said, "I don't care if we ever go back."

Two-Fingers and Veronica were sitting at the kitchen table patiently drinking coffee when Vicki and I finally emerged from the bedroom. Vicki poured us both a cup of coffee and leaned up against the counter next to me. Nobody said a word for a long time before Two-Fingers finally said, "I thought there was a bear in your bedroom last night, I never heard so much grunting in my life." "Gee you're pissy, Two-Fingers." Veronica said. "I couldn't hear nothing over your snoring, aenet." "Well, I was worn out from catching all them damn fish." Two-Fingers said before lighting up a joint. "Getting started a little early this morning, aren't you, Two-Fingers?" Vicki asked as she rinsed her coffee cup in a basin filled with water. "Shit, it's five o'clock somewhere in the world." Two-Fingers said before standing up and handing me the joint. I gladly accepted the joint and said, "Well, If we are going to go, we better go now before it gets too late."

After walking the entire five miles into Heart Butte, we finally caught a ride with an old cowboy in a pickup truck who was headed to Browning. I helped Veronica and Vicki into the cab before climbing over the tailgate and sitting next to Two-Fingers in the bed of the pickup. "So, White Guy, how is that?" Two-Fingers asked as he nodded his head in Vicki's direction. "A gentleman never says, Two-Fingers. How is Veronica?" I asked. "Shit, I don't know, I thought we were taking them there to cool off not to get them all heated up." Two-Fingers said. "Look on the bright side," I said. "At least nobody's chasing you down the road throwing rocks at you." "Crack you, White Guy."

It was a quiet ride to the fairgrounds in Browning, I was actually able to doze off for awhile. The old cowboy drove us right up to the entrance and dropped us off, we thanked him before walking to the center of the Encampment. We were walking along minding our own business when Two-Fingers noticed Juanita and Johnny Kills-at-Night staggering towards us, arm in arm. He desperately tried to steer the girls away but was unable to do it in time. Juanita saw us and yelled, "Hey, Tony, what are you doing with that whore?" Vicki turned around, and without saying a word, she walked right up to Juanita and slapped her in the face and started pulling on her hair. Juanita, initially stunned, finally shook free of Johnny and punched Vicki in the face. Vicki, still holding onto Juanita's hair, yanked on the hair as hard as she could and they both fell to the ground kicking and clawing at each other. I rushed over and tried to break up the fight and that only caused them to fight harder. Johnny staggered into the fray and took a swing at me, he missed badly and fell to the ground. Soon, a large crowd gathered and Two-Fingers walked over to Johnny and said. "Johnny, there are a lot of voters looking at you, what do you think they are going to do come election day if they see you are involved in this?" "I don't give a shit." Johnny said as he struggled to his feet. "Well, what about Charley, do you think Charley is going to give a shit?" Two-Fingers asked as the fight raged on.

Johnny, suddenly looking pale, seemed to understand the situation a little better. He brushed himself off and slowly walked away and didn't look back. "Just like a fucking politician to run away when the going get's tough." Two-Fingers yelled to the crowd before walking over and helping me break up the fight.

I held Vicki in my arms as she continued kicking and spitting at Juanita. Juanita was held back by Two-Fingers but she still tried to break loose. Just then, Veronica calmly walked over to Juanita and slapped her as hard as she could, blood flew everywhere. Juanita was furious and she grabbed Two-Fingers arm and bit down on it as hard as she could, Two-Fingers was forced to let go as blood poured from his wound. Juanita charged Veronica and they both tumbled to the ground. "Who you calling a fucking whore, you bitch." Veronica yelled as she straddled

Juanita and started pounding her with closed fists. Two-Fingers dove on Veronica and pulled her off of Juanita. Juanita slowly stood up and looked at Veronica and then over at Vicki, she was breathing hard as she walked up to me and punched me squarely in the eye. Vicki tried to break loose and I held her with all my strength, finally she settled down. Juanita, looking dazed, focused in on the crowd around her before she turned and walked away. Two-Fingers laid on the ground with Veronica in his arms panting like a dog in heat when he finally said, "Well, I'm glad we let them cool off."

The crowd, sensing the main event was over, slowly began to disperse. Vicki and Veronica brushed each other off and fixed each other's hair. Vicki had a bloody nose and a few scratches on her neck. Other than that, she was fine. Veronica didn't have a scratch on her.

After all that, Vicki and I decided to call it a day and the two of us went to her Teepee. Before we entered the Teepee, I took her in my arms and hugged her and she slowly began to relax and then she buried her face in my chest and began to sob. "Are you hurt?" I asked as I gently stroked her hair. Vicki, still sobbing, shook her head and buried her face a little deeper. "Well, what's wrong then?" Vicki lifted her tear streaked face and asked, "What's between you and her, Tony?" I turned and raised the flap of the Teepee so we could enter and after we were seated, I slowly began to tell her most of the story.

Like it wasn't bad enough that I had to explain my actions to a girl I liked, I found out Charley was mad as hell at me. But, I am getting ahead of the story. Incidentally, the following part of the story is based on information I gathered up over the years, details which were mainly provided by my dad.

The next day after the fight, Charley returned home from his business trip to Chicago. He arrived at the Great Falls Airport around noon and immediately called my dad and asked if he had seen Juanita lately. My dad told him he hadn't seen her and he could tell that Charley was very stressed. Evidently, Charley drove the one hundred and twenty miles to his ranch from the airport in record time. He was tired and in a hurry to get home, he was worried about Juanita. When he got to the ranch, he asked Ivan if he had seen his daughter lately, Ivan had not. He was unloading his Cadillac when his father Bob rushed out the front door and yelled, "I am glad you are home, that wife of your's has been drinking and raising hell up in Browning since the day you left, I heard she was in a big fight yesterday. I have told you before about her, she is drinking and running around and you don't do a damn thing about it." Bob said. "I'm fed up. It's all over town, she is a damn embarrassment." "Was she hurt? Where the hell is she?" Charley asked. "She's in Browning at Indian Days and I don't give a damn if she is hurt." Bob said as he walked down the porch to his pickup. "Where the hell you going?" Charley asked. "None of your business, you better do something about her, I won't tolerate much more of this bullshit."

Charley stood on the porch and watched his father drive away and after leaving his suitcase on the porch, he walked to his car and drove the forty-five miles to Browning. When he arrived, he stopped to get gas at our Chevron station and filled dad in on what had just happened with Bob. Dad said he tried to settle Charley down put he was clearly agitated. Dad and Charley talked while his car was being filled up. "Any news about Stan?" Charley asked. "Nothing new really, I guess the good news is they don't really know where he is." Bud said. "At least they haven't found his body." "I've heard there are a lot of POW's over there, maybe he has been captured." Charley said. "Either way, it is causing Ruby and me a lot of sleepless nights, we miss him so." Dad said. "Well, stay strong partner, I am sure everything is going to be all right." Charley said. "Wish me luck, I am going to Indian Days." "You will need it. Say, if you see my son, let him know his parents are still alive."

The Encampment was very busy when Charley arrived. He found a parking place near the entrance and began walking towards the center of the festivities. Charley stopped people he knew and asked them if they had seen his wife, nobody had seen her. He eventually found someone willing to talk and they gave him directions to Juanita's Teepee and it was easy to locate, there was a trail of empty liquor bottles leading up to it. Charley pulled the flap back and entered the Teepee only to find Juanita passed out on the dirt floor. She was surrounded by half-empty bottles of Southern Comfort and was snoring loudly.

Charley leaned down and shook her awake, Juanita bolted upright and started swinging, Charley held her firmly until she stopped. When she finally settled down, Charley let go and said, "Get your things, we are going home." "I am not going back to that fucking place. Do you hear me?" Juanita asked as she fell back to the ground. "Juanita, I am not arguing with you, just get your shit and lets get out of here." Charley said as he picked up her purse. "I hate your old man and I ain't never going back there." Juanita said as she picked up a bottle of Southern Comfort and took a long satisfying drink.

Charley reached over and took the bottle from her as she slipped in and out of consciousness. Too heavy to lift, Charley decided to drag her out of there and he had her halfway out of the Teepee when he noticed Vicki and I standing there, we had come to look in on her and we saw and heard everything. "Tony, I am glad you are here, help me with Juanita." I quickly stepped forward and put Juanita's left arm over my shoulder. Charley took hold of the right arm and handed Juanita's purse to Vicki asking, "Would you mind holding this?" We slowly began to walk Juanita to Charley's car as tourists and locals stopped to watch us pass by. When we got to Charley's car, we put her in the passenger seat and shut the door. "Tony, I need you to find Juanita's pickup and drive it up to your place, I will have someone pick it up later." Charley eventually found the keys in Juanita's purse and handed them to me. I stood there looking down at her keys as Charley and Juanita drove off. "Well, that fancy red pickup of hers shouldn't be too hard to find." Vicki said as she took me by the hand.

It wasn't long before we found Juanita's pickup parked behind Shriver's Museum. "Let me drive." Vicki said as she grabbed the keys from me. Vicki drove past the Junction on her way towards the Park and after driving a few minutes, she pulled off the paved highway and followed a small dirt road until it came to a wide spot in the road. Hidden from view by a small stand of birch trees, Vicki slowly began to remove all of her clothes except her panties and bra. She then stripped me down to my underwear and we held each other tight as the sun rose high over the Rocky Mountains.

According to Juanita's parents, when Juanita finally sobered up, she and Charley had a huge argument. Juanita demanded her pickup back and Charley said that if she ever acted like that again he would divorce her, Juanita told him to go to hell and spent the night with her parents. The next day, Charley gave in and drove her to our place to get her pickup. That was Thursday morning. Thursday afternoon, the Montana Highway Patrol found Juanita's body inside her pickup at the bottom of the ravine east of East Glacier.

Witnesses to the wreck claimed Juanita was driving extremely fast as she approached the quarter mile long bridge leading to East Glacier. Evidently, she had passed a number of vehicles and her speed was estimated to be over one hundred miles per hour and as she approached the bridge, she lost control of her pickup and it slammed into the cement railing before flipping twice and eventually jumping over the two foot retaining wall and falling two hundred feet to the bottom of the ravine, there were no skid marks.

Ivan, Charley and my dad stood on the bridge watching in silence as the workers tried to haul the pickup out of the ravine. After several hours, Juanita and her pickup were finally retrieved and her body was taken to Cut Bank in an ambulance and her mangled pickup was loaded onto a flatbed truck and taken to the Hoyt's car graveyard. It took several days for the investigation and the autopsy to be completed.

Chapter 25

The Blackfeet community was shocked by Juanita's death. Car wrecks are an all too frequent occurrences on the Rez and, after a while, the news of another wreck was viewed as an inevitable consequence of everyday life. Unless, of course, it is a relative or close friend that was killed. Then, the inevitability of it all is swept away, leaving the survivors with a loss that is all too real and everlasting. Years of such tragedies have had a numbing affect on the community. However, Juanita's death seemed to shake everybody to their core.

Juanita was not raised on the reservation. In fact, she had never spent much time on the Rez before the year leading up to her death. Nonetheless, she was viewed as a Blackfeet women who had made it in the white world, she was looked upon as being successful and her success had given them hope, even her recent behavior was excused; on the Rez, there's always an excuse.

Two-Fingers and I were at the Sweat Lodge tending to the fire and the rocks when we heard of Juanita's death from two horseback riders who were passing by. After hearing the news, we looked at each other and shook our heads in disbelief. I remember feeling like someone had kicked me squarely in the nuts and as the feelings of guilt and loss washed over me, I had to sit down. Two-Fingers remained standing but was leaning against his shovel when he asked, "Shit, what else is going to happen this summer?"

Billy, frantically tried to cover himself with a breech cloth as he emerged from the Sweat Lodge and walked over to where we were, "Is it true? Is Juanita dead?" Two-Fingers nodded his head before sitting on the ground next to me. "She always seemed like she was lost, aenet." Uncle Billy said. "She lost her way and that's what happens when you abandon your roots, your heritage." Two-Fingers and I were barely listening, we were absorbed in our own thoughts. Billy continued, "We are all losing our way, aenet." Billy walked back to the Sweat Lodge and before he entered, he untied his breech cloth and threw it in the fire.

Two-Fingers and I sat there watching the cloth turn into ashes before we finally stood up and walked back to the Encampment. We deliberately avoided walking past Juanita's Teepee and, following an all too familiar pattern, began to look for some alcohol. Soon, we were in Fred's Teepee working hard on a bottle of Black Velvet. "You got a joint, Two-Fingers?" Two-Fingers reached deep into his boot and pulled out the baggie with one remaining joint and handed it to me saying, "That's the last button on old Gabe's coat." I quickly lit the joint and took a big hit and chased it with whiskey, I passed the joint to Two-Fingers and he did the same.

We sat in silence for awhile before I said, "I wonder if I had anything to do with her death? I mean, hell I never understood her at all, we barely even talked. Maybe I should have gone with her the other day." I took another hit and chased it with more whiskey. I was anchored against Fred's saddle and smoking the joint when Two-Fingers said, "Brother, you can't blame yourself for this shit. Uncle Billy is right, she was lost a long time ago, looks like bad shit happens to rich people too." Two-Fingers said as he reached for the joint. "Besides, I knew for sure there was going to be a fight and I should have kept them girls apart, looks like there is enough guilt and blame for everybody."

Just then, the flap of the Teepee was thrown back and Fred stepped inside the Teepee. "Well, it looks like you have heard the news, no sense crying over it." Uncle Fred said. "Get up, we are going to my ranch for a few days, do you all some good. We'll come back and pack this shit up later." Before leaving the Teepee Fred said, "What the hell is that smell?"

Fred stopped at the Businessmen's Club to replenish his supply of whiskey while Two-Fingers and I waited for him in his pickup. We were looking across the street at his house when we noticed Stogie Man slowly walking in front of it. "Dumb fuck, talk about somebody who is lost, aenet." Two-Fingers said as he stared at Stogie Man. Stogie Man briefly stopped at their gate before he turned and quickly walked away.

Fred was driving past the Legion Club headed out of town when Two-Fingers noticed Big Man Bear Claw sitting in his car in the parking lot. Two-Fingers had his uncle pull over and he jumped out of the pickup and ran over to talk to Big Man. "Hey, Big Man, you got any weed I can buy?" Two Fingers asked. "Yeah sure, Two-Fingers, I got an ounce left." Two-Fingers paid him fifteen dollars and jumped back into Fred's pickup.

Fred, Two-Fingers and I were sharing another bottle of Black Velvet as we drove to the ranch. Two-Fingers, feeling no pain, took out his pot and began to roll a joint. Fred glanced over and asked, "Is that some of that Maryjuanna shit?" "Yes indeed Uncle, yes indeed." Two-Fingers said before lighting the joint and passing it to me and I took a big hit before passing it on to Fred. Fred looked at it suspiciously for a second before taking a puff. "Damn, that's all right, aenet, Nephew." Fred said as he handed the joint back to me, I was sitting in between them so I was getting two hits to their one. Soon, I was higher than a kite and as I handed the joint to Fred, Fred let it slip through his fingers and it fell on the floor board. Two-Fingers said, "Damn Uncle, be careful." I reached down and found the joint and gave it back to Fred. Again, it fell to the floor. Fred said, "I can't help it, you guys got those skinny little fingers and I have these big, fat ones." "I think you are just getting all fucked up, Uncle." Two-Fingers said before rolling another joint.

As we drove slowly through Heart Butte, Fred suddenly decided to stop and get some groceries. While Fred was in the store, Two-Fingers and I got out of the pickup and stretched our legs. "I think Uncle is getting the munchies, aenet, White Guy." Two-Fingers said. "Damn, are you all right partner? You don't look so good." "Food doesn't sound too good to me right now." I said as I leaned over the back of the pickup, my head was spinning out of control. "Now don't you start puking." Two-Fingers yelled. "Just then, Fred walked out of the store with two cases of beer and a bag of barbecue potato chips and asked, "Hey, you guys want some Copenhagen?" With that, I started puking my guts out. "What's wrong with White Guy?" Fred asked as he gave Two-Fingers the groceries. "I don't think he cares much for snuff, aenet." Two-Fingers said.

The five mile drive to Fred's ranch passed very slowly, Fred had to pull over a few times so I could puke. We finally got there and when we did, they both helped me into the cabin and I propped myself up on a chair at the kitchen table. "Drink this, you'll fell better." Fred said as he handed me a cold Rainier. Soon, we were all seated at the table drinking beer and smoking dope. We told Fred we used his cabin and he seemed okay with it. "So, you guys brought some women out here the other day, I hope there aren't any pecker tracks in my bed." Fred said as he looked at Two-Fingers. "Hey, don't look at me." Two-Fingers said. By that time I had gotten my second wind and I said, "Two-Fingers hasn't gotten any pussy in so long his wrist is beginning to swell, aenet." Fred said. "I am going to have to find my old lady pretty soon or my wrist is going to start to get a little puffy too." "I thought you said you kicked her ass out?" Two-Fingers asked. "I did, but only for Indian Days. Shit, we both like to be free to do what we want then, aenet." Fred said. "Everybody in the Tribe splits up for ten days." "Well, this Indian Days seems like it has already lasted a month." Then I asked. "What day is it anyway?" "Lets see." Two-Fingers said as he began to count on his fingers. "I think it is Friday, aenet." "Try Tuesday. Five more days left after today." Fred said. "I think we ought to hang around here and head back on Saturday, you can help me do a few chores." "Sounds good to me." Two-Fingers said. "What do you think White Guy?" "Best idea I have heard in weeks." I said as I reached for the bottle of Black Velvet. There is nothing like throwing up to make you feel like a new man.

We stayed up most of the night partying and telling stories on each other. Two-Fingers finally passed out on the kitchen floor and I passed out on the couch, I think Fred actually made it all the way to his bedroom.

Around noon the next day, we all came to about the same time. Fred was the first one up so he started the coffee. Soon, Two-Fingers and I joined him at the scene of the crime, the kitchen table. "Don't start talking food right now, Uncle. "Two-Fingers said when Fred mentioned he could cook a little breakfast." I just want a little coffee and a smoke." "All right, you do that and then let's get outside and get some fresh air." Fred said. "I need to check on my cows."

After finishing our coffee, we started doing some chores. I went over to the woodpile and started chopping some wood for the fireplace and after about a dozen swings I began to feel almost human again. Two-Fingers and Fred went to the pasture to get three horses rounded up, they were able to get them quickly, Fred just whistled and offered them cubes of sugar. "You better let me tie that knot, Uncle." Two-Fingers said. "We can't afford to lose anymore horses this week." "Never going to let me forget that are you, Nephew?" Fred asked as he walked the horses towards the corral. "Never." Two-Fingers said.

I finished chopping the wood and was stacking it inside the cabin when Two-Fingers and Fred came riding up to the cabin leading an extra horse. "Saddle up, son. We are going to go round us up some cattle." Fred said as he pointed to the spare horse.

We rode off and before too long, we had about twenty head of Fred's Herefords rounded up, that is when Fred decided to stage a mini-rodeo for us. We got the cattle into the corral and Fred chased one of then into the chutes. "Okay, Two-Fingers, you first." Fred said as he nodded towards the cow. Two-Fingers slowly lowered himself down onto the back of the cow and grabbed a handful of its hair. He raised his left hand above his head and nodded to Fred to open the gate and as the gate opened, the cow jumped straight in the air and landed hard before she started spinning around in circles. Two-Fingers crumbled to the ground after the second jump and narrowly avoided getting kicked in the head. "I probably should have warned you, these cows are a little rank." Fred said as he loaded another cow into the chute. "A little rank, what the fuck do you mean, a little rank?" Two-Fingers said as he dusted himself off. "They are crazy."

I reluctantly climbed onto the back of the next cow and motioned to Fred to open the gate but I wasn't taking any chances, I held on with both hands. After the gate opened the cow, instead of jumping and twisting, ran straight across the corral at full speed and just before it ran into the fence, it suddenly stopped and I literally flew over its head and into a fence post. I was laying on the ground digging splinters out of my hand when Fred approached. "You okay, White Guy?" Fred asked. "I am fine." I said as I picked myself up off the ground. "Your turn, Uncle." Two-Fingers had already herded the biggest cow in the corral into the chute. Fred walked over to the chute and gently lowered himself onto the back of the cow. After adjusting his hat, he raised his left arm, leaned back and motioned to Two-Fingers to open the chute. The gate swung open and the cow took off, it began to run like a bat out of hell when it suddenly stopped and started to spin. Fred hung on precariously as the cow continued to spin in a desperate attempt to shake free of the intruder. Two-Fingers and I watched intently as Fred held on for all he was worth. After a few seconds, the cow started to run again and Fred took his hat off and started to whip it across the back of its head. "Open the gate!! Open the gate!!" Fred yelled as he continued whipping the cow with his hat. I ran over to the gate and swung it wide open as Fred and the cow went racing by. Two-Fingers walked over and we stood there watching Fred and the cow running across the meadow. "I am the last of the wild bunch!! I am the last of the wild bunch!!" Fred yelled as he disappeared from sight. "He's the last of something." Two-Fingers said as we chased the rest of the cattle out of the corral.

Two-Fingers and I were sitting on the front porch sipping beer when Fred finally showed up. "Damn, that was fun, aenet." Fred said as he stretched out on the porch. "Tomorrow, we need to get some work done."

We spent the rest of the day drinking beer and laughing about our rodeo and when the beer was all gone, Fred stood and said, "Six o'clock comes awful early in the morning, boys. You better get some sleep because we have a full day ahead of us."

The next morning, Two-Fingers and I were awakened by the smell of bacon and eggs. We were both starving so it didn't take much prodding to get us to the breakfast table. "Well boys, you better eat good, we won't be eating again until nightfall." Fred said as he poured himself a cup of coffee.

Over breakfast, Fred laid out his plans for the day. He had a hay meadow a half mile west of his cabin where he had recently mowed and bailed about twenty acres of hay. He wanted the hay moved from that location to the barn, it was going to be used for winter feed. "Uncle, how the hell do you get back up in there?" Two-Fingers asked.

"There isn't even a road going back there." "Very carefully." Fred said. "Actually, there is a small trail I take, we just have to drive slow."

After we ate, Fred drove to the barn and began attaching railings around the bed of his pickup, we needed to stack the hay high and the railings would help hold it in place. Once this was done, we drove to the hay meadow and as we made our way slowly through the trees, we noticed a small herd of elk grazing in the meadow. The elk slowly lifted their heads and watched as we drove past them, they seemed unconcerned by our presence. "Damn, the grass is growing fast this year." Fred said. "It will be ready for another cutting soon." Fred stopped the pickup and we removed a section of the railing and began to load the hay, Fred was in the bed of the truck stacking and I was on the ground lifting the bales up to him, Two-Fingers primary duty was to drive the pickup. After a sufficient amount of hay was loaded, we re-attached the railing and drove back to the barn to unload and stack the hay, that process was repeated until nightfall. After Fred and I stacked the last bale, I collapsed on the floor of the barn and said, "Oh, shit I hurt all over." "Well boys, I really appreciate your help. We didn't get it all, but damn near." Fred said as he took a pinch of snuff. "I'll get the rest on Monday." "What's the matter with you White Guy?" Two-Fingers asked as he helped me to my feet. "Can't take it, huh?" "What, you're not tired from doing all that driving?" I asked as we walked back to the cabin.

That night, we feasted on venison and fell asleep shortly after eating. We slept until midmorning the next day and when I woke up I was as stiff as a board and my arms and hands felt like they were on fire. I sat at the coffee table trying not to spill coffee on myself while Fred cooked breakfast. "You are a good hand, Tony. You got a place out here anytime you want it." Fred said as he placed a couple of eggs on my plate. "You too Nephew, you do pretty damn good with what you got." "Damn Uncle, that's nice of you to say but where the hell are my eggs?" Two-Fingers asked as he looked down at an empty plate. "Coming right up, coming right up." Fred said.

After I ate, I stripped off all my clothes, grabbed a towel and walked down to the creek and jumped in. The water was ice cold and it took my body a few seconds to adjust to the temperature. Soon, the burning in my arms and legs began disappear. I took a handful of sand from the bottom of the creek and began to scrub my entire body with it. Then, I lowered my head into the water and I was instantly rejuvenated. After my bath, I climbed out of the creek and quickly dried off with the towel. On my way back to the cabin, I noticed a large cloud of dust in the air and a car driving in our direction. It took me awhile before I was able recognize the vehicle, it was Bitsy's Volkswagen.

"Shit." Bitsy said as he jumped out of his car. "I got drunk and I forgot about you guys." I just stared at Bitsy and shook my head in disgust. "Shit, I'm sorry, man." Bitsy said as he walked up to me. "The women got ate by bears and all you got to say is, I'm sorry?" I asked. Two-Fingers stepped off the porch and he yelled, "Is that Indian time you are on, Bitsy?"

After making Bitsy feel as bad as we could, we finally let him in on what happened. "Well, shit, I was worried, this being the last day of Indian Days and all." Bitsy said. "Last day?" Two-Fingers asked. "Yes, it's Sunday." Bitsy said as he sat down on the porch. "Sunday? Doesn't anybody know what day it is around here? We better head into Browning then, aenet." Two-Fingers said. "Better get some damn clothes on White Guy, all you do is run around naked."

I dressed as quickly as possible and when we told Fred we were driving back to town with Bitsy, he told us not to wait up for him, he was going to go find his old lady. We jumped into Bitsy's car and drove to Browning, a cloud of dust rose behind us as we sped down the dirt road.

After Bitsy dropped us off at the fairgrounds, Two-Fingers and I decided to go watch the dancers for one last time. On our way to the dancing area, we passed a couple of pretty Indian girls who were wearing their traditional garb. Two-Fingers stopped to watch them pass when they both suddenly stopped and looked at him. "Oki, where you girls from?" Two-Fingers asked. "Lander, Wyoming-we are Arapahos." The tallest of the two girls said. Two-Fingers and I were staring at them when the other girl said, "Oh my, what happened to your hand?" Two-Fingers lifted his left hand high in the air and said, "Garbage disposal."

The two girls looked at each other and then turned and ran away. "Shit, I never had that happen before. Those Arapahos must have some serious mental problems, aenet, White Guy." "I don't know, maybe they are just a more intelligent breed of woman than you are used to." I said. "You always got an answer, aenet, White Guy." Two-Fingers said as we turned around and found Vicki and Veronica glaring at us with their arms crossed. "So, you two running with those girls all this time?" Veronica asked as they walked towards us.

Seeing Vicki suddenly brought back the feelings of guilt I had suppressed over the last few days. I was able to put Juanita's death out of my mind, until then. As Vicki approached, I sensed that she was guilt ridden over Juanita's death too. "Damn girl, I didn't know you owned me." Two-Fingers said to Veronica. "Besides, you know I only have eyes for you." "Bullshit, me and half the other women around here." Veronica said. "Hello, Tony. We need to talk." Vicki said as she looked down and kicked at a small rock. "Sure, let's get some pop and go over to your Teepee."

Just then, Two-Fingers noticed his uncle Billy walking our way, he was dressed in his dancing outfit. He wore eagle feathers in his hair, a chest plate, a loin cloth and moccasins. He jingled as he walked; dozens of tiny bells were attached to his outfit. "Damn, you got knobby knees, Uncle. You shouldn't be going out in public dressed like that." Two-Fingers said when Billy was in hearing range. "Oh, my wayward Nephew, what am I going to do with you?" Billy asked. "Tomorrow morning I am tearing down the Sweat Lodge with a couple of Indians who are with the American Indian Movement. I want you there, bring your friend." Billy said as he passed by. "Nine A.M. sharp and don't make me come looking for you."

After getting our pop, Vicki, Two-Fingers, Veronica and I went to Vicki's Teepee and sat down in a circle. Vicki was distressed over her recent fight with Juanita. Veronica, on the other hand, showed absolutely no remorse. After about an hour of discussing the matter, I stood up and said, "Listen, for the last time, there is nothing we can do about it. I feel bad too. What if this, what if that. Shit, it's useless." Without saying another word, I abruptly left the Teepee.

"Hey, hey. Where you going?" Two-Fingers asked as he ran after me. "I am going over to Fred's Teepee to sleep." "I am worn out." "Well, don't wait up for me." Two-Fingers said. "I am feeling lucky tonight."

The next morning, I was startled out of a deep sleep by Two-Fingers gently poking my head with his left hand. "Hey, White Guy, it is eight thirty and we have just enough time to get some coffee before we go help Uncle Billy." I slowly sat up and got my bearings. I had a great sleep, there is just something about sleeping in a Teepee. "So, how did it go last night with you and Veronica?" I asked as I stretched my arms. "Well, let me put it this way, you don't see her chasing me with rocks, do you?" Two-Fingers said before standing. "Finally, a sexual escapade of your's that doesn't end in bloodshed."

Chapter 26

As usual, Billy was up early. He made Two-Fingers and me a breakfast of dry meat and tea and then he sat down and talked to us about Lenny Iron Horse, an Ogala Sioux from the Pine Ridge Indian Reservation in South Dakota and Jack Little Wolf, a Northern Cheyenne from the Northern Cheyenne Reservation in Montana. They were going to help him take down the Sweat Lodge as repayment for using it. Jack was the head of AIM in Montana. Lenny was the head of AIM in South Dakota and was very instrumental in the policy making of AIM. Jack and Lenny both advocated a peaceful form of resistance to the current American Indian Policy, they sought change. They were both strong environmentalists who wanted to protect all land, not just Reservation land. During their sweats, Billy listened intently to Lenny and Jack and he was impressed with their spiritualism and social activism.

Billy sipped on a second cup of tea when Jack and Lenny arrived. Lenny was tall, lean and muscular and his long hair flowed freely and reached his shoulders. Jack, on the other hand, was short and plump and wore his hair in braids kept in place with a rubber bands. Billy introduced them to Two-Fingers and me. "Oki, Billy" Lenny said. "Good day to get some work done." "Glad you could make it Lenny, Jack." Billy said as he nodded in their direction. "Can I get you a cup of tea?" After declining the offer, Billy, Jack, Lenny, Two-Fingers and I busied ourselves with removing the buffalo hides and placing them in the back of Billy's pickup. We worked in silence until Lenny stopped working and said, "You have a good group of young men on this reservation, I believe they are going to rock the status quo." "Yes, the old men running all our reservations had better pay attention, aenet." Jack said.

They talked in length about how the older Councilmen were only in it for themselves, they say and do what they have to get elected and then do nothing but put money in their own pockets and the pockets of their friends and relatives. The problem, as they see it, is not Tribe against Tribe, it is young against old. Those with vested interests versus those with interests; relevant social change versus no change.

"What do you two think?" Lenny asked Two-Fingers. "Are you going to become an AIM member and fight for your rights?" Two-Fingers looked at me before he said, "What you say is true, but it has been true forever. How are you going to change it?" "I am not going to change it." Lenny said. "We are all going to change it because it must be changed. The old men know it and they are running scared. They have been good apples for a long time and when the Bureau of Indian Affairs tells them to jump, they say, "how high," aenet." "Apples, red on the outside and white on the inside. We need our independence. Indians, all Indians, must have more of a say in our destiny." Jack said. "The Federal Government has never given a shit about us. We are Native Americans, fuck this Indian shit." "But, they give a lot to the reservation like commodities, housing-lots of things." I said sheepishly. "That's right, they give it." Lenny said. "It is never earned and therefore it is never appreciated. We all have been living on handouts for so long we don't even know how to work for a living anymore." "There are no fucking jobs on the Rez." Two-Fingers said. "That's what AIM is all about, we say make our own jobs and take care of our own people and our land and let the crazy white people fuck up their own place." Lenny said. "We do not have much left so we must fight hard to keep what we have."

"Aenet." Billy said. "The white's are greedy and destructive and anybody who cares about the land is a "tree hugger" to them. Their rivers are on fire, their air is polluted and their minds are tormented. Everybody is chasing the almighty dollar and they all make excuses on why they do it. We need to live as Native Americans, not as the Indians we have become. Jack and Lenny are right, we must embrace our old ways, our own culture. Not the culture of the white man. We have become just like them, everybody trying to get ahead of the other guy and nobody caring how they get there, they have no honor. They are selling their souls so they can have more trinkets, aenet. If we do not change, how will they?"

With that said, we returned to the task at hand and soon the Sweat Lodge was completely dismantled and stacked into the pickup's bed. Two-Fingers and I sat on the tailgate and listened as Billy continued, "You two need to understand that changes are in the wind. You both go through life like the rest of the young, oblivious to all the problems in the world. But, you are both old enough now to start thinking of these things. Changes are coming, embrace them." With that, Billy, Lenny and Jack turned and started to walk towards the main Encampment area. Two-Fingers and I sat in silence and then slowly walked off in the same direction.

The day after the Indian Days Celebration ends is always a busy day. The Encampment area is vacated and that meant all the temporary structures had to be taken down and removed. Two-Fingers and I were walking through the area looking for someone to help when we heard a voice behind us say, "Hey, you guys, you want to buy some Peyote?" Two-Fingers and I turned around and watched as this skinny, long haired Native American wearing a red bandana approached. "What the hell is Peyote?" I asked. "Man, it's a hallucinogenic kind of like Mescaline, us Apaches use it all the time." The stranger said as he stopped in front of us and opened his hand to reveal four red buttons. "It comes from the cactus down in the desert where I come from."

Two-Fingers picked up one of the buttons and examined it. It was round, hard and had a disgusting pungent smell to it. "This is the shit you use for rituals, right?" Two-Fingers asked. "I remember my grandfather talking about this stuff." "That's right, take that and you will see the light, man." The stranger said. Two-Fingers and I looked at each other before I asked, "How much?" "Five dollars a piece, they are worth more than that but I am out of money and I need to get back to Arizona." "I can buy four cases of beer for that kind of money." Two-Fingers said as he handed back the Peyote. "Yeah, but this shit will kick your ass like you drank a hundred cases of beer." The stranger said as he began to put the Peyote away.

Two-Fingers, always on the lookout for a bargain, quickly figured out this was a hell of a deal and said, "Better give us all four." I reluctantly handed the stranger twenty dollars. The stranger placed the Peyote in my hand and before he left he said, "Take it at night, it works best at night."

"Tonight? Shit, I say we take it now." Two-Fingers said as he turned and started to walk to a nearby hill. When we reached the top of the hill, we sat down on top of a large boulder and was able to see in all directions. I took the Peyote out of my pocket and gave Two-Fingers two buttons. After we each examined our buttons, we placed them in our mouths and slowly began to chew, the taste was bitter and acidic. I swallowed hard and soon the taste was tolerable. We sat in silence watching as the Encampment slowly disappeared.

After awhile, we drifted off into a deep trance like state. I was still able to recognize what was going on around us but I began to drift further and further away. Two-Fingers looked rather possessed when he reached into his pocket and removed his knife. He slowly opened the blade and whispered, "blood brothers." With that, he cut a four inch gash in his deformed hand's palm, blood flowed freely from the wound as Two-Fingers handed me the knife. Without hesitating, I cut an identical wound in my right hand and after I did that, I took the knife and threw it as high into the sky as I could and then I reached over and took Two-Fingers hand and our blood soon flowed together. Within a matter of minutes, we both started to vomit. Puke flowed down the front of our shirts and pants like lava from a volcano. The vomiting caused us to go deeper and deeper into our trances, the mixture of blood loss and the effects of the Peyote caused a hallucinogenic effect that was totally overwhelming.

We drifted off into the sky and soon we came swooping down out of the clouds and crashed to the earth. Our blood formed a river that washed over us and cleansed our minds and bodies, time stood still. What seemed like minutes was actually hours passing us by and as we sat on the boulder we were taken places that we did not even know existed, we both experienced things in our own separate ways yet they were similar.

I saw Stan but I could not get to him. Juanita appeared and then she turned her back on me. Two-Fingers was young and then old; standing tall and proud, but old. Our minds left our bodies and we were unable to move, we were prisoners to the overwhelming impulses that rushed over us. Neither of us wanted to move, moving was the last thing on our minds.

We were now on a river together rushing head first down a series of steep rapids and our blood ran together and so did our thoughts. We became blood brothers, brothers. The Peyote strengthened the bonds of our friendship, we both felt a kinship for each other that was now stronger than anything we had ever experienced. A friendship that was strong suddenly got stronger and our journey continued for hours.

By the time we emerged from the trance, the sun had disappeared behind the mountains. We looked at each other and slowly let go of each other's hand. Through the dim light, we saw blood and vomit everywhere. After awhile, we were free of the effects of the Peyote and able to walk home. It may be my imagination, but since that day I have always thought Two-Fingers looked a lot whiter.

When I got home, dad was sitting alone in the kitchen drinking beer. He took one look at me and asked, "What the hell happened to you? You been fighting again?" I just shook my head before walking over to the sink to clean up. My right hand had a deep gash in it but it wasn't bleeding much. I dried my hand and then wrapped the towel firmly over the cut. "Where is mom?" "She's in bed. You better go to, Juanita is being buried tomorrow in Cut Bank and we will be leaving early." Dad said as he finished his Oly.

The line of cars driving from Browning to Cut Bank stretched for miles, the funeral was very well attended. The graveyard was located on a hill overlooking a stretch of Cut Bank Creek. It was a cloudy day and as the mourners made their way to Juanita's grave site, a cold wind swept upward from the creek and caused a chill to spread amongst them.

Charley, dressed in black, stood over Juanita's coffin. Just behind him, Ivan, Helen and Bob were seated in folding chairs with my family seated next to them, the rest of the mourners were standing. Father Ian Kelly was also standing and seemed amazed to see all the people that were there, half the Rez was in attendance.

Charley stood the entire time and when the ceremony was over and Juanita's body was lowered into the ground, he threw a rose onto her coffin and slowly turned and walked to his car, not stopping to talk to anyone. The crowd stood in silence and watched him leave before they returned to their vehicles.

We drove home and spoke very little. Dad was deeply concerned about Charley and a little surprised that he hadn't stopped and talked to him after the funeral. When they spoke the day before, Charley told dad that Juanita's autopsy showed that she had not been drinking the day of the accident and the Highway Patrol investigating the crash were concerned by the lack of any skid marks, they told Charley that may have meant the brakes were tampered with. However, her pickup was so badly damaged nobody would ever know for sure. So, the investigation ended unceremoniously when they could not find any conclusive evidence of foul play. Charley told dad that he was going to do his own investigating, he had heard that Juanita was having an affair and he was going to find out who the son-of-a-bitch was. Dad asked me if I knew anything about it and again I lied and said no.

The morning after Juanita's funeral, I was startled out of a deep sleep by my Dad. "Wake up." He yelled. "Charley is out in the kitchen and he wants to talk to you." I quickly dressed and walked to the kitchen where I found mom, dad and Charley sitting around the kitchen table. I sat down next to my Mom and said, "Hi, Charley. Dad said you wanted to talk to me about something." Charley looked down at his hands before saying, "I have spent the last couple of days going all over this godforsaken place asking questions, I needed to know who it was that was sleeping with my wife." Charley looked up at me before continuing, "I have heard from a number of people that it was you, Tony." I sat there looking at Charley as my world crumbled around me. I had never seen such hatred before, he stared at me with a look of disgust on his face. I actually hoped he would climb over the table and choke my lights out. "Tony, is this true?" Dad asked. Before I could say anything, mom stood and walked to the kitchen sink for a drink of water. My silence must have told Charley all he needed to know. "Well, it looks like you were man enough to fuck my wife but aren't man enough to admit it." Charley said as he stood and walked to the front door and opened it. Before leaving, he turned to my dad and said, "You can forget about any loan from me, you can all forget that you even know me." Charley walked out and slammed the door behind him.

Before I was able to say anything, dad said, "We are selling this place and leaving here as soon as possible." He then stood up and walked out the front door, mom just stared at me. Then, without saying a word, she slowly walked back to her bedroom and closed her door. I sat there by myself for a long time thinking about what I could have said, Charley already knew and nothing I could say was going to change what I had done or the fact that he knew about it. I was not afraid of getting a beating. In fact, I preferred it to the unrelenting quilt I felt.

Events over the weeks following Juanita's funeral brought a number of changes to both our families and Two-Fingers and I rarely saw each other over that period of time. I stayed close to home and spent most of my time working at the station, I desperately tried to repair the damage I had done to my parents. Nothing I did helped, I hurt my parents real bad and there was little I could have done about it, it took them awhile to get over what they perceived as the ultimate betrayal.

When I mentioned that I was going to stay in Browning and finish my high school education, I received little resistance. Dad actually thought it was a good idea to stay and face the music and Max and Pam agreed to give me a place to stay if and when we were able to sell the station.

Speaking of Max, he had been released from the hospital and was trying to get around on his new artificial leg. That was the good news, the bad news was Max was drinking constantly. Evidently, he became addicted to the pain pills he was given in the hospital and once they were taken away, he turned to alcohol to ease the pain. Max, who had been a social drinker, was letting his drinking get out of control.

During the time I lived with the Schwartz's, I did a lot of work for them and that allowed Cindy Ann to take her two girls and move to Missoula, Montana with Paula where they both attended the University of Montana. Cindy Ann was still married to Stogie Man at the time but she was going through with a divorce. When Stogie Man was served the divorce papers, he snuck into Cindy Ann's room and tried to attack her. Two-Fingers intervened and kicked the shit out of him. Shortly after that, Stogie Man was seen living with the winos. Pam tried to cope with all the problems the family faced that summer. In addition to the family problems, business was off badly at the curio shop, not as many tourists stopping with all the unrest going on and her beloved husband drank to kill his pain. Pain, on the Rez there is always so much pain.

To the best of my knowledge, Charley never came back to Browning after Juanita died. Rumor had it that he and his father had a huge fight and Bob moved to Cut Bank to live and Charley stayed on the ranch. Ivan and Helen left the Owen Ranch shortly after the funeral and they now live in a cabin they built in the mountains near Heart Butte.

Summers on the Rez were usually a time for the Blackfeet to renew and strengthen themselves before the ravages of winter descended upon them. That summer, the hope of renewal fell considerably short of expectations, hope was replaced with a large dose of heartache and despair. Close knit families were divided over the issues of the day, the young were seeking change and they did not understand why the older Blackfeet were so resistant to it. The Tribal elections did not help soothe that division, four of the seven council seats were won by young, college educated Blackfeet and all hell broke loose as they gained control over the Tribal Council. Like it or not, change was on it's way.

Chapter 27

Over that summer, the Bureau of Indian Affairs finished building the Blackfeet a new high school. It is a large, round brick building without any windows. The Blackfeet have a thing about breaking out windows and the BIA finally figured that out. Two-Fingers and I were checking it out on our first day of our senior year when Two-Fingers said, "Damn, I'm already feeling claustrophobic in this place, I feel like a mouse in a maze, aenet."

Two-Fingers and I were assigned to the same homeroom and it didn't take us long to find it. We walked around the room greeting our friends and avoiding our enemies, Vicki and Veronica looked the other way as we passed. They felt neglected over the last days of summer and they were pissed off and as Two-Fingers and I found our seats I whispered to Two-Finger, "Oh well, there are plenty of other fish in the sea." Two-Fingers nodded his head and said, "Yeah, but with our luck, they will turn out to be sharks." The morning bell rang and our senior year in high school began.

During the first few months of the new school year, Two-Fingers and I worked hard at getting good grades. In the past, neither of us worked real hard at school and our grades showed it. So, we both decided to spend more time on our studies in case we decided to go on to college. In short, Two-Fingers and I grew up a lot over the summer.

Our attitude towards school had changed and so did our attitude towards our appearance. We got rid of the collared white shirts and Levi's that we always wore to school and replaced them with fatigue jackets, T-shirts and khaki pants. My short cropped hair became a thing of the past too and we occasionally wore bandanas on our heads and chains around necks. We were both very athletic but neither of us participated in organized sports, too busy working. While the other school kids were busy with sports, Two-Fingers and I were concentrating on our studies, jobs and families. We tried to avoid the petty arguments and fights that occurred on a daily basis and mainly kept to ourselves.

One bright spot for me personally was the addition of another white person in my class. His name was Michael C. Brown and he was the only son of two employees of the Great Northern Railroad. The Great Northern is known for its symbol of a mountain goat that is emblazoned on all of the railcars. His dad and mom both worked out at the train depot east of town and they lived downtown near the Catholic Church.

The first day of school Mike got chased home by some rowdy Blackfeet and he was given the nickname "Brownie." Turned out that was a very deft nickname because Brownie loved his pastries. Whenever I wanted to find him, I just went down to the local bakery. Two-Fingers and I took him under our wings when he finally reappeared at school. We both told him the worst thing you could do was to run, he needed to stand his ground like I did or his life was going to be a living hell.

The usual bullies on the Rez were merciless to Brownie. They hurled racial slurs, attacked his manhood and threatened his existence. One day I pulled him aside and told him, "When they start that shit with you, go up to the biggest one in the pack and bust him square in the face." After school that day he got his chance, a group of thugs jumped him and they were making all kinds of noise when, all of a sudden, Brownie walked up to the biggest guy in the crowd and punched him right in the face. Well, that only made the guy madder than hell and he proceeded to beat the holy crap out of Brownie. When he was finished, I helped Brownie up and he asked me, "What did I do wrong?" As I was brushing him off Two Fingers stepped up and said, "First of all you listened to the White Guy, I personally would have punched the littlest guy and then ran like hell." The three of us became good friends after that and Two-Fingers and I protected him the best we could.

Thankfully, Brownie cut down on the food and discovered the new weight room at high school and he soon turned the fat into muscle. In short, he turned into one hell of a load.

During most of our senior year, Two-Fingers and I rarely spent time together outside of school. I was still trying hard to make amends with my folks by helping out around the station and at home. Mom was very despondent and spent most of her days in her bedroom and dad was quiet and reserved, he suffered from the absence of Stan and his best friend Charley. From mom and dad's standpoint, the only good news was Bobby Racine's loan came through and he was able to buy our station.

Two-Fingers spent a lot of time with Max. Max was walking better with his prosthetic leg but he was still unable to drive. Max hated being cooped up in his house so Two-Fingers drove him where ever he wanted to go, they were constantly driving around the Rez.

As winter approached, the days got colder and darker and Max became extremely depressed and was drinking more with each passing day. On the first Saturday in November, Two-Fingers, in an attempt to cheer Max up, suggested they go deer hunting. Max hesitated but was finally persuaded by Pam to go. Two-Fingers loaded their car with their 30/06 rifle, shells and a couple of sandwiches. Two-Fingers was driving and Max was seated in the front passenger seat as they off. Before leaving town, Max insisted on stopping at Buttries for a cold case of beer, Two-Fingers hesitated and then decided to do as he was told.

Two-Fingers and Max spent most of the day on the Rez looking for deer. It had snowed heavily during the night and the roads were snow packed and icy. They decided to drive in the direction of Heart Butte, they figured the deer would be coming down from the higher elevations because of all the snow and with any luck, they would be able to shoot one from the road.

Max drank his beer and sipped on a pint of Seagrams he had stashed in his coat pocket. Before too long, he got drunk and started feeling sorry for himself, he complained about how fucked up he felt and how useless he was and all the while he continued to sip on his booze. This went on for hours and Two-Fingers tried to console him and that only seemed to make matters worse. Max repeatedly told Two-Fingers he was tired of living and wished he was dead. Two-Fingers consoled him some more and Max continued to drink. They drove on and on and before long, Max was crying hysterically and demanding that Two-Fingers pull the car over and shoot him, he wanted to be put out of his misery. Two-Fingers continued trying to calm him down and Max finally did calm down a little but he kept right on drinking.

As they approached Heart Butte, Max suddenly and completely lost it and demanded Two-Fingers pull over and put a bullet in his head. Two-Fingers stopped the car on the shoulder of the road and wrapped his arms around his father and after a while Max calmed down and they resumed their journey.

On and on they drove until Max began to lose it again. He pleaded with Two-Fingers to kill him and he was inconsolable. Two-Fingers stopped the car and spent several minutes trying to talk his father out of it. But, he was unsuccessful, Max insisted on being put out of his misery.

By then, Two-Fingers was fed up with the whole damn mess and decided to teach his father a lesson. He yelled at Max to get out of the car and to go lie down in the ditch next to the road. "If you want to end your rotten, miserable life I will help you do it." Two-Fingers said he grabbed his rifle and jumped out of the car as Max slowly slid out of the car and haltingly limped down the embankment before laying flat on his back in the snow, exposing his prosthetic leg to Two-Fingers.

Max laid on his back with his hands folded over his chest and quietly prayed. Two-Fingers walked around to the rear of the car and steadied himself against the trunk. He raised the rifle and adjusted the sights when Max suddenly looked up at Two-Fingers and all of a sudden there was a loud BANG!! Two-Fingers, with smoke coming out of the barrel, watched as Max's prosthetic leg flew end over end until it reached the top of a nearby telephone line where it hung for a second or two before falling to the ground.

Max laid on the ground as the blood drained from his face. Then, he slowly propped himself up onto one elbow and looked around before yelling at Two-Fingers, "What the hell are you trying to do, kill me?!!" He laid back down and was quiet for about a minute or so before Two-Fingers walked over and helped him back to the car. Two-Fingers gently placed him onto the passenger seat and before he closed the door, Max threw the remaining beer and whiskey into the ditch.

After taking Max home, Two-Fingers drove to see me so he could tell me the story of how he got his father to quit drinking. I was shocked to the core when he told me what happened. "How did you know you weren't going to hurt him?" I asked. "I didn't." Two-Fingers said. "All I know is he isn't much good to anyone the way he is and something needed to be done. On the way home he swore he would never drink again and I believe him, he has never promised that before." "Well, I hope he quits. Man, that is the wildest thing I have ever heard." "Yeah, I cured him." Two-Fingers said proudly. "Alcoholics Anonymous uses a ten step program to help someone quit drinking, I use a one legged approach."

Chapter 28

Holidays are always tough times on the Rez, depression is at its pinnacle during these times. The week leading up to Thanksgiving that year saw a number of suicides. One death in particular deeply affected Two-Fingers and me. Three days before Thanksgiving, Rubber Joe's body was found at the base of the City's water tower, he had jumped over one hundred feet to his death; the cold, hard, unforgiving ground took away what life he had left.

Evidently, he and the Governor had been drinking especially hard that day and just before he took the fatal dive, they were laying underneath the tower sharing a bottle of wine and trying to keep warm. That's when Rubber Joe suddenly stood up and started mumbling, "There are just too many ghosts, too many ghosts." Before the Governor knew exactly what was happening, Rubber Joe started to climb to the top of the water tower. When Rubber Joe got to the top of the tower, the Governor started to scream for help and soon a small crowd gathered just in time to watch Rubber Joe plunge to his death.

That night, shortly after his body was taken away, a terrible blizzard descended upon the Rez, it snowed for forty-eight hours. After the snow stopped, the temperature dropped dramatically. Schools, roads and businesses were closed and Browning became a virtual ghost town, nobody went outside unless it was absolutely necessary.

On Thanksgiving Day, the weather situation was still very bad so my parents and I dined alone. No need to worry about customers, there weren't any. We sat at our kitchen table and feasted on a traditional Thanksgiving dinner. Mom was more cheerful than usual and dad seemed to be getting back to normal. Maybe he realized the love of his son was more important than any friendship, at least I hoped that was what he was thinking. Dad was helping himself to a piece of pumpkin pie when he said, "Your mother and I will be leaving for New Jersey before the end of the year. The new Tribal Council wants to see all the white merchants out of here, I guess it is a blessing in disguise." "What about Stan? How will he know how to get in touch with you?" I asked. "I will notify the War Department as soon as we know where we will be living." Dad said. We finished the rest of our meal in silence and then I asked permission to go see Two-Fingers. "Sure." Dad said. "Just be careful walking in this crap."

I dressed up warmly and began my walk to Two-Fingers, there wasn't a car on the road. Off in the distance, I could hear the roar of snowmobiles but there weren't any cars driving around. There were a lot of them abandoned along the side of the road, but none of them were moving. I trudged slowly through the waist high snow and eventually arrived at Two-Fingers where I was greeted at the front door by Max. Max had his new leg on and a new attitude as well, I hadn't seen him that happy in months. True to his word, he had not had a drink since Two-Fingers shot his leg off. Pam rushed in from the kitchen and gave me a hug. She was wearing an apron with flour on it, she was baking pies. I took the opportunity to inform them that I would soon be taking up permanent residency at their place. They seemed very pleased and invited me to sit and eat with them. I did not want to appear rude so I said yes and as Pam placed the turkey on the table she said, "I wish our girls were here, this blizzard has caused most of the roads in Montana to shut down."

The Schwartz's said a prayer before we began to eat and they were right, we had a lot to be thankful for. They were in a festive mood and soon we began to talk about a number of events that had recently taken place on the Rez. We all agreed that Rubber Joe's death was a terrible thing, Pam believed his soul was finally at rest. Before long, the conversation turned to politics and Max said, "Looks like I am going to have to run for Council, these young bucks are going to ruin the place. Hell, they are going to scare off all the tourist trade." "Pop, things have got to change around here." Two-Fingers said. "There is no way they can make it any worse than it already is."“Yeah, but they are moving too damn fast." Max said. "Too damn fast? Hell, if you ask me, they are a hundred years slow." Two-Fingers said. "I hope they burn the whole place down and we start from scratch."

Pam and Max stared at Two-Fingers before they resumed eating. I just sat there soaking it all in wondering if it was too late to go to New

Jersey. Before I got too far into my thoughts, Two-Fingers nudged me and said, "Let's go walk off some turkey."

The wind was blowing the snow in all directions as Two-Fingers and I walked towards the Government Square and as we approached the alley behind the theater, we were both startled by the sound of growling. Up ahead, Old McGraw and a big German Shepherd were circling each other. We watched them in silence as the German Shepherd jumped on Old McGraw and bit him on the neck, Old McGraw shook his head violently but the German Shepherd held on tight. Old McGraw, slowed by age, was unable to get loose but he kept trying. They were spinning around and around in the snow, blood flew everywhere. Soon, Old McGraw stopped struggling and laid down and slowly died. All the snow in the immediate area turned a bright red color, it looked like a big cherry snow cone. The German Shepherd looked around and then slowly ran off, his tail wagging. Two-Fingers and I were amazed at what we had just witnessed, Old McGraw had finally met his match. "No one and nothing lasts forever, aenet." Two-Fingers said as we turned and started walking back home.

Mom and dad left Browning shortly after Christmas and I remember their leaving like it happened yesterday. They left town on December 28, 1970. There was a break in the weather and they wanted to get going while the getting was good. We said our goodbyes and as they slowly backed out of the driveway, a feeling of despair and loneliness suddenly swept over me.

I stood there watching them drive away as I waved weakly back at them and then I heard myself saying, "You can't stay and I can't go, you can't stay and I can't go." Tears ran down my cheeks as I repeated this over and over again and as they began to disappear from view, I started to run after them while I continued saying, "You can't stay and I can't go, aenet." I was about a mile or so down the road before I finally stopped running after them and turned around and slowly started to walk back into town. I remember stopping briefly to admire a new sign that read, "Welcome to Browning-Headquarters of the Blackfeet Indian Nation." That sign replaced the old sign that said, "Welcome to Browning and enjoy your stay."

Chapter 29

After my parents moved away, I fought the loneliness by keeping busy. I worked hard at school and got good grades and I continued working at our old gas station for Bobby Racine and at the Schwartz's. Two-Fingers and his family were now my family so I really didn't suffer too bad.

Two-Fingers kept busy too and our senior year of high school flew by. Vicky and Veronica had long since moved on from us and Two-Fingers and I briefly dated girls from the Babb area; beautiful Blackfeet girls who were truly wild in every way. Babb is on the Rez not too far from the Canadian line, it is so desolate and poor it makes Browning look like Hollywood.

Anyway, on our graduation night, after partying into the wee hours of the morning, Two-Fingers, Brownie and I decided to continue our partying in Glacier Park not far from Babb. Brownie had received a beautiful 1957 Ford Crestline Skyline convertible for his graduation present, the model is famous for being the first retractable hardtop convertible. It was absolutely gorgeous, why anybody would drive such a nice car on the Rez was beyond me.

The three of us were drinking and driving through the Park near the newly rebuilt Many Glaciers Lodge on a warm, beautiful night. We didn't bother a soul all we did was drink, smoke and drive around, it was all very blissful.

The next thing I remember was getting startled out of a deep sleep by a baby mountain goat. Evidently, mountain goats are plentiful in the Park but it was the first time I had ever seen one. Anyway, this baby mountain goat was drunk as hell, he had gotten into one of the whiskey bottles we left open when we all passed out. I was laying on the ground behind the Ford, Two-Fingers was sleeping in the back seat and Brownie was stretched out in the front seat.

There I was trying to get the bottle away from this goat when the two of them woke up and wondered what the hell was going on. The baby goat was laying on the ground licking up the whiskey it spilled as quickly as it could.

When he finished drinking up all the spilled whiskey, he started to stumble around the meadow we were parked in. That's when Brownie thought it would be a good idea to give the goat a beer chaser. So, he opened up the driver's side door and waved a beer at the baby goat. Well, the goat quickly regained it's balance and jumped into the car and sat down next to Brownie who held a bottle of beer for him. Two-Fingers rummaged around and found a pair of sunglasses and a baseball cap and put it on the goat. The goat sat there real social like drinking his beer, he had very good manners for a goat.

We all had a good laugh and decided it was time to go to town but the goat would not get out of the car. Two-Fingers finally grabbed it and pulled it into the back seat with him. Brownie drove off with me in the front passenger seat and Two-Fingers in the back with this goat sitting on his lap.

Before going too far, Brownie pulled off the road and put the top down on the convertible, it was a beautiful morning. As we got close to exiting Glacier Park, a park ranger in his green government issued pickup met and passed us before suddenly making a radical U-turn. He must have noticed something was not right, who said you can fool a government employee?

Anyway, he chased after us and we eventually pulled over just outside the Park entrance near St. Mary. He got out of his vehicle and slowly walked around the Ford before stopping and staring at the drunk goat wearing sunglasses and a hat. He began to threaten us with all types of legal action for stealing a Federally owned goat. He also was going to charge us with underage drinking, we were not sure if he meant us or the goat. When we asked him about that he went ballistic. I thought for sure we were going to prison until Two-Fingers perked up and reminded the park ranger that we were no longer in the Park so he did not have legal jurisdiction, that seemed to put an end to it. So, Two-Fingers gently handed the goat to the park ranger and the goat promptly puked all over the ranger's nicely ironed lime green park ranger shirt.

Out of booze and thirsty, we stopped at a store in St. Mary and bought a case of cold beer. Two-Fingers was riding shotgun and I was now sitting in the back seat enjoying the fresh air. As we drove down a steep hill headed towards Browning, Brownie thought it would be funny to see how far down the switchbacked, windy mountainous road we could go before he had to apply the brakes. We picked up speed quickly and the trees began to fly by and the tires squealed as we went into the curves and, about a third of the way down the hill, I looked over at Two-Fingers and noticed he was bracing himself by putting both of his feet firmly into the dash.

I was looking for something to hold onto when I noticed a red Park bus coming around the curve in front of us. At the very last second, Brownie hit the brakes and swerved out of the way of the bus and we launched off the road into a meadow with one lone pine tree. Brownie slowed down considerably but was unable to avoid hitting the pine tree and the whole drivers side of the car caved in. The force of the collision caused the steering wheel to imbed itself squarely into Brownie's chest, no air bags on a 1957 Ford. In fact, there were no seat belts either. Two-Fingers didn't receive a scratch but I received a whiplash that I still feel to this day. Brownie was not as lucky, he died that day in an ambulance headed for the Cut Bank Municipal Hospital. The autopsy revealed he bled to death as a result of numerous internal injuries.

Brownie was buried in his parents hometown somewhere in Nebraska, Two-Fingers and I did not go to the funeral but we did see him off. We helped load his coffin into a dark and musky Great Northern freight car with a picture of a mountain goat on the side and as I stood on the tracks watching the freight car disappear from view, I couldn't help thinking of my parents and Stan.

Chapter 30

One of the few good things that happened that summer was the construction of the Pencil Factory. It was the Blackfeet's first major endeavor to create jobs for the populace. They had received the funding through various Federal aid programs and they were also given contracts to supply a number of Federal agencies with pencils. Everybody in town was excited about the new economic possibilities.

Two-Fingers and I went in and applied for jobs and after we completed filling out the paper application, we sat through an interview process. We were in a room packed with Blackfeet and the interviewer, Edward Bear Child, was making short work of who was hired. Basically, if you could walk and chew gum at the same time, you were hired. Two-Fingers was asked a couple of questions and then he was hired on the spot.

He sat next to me during my interview with Edward and by that time, the room was virtually empty because all the other applicants had been hired and were out partying. I sat there patiently watching Edward go over my application and after about 30 seconds he looked up at me and said, "Sorry, White Guy you are not qualified." I stared at him for awhile and finally asked, "Not qualified, what do you mean not qualified?" Edward seemed to be in a hurry to get out of there but he did take the time to tell me one more time, "You are not qualified." With that he stood up and started to leave when Two-Fingers put his hand on his arm and asked, "Not qualified, what do you mean? How can anybody screw up a pencil?" Edward got agitated but instead of going ballistic, he leaned over and whispered into Two-Fingers ear, "I decide who is hired and I am not hiring him." I do not have the best hearing in the world but even I was able to hear that. I stood up and said, "So you are not an Equal Opportunity Employer? So much for Affirmative Action, aenet. I always knew your were a racist Eddie." Edward looked at me and said, "Tough break, aenet, White Guy." With that he stomped out of the room leaving Two-Fingers and I to debate the merits of his decision. Two-Fingers could tell I was pissed off but all he could say was, "That's what you get for stealing our land." He's repeated that many times over the years and it always makes me sick.

It all worked out for the best, I was able to work full time for Bobby Racine and the night shift allowed me to go to the Blackfeet Junior College during the day, Two-Fingers and I decided to eventually go off to a four year college and make something of ourselves. Neither one of us worried about being drafted, not a lot of demand for a one handed soldier and I was number three hundred and fourteen in the draft lottery. Back then, as Vietnam was winding down, the government decided to go to a lottery system to see who was going to be drafted. Number one had the highest probability and number three hundred and sixty five had the lowest. Like I said earlier, I was three hundred and fourteen so there was no way I was going to be drafted, I thought about enlisting but was unable to imagine how I would tell my parents. So, Two-Fingers and I worked at our jobs and saved our money the best we could, Two-Fingers always had a hard time retaining money. Too many people on the Rez with bigger money problems than him and he was always generous to a fault.

Two-Fingers really did well at the Blackfeet Junior College night school. He loved American History and Native American History, he seemed to always have a history book of one kind or another in his hand. He found a calling for himself, he wanted to teach history. I was a good student too but I really didn't have the same passion for studying as he did. We still partied a lot but Two-Fingers really was driven by History, Democracy and Capitalism. He studied it endlessly. He even studied the Constitution, who does that?

During this time, the Rez was continuing it's renaissance, out with the old and in with the new. There was a big push for self governance and independence, young Blackfeet wanted to shake the chains of government dependency and they were hell bent on taking control of the Tribal Government and they were sick and tired of the Bureau of Indian Affairs telling them what to do. The Bureau of Indian affairs is a Department within the Department of Interior and some of the younger Blackfeet referred to them as the Department of the Inferior.

In particular, they hated the local head of the Bureau of Indian Affairs (BIA). His name was Trevor Kanowski and he was a new arrival who was already despised by everyone that came into contact with him, nobody on the Rez liked him, nobody.

Evidently, Kanowski came from Poland and ended up getting a cushy job with the BIA through marriage. After World War II, he ended up in Washington, D.C. where he met the sister of the current head of the Department of the Inferior. They ended up getting married and as Trevor's brother-in-law rose up the food chain, so did Trevor. Isn't nepotism a wonderful thing? Trevor's wife, Roberta, lived with him on the Rez but she was seldom seen. I saw her once at the Post Office and she was wearing sunglasses when she picked up her mail, I thought that was weird because it was a dark, cloudy day. Anyway, she dropped some letters and as I picked them up and handed them to her, I noticed she had heavy makeup on in a vain effort to conceal bruises around her eyes.

The rumor around town was that Trevor was a wife beater. It was also rumored that Trevor was a Nazi collaborator during World War II who switched sides when the Russians invaded Poland. Nobody knew for sure but everybody agreed on one thing, Trevor was a prick. He was a petty Bureaucrat that used his position of power to terrorize the Blackfeet at every opportunity, Trevor was a nickel living in a dime world. He was one of the main reasons the Blackfeet sought change, Trevor had to go.

Chapter 31

In the early 1970's, there was a lot of social unrest, people were marching and protesting throughout the United States of America. From a Native American perspective, AIM elevated the fight against injustice to a new level when they invaded and occupied Wounded Knee in South Dakota in February of 1973. A bunch of AIM members on the Rez wanted to go to Wounded Knee to join the occupation and as it turned out, 1973 was a pivotal year for the movement.

By then, Jimmy B was already out of the Army but no one knew exactly where he was. When he finally showed up in Browning, the three of us decided to go to Wounded Knee and fight for the cause. That is how we ended up there but I am getting ahead of the story. Let me take you back to February of 1973 and some of the events that lead to the Occupation of Wounded Knee.

The City of Wounded Knee is the headquarters of the Lakota Pine Ridge Reservation in South Dakota. Pine Ridge is the home of the once gallant and brave Sioux Indians, the free and independent Sioux who lived in harmony with nature; the Sioux that fought their enemies and who provided for their families. The sick, the old and the young were all cared for. They were a proud and strong people who were led by Chiefs who cared for their people more than they cared for themselves. Chiefs who did not eat until all of the people had eaten, Chiefs who were selected because of their courage and honor.

The Sioux Tribe is a combination of many bands of Sioux. Crazy Horse was the Chief of a Band of Sioux. Just as the great warrior Sitting Bull was a Chief of a Band. Prior to the invasion of their lands, the Sioux lived free and honorably. In 1973, the Sioux lived on a reservation that had shrunk in size since it was established by the 1868 Treaty of Fort Laramie. This is the treaty that stated, "This land will be yours forever more. As long as the grass grows and the sun shines." Or, as it turned out, until white settlers found gold in the Sacred Black Hills and they demanded the land. Once greed enters into things, all bets are off.

On June 25, 1876, in the Battle of the Little Big Horn, Armstrong Custer and members of the 7th Calvary paid for that sin. In the battle that is also known as Custer's Last Stand, Indians from several Tribes won a major victory in a last ditch effort to survive. Lies and broken treaties led to a battle that brought a small victory but it also brought an end to a way of life that is forever lost, a life of freedom and independence that was beautiful in its simplicity. A life built around the preservation of Mother Earth and family, a life of honor and pride. In its place, a life of government dependence and heart break began.

On February 28, 1973, The American Indian Movement (AIM) went to Wounded Knee to right a number of wrongs. The American Indian Movement was the Native American version of the Black Civil Rights movement. AIM was actually formed in the late 1960's during a period of time when radicalism was sweeping America. Fueled by years of injustice and the events going on in Vietnam, a number of city dwelling, college educated Indians began a movement to unite all Indians across America to stand up and fight back against the Federal Government.

In 1972, AIM and other activists called for a Trail of Broken Treaties march on Washington D.C. Large numbers of Indians from all over the Country descended on the Capital. Their main demands were for the re-establishment of their own sovereignty and the revalidation of treaties entered into back in the 1860's and in particular, the 1868 Fort Laramie Treaty. This treaty was problematic for the Federal Government because it was favorable to the Indians. Chief Red Cloud, Chief of the Ogala Lakota Sioux, had waged a very successful and protracted war against the United States Army which forced the Federal Government to enter into the treaty to stop further bloodshed.

From 1866-1868, against great odds, Chief Red Cloud fought the United States Army in an effort to maintain the Indian way of life. He fought to rid the Plains of the White Man and his forts. One battle in particular stands out, in December of 1866, the Ogala Lakota Sioux, along with their Cheyenne and Araphoe allies, attacked a group of 81 men who were sent out of Fort Phil Kearney on a mission to gather wood. Fort Phil Kearney is located in the north eastern part of

Wyoming near the present day town of Story, Wyoming. The Indians set a trap for them by using Crazy Horse as a decoy. Crazy Horse enticed the soldiers to chase him and they did. Thinking Crazy Horse was alone, they chased after him and rode head long into an estimated two thousand Indians, these Indians were under the leadership of Chief Red Cloud and the ambush has become known as the Fetterman Massacre. Captain William Fetterman was the commanding officer who disobeyed direct orders to not chase after Indians and the 81 deaths resulted in the most military casualties of any Indian battle to date.

For years, the Federal Government mistakenly believed that Indian Tribes would not band together to fight them. This belief was based on the fact that Tribes had traditional enemies that they hated more than the Whites. Chief Red Cloud was instrumental in galvanizing various Tribes into a fighting unit with the knowledge that the Whites were a bigger threat to their way of life, their very existence, than the Indians from other Tribes. Unified, they posed a serious threat to the Federal Government and its desire to expand westward. Divide and conquer was no longer viewed as a viable strategy.

Soon after the Fetterman Massacre, a U.S. Peace Commission was established and sent to Indian country to gather information and try to find a resolution to the "Indian problem." The Commission determined that white encroachment of Indian Territory had provoked the war and they concluded that the solution was to assign definite territories to the Plains Indians. The Tribes and the Federal Government entered into negotiations that resulted in the 1868 Fort Laramie Treaty.

That treaty resulted in the establishment of the Great Sioux Reservation. At the time, this reservation encompassed over half of what is now known as South Dakota. Over the years, through various changes in Federal Government policies, the reservation has shrunk by more than half it's original size. The unilateral taking of Indian land was not unique to the Sioux, it happened to Tribes all across America. The violation of treaties and the fact that Indians were treated like second class citizens helped to propel interest in joining a movement, any kind of movement. Native Americans were trying to find a voice, a unified voice against these injustices. That was the driving force in the creation of the American Indian Movement.

So, in February of 1973, a number of AIM members traveled to the Pine Ridge Reservation in the southwest corner of South Dakota. At one time, Pine Ridge was part of the Great Sioux Reservation. In 1889, the Federal Government decided to abolish The Great Sioux Reservation and establish five separate reservations. This resulted in the net loss of reservation land and the establishment of Pine Ridge and four other reservations. AIM decided to occupy Wounded Knee and use its occupation as a protest against the past and current wrongs being perpetrated against them by a society that had turned a deaf ear to their cries for help. Since the inception of AIM, their protests had been peaceful and they had not gotten anywhere, they were now willing to do whatever was necessary to be taken seriously.

Another factor that caused the eventual Occupation of Wounded Knee was the racist beating of Raymond Yellow Thunder. He was beaten to death for no reason other than the fact that he was an Indian. An Ogala Lakota Sioux Indian who became an alcoholic. He was a 51 year old man who was good natured and peaceful. Raymond was stripped naked to his waist and paraded around Gordon, Nebraska and killed by two white brothers who were eventually convicted of manslaughter. The oldest brother was sentenced to six years and his younger brother was sentenced to two years. Manslaughter, not first degree murder. These lenient sentences infuriated many Native Americans. AIM organized a two hundred car caravan and drove from Pine Ridge to Gordon to voice their concerns over the light sentences. Their protests were ignored.

Tensions simmered throughout the latter parts of 1972 until a new racist attack in January of 1973 brought things to a boiling point. A young Indian named Wesley Bad Heart was stabbed to death in Buffalo Gap, South Dakota. The man who was accused of the killing was the local town bully who was heard the day of the murder to say, "I am going to kill me an Indian." Once again, manslaughter charges were filed, not first degree murder charges. AIM stormed the courthouse in Custer, South Dakota and demanded justice. Police cars were overturned and burned, Justice was repeatedly demanded and it got physical. It was the first uprising and outbreak of violence since the Massacre at Wounded Knee in 1890. Several arrests were made and a small group of AIM members returned to the Pine Ridge Reservation.

The Massacre at Wounded Knee in 1890 is another illustration of the brutality that was inflicted on the Sioux Indians by the United States Army. In the years following the 1868 Fort Laramie Treaty, the United States Government continued to seize Sioux land. Buffalo, the Sioux's primary food source, were hunted to near extinction. Broken government promises to protect reservation lands from settlement and hordes of white gold miners invading their lands resulted in wide spread unrest on the reservation.

The Massacre at Wounded Knee occurred on the morning of December, 29, 1890. Earlier that month, Sitting Bull was killed at his home on the Standing Rock Reservation. Standing Rock was one of the reservations created when the Great Sioux Reservation was divided. Forty Indian policeman were sent to bring Sitting Bull back to the Agency's headquarters for questioning because reservation officials believed he was behind the unrest that was sweeping across the Sioux and Cheyenne reservations. The fact was, the Indians were starving, promises of food and shelter were broken. Dishonest reservation agents were stealing their food and selling it and for two straight years, their crops failed and they were hungry.

When the police arrived at Sitting Bull's home, his supporters tried to intervene on his behalf and when Sitting Bull resisted arrest, shots were fired resulting in his death and the death of eight of his supporters and six policeman. Fearful of reprisals, two hundred members of Sitting Bull's band fled the Standing Rock Reservation to join up with Chief Spotted Eagle and his band on the Cheyenne River Reservation. On December 23, 1890, Chief Spotted Eagle left the Cheyenne River Reservation and began to travel to the Pine Ridge Reservation and the protection of Chief Red Cloud. The group included over three hundred members of Chief Spotted Eagle's band and thirty eight members of Sitting Bull's band. On their way to the Rez, they were intercepted by the 7th Calvary Regiment and detained, the 7th Calvary was Custer's old Regiment.

As the sun rose on December 29, 1890, this group of Indians were peacefully camped beside Wounded Knee Creek. They were waiting to be transferred back to their reservations by train and they were surrounded by more than five hundred troopers of the 7th Calvary. The 7th was heavily armed and they feared that the Indians were armed too. During their search for weapons, the 7th Calvary began to scuffle with a deaf Indian who did not understand why they were taking his rifle. During the struggle, the rifle discharged a round into the air and the 7th Calvary opened fire and panic and chaos ensued, Indians grabbed their rifles and began to shoot back. The so called battle did not last long and when the death toll was added up it came to over one hundred and ninety Indians dead. Men, women and children were indiscriminately killed that day. 25 members of the 7th Calvary also died, the exact number killed by their own fire is unknown.

Wounded Knee added an additional degree of symbolism to the occupation by AIM in their fight against injustice. They fully understood that their Occupation of Wounded Knee may very well end the same way as the battle of 1890.

As news of the Occupation of Wounded Knee began to spread, hundreds of Native Americans from across America began their journey there to show their solidarity for the cause. Indians who were once good little apples were now militants ready to fight back against the recent atrocities. This was the place where Two-Fingers, Jimmy B and I found ourselves on March 8, 1973.

Again, I am getting ahead of the story. Let me back up a little bit and explain how the three of us ended up there.

Jimmy B had been discharged about six months earlier. Instead of coming home to Browning he decided to go to Long Beach, California with an Army pal who was from there. Jimmy B ended up getting work in the shipyards painting and restoring older ships. Evidently, he spent a lot of time in the hull of those ships sanding and repainting them. He said the job sucked because he was always breathing in fumes from the paint, the ventilation was very bad down there and he was high on fumes all day long and it really messed him up. When he finally had enough and came home to Browning, it took him days to regain any semblance of normal. With Jimmy B normal had always been a stretch but Two-Fingers and I both noticed he was just not all there.

Anyway, Two-Fingers hatched this scheme whereby the three of us were going to go to Wounded Knee and help our brothers in arms. Jimmy B was all for it and against my better judgment, I decided to go along with them.

The night before we left, we ended up getting plastered and I mean lit up like a torch. We were in Two-Fingers pickup he had recently bought from his uncle Fred and, as usual, we were out driving around the Rez drunk. The exact details of that night have been lost to an alcohol induced haze. All I remember was getting stuck in a huge snow bank near East Glacier and waking up the next morning and wondering how the hell are we going to get out of this mess? As it turned out, Jimmy B and Two-Fingers were wondering the same thing and after careful consideration, Two-Fingers decided Jimmy B and I needed to get out and push. We were in a hurry, we needed to get to Browning so they could pick up some money the BIA owed them.

It was very unusual that the Bureau of Indian Affairs handed out checks on a Saturday. But, they were forced to do so. Evidently, there was some accounting irregularities and once they were discovered the Blackfeet demanded immediate payment. Two-Fingers and Jimmy B planned on being the first in line to receive their $2,000.00 share, each enrolled Blackfeet had that amount owed to them. So, we needed to hurry up and get to the BIA office at the Government Square as quickly as possible. Two-Fingers paid $300.00 for the pickup and he promised to pay his uncle as soon as he got his check cashed. Plus, we needed to get to Wounded Knee so we could save the world.

So, Two-Fingers started the pickup and Jimmy B and I moved to the back of the pickup to push. We leaned down and placed our hands under the tailgate and pushed with every fibre of our being, nothing moved except a few discs in my back. It was freezing cold out and Jimmy B and I were both sweating like crazy. We finally got the pickup rocking and it broke free of the frozen ground, the tires were literally frozen to the ground. When the pickup started to move, Two-Fingers gunned the engine and the pickup finally escaped the snow bank and lurched about thirty yards down the road. Jimmy B and I ran to the pickup and jumped in. Jimmy B looked over at Two-Fingers and said, "Next time you get us stuck, you are pushing."

We arrived at the Bureau of Indian Affairs an hour before the doors opened and they were third in line to get their checks. After all, it was Saturday morning after a hard Friday night and the Blackfeet were moving a little slow.

After they received their checks, we hightailed it to the Cowboy National Bank in Cut Bank. Special arrangements were made to have the bank open on Saturday so all the Federal checks could be cashed. They were charging $10.00 per check to cash them, the Blackfeet were used to paying to get their money.

We were the first one's out of town and Two-Fingers was driving as fast as his old pickup would go. Suddenly, he looked in his rear view mirror and yelled, "Oh shit, here they come." Car after car passed us by, Blackfeet like to drive fast and they never give safety a second thought. Soon, a newer pickup overflowing with Blackfeet rushed by and one of the Blackfeet struggled to his feet and saluted us from the bed of the truck. He eventually sat back down and passed a bottle of wine to one of the other occupants before they disappeared from sight.

It took us about thirty minutes to drive to Cut Bank and when we got to the bank, the parking lot was jammed full of vehicles. Two-Fingers finally found a place to park and we walked into the bank with our heads held high. The place was literally packed, standing room only.

The tellers moved quickly and all the bank employees were on duty. Checks were cashed at a feverish pace, each check holder received $1,990.00 for a $2,000.00 Federal check. Over in the corner, the bank President was puffing on a cigar and pacing around, a small bead of sweat ran off his forehead and fell to the floor before he mopped his head with his handkerchief. He was having a hard time containing his joy, he wore a shit eating grin as he made a mental note of his profits.

Two-Fingers and Jimmy B finally made their way to the front of the line and got their checks cashed. Two-Fingers made them count out his money several times before he gathered it up and slowly walked over to the bank President and said, "You always got to make money off of us Indians aenet, you steal our land, you steal our money and you turn your back on us when we need a loan. You bankers are all a bunch of thieves." The bank full of Indians yelled their support when the bank President, now standing nervously behind a closed metal gate said, "It is just business son, it is just business." Two-Fingers walked over and slid a ten dollar bill through the bottom of the gate and said, "Well, here is another $10.00, go buy yourself a personality it will be good for business." The lobby full of Blackfeet begin to chant as we walked out the door.

After leaving the bank, we walked down the street to the Western Union where Two-Fingers wired his uncle $300.00 for the pickup along with a short note asking him to let his parents know where we were headed, we were leaving immediately for Wounded Knee and there was no way of knowing how long we would be gone.

Edward Still Smoking, the head of AIM on the Blackfeet reservation was already at Wounded Knee along with several Blackfeet who traveled there before the actual occupation began. Like I said earlier, now that the occupation was in full swing, Native Americans from all over the Country were headed there to lend their support.

A lot of the support was coming from Native Americans who served in Vietnam and Jimmy B was one of those. Jimmy B was no longer the brainwashed Indian boy who willingly went off to war to fight for his Country, long gone were his thoughts of heroism and a sense of duty. That was replaced with the reality that wars are ran by a bunch of politicians that have no skin in the game, self serving politicians who only advanced their agenda and were okay with sacrificing the lives of Patriotic Americans who were called to battle. Jimmy B gladly went to war just as thousands of other soldiers have, only to be betrayed by the very government that sent them.

The government that could find no answer other than to go to war and when these brave soldiers returned from the war, they could not walk down the streets they fought to defend without being called names and being vilified, people spat on them and called them warmongers. Vietnam cost America more than the lives of our soldiers, it took away our very soul. Protests bordering on anarchy raged across America. Vietnam, at the risk of overstating the obvious, was a very unpopular war.

Jimmy B had let his crew cut grow out and he braided his hair Indian style, he desperately needed to be Indian again. He tried to heal up from all the experiences he had in 'Nam and was sleeping better after months of nightmares that woke him in the middle of the night.

Jimmy B wore the look of a man much older than he actually was, the joy of life had been stomped out of him; the booze helped ease the pain but it was the grass that helped him sleep at night. Jimmy B knew he was one of the lucky ones, so many of his comrades came home in body bags. Too many of his comrades were injured, horrific injuries that were almost unimaginable. Maimed and twisted bodies; limbs blown off, faces disfigured, souls destroyed, Jimmie B had seen a lot and he suffered from it.

His closest friend in 'Nam was a white guy from Torrington, Wyoming by the name of Mike Edwards. Mike was a platoon leader in 'Nam and he took the safety of his men very seriously, more than once he put his own personal safety at risk to save and protect his men. His unit, which included Jimmy B, was deep in country one day when they were ambushed by a sniper. One of his men was shot and as Mike moved in to help him, he was shot in one of his elbows. According to Jimmy B, his whole arm was practically shot off but Mike kept moving to help his fallen comrade. Jimmy B was able to find the sniper high up in a tree and with one shot he brought him down, Blackfeet are very good shots.

Helicopters were sent for and soon everyone was evacuated and returned to camp. To save Mike's arm, the field doctors opened up his stomach and placed his elbow inside it and then they grafted skin and stitched around the opening until the elbow was secured to the cavity of the stomach.

Jimmy B visited him in the hospital several time before Mike was shipped back home and when Jimmy B was released, he contacted Mike and was told the procedure helped with circulation and his arm was saved, he had limited mobility but he still had his arm. Jimmy B considered himself lucky, no missing parts or outward injuries; the reality is nobody goes through war unscathed.

After wiring the money to his uncle Fred, we stopped and got a case of beer and a bag of chips before heading off to Wounded Knee. We planned on buying whatever else we needed on the way and as we left the city limits of Cut Bank, a carload of Blackfeet going to Wounded Knee passed us and gave us the finger. Two-Fingers just shook his head and reached for another beer.

We drove slowly across the great expanse of Montana only stopping for gas, supplies and the occasional piss and as the sun sat and darkness enveloped us, we drove on through the night. As we approached the South Dakota state line, our conversation ended and an uneasy silence filled the cab of the small pickup.

Chapter 32

We arrived at the city limits of Wounded Knee on the morning of March 8, 1973. By the time we arrived, the city had already been under siege for over a week. All roads in and out of town were sealed off by the Federal Government, hundreds of well armed Federal agents made entry into Wounded Knee virtually impossible.

In addition to the Federal agents, there were the local Tribal Law Enforcement agents who were beholden to the older Tribal Council members who wanted AIM off their reservation. The leaders on the Tribal Council desperately wanted things to return to the way they were before the occupation began because they had a vested interest in maintaining the status quo. They were no help to AIM. On the contrary, they were a hinderance.

The situation got worse with each passing day as shots were exchanged between the agents and the occupiers. The occupiers had their hunting rifles and the agents had automatic weapons, grenade launchers, helicopters and armored vehicles at their disposal, the agents were ordered to show restraint while high ranking government officials tried to negotiate a peaceful resolution to the problem. AIM leaders wanted action and were not interested in anymore lies, both sides were at an impasse and patience was running out.

Electricity and water was cut off and it was desperately cold and food and medical supplies were not allowed in. Added to that, anyone trying to enter Wounded Knee risked being arrested and anyone leaving was stopped, searched and questioned.

Two-Fingers, Jimmy B and I were turned away at one of the roadblocks set up outside of town. Unfamiliar with the terrain, we drove north until we came upon the town of Anderson. Anderson is a typical reservation town; full of despair and desperation. No urban or rural planning, a dirt road for a main street and houses scattered about haphazardly. Cars piled up in the front yards created a buffer zone between the streets and the houses and the only business in town, other than the Post Office, was the Palomino Bar, Cafe and Motel. It had a large, freshly paved parking lot and a fresh coat of paint. A large neon sign above the parking lot was still on even though it was mid-morning; the Palomino was a welcome sight for three weary travelers who were lost and all alone.

Jimmy B and I followed Two-Fingers into the bar and as we entered, we were immediately overwhelmed by the strong smell of cigarette smoke. It took us awhile for our eyes to adjust to the dimly lit interior and when we regained our sight we noticed a large, hand carved mahogany bar awaiting us, the place even had bar stools to sit on and booths with cushions. Over in the corner was a Juke Box playing a country tune that helped create the mood of the place, mournful and somber. In the middle of the dance floor was a pool table with a bright light shining down onto it, it was also very welcoming. The place was clean and well taken care of, not your typical reservation bar.

As we approached the counter, we were meet with a warm "hello" from the owner of the Palomino, Faye Spotted Eagle. As it turned out, Faye had recently bought the place and spent a lot of money fixing it up, more money was spent on the place than she would probably ever make. Faye was a widowed women with a lot of money. She was around forty years old but she had already lost three husbands. Each rich, white deceased husband left her a sizable inheritance. Evidently, losing them had driven her back to the Rez where she grew up.

At the far end of the bar sat an old cowboy nursing his beer, he had the look of the town on his face, worn out and tired. We quickly bellied up to the bar and ordered beer, we were thirsty from the weed and the long drive. After a few beers, we began to feel almost human again. When the music finally stopped, Faye walked down to the end of the bar and struck up a conversation with the old cowboy. "Yeah, I lost three good men." Faye said loud enough for everyone in the place to hear. She slowly looked around to see if anyone would respond to that statement when the cowboy asked, "What did they die of?" With that, Faye stood up a little straighter and said, "Well, the first two died from eating bad mushrooms." The place remained deathly quiet until the cowboy asked, "That is terrible Faye, just terrible, what did the third one die of?" Faye looked over at Two-Fingers, Jimmy B and me as we sat there staring at her with our beers raised to our lips, "Crushed skull....he wouldn't eat the mushrooms!!" Jimmy B started to choke and gag before he finally spit up beer all over the bar. Turns out, she was only joking. She had been asked so many times about her dead husbands that she came up with that story. Remember, fiction is always better than reality on any Rez.

After Jimmy B finally got control of himself Faye asked, "Do you fellas want anything to eat?" Two-Fingers took his last swallow of beer and said, "I will take a steak with fries, hold the mushrooms."

After we ate, Faye sat down in front of us and struck up a conversation. Soon, we were telling her all about why we were in South Dakota and she listened to all we had to say without voicing any objections or dousing the moment with reality. We told her about the roadblocks and our desire to get into Wounded Knee and she told us there were a lot of Native Americans picketing and demonstrating on the roads leading to Wounded Knee and to her knowledge, the only Native Americans actually in Wounded Knee were those that arrived before the occupation.

Evidently, most of the recent arrivals were staying in the town of Pine Ridge because there was more lodging there, a few Native Americans stayed in her motel the night before we arrived but they had left before she opened the bar. It was relatively quiet now, but she did not think that would last long. The area was a media mecca, news teams from all the major networks had descended and places to stay were going to get harder to find. She served us one last beer and said, "Drink up and go get some rest, you look like death warmed over. $10.00 a night and you can stay in my motel for as long as you like." After the long drive without much sleep and too much beer, she didn't have to twist our arms.

In the middle of the night, I was roused from a deep sleep by chanting and the beating of drums. I remember crawling out of bed and taking a good, long piss before walking over to the motel window and looking outside. It was pitch black outside except for a big bonfire that was burning in the middle of Faye's newly paved parking lot. I took a nice long, hot shower that helped wash away most of my drowsiness and after brushing the grime from my teeth, I splashed on some Old Spice and put on my cleanest change of clothes. I couldn't find my coat so I borrowed one of Jimmy B's green Army jackets.

I recognized a number of familiar faces as I approached the bonfire, it appeared as if half the Blackfeet Tribe had descended on the place. In the middle of the crowd stood Two-Fingers and Jimmy B smoking joints and drinking beer, Faye was smiling and busily handing out sandwiches. Two-Fingers stepped closer to the fire and yelled, "About the time I think I have gotten away from you sum bitches you show up on my doorstep, aenet." Someone in the back yelled, "You were easy to track, we just followed all the empty beer cans." Two-Fingers walked over to where Faye and I were standing and said, "Sorry about your new parking lot." Faye responded by saying, "Ah what the hell, it gives the place a lived in look. Besides, you Blackfeet are a fun bunch, just consider it my contribution to the cause." Fun bunch? Two-Fingers shook his head and let it drop. Faye turned around and walked back to the Palomino as Jimmy B approached Two-Fingers with a joint in his hand. I stood next to them patiently waiting in vain for a hit of the weed, the white guy was always the last person to get a hit.

"What the hell time is it Jimmy B?" Two-Fingers asked as he peered up at the cloudless sky. "I thought you didn't need a watch to tell the time?" Jimmy B said as he handed Two-Fingers the joint. "I usually don't when the sun is out, my guess is it's about midnight." Evidently, Two-Fingers woke up shortly before I did.

"Close, it's only 11. You and White Guy were snoring so loud I couldn't sleep so I decided to find us a way to get into Wounded Knee without getting shot. I found a spot that may work and as I was headed back this way, I ran into this crew demonstrating at one of the checkpoints and I talked them into coming back here and staying so we can get a plan of action figured out. Most of them want to go back home, they are pretty frustrated and tired, they got kicked out of a white owned motel a few nights back and they have been sleeping in their cars ever since. Too cold and miserable out for that shit and when I explained the situation to Faye, she agreed to let them stay if we all behaved. She even said it was okay to build a small fire, just kinda got out of hand. Good woman Faye, it's hard to beat a woman that owns a Bar, aenet Two-Fingers?" I stood next to them as they continued to pass the joint between themselves, I figured I must have said something bad about them in my sleep.

Two-Fingers stood there listening but he was staring at Faye who was standing on the other side of the fire with a beer in her hand, she was staring intently into the fire and seemed to be in a trance. Her hair was pulled back from her face and held in place by a beaded barrette, this accentuated her high cheek bones and coal black eyes. She was not wearing any makeup but her lips glistened red as she sipped on her beer. She wore a beaded buckskin jacket over a aqua blue blouse and her Levi jeans were tight on her body yet they fit loosely over her boots. She was a beautiful Sioux Indian who looked younger then she was, much younger.

She slowly raised her eyes and smiled softly when she noticed Two-Fingers staring at her. Then, she raised her index finger and motioned for Two-Fingers to join her. As he approached her, he started to say something and she just put her finger on his lips and said, "Do you dance? I feel like dancing." With that, she took his hand and they walked to the Palomino Bar. I stood alone next to the fire, the only white person in the crowd. Finally, I decided to go to the bar and get a beer and as I turned to walk away, the crowd yelled, "Just messing with you White Guy, come back." It's a lot of fun being the only white person in a crowd of Indians, you should try it sometime.

As I entered the bar, I noticed that the pool table was moved off to the side of the dance floor and a few couples were dancing to an old country and western tune. Faye and Two-Fingers were in center of the dance floor moving rhythmically to the music as they slowly melted into each others arms; they were so close, Two-Fingers belt buckle began to shine. They danced, drank beer and laughed until closing time. The party outside was still going strong when Faye took Two-Fingers by the hand and led him to her room. I sat at the bar thinking it probably had been a long time since either one of them had sex. Faye by choice, Two-Fingers because he could never find anyone hard up enough. Drunk on free beer, I stumbled outside and partied until morning with my Blackfeet brothers and sisters. Booze can either make you social or ringy. Me, I have always been a very social guy in a ringy world.

Years later, Two-Fingers told me about the night he and Faye spent together. Evidently, they made love several times and each time they did, Two-Fingers learned a little more about what a woman liked. Faye showed him things he had no knowledge of, his previous sexual encounters were always with eighteen year old girls. Faye was a women and she knew what she liked and what she wanted, he said it was a night of learning, experimentation and pleasure. She taught him to slow down and take his time, not to rush. He turned out to an able and willing student and Faye a very thankful teacher. As the sun came up and before Two-Fingers left, Faye raised herself up on one elbow and asked, "Will I see you again? If not, I will understand. I know all there is to know about loss, you could say I am currently between heartbreaks." Two-Fingers told me he was confused by that statement and all he was able to do was softly close the door behind him.

Later that day, Jimmy B took us to the spot he had chosen for our entry into Wounded Knee. "So let me see if I have this correct, we are going to load up my pickup with provisions and we are going to bust into Wounded Knee." Two-Fingers said as he tried to wrap his mind around the plan that Jimmy B came up with. We were seated in his pickup on top of a hill overlooking Wounded Knee and to get there, we had to take a small, narrow cattle trail. "That's right, you got it." Jimmie B said as he gave a fifth of Jim Beam back to Two-Fingers. "We wait until three in the morning and then we make a mad dash down the hill and onto the streets of Wounded Knee, I talked it over with the guys at the bonfire last night and that is what we came up with."

Two-Fingers took a long pull on the whiskey, shook his head and said, "The best you guys could come up with is that we are going to risk our lives, my pickup and any future government payouts by crossing this open range in darkness to get into Wounded Knee?" "Oh yeah, it has to be at night and in the darkness or they will see us. You will have to turn your headlights off so it is totally dark." Jimmy B reached across me to take the whiskey from Two-Fingers but he would not let it go.

"That's the plan?" Two-Fingers asked as he took another drink of whiskey. "Where will our Blackfeet brothers in arms be while we are committing suicide?" "They are going to help with a diversion." Jimmy B said as he finally wrenched the bottle from Two-Fingers hand. "It is all worked out, there will be a commotion at that checkpoint down there at three in the morning. Jimmy B pointed down to the roadblock. "While the Feds are trying to figure out what is going on, we take off down this hill as fast as we can." "Without any lights on?" Two-Fingers then asked another question, "What about the helicopters?" Jimmy B was clearly getting frustrated when he replied, "Look, if you want to head home, we can go home. I thought you wanted to help make a difference. Besides, you haven't heard my entire diversion idea." Jimmy B then lit a joint and handed it directly to Two-Fingers. "Fair enough, what is your plan?" Two-Fingers asked as he accepted the joint. I sat there watching these two drink whiskey and smoke pot until I finally had enough and took the bottle and the joint away from them. They both smiled and said, "Just fucking with you, White Guy." Of course, neither one of them asked me what I thought of the idiotic plan so I just sat there and got stoned.

"Well, while you and Faye were dancing the night away last night, I was doing some additional investigating. At the bonfire, I ran into a Sioux by the name of Arthur Lone Elk and it turns out that Arthur works for the Sioux Tribe as a wrangler of the Tribal Buffalo herd. It also turns out that the Sioux have one of the largest buffalo herds in all of America, thousands of buffalo. As he and I were talking, an idea popped into my head. What would happen if a few buffalo stampeded through the checkpoint I saw yesterday? That checkpoint down at the bottom of the hill." He said as he reached in vain for the joint. "As we spoke, it became obvious that Arthur wanted to do something for the cause but he didn't want to quit his job and join the Occupation. There are a lot of our Native American brothers thinking the same thing. So, after a few beers and a couple of joints, Arthur and I came up with the stampeding idea. Here is what is going to happen, Arthur and a couple of Sioux buddies are going to round up a hundred head or so of the buffalo and at precisely three in the morning, they are going to stampede them through that checkpoint." Jimmy B said as he pointed to the checkpoint at the bottom of the hill for the third time. "It should cause one hell of a ruckus and that is when we drive into Wounded Knee."

Two-Fingers thought on it for awhile before he said, "It would be easier if we just snuck in on foot and left the pickup with Faye." "Yeah, it would be, but the story on the street is that the occupants are running out of food and we can be of great help bringing in a few essentials." Jimmy B said as he slowly nodded his head.

We sat there on top of the hill for a long time surveying the scene in silence. We smoked a couple more joints and pondered the situation before Two-Fingers finally said, "Well, what the hell, it is a good day to die." "Well, technically it would not be today that we die, Two-Fingers. It would be more like 3:10 tomorrow morning that we would die." "Crack you, Jimmy B." Two-Fingers said as he started his pickup, we needed to get some supplies so we drove off in search of a grocery store.

We found a grocery store thirty miles away in Hot Springs, South Dakota. Hot Springs is not a reservation town and that became quite obvious when we parked in the grocery store parking lot and noticed a group of white citizens staring at us and pointing fingers. It just so happened that the locals were tired of all the commotion and publicity and wanted things to settle down.

We jumped out of the pickup and hastily entered the store where we each grabbed a large grocery cart and started loading up sugar, flour, coffee, canned meat and sacks of potatoes, we paused briefly at the beer cooler before deciding against it. As we were paying for the supplies, I glanced out the front window and noticed a mob forming around the pickup, white men and women of all ages were talking loudly and waving their arms in the air.

We were loading all the provisions into the bed of the pickup when someone in the crowd asked what we were going to do with all those groceries. We didn't say a word, we just quickly finished loading everything and as we started to get into the cab a big cowboy got in front of Two-Fingers and said, "You deaf Indian? I asked what are you doing with all those groceries?" Two-Fingers started yelling at the top of his voice, "We are going to go for a picnic, do you want to come?!!" Before anyone could answer, Two-Fingers jumped into the driver's seat and started the pickup and began to back up very slowly. "Watch your toes." He yelled, "You got to be careful around vehicles, I lost most of my hand when a drunk cowboy ran over the top of me." Two-Fingers was waving his hand out the window as the crowd slowly backed away with a look of horror on their faces. "Saved by the claw again, aenet, Two-Fingers." Jimmy B said as he glanced over his shoulder.

Around 2 A.M. the next morning, we were strategically parked on top of the hill trying not to doze off when we noticed the earth was shaking. Even though it was very cold out, we rolled down the windows so we could listen to what was causing all the racket. As the pickup trembled, the roar got louder and louder, deafeningly loud. It was a dark, cloudy night and we couldn't see five feet in front of us and as we strained to make out the sound we suddenly and simultaneously screamed, "BUFFALO!!!"

Two-Fingers tried to start the pickup but he was shaking so badly the keys kept falling to the floorboard. Finally, on his third attempt, he started the pickup and drove down the cow path towards the open meadow, the roar from the stampeding buffalo was deafening and the visibility sucked.

Buffalo after buffalo began to run past us and the dust was so thick we could not see anything except buffalo, hundreds of buffalo tore up the ground as they stampeded into the night. We were driving on the trail with our lights off when all of a sudden a huge bull buffalo landed on top of the hood and stared at us through the windshield before falling off and running away. Two-Fingers turned his lights on just as we went airborne and as we were falling from the sky, a bullet hit the windshield and wedged itself into the seat between Two-Fingers and me. When we landed, we landed hard and it took us awhile before we realized we were in the middle of Wounded Knee.

Native Americans in various stages of dress came running towards us waving their hunting rifles and screaming obscenities. Three very large Native Americans opened the doors and pulled Two-Fingers, Jimmy B and me out of the pickup and threw us to the ground. Soon, a larger group of Native Americans were gathered around staring down at us, some of them had their rifles aimed at our heads. It was pitch black outside except for the dim light coming from the pickup's headlights.

We were laying on the ground when Two-Fingers stared into one of the rifle barrels and said, "You Sioux have been shooting at us Blackfeet for centuries, still haven't killed any of us." He smiled and slowly stood up and brushed the dust off of his pants. As the crowd moved in towards us someone yelled, "Is that you Two-Fingers? It has to be you, no one else in the world is that mouthy." Eddie Still Smoking pushed his way through the crowd and said, "Don't shoot these three fools, it would be a waste of bullets."

It was right around then that Arthur Lone Elk and three other horseback riders came racing down main street towards the assembled crowd. He slowly got off his horse and walked up to Jimmy B and said. "Well, it looks like I am going to be joining the cause after all. We tried to cut out a hundred head of buffalo and we ended up spooking the whole damn herd and the next thing I knew, we had 3,000 head on the run and no way to turn them. Once a buffalo decide's to run, they run. They tore up fencing, the roadblock and everything in between and they are still on the run. I figure I am either going to get fired, arrested, ran out of town, tar and feathered or banished, so I am staying in here where it is safe." "Well, I don't know how safe it is in here but you are welcome, you are all welcome." Eddie Still Smoking said as he swept his arm in the air in a wide arc. "Even you three." As he disappeared into the night, the crowd slowly dispersed leaving us new recruits standing there looking at each other.

As it turned out, we were very popular once they found out we brought in a bunch of provisions, supplies were limited and every little bit helped. The first few days we were in Wounded Knee were not too bad but that all changed when our food ran out. We were under constant pressure from the authorities, gunfire would just randomly break out. Luckily, nobody had been killed but tensions were high, real high.

Chapter 33

A week quickly passed and I was freezing as my night shift ended, another bitterly cold night in Wounded Knee had come and gone. In the distance, a reservation dog howled mournfully. It's sorrowful moaning was soon eclipsed by the howling of dogs from all around town. The howling was a nightly ritual from a bunch of dogs that were not completely domesticated nor were they truly wild and free. In that way, they were like the human inhabitants on the Rez. As the sun began to rise and the last reservation dog stopped howling, the town of Wounded Knee slowly began to show signs of life; the freezing cold made it hard to stir from a comforting bed.

Life on the Rez wasn't the same after AIM took over Wounded Knee and many of the permanent residents were beginning to resent their presence, their initial enthusiasm was beginning to wain. Two-Fingers, Jimmy B and I were wide awake by the time the last dog stopped howling. We were assigned night patrol duties and we took the assignment very seriously, it was an important task and we wanted to do the best we could. We were not getting much sleep but once we were awake, the adrenaline took over.

The longer the Occupation lasted, the more determined the government was to end it. Like I said earlier, they had cut off the power and water along with our food supply hoping to either freeze us into submission or to flat out starve us. Still, AIM had galvanized the volunteers into a tight fighting unit, we were outgunned but we all were dedicated and committed to the cause.

Jimmy B was especially vocal and active. He walked around town with a hunting rifle that was assigned to him and when he was on patrol, he constantly snapped the rifle in place and aimed it at everything that moved, seldom firing but always on the ready. Two-Fingers and I watched him do this time and time again and we both worried that Jimmy B was reliving Vietnam and feared he could come unglued at any time. Just a few days into our stay, Jimmy B had taken a shot at a helicopter and he wanted another shot at it, he was sick and tired of the light that beamed down from the helicopter and swore that if it held still long enough, he was gong to shoot it out.

That night, the three of us were walking around the perimeter of the camp trying to stay warm when Two-Fingers and I decided to go to the bonfire to get some coffee and warm up. As we approached the fire, a helicopter suddenly appeared and turned on its spotlight. We both glanced over at Jimmy B just in time to see him raise up his rifle and take a shot. Seconds later the light went out and the helicopter suddenly veered off and headed towards the south of town.

"Jimmy B is bound and determined to shoot down that helicopter," Two-Fingers said as he lit a joint and handed it to me. He exhaled a cloud of smoke into the cold night air before continuing, "He has gone full blown military over the last couple of days and his nightmares are getting worse and he is not sleeping much, I think he is beginning to lose it. He constantly talks about 'Nam and killing gooks." I pondered the situation before answering, "I know, I think we should seriously consider getting him the hell out of here before he goes completely ape shit."

The next morning, Jimmy B, Two-Fingers and I were summoned to the command center by Edward Still Smoking the head of AIM for the Blackfeet Nation. We made the short walk to the Catholic Church which served as headquarters for AIM. We walked up the cement and stone steps and opened the door to the church, it was dimly lit and smokey inside. There were a few candles burning by the alter and the leaders of AIM were standing under a stained glass window absorbing the sunlight. Standing next to Edward was Jack Little Wolf, the AIM leader for the Northern Cheyenne and Lenny Iron Horse the AIM leader of the Sioux. They were dressed in their traditional Tribal garb and their long, black hair rested freely on their shoulders.

"We called you here this morning so we can have a good talk. It has been awhile since we were all together in Browning at your uncle Billy's Sweat Lodge." Jack said as he nodded his head towards Two-Fingers. "A lot has changed since that time. Change is what we want to talk about with you." Lenny interrupted by saying, "We are trying to draw attention to our plight as Native Americans. We are here to fight against the injustices that have been perpetuated upon us for over a hundred years. We are asking the United States Government to live up to their own laws." Two-Fingers, Jimmy B and I looked at each other and realized we would be there awhile so we sat down in the front row of pews and stretched out. "We are not trying to kill anybody but we will die for the cause." Lenny looked over at Jimmy B who stared back without blinking. "It is not a good idea to start shooting at helicopters, we understand that the government can wipe us out at any time. The purpose of this occupation is to bring national attention to our Treaty Rights, the oppressive nature of Federal and Tribal Governments and our desire to be treated as human beings." Lenny took a deep breath and was interrupted by Edward, "Brothers, we appreciate your help, it is good to have a white guy fighting with us but do you really know what you are fighting for? You need to understand why you are here. This is not a game, we want to be recognized as a sovereign people. That is what was established by the Fort Laramie treaty of 1868. This is our last chance at sovereignty, we are not asking for anything more than what the law say's is ours." "So, what you are saying is, I don't get to shoot anybody?" Jimmy B asked as Two-Fingers and I fidgeted in our seats. "Only if we are shot at first." Lenny said as he stared back at Jimmy B. "The Federal Government wants this to end peacefully and they are sending a couple of Senators for more peace talks. We need to chill out and hear what they have to say and if they lie to us like in the past, I will be the first one to shoot."

Lenny sat down next to us and talked about the allegedly corrupt local Sioux Tribal Council and their leaders and how they favored their friends and family for jobs and benefits. He spoke of the unbearable hardships the Sioux Nation had endured for decades. He spoke of Red Cloud, Black Elk, Sitting Bull and Crazy Horse and how they fought for the sovereignty of the Sioux. Lenny wanted to restore dignity and pride to his people by shaking off the chains of Federal Government dependence, his was a broader message than just occupation. He envisioned the support of all minorities in his quest for equality. The support had not yet appeared but he was still hopeful. He talked about the spirituality of his quest and the importance of traditionalists like Billy Spotted Eagle, Two-Fingers uncle. He talked about the importance of being a human being, an Indian. The threat of violence was important in getting the public's attention but he did not want to see his brothers sent home in body bags, he too had seen enough of that in 'Nam.

He spoke for over an hour and as he prepared to leave he extended his hand to each of us and quoted Red Cloud by saying, "I will fight no more forever." He then turned slowly on the heels of his moccasins and walked down the row of pews and out into the morning air.

We later found out that the Sioux Tribal Council was growing increasingly frustrated with the occupation of Wounded Knee by the members of AIM. They depicted them as trouble makers and wanted help from the military to rid the area of these "rabble rousers." Their interests were being challenged and they had no qualms about using fire power to rid themselves of the nuisance. They opposed any efforts that would bring a peaceful settlement of the problem, they wanted the Federal Marshall and the FBI to use force in taking care of the problem.

After the helicopter was shot, tensions in and around Wounded Knee grew exponentially with each passing day. The meeting Lenny spoke about between AIM and the Federal Government officials did not result in a peaceful resolution to the problem. The AIM leaders were told that the Congressional Act of 1871 prohibited negotiations between Indians and the government and when they pointed out that the Fort Laramie Treaty of 1868 pre-dated the legislation by three years and should take precedent, the Senators got up and walked out of the negotiations; the U.S. Government had too much to lose if that treaty was fully recognized.

Once the government shut down the negotiations, random gun shots increased dramatically. The public outcry for past injustices and the support from other minorities was virtually non-existent. The press labeled the occupiers as romantic primitives that were living in a dream world, they did not appreciate the fact that Indians fought and died in 'Nam only to come home and be treated as second-class citizens.

This irony did not escape Jimmy B and as each night passed he grew more and more aloof. He never slept, all he wanted to do was patrol and carry his rifle. He exchanged gun shots with people he could not even see and this became a nightly ritual so Two-Fingers and I decided to get him out of Wounded Knee and back to Browning.

We had very little to pack, all we had to do was convince Jimmy B to leave and that was not going to be easy as I pointed out to Two-Fingers, "Jimmy B is a warrior and we are going to have to trick him to get him out of here, he will not go willingly. He hasn't let go of that rifle in days." Two-Fingers was looking at the sun setting behind the distant hills when he said, "I know and he is too big and strong to kidnap and too smart to be easily fooled. I say we tell him we have to go get supplies and that we can stay at the Palomino while we round them up. He likes that place, it was the last place he was semi-normal, at least it is worth a try. We have to do something he walks around out in the open firing into the hills."

Soon after our talk, a helicopter suddenly appeared from out of nowhere. It flew towards us with the setting sun directly behind it. As it got closer, Jimmy B crouched down and took aim, he shot several times before someone in the helicopter started shooting back. He was firing as fast as he could when all of a sudden he stood straight up and dropped his rifle, blood gushed out of his green Army fatigue jacket. Jimmy B looked up towards the sky and raised both of his arms into the air before falling over backwards. Two-Fingers and I ran over to him as all hell broke loose, Native Americans began to return fire with a vengeance.

The helicopter pilot must have been shot because the helicopter began to spin out of control before it crashed into the Catholic Church and as soon as that happened, the place became eerily quiet and all shooting stopped. Two-Fingers ran towards the burning helicopter and was getting close to it when it exploded, his attempt at providing help went up in smoke. The church quickly burned to the ground as a group of Native Americans gathered to watch, the water had been turned off weeks before and there wasn't much they could do about it.

Two-Fingers quickly recovered from getting knocked on his ass from the explosion but he and I were both stunned, Two-Fingers from the blast and me from losing Jimmy B.

We carried Jimmy B's lifeless body to the bed of Two-Fingers pickup and carefully lowered it in. Two-Fingers went to look for some blankets to wrap his body in and I climbed up on the bed of the pickup and gently cradled Jimmy B's head in my lap. Two-Fingers returned with blankets and a canvass tarp and we wrapped Jimmy B in the blankets and tied wire around his body to keep the blankets in place and then we placed the tarp over his body. After we were finished, we sat on the tailgate and surveyed the scene.

As the church smoldered in the distance, Indians from all of the Tribes came by and offered a few kind words and their condolences. The leaders of AIM were initially busy with the wounded and only stopped by after giving aid to the living. "Jimmy B was a great warrior and will be missed. He is now with the Great Spirit in the Sky and is at peace." Edward Still Smoking said as he stared up into the stars. Two-Fingers listened to him for awhile and then abruptly jumped off the tailgate and said, "Ah bullshit, he is dead and I am taking him home. Get in the pickup White Guy, we are getting out of here."

I jumped down from the bed of the truck and walked over to the driver's seat and sat down, Two-Fingers secured the tarp and then jumped into the passenger seat. Edward yelled at us to stop and think about what we were doing. He said it was a crime to remove a dead body from the scene of a shooting and we would go to jail, all of this fell on deaf ears.

He continued to yell as I slowly drove across the prairie with the lights off and as we approached a small hill we could still hear Edward yelling, "It's illegal to take a dead body across state lines, you are going to get arrested." His voice faded away as we reached the top of the hill surrounding Wounded Knee. Two-Fingers looked at me and said, "Fuck a bunch of laws."

To my complete amazement, we were not shot at or stopped. Must have been because of all the confusion back at Wounded Knee, both sides were probably wondering, now what? I was able to steer the pickup onto an isolated dirt road before needing to turn the lights on. We drove west and soon we were passing through Anderson at around 3 A.M., the Palomino was closed for the night. The only light on was the neon light above the billboard that advertised the Palomino Bar, Cafe and Motel and as we drove by, the sign flickered a few times and then suddenly went dark. I drove slowly onward and Two-Fingers stared straight ahead, he never said a word. Soon, Anderson was in our rear view mirror and Browning was on our minds.

We drove in silence, each of us in our own world of contemplation and we did not stop until we hit the Montana state line where a big blue sign welcomed us to, "Montana, The Big Sky Country." The sun was rising steadily behind us as we pulled into the first gas station we saw. We quickly filled up the pickup and took turns using the bathroom, Jimmy B was never left unattended. Two-Fingers adjusted the tarp that covered him, it was still desperately cold out so we decided against getting ice for the body. We drove straight through to Browning, each taking our turn at the wheel.

As we drove across Montana, we each shared our quilt for not getting Jimmy B out of Wounded Knee sooner. Two-Fingers was taking it extra hard and kept saying he should have said no to Jimmy B when he wanted to go fight for the cause, he wasn't the same since he came back from 'Nam. "Don't blame yourself, Jimmy B needed to go. He needed a cause like Stan needed a cause, some people need causes. They fight for all of us and that is just the way they are, thankfully. My dad fought too but he never talked about it, World War II veterans seldom do. Has Max ever talked about his war experience?" "Pops? Hell no, he never spoke of it, at least not to me. You are right about that generation, they never talk about what they had to do or anything, they all seem to suffer in silence. Tough dudes all of them, makes me proud to be an American." Two Fingers said as he pulled out his last joint from the front pocket of his Levi jacket. "At least they were treated as hero's when they came back home from fighting the enemy. 'Nam vets are treated like shit and are no less the hero's, not their fault the war is so unpopular, they did their duty nonetheless." Two-Fingers took a hit and passed the joint to me and I took a long, satisfying hit before saying, "I hope Stan is released soon, it must be hell being in a P.O.W. camp in 'Nam. The stories I have read about how prisoners are treated makes me sick to my stomach." Two-Fingers took the joint from me and said, "The thing I do not get about all these wars is once they are over all the people we helped quickly forget about American sacrifices. Look at Russia, we saved them from speaking German and they threaten us with nuclear war. I remember in grade school they taught us to get down on the floor and hide under our desks in the event of a nuclear attack." Two-Fingers re-lit the joint and took a long hit before continuing, "I am tired of hiding on the floor, screw all of them."

Day turned into night as we travelled on, we drove at a pretty good clip considering we were in an old, beat up pickup. We stopped in Great Falls and gassed up for the last time before getting to Browning. Two-Fingers was driving and I was curled up against the passenger door trying to sleep when we passed through the town of Dupuyer. Soon, we were in the heart of Blackfeet Indian Country and not far from Jimmy B's parents house near Badger Creek.

As we pulled off Highway 89 and travelled down the dirt road leading to Jimmy B's house, Two-Fingers was reminded of their childhood together and he began to shake and it took him awhile to gather himself. We sat in their front yard staring up at their house for quite awhile in complete silence.

There was a lone light on in the kitchen and smoke was coming out of the chimney, it was March and very cold in the Northern Rockies. I was wide awake and apprehensive about giving Jimmy B's parents the bad news. After Two-Fingers turned off the ignition, we looked at each other and slowly got out of the pickup and walked up the front steps of their house.

We wiped our feet on a small mat that said, "Welcome" and then we entered without knocking. Jimmy B's parents were awake but not yet dressed for the day, they were sitting in their robes at a round coffee table in the middle of their small, wood stove heated kitchen. They smiled at us and looked behind us expecting to see Jimmy B and when they did not see him their blood drained from their faces as they slowly rose from their chairs to greet us.

They had lost loved ones all too often on the Rez and they instinctively knew something was wrong. Two-Fingers and I were offered food and coffee and a place to sit before we tried to explain what had happened to Jimmy B. How can you possibly explain away the death of someone's child? Jimmy B's mother was inconsolable and his father was hard faced and stoic. They held each other and tried to make sense of it all as Two-Fingers explained what had happened and that we had brought Jimmy B home for a proper Blackfeet burial, he could not bear the thought of Jimmy B being buried anywhere but in Blackfeet Country.

After listening to all she could stand to hear, Jimmy B's mother rushed outside to be with her son while Jimmy B's father thanked us both for bringing him home. He then started his long walk to the pickup as Two-Fingers and I stood looking out their front window. As he approached the pickup, he stopped suddenly and grabbed onto the front bumper in an effort to steady himself, he needed to gather all of his strength before he looked down at his only son laying dead in the bed of an old, worn out pickup.

Chapter 34

Arrangements for Jimmy B's burial were made quickly, death is a too common feature of life on the Rez and the whole Tribe rallied around to offer assistance. Jimmy B was buried near where he had lived, at the cemetery in Heart Butte.

The cemetery has been used by the Blackfeet for nearly a hundred years. In the old days, long before the Blackfeet got "Religion" the dead were laid to rest above ground so that their Spirit could easily soar to the sky. There have been laws in place for decades that no longer allow them to do that so Jimmy B was buried in the cold, hard ground that is the Heart Butte cemetery.

Actually, it is a beautiful spot as far as cemeteries go. It is in a large open meadow surrounded by pine trees and it lies at the foot of the Rocky Mountains surrounded by a barb wire fence and a cattle guard at the entrance keeps the large animals out. As you drive into the cemetery, there is an arched wrought iron entryway with a sign at the top that simply says, "Cemetery." There are hundreds of white wooden crosses that dot the landscape and occasionally you will find a granite headstone, granite headstones are expensive and the Blackfeet are poor. Each Memorial Day you will see the Blackfeet cleaning and repairing crosses at all the reservation cemeteries; plastic flowers are tied to the crosses in a vain attempt at keeping them there, the high winds eventually blow them away leaving behind the unceremonious reality of death. The final resting place; cold, heart breaking and forever.

Jimmy B's funeral was well attended, the small Catholic Church was filled to capacity and the overflow stood outside the church in silence. The Catholic priest, Father Ian Kelly, waxed poetically about Jimmy B and his contributions to society and this seemed to provide great comfort to his parents. Two-Fingers uncle, Billy Spotted Eagle performed an old, traditional ceremony that was appreciated by all. Over the previous couple of years, the Blackfeet came to embrace their old traditions and their response was sincere, the ceremony was a mixture of old and new.

Outside the church, the drummers and singers chanted a welcoming song as Jimmy B's casket was carried down the church's front steps. Two-Fingers and I were at the front of the casket holding it firmly on our shoulders with the help of four other pall bearers. We gently carried the casket across the parking lot and over the cattle guard and into the cemetery where we placed it on some outstretched ropes laying on the ground. In unison, we lowered the ropes and gently placed Jimmy B's body into the hole that was dug by the burial committee.

The Blackfeet crowded to the front of the procession as Billy spoke soothing Blackfeet and burned sage and blew the smoke in all four directions. Just as he finished, the crowd was startled by a twenty-one gun salute that was performed by the local Veterans of Foreign Wars Committee. The smell of smoke and gunpowder lingered in the air as Jimmy B's parents accepted an American flag from the head of the committee. Jimmy B's dad shook his hand vigorously and returned a sharp, crisp salute as his wife wept softly and the drummers and singers wailed and chanted loudly as the crowd slowly turned and walked to their cars.

The burial committee was shoveling dirt onto Jimmy B's casket when Two-Fingers intervened, he insisted that the two of us would finish burying Jimmy B. The head of the committee strongly objected until Billy Spotted Eagle said it was okay. Billy told him that he would stay with us and make sure it was done right, no sense in everybody staying when two could do the job. Billy won the argument and Two-Fingers and I removed our coats and ties and started to shovel dirt onto Jimmy B's casket. We shoveled fast and furious as Billy looked on. We were drenched in sweat by the time we smoothed the last of the dirt onto Jimmy B's grave. After doing so, we leaned on our shovels and admired our handy work.

"That should be enough for today, aenet. It will be getting dark soon and you can come back tomorrow and finish up. I made a special cross for Jimmy B and you can place it tomorrow." Billy said as he gathered up his supplies. "Not yet Uncle, we are not finished." Two-Fingers and I ran over to his pickup and gently removed a granite headstone that we purchased with the little money we had left, we had wrapped it in the tarp that covered Jimmy B on his trip home. It was a special rush order and we had just picked it up from Cut Bank earlier that day, Jimmy B was going to have a proper granite headstone compliments of his two best friends.

Two-Fingers and I unloaded a bag of cement and a bucket that we had brought along especially for this occasion. From a nearby stream, we gathered enough water to mix with the cement and when the texture was just right, we carefully positioned the headstone. It laid at the head of the grave flat on the ground. Most granite headstones rise into the air but not Jimmy B's, it would lie flat, out of the wind. Hopefully, it would not erode as quickly as the upright ones do. When we finished placing the headstone in its new, permanent home we stood back and took a look. Billy walked over to the headstone and nodded his head. The inscription on his stone says:

Here lies James Bailey No Runner
A Blackfeet Warrior
Who died Fighting for his Country

"No dates or anything, Nephew? Uncle Billy asked as he stared at the stone. "Ran out of money. Besides, Jimmy B never knew what time it was or what day it was and now it really doesn't matter, aenet." Two-Fingers said as he packed dirt around the stone.

After we buried Jimmy B, Two-Fingers and I went on a three day runner. We partied all over the Rez and if we couldn't find anyone to party with, we partied alone. We drank and drank until we drank ourselves dry and when we finally sobered up, we found ourselves in the basement of Two-Fingers parent's apartment house. After three days of hard drinking we went looking for a refuge and we found it there. Sleepy, hungover and hungry we walked up the stairs to the living quarters to face the music.

"Well, look what the cat drug in, aenet. Nice to see you could come by and say hello to your family. Did you drink the bootleggers dry or are you hiding from the cops?" Max asked as he lit a Camel cigarette while sitting in his wheelchair. The smell of the smoke caused my head to spin and my stomach began to churn; his loud voice sounded like a thousand buffalo stampeding through my brain. I quickly found a place to sit down just as the living room began to spin out of control. In a voice that was barely audible, Two-Fingers said, "I think we drank the whole Rez dry, must have. I can't remember leaving any booze behind. Have you seen my pickup? I think I misplaced it somewhere." Two-Fingers asked as he leaned his head back against the sofa.

"Nobody's seen your pickup, Donny R." Pam said as she handed him a large glass of water. She gave one to me too but I was unable to hold onto it, I was barely hanging onto my seat. Finally, I took the water and with both hands on the glass, I slowly raised it to my lips and drank it down in one long, satisfying gulp. Unable to speak, I handed the glass back to Pam who offered a refill. I just nodded my head and leaned back against the sofa. Pam returned with two more large glasses of water and said, "Maybe I should hook up the garden hose for you two."

"Now you know the main reason I quit drinking." Max said as he stomped out his cigarette in the ashtray on his lap. "You are young and will heal physically in a day or two. At my age, hangovers last forever. The sickness eventually fades but the damage caused by all the years of drinking never does. You hurt yourselves, your family and your friends. This damage never goes away. How long are you boys planning on punishing yourselves with drink? When you are young you drink to have fun but eventually it turns to punishment. You see all the winos around town? They are all punishing themselves for something."

The living room fell quiet as we contemplated the advice and with slightly trembling hands, we raised our glasses to our mouths and savored the cold water like two lost travelers who found an oasis in the middle of the desert. Eventually, the room quit spinning but it remained slightly tilted.

"Oh, I almost forgot. A letter from your father came a few weeks ago, Tony. I meant to give it to you at Jimmy B's funeral but forgot all about it." Max slowly rose from his wheelchair with the help of his prosthetic leg and a cane. He shuffled over to a bookcase in the corner of the room and searched through some papers until he finally found the letter and then he handed it to me before making his way back to his wheelchair.

I glanced down at the letter but had a hard time opening it. Two-Fingers reached for it with his left hand and ripped the envelope open before handing it back to me. I struggled to focus on the writing until my eyes adjusted to the morning light that peeked in through the window behind me.

Dear Son,

I hope this letter finds you well. I have no way of contacting you in Wounded Knee so I am sending this letter to Max and Pam. I wish I could talk to you in person about this but that is not possible.

Your mother and I found out the day after you left for Wounded Knee that your brother is dead. It is with the greatest sense of sorrow that I have to tell you this. This is something no brother or parent should ever be told but it is a fact, a fact that I am desperately trying to deal with.

An Army Captain from the Department of War came to our home and gave us the news. It seems the prisoner camp your brother was in was bombed by the U.S. Air Force, they claim they had no idea that it was a prison camp. When the ground troops arrived they found the remains of several Americans but they did not find Stan's body. However, they did find his dog tags which he gave to us before leaving.

Your mother and I are holding up as well as possible. Please be safe and say a prayer for your brother. We miss you. Love, Dad

Two-Fingers stared at me while I read the letter and he noticed my hands were shaking violently. I remember running into the kitchen and vomiting into the sink, all the while anchoring myself to the counter so I did not fall over. I could hear Two-Fingers reading the letter out loud to his parents and when I returned to the living room, Pam quietly wept and Max stared at the letter before he said very quietly, "And they wonder why a man drinks."

Chapter 35

For Two-Fingers and me, the spring of 1973 seemed particularly gloomy. In addition to the cold weather, cloudy skies and the late snow storms, the cloud of death hung in the air. Before that spring neither of us gave much thought to death and the finality of it; our own mortality and the ominous realization that we could go at any time weighed heavily on our minds. Jimmy B's and Stan's death shook us out of our comfort zones and the bad weather wasn't helping our moods. In addition to feeling on edge and slightly uncomfortable, we both had cabin fever and a strong desire to get on with our lives.

By that time, we were both working at the Blackfeet Pencil Factory, I am not sure exactly why I was hired. Maybe, they thought I was Indian enough after participating in the Occupation of Wounded Knee. Or, perhaps Max helped me get on, he was always raising hell with management and that probably was the main factor. In any event, I was happy to have a well paying job and the Pencil Factory actually proved to be a success. The Blackfeet secured additional contracts to supply pencils to all the Federal Government agencies. As I said earlier, it was the Tribe's largest investment in the future economic survival of the Tribe and everybody wanted to make a success out of the endeavor.

Two-Fingers and I both worked on the production line and even though the work was tedious, we both felt as if we were accomplishing something. We had a purpose and felt pretty good about things as May approached, working is a wonderful thing.

Sunlight finally made an appearance the first week of May, 1973. The whole Tribe seemed to light up, they were happy to shake the cold out of their bones and have some fun. It had been a hard winter and spring for everybody, especially the elder Blackfeet who worried about their sons and daughters coming home safely from either Wounded Knee or 'Nam.

On May, 10th, Two-Fingers and I were hard at work at the Pencil Factory when the overhead siren blared, it was lunchtime. All the workers located their homemade lunches and walked down the hall to the lunchroom. The employees only had a half hour lunch break so everybody moved quickly to find a seat at the long tables that occupied the center of the dining hall. Two-Fingers and I sat at our usual places next to the coffee pots and quickly began to devour the peanut butter and jelly sandwiches Pam made for us. The foreman of the place was Eddie Racine. Eddie is Old Man Racine's youngest son and he really liked his job, he was 45 years old at the time and it was his first full time position. He, like most of the other workers, were finally working and were no longer dependent on the government handouts that plagued the Rez.

Eddie had a habit of always standing at the entrance of the lunchroom and nervously checking his watch to make sure everybody was back to work in precisely one half hour. Eddie took ownership of the place and he was serious about getting a full day's work for a day's pay, it was as if the money came out of Eddie's pocket and he had a death grip on it.

Every day Eddie said virtually the same thing, "You work at a pencil factory so let's get the lead out." It was sort of funny the first time we heard it but eventually all the workers turned a deaf ear to Eddie and tried to ignore him. Nobody knew why he stood in the doorway because when the half hour was up, the siren blared and everybody went back to work right on schedule, nobody ever attempted to escape or run off with a handful of pencils.

Anyway, it generally took everybody about fifteen minutes to eat their lunches and then it was smoke time. Cigarettes were bummed from those that had them and once they were handed out, matches were struck simultaneously and the smokefest began. I usually grabbed a couple pots of coffee and made my way around the room refilling coffee cups. After doing so, I would walk back to my seat to a chorus of, "Fuck you, White Guy." On this particular day, Two-Fingers, in his never ending attempt at bettering himself, was reading the latest edition of the Big Sky Reporter out of Great Falls. He was leaning back with his head slightly cocked and was smoking a cigarette he "borrowed." When he got to page six, he saw a headline that read, "Wounded Knee

Occupation Ends." He quickly spread the paper out in front of him and began to read the article out loud so I could hear.

"On May 9, 1973, the Occupation of Wounded Knee came to a peaceful conclusion. After 71 days of unrest and occupation, representatives of the Federal Government and the leaders of AIM settled their differences and the Occupation is officially over. As always, when more information becomes available, we will report it to you in a timely and thorough manner."

Two-Fingers stared at the article and slowly read it again. Finally, he looked up from the article and stared at me as he shook his head in disbelief and said, "Is that all they have to say? Thorough manner? What the hell do they mean, thorough manner? Nothing about a downed helicopter or a burned out Catholic Church or Jimmy B's death? What kind of reporting is this?" I shook my head and said, "Well, in all fairness, we took Jimmy B out of there and I doubt they know about it. The downed helicopter and the church, well, that is another matter, not sure about that one. It seems like they are trying to downplay the entire episode if you ask me. You know, the less people know about it the better." Two-Fingers stomped out his cigarette on the cement lunchroom floor and stood up and stretched. When the siren blared signifying the end of the lunch break, the Blackfeet slowly rose to their feet and walked single file back to their workstations. As always, Eddie Racine checked his watch one last time before turning out the lunchroom lights.

That weekend, it began to rain, sheets of rain poured down from all angles. The cold, hard ground began to thaw quickly as the rain kept on coming. For three days and three nights it rained nonstop. Everybody was ass deep in mud by the third day and all the Blackfeet who survived the flood of 1964 were worried.

The flood of 1964 was the worst flood in Montana history. For several days back then the rain poured down on the Rez and Glacier Park. The heavy rains caused the larger than normal snowpack to melt very quickly. So quickly, that people in several communities were caught off guard. When the dams on Birch Creek and the Two-Medicine River burst, a twenty foot wall of water roared down the countryside and flooded everything in it's wake. Trees were uprooted and carried sixty to seventy miles before coming to rest. Cars were swept off the roads and carried along the swollen rivers and streams as the occupants desperately tried to get out of them. Houses were pulled into the raging torrent that built up steam as streams and rivers merged, destroying virtually everything in it's path. Debris was carried off downstream, people drowned, houses were destroyed and lives were ruined. Of the 31 deaths, 30 occurred on the Rez. 8,700 people in the area were evacuated and a lot of Blackfeet families had no choice but to live in Teepees and tents that summer.

Fortunately, the three days of hard rain in 1973 did not create any major flooding. Evidently, The snowpack was not as large in the Rockies as it had been in 1964. Plus, the replaced dams were stronger and better built.

The only major downside to the hard rain was the loss of power in Browning. The antiquated power system could not handle that much water and transformers all over the Rez blew up and that meant that the Pencil Factory would be closed until further notice, it takes a lot of power to make pencils.

The Junction Drive In had recently opened for the summer. The owner, Clyde "River" Cross Guns invested in a generator after the 1964 flood and was well prepared to do business when most businesses were not, the Junction was one of a handful of businesses that were not in the dark.

Two-Fingers and I walked the three blocks from home to the Junction and were sitting at the counter nursing our cups of coffee when River gave us the evil eye and threatened to throw us out if we did not order some food real soon, the place was getting busy and he needed to sell something. So, we each ordered cheeseburger deluxe's and milkshakes. Just as we were being served, Edward Still Smoking and Johnny Skunk Cap came walking in and muscled their way to the counter next to us. The Junction only had hard wood bench seating so Two-Fingers and I skinnied up so they could sit down, Two-Fingers was smashed up against the wall and I was smashed up against him.

Edward and Johnny had plenty of room, one of the perks for being elders.

Right off the bat they started talking about Wounded Knee. They said they had just gotten home the previous night from South Dakota. Evidently, they spent a couple of nights in jail after the occupation ended or they would have been home sooner. As it turned out, Johnny had gotten into a fight with a couple of white ranchers at the Palomino Bar and Edward stepped in to break it up and they both ended up in jail. Johnny has a bad temper and was one of the more militant Blackfeet at Wounded Knee. He never was in the Army or anything like that, he just was always warring against white people. Anyway, they both cooled their heels in the jail at Pine Ridge for a few days before being released.

"So what the hell happened after we left?" Two-Fingers asked as he dipped a french fry into his ketchup. "I read in the newspaper that there was some type of peaceful conclusion and that you had settled all your differences, what is up with that?" "Yeah, like we could settle our differences. You might say that we were left high and dry. We had hoped the occupation would raise the consciousness of our plight. With all the civil unrest going on regarding the Civil Rights Movement and 'Nam, we mistakenly thought we could bring attention to the injustices we suffer and everybody protesting would rally to our cause." Edward said as he took a bite out of my cheeseburger. "That didn't happen and the Federal Government won the war of attrition, beat us down and finally starved us out, they always starve us out, aenet."

I was looking at Johnny as he stared out the front window at a couple of white tourists on bicycles when he suddenly jumped up and said, "Follow me." He kicked open the screen door and ran after the two bicyclists who were laboring to get up the hill leading out of town. We got up and ran after him and by the time we caught up to him, he had already stopped the bicyclists and was holding their handlebars with a death grip. He was physically shaking with anger, his face was bright red and he was drooling slightly as he yelled, "How long are you two going to be squatting on my reservation?" Johnny shook both of the bicycles so violently that the bicyclists fell to the ground. Johnny tossed their bikes in the ditch and yelled again, "I asked you how long are you going to be squatting on my reservation?" A crowd formed as the two bicyclists slowly got to their feet. Simultaneously, they both said, "We are just passing through, we are headed to the Park." That seemed to really piss off Johnny who grabbed them both by their jerseys and said, "If you are not off my reservation in ten minutes you will never see the Park." He pushed them back as he released his grip and they ran over and retrieved their bikes from the ditch, they did not seem too labor much as they flew up the hill and out of town. Johnny turned to face the crowd and said, "That is what I am going to do every time a find a white squatter on my reservation." He turned and walked back to the Junction to a chorus of chants. The younger Blackfeet surrounded him and slapped him on the back as the older Blackfeet shook their heads in disgust.

"Times are changing but they are not changing fast enough to suit all the young bucks. They blame me for not being militant enough at Wounded Knee, maybe they are right. There are just too many of them and not enough of us." Edward said before walking across the road and re-entering the Junction. Two-Fingers looked over at me and asked, "How long are you going to be squatting on my reservation?" "Bone you, Two-Fingers. I will squat here as long as I want. However, I will pay for your cheeseburger as a sign of my respect." "Fucking white people, always buying us off with cheese, aenet." Two-Fingers and I started to walk back to the Junction when suddenly a truck stopped in front of us and two older Blackfeet jumped out and started pounding a political campaign sign into the ground. We stopped and watched and when the truck drove off to its next destination, we leaned forward and read the sign, "Vote for Robert "Stubby" Grant for your Tribal Chairman." In smaller print at the very bottom it read, "A vote for Stubby is a vote for the future." Two-Fingers laughed and said, "Future? Stubby doesn't know what day it is and if Stubby is the future, we are royally screwed."

When I was younger, racism on the Rez never really bothered me. I was the only white kid in my class for quite awhile and I was teased a lot and I had more than my share of fights, but it never really bothered me. As time passed, the teasing and fighting slowed and I was treated pretty well. But, In the early 1970's, people were angry. The younger, college educated Blackfeet were desperate for change and they began to strike out. Fortunately, I was well liked around town and by the Schwarz family, they treated me like family.

They liked me so much, they invited me to Paula's and Cindy Ann's graduation from the University of Montana. They both finished school in less than three years by taking extra classes and going to summer school. Once they sat their minds on doing something, it got done. Cindy Ann divorced Stogie Man and she put all of her energy into raising her girls and getting a college degree. During their time at Missoula, Paula, Cindy Ann and her two little girls all lived together in a large house they rented near the campus.

Is was during this time that Stogie Man fell deeper and deeper into the depths of alcoholism and was rarely seen in Browning. Rumor had it he lived north of town near the Canadian border with a Chippewa Cree from Alberta, Canada.

Anyway, on the day before graduation, Pam and Max drove to Missoula in their Buick and Two-Fingers and I followed in his pickup. We hoped that by the time we to got back the Pencil Factory would be up and running and we could get back to work. Until then, it was time for a road trip and we were eager to get out of town.

After spending five hours driving, Two-Fingers and I were glad when we finally got to Missoula. It is a beautiful place, lots of trees and a beautiful river running through the center of town. The campus of the University of Montana is spectacular, it is full of well maintained buildings and beautifully manicured lawns and it looked like paradise to me. There is a big M made out of rocks and painted white that looks down on the campus and the entire valley. Two-Fingers and I hiked up the hill to the M and smoked a joint and daydreamed about going to college there. Cindy Ann and Paula's house was not far from the M so we decided to walk there and worry about his pickup later.

When we arrived, the kids were happy to see their uncle and they even seemed pleased to see me. The backyard was filled with tables and chairs and they had a fire pit going with venison cooking slowly,

Max was in charge and he seemed happy about that. We drank pop and played with the kids and told stories on each other, it was a great day and we were all happy to be together. I spoke to Paula about Stan and that seemed to cast a pall over the festivities, but it did not last long. She had moved on from Stan years ago and was more interested in comforting me than rehashing any sad memories. So, I never mentioned it again.

The next day, there was a big graduation celebration at the Field House. Caps were thrown in the air and hugs were exchanged, a typical ceremony I guess. Two-Fingers and I felt right at home and decided right then that we were going to college there.

Cindy Ann was moving back to Browning and running for the Tribal Council. Paula was staying in Missoula and preparing to go to the Montana School of Law, she was going to be an attorney. Paula told us that she had plenty of room in the house she rented and would like us to stay with her as long as we behaved. She kept referring to Two-Fingers as, "little brother."

So, that is how we ended up in Missoula. Before we moved, we helped Cindy Ann get elected to the Council. She was the first women on the Council and one of the most educated Blackfeet to ever serve. Two-Fingers ended up getting a free place to stay and free tuition, he qualified for enough grants to choke a mule. Affirmative Action, Tribal money, Federal grants and all kinds of other assistance. I had to work at night and go to class during the day to afford the place. When I brought this up to Two-Fingers all he would say was, "That's what you get for stealing our land." Then, he would laugh hysterically.

Personally, I never found much humor in that. Especially not at three A.M. in the morning when I was loading packages onto a UPS truck in the dead of winter.

Chapter 36

Under the advice of counsel, I can't go into a lot of detail about Paula and I falling in love and all the events that happened during our courtship, I have been sworn to secrecy. Besides, this is the story of Two-Fingers and how he became the most beloved and revered Blackfeet leader in modern history and I have already given out too many intimate details of events I witnessed and was a part of.

As you can tell, up until Two-Fingers went off to college, there wasn't any evidence that he was anything special. Far from it, he was a young Indian boy growing up on an Indian reservation, the odds of success were not in his favor. All I know is that he was socialized in a very unique way and that may have had something to do with it. He was the most honest person I have ever known, he always lived by a code that was more important to him then personal achievement. Meaning, if he had to lie to get something he would go without, he always said if you had to lie to achieve success you were a loser and you just didn't know it.

Plus, in all the years I knew him he never used his race to define who he was. He did not want his people to use race as an excuse for failure, he had more pride than that and he refused to play the race card. Once the race card is played, personal accountability goes out the window. He grew up surrounded by people that blamed being an Indian on their failures. He never blamed white people for his plight, he just made fun of us. He succeeded and was a stronger person because he did not allow himself to be preyed upon by those that wanted to use Indians as an excuse or rationale for the need for government intervention. He grew to hate the Federal Government and he fought against it his entire adult life.

As I have repeatedly said, he witnessed the deprivation brought on by government dependency and he also witnessed what happens when you are not dependent, when you are free. Government dependency is like a cloud hanging over your head. It does not provide hope, it just helps take away the drive that is needed to succeed and it kills independence and freedom. He understood that people had to take personal responsibility for their actions. Big government provides excuses for failure instead of holding people accountable, they enable people to shirk their responsibility; big government is never a good idea.

He honed this philosophy over the years by combining large amounts of book learning with practical experience. Two-Fingers had common sense and an encyclopedic knowledge of the History of America and America Indian History. He studied these as an undergraduate and when he went off to law school, he studied the Constitution along with the caselaw that derived from the interpretation of the Constitution.

The Constitution is the genesis of our entire legal system and strict adherence to it must be maintained at all time. Without it, America is just another land mass filled with rudderless people, it gives all Americans a track to run on. Two-Fingers believed the Constitution is why America is the greatest country on earth. He spent his entire life defending the Constitution against those that used it for their own evil intentions. Over the years, he saw too many politicians violate it and too many criminals hide behind it. So, if you ask me to point to the one thing that made Two-Fingers exceptional, I would point to his patriotism and his love for the United States of America. I will try to put that into greater context later.

Right now, I believe it is meaningful to tell you that Two-Fingers knew that Indians were fully aware of the Right of Conquest. He would often say that is how the Blackfeet ended up with Crow territory. Indians knew about Conquest and respected the right of Tribes to battle other Tribes for land, horses, women, food, etc. He also knew that the Spanish were conquerors of Mexico and inhabited that land for over three hundred years. Over the years, virtually all lands have changed hands and who can say who was really there first? First does not matter to an Indian, the power to fight and conquer does. In the olden days, Indians did not cry about being conquered, they understood that. What they did not understand is why the White Man lied and broke all the treaties, lying and dishonorable conduct was foreign to them. In their world, anybody who lied or cheated was banished from the Tribe. If you were a coward and brought shame upon yourself and your family you were banished. Honesty, courage and leadership qualities were revered and honored, America may have these same ideals but they are quickly disappearing and he knew it.

Politicians, above everyone else in society, must be honest and trustworthy. Their dishonest acts will kill America dead and they must be held accountable for their actions. Oh well, I am getting ahead of myself but hey, I warned you I wasn't much of a writer.

I can tell you this much, Paula and I ended up getting married after she graduated from law school and she immediately went to work for a local law office and I followed in her footsteps and went to law school too. Two-Fingers decided against being a history teacher and decided to go to law school with me. So, there you have it, Two-Fingers and I went to law school and I am happily married to his sister. There is more to the story than that but I figure you have better things to do than to listen to me go on and on about my private life. All I can tell you is Two-Fingers really came alive when he hit law school.

Chapter 37

The first year of law school is when they try to scare you to death. They put a lot of pressure on you to see if you are cut out for law school and the practice of law. They try to weed out all the weaklings and they do that by making you study Torts, Contracts, Constitutional Law, Evidence, Criminal Law and Civil Procedure and then calling on you in class to discuss the subject matter. If you think my writing is boring, just crack open a copy of Civil Procedure in America, you will want to cap yourself.

Two-Fingers liked all of that stuff but he especially liked Constitutional Law. He was the wunderkind when it came to Constitutional Law. In class, he would challenge the Constitutional Law professor on something and they would debate it forever. The other students loved him for doing that because it took the pressure off of them, the last thing a first year law student wants is to be called on to recite some case that interprets a Constitutional Amendment. Every time I was called on, my ass puckered up and I could not spit out a sentence. As soon as that happened, Two-Fingers came to my rescue and off to the races he and the professor would go.

The second year of law school is where they try to work you to death, about twice the work load as the first year. I can't remember what they try to do to you during the third year, all I can say is by then I was bored to tears and ready to get the hell out of there.

Anyway, Paula was very helpful and I breezed through law school and passed the bar on my first attempt, so did Two-Fingers. The only really interesting thing that happened during our time in law school was when Two-Fingers decided to get married.

During our first year in law school, Two-Fingers met a fellow student by the name of Margaret Johnson. She was known to everybody as "Maggie." Maggie was a little hippie girl who was going to change the world. She was hell bent on fighting every injustice known to mankind, real or imagined. Maggie, in addition to being an advocate for justice, was a drop dead gorgeous blond with an ass that would stop traffic. Probably a little more information than you needed to know but I am all about transparency.

Anyway, Maggie's dad was the Governor of the great state of Montana at the time. Actually, Franklin T. Johnson was just starting his second term when Two-Fingers and Maggie started dating. Franklin, Frank to his many friends, loved being Governor. Before taking office, he was a rancher near Butte. Do you want to know the prettiest place in Montana? Butte in your rearview mirror. Anyway, he was a humble guy back when he was first elected. He was dedicated to being a public servant and promised to serve only two terms. But, like most politicians, he began to enjoy the power that went along with his office and he broke his promise. Over the years, he employed a number of devious tactics to remain in power. In short, he was no longer a public servant, he was a professional politician.

Maggie and Two-Fingers fell for each other hard and moved in together at the end of our first year of law school. Frank proved to be a real racist when it came to Two-Fingers and he went ballistic when his daughter, his only child, moved in with him. I suspect he did not think it looked good politically, with Frank, it was always about the politics. Two-Fingers tolerated Frank's endless interference and finally wore him down.

After graduation, Two-Fingers and Maggie eloped and when they returned to Montana, as soon as they crossed the state line from Idaho, the Montana Highway Patrol was waiting to escort them to the State Capital in Helena. Upon their arrival at the Governor's Mansion, Frank preceded to lecture Two-Fingers on a variety of things. When he came around to belittling his ancestry and heritage, Two-Fingers kept his cool and adeptly pointed out the fact that Montana has seven reservations filled with Indian voters and it may not be such a bad thing having an Indian for a son-in-law. According to Two-Fingers, it took Frank awhile to figure out the obvious importance of such a thing. Of course, Frank was a professional politician and he could be excused for being dimwitted and slow. Somehow, as soon as politicians are elected they begin to lose their common sense. Frank, after digesting the idea that the marriage may get him some extra votes, put down his whiskey glass and cigar and began to slap Two-Fingers on the back. The number one priority for all politicians is getting re-elected. They will sell their souls and the souls of their constituents just to get re-elected. His daughter's happiness was irrelevant.

Frank warmed to the idea but still did not take any chances. So, He appointed Two-Fingers to a high paying job as the head of the newly created office of the Montana International Trade Organization. The primary duty of the head of this organization was to travel the globe promoting trade. Two-Fingers ended up spending six years traveling virtually nonstop promoting the sale of Montana products to foreign countries. He travelled to Africa, Russian, Europe, the Far East, Canada and Mexico. The program worked so well that Montana exports to these countries skyrocketed. Of course, Frank took all the credit and was easily re-elected to a third term.

Meanwhile, Maggie became despondent because Two-Fingers was never home so she took to drinking. The occasional martini with dinner became a nightly ritual that spilled over into the wee hours of the morning. Booze followed her every step of the way as she descended into the depths of her alcoholism. They tried to have children and every time she got pregnant, she miscarried. Two-Fingers threatened to quit several times but Frank would not hear of it. Besides, he couldn't quit, he had been bitten by the disease called consumerism. He had car payments, a house payment and credit card bills that would choke a maggot, he was indebted. Then, one cold winter morning, while he was away promoting trade, their maid found Maggie hanging from the center beam of their horse stable. Two-Fingers, wracked with guilt, left his career behind and moved back to Browning. He never talked much about that time in his life and I respected him too much to pry. All I know is a man spends a little time living and a lot of time sorting things out.

We never saw too much of Two-Fingers or Maggie during this time, everybody was busy with their own lives I suppose. Paula and I were living in Missoula working for a law firm that specialized in Contract and Corporate Law. I consider myself a good attorney but Paula is a great attorney, there was never an issue that was too complex for her. During our years in Missoula, she developed an interest in Gaming Law. She saw how Tribes from across the Country were improving their lot in life with the revenues from gambling. Casino's were popping up all over Indian Country and reservations that once suffered unspeakable poverty were becoming prosperous, Indian reservations were able to enter into gambling accords with the State they resided in. The way it works is, if a state allows a particular kind of gambling, Reservations could not be precluded from establishing that same type of gambling. White entrepreneurs flooded reservations and set up partnerships with different Tribes where they would provide the knowhow and capital for a large piece of the action. Paula wanted the Blackfeet to be the first Tribe in Montana with large scale gaming.

When she approached the Tribal Council in Browning, she was initially met with a lot of resistance. She was finally able to get their approval when she pointed out that the Pencil Factory could be converted into a casino that would employ a lot of Blackfeet. The Pencil Factory had sat vacant for a couple of years because pencils were mostly obsolete, new technologies had replaced the need for pencils. When it shut down, it put hundreds of people out of work and the Tribe was really hurting financially. Finally, the Tribe agreed to put money into the venture on one condition, Paula had to come back to the Rez and run it. So, after weighing the pro's and con's, we decided to move back to the Rez. I remember sitting at our kitchen table when the decision was made and Paula saying, "The White Man's greed took most of our land away and the White Man's greed is going to give it all back."

By the time we moved back home, Two Fingers had already been back a few months. He lived a very solitary life, he had lost his way in the wilderness of life and was trying to heal up. He built a small log cabin four miles outside of town on Willow Creek and was trying to get over his guilt and loneliness. When I went to visit him, I noticed right away he was a changed man, his zest for life was replaced by introspection. He questioned his every move and thought, he was filled with self doubt and confusion. All the things he thought were right, turned out to be wrong. His attempt at being a good little apple by pursuing wealth and power was an unmitigated disaster for him. He could not escape it and he refused to drink it right. He was sober for the first time in his life and it was taking a toll on his reasoning, he actually began to have clarity. He told me he was having visions and I jokingly asked if any of the visions featured snakes? He stared at me for the longest time before he finally laughed. That is when I knew things were really serious, Two-Fingers had lost his sense of humor and his sense of being.

Over the months after my initial visit with Two-Fingers, Paula and I would go see him and try to shake him out of his malaise. Paula kept telling him he needed to go back to work and find a purpose in life, she was largely unsuccessful. Then, out of the blue, Two-Fingers announced to us that he was going to run for the Tribal Council. He hated politicians in general but thought the only way to beat them was to beat them. He was going to be a leader no matter what that cost him politically. He would help his people rise above the abject poverty that still existed on the Rez and he would rid the Rez of all corruption and dishonesty, he would be an Indian leader not a politician. He laid out his entire plan and when he was done I asked, "Do you have any room for me in your master plan? I am tired of working for the old lady and I could use a job." In reality, I was worried about him and wanted to help him in any way I could.

So, that is how I became his campaign manager. Paula, much to my surprise, did not miss working with me. She was absorbed with getting the gaming operations up and running and she liked complete autonomy. To be successful, all ventures must have that one leader with vision. Tireless, endless dedication to the cause is necessary for success. When you start having a lot of people injecting their ideas and wishes into something, nothing ever gets done. Paula lived by one principle in that regard: lead, follow or get the hell out of the way.

That is one of the main differences between a successful business and government. Governments are bogged down by bureaucracies and they seldom get things right. Eventually, things get done but they are seldom done right. Too many Chiefs and not enough Indians is never a good thing. Paula got it done right and soon money poured into the Tribal coffers. She ran things and hired consultants who were paid a salary. Then, she hired capable Blackfeet to learn from the consultants and as soon as they had the knowledge necessary to run their department, she got rid of the consultants. Soon, gambling on the Rez was controlled one hundred percent by the Blackfeet.

The elections were about a year off when Two-Fingers announced he was running and he was apprehensive about how to mount a campaign, he was actually worried he might lose. I told him his fears were unwarranted but to ease his mind, we would come up with an effective way to get his message across. Luckily, the Rez is not that large and consists of just a few populated areas and Browning was the key, you win in Browning and you will be elected. Cindy Ann was still on the Council and more than eager to explain the current situation on the Rez and to help with campaigning, Two-Fingers and I had been gone a long time and we were not that up on the issues of the day.

Turns out that it was the same old issues that always plagued the Rez. Cindy Ann explained to us that even though there were two other young members on the Council, the majority of the members were the same old guys that had always been in control. After a very brief time in the majority, two of the young Council members were voted out of office. So, of the seven seats, four were controlled by the old professional politicians and three seats by the younger members. Majority ruled on the Rez and the four members always voted in lockstep with each other and nothing on the Rez changed. Allegations of graft, cronyism, distrust and greed still ruled the day. The older members were in bed with the BIA and Trevor Kanowski and they were allegedly bleeding the Rez dry, the Rez's dependency on the Federal Government was at an all time high.

After our meeting with Cindy Ann, Two-Fingers decided that the Federal Government and their chains of dependency had to go once and for all. Over one hundred and fifty years of their policies towards the Indians had left them worse off than ever. They were still dependent on handouts and the effect of that policy was evident in the destruction of the human spirit which manifested itself in the alcoholism, deprivation and short life expectancy that was so prevalent on the Rez. But most importantly, it was an affront to individual growth and freedom. The chains had to be removed but how do you do that when several generations of people were used to the dependency? That was the challenge, Two-Fingers never met anybody that turned down free commodity cheese. So, Two-Fingers campaigned on the notion of liberty, freedom and self respect, all of these things were forgotten concepts on the Rez.

Chapter 38

The Rez never saw a campaign like the one Two-Fingers ran. He met with virtually every voter and talked to them individually, face to face. He talked of getting honor back into their lives, self respect and pride were the themes he pushed. He wanted to get back to the ideals of governance that were key to the Indian way of life centuries ago. He promised to be a leader and he would not be swayed from doing all he could do for his people. He talked of sacrifice and how change was necessary and that it would not be easy and it would not come overnight. He spoke about the failures of the current political system and the effects it had on the entire Rez. Children saw their leaders doing and saying dishonest things and that could not help but create an atmosphere of dishonesty throughout the entire Tribe.

It is a disgrace to lie but politicians somehow are excused for their lies, what kind of system is that? Politicians have to be held to the very highest standards because if they are dishonest and their lies are accepted, the entire Tribe suffers. He would quote Chief Joseph the great Chief of the Nez Perce whose Indian name was, "Thunder Rolling From the Mountains." Chief Joseph is a great example of what a Leader is and was well known for saying, "It is a disgrace to lie, a real Leader is always honest." He is also known for saying, "Never be the first to break a bargain." In short, Two-Fingers preached ethics and it worked, he won by a landslide and the good guys regained a majority of the seats on the Tribal Council.

The first thing he did as a Council member was to open a job up for a Tribal lawyer. The Tribe had never had their own lawyer, they always relied on the BIA for all their legal advice and that was like having the fox guard the hen house. Two-Fingers changed all of that, he was convinced that the BIA had to go. So, I was hired to be the Counsel for the Tribe and my main duties were to sit in on all Council meetings and come up with a plan to get the Federal Government out of their hair and off their backs. The majority of the Council members saw the wisdom in Tribal autonomy and were happy I was hired. When I thanked Two-Fingers for hiring me he said, "Don't thank me, you were the only one that applied."

The Tribal Council and his people became his life and he gained strength from them and they benefitted from that strength. He became known as a man of his word and that was more important to him than anything else in the world. As he grew older, he would refer to all the residents on the Rez as "his children." He told me once you decide to become a parent, life is no longer about you it is about your children. He said that once he decided to get involved with Tribal politics, life was no longer about him, it was about his people. He made many personal sacrifices and provided the type of leadership that was desperately needed and when the elections rolled around two years later, he won handily and ended up getting the most votes out of all the candidates which meant he was the new Chairman of the Blackfeet Nation.

As Chairman, his number one priority was changing the attitude on the Rez. For decades, the Tribe was told they were inferior and irrelevant, that was evident by the government programs that were forced upon them. He set out to change everybody's view on who they were. He spoke of all the great virtues of Indians; honesty, integrity and self respect qualities were preached, he told everyone that would listen that they were exceptional. He told them if a Tribe or a people don't believe they are exceptional, they just as well stay in bed. He preached unity, hard work and dedication to task and it worked. Attitudes changed and people looked at things in a positive light, not in the dreary light that flickered from Washington, D.C. Believing you are exceptional leads to exceptional results and if you think you are inferior, you probably are.

Being the Chairman gave him enormous power to effect change on the Rez. Like I said earlier, The Council consists of seven members and the majority ruled so there was not a lot of back and forth when it came to deciding on the issues of the day. Two-Fingers presided over the Council fairly and adeptly, he was always willing to listen to any opposing view and everybody was allowed to talk freely and honestly. The older Council members were constantly opposing change but that did not deter Two-Fingers from listening. Over the course of his time as Chairman, Two-Fingers and the majority of the Council were able to implement a number of good programs, it helped a lot to be flush with cash from the gaming operations. Capitalism at it's finest, Two-Fingers knew that wealth fuels democracy and hope.

Gaming also provided much needed jobs, everybody who wanted a job was able to find one. The Tribe invested in all types of new businesses and most of them proved to be money makers. One of the projects that was near and dear to Two-Fingers heart was the establishment of a buffalo herd on the Rez. He worked out a deal with the Sioux Tribe in South Dakota to buy a hundred head of their buffalo. On the day they arrived, Two-Fingers and I were watching them being unloaded when he leaned over to me and said, "I think I recognize a couple of them." It had been awhile but it was nice to see his sense of humor finally return, he was no longer grief stricken and desolate. He hadn't drank in years and he even quit smoking weed. He was all about building a better life for his people and he said he needed to keep a clear head to do that. He always said, "Everything in moderation, everything in moderation." I would always say, "Moderation yes, abstinence no." I smoked a lot of pot by myself during those years.

The thing that impressed me most about Two-Fingers is he got things done. We all know people that have all these great ideas and then they never get up off the couch long enough to get them done. All the good thoughts in the world are useless without action, Two-Fingers was all about action. By the way, not everything he tried worked but that never stopped him from trying.

During one of our many Tribal Council meetings, Stubby Grant was lamenting on how America was such a terribly racist country and that we should sell the Rez to the Russians. Stubby, like most of the Tribe, had no idea what an average Russian's life was like. He just hated all things American and figured it was the best alternative. Stubby had actually served as the Chairman of the Tribe until Two-Fingers unseated him and he was still on the Council because he got enough votes to be there but not enough to be Chairman, thankfully. He was constantly bringing up horseshit like that and Two-Fingers and the other Council members would always sit there and patiently listen to his whining.

Of course, all of his whining was recorded in our minutes of the meeting. The stenographer would always have to have Stubby repeat what he said because he talked so fast she could not get it all down the first time. So, we would all sit there and listen to him repeat the horseshit over and over again. Two-Fingers finally had enough of his rambling and asked, "Stubby, have you ever been to Russia?" Stubby looked perplexed and said, "Of course not, the farthest I have been away from the Rez is Great Falls." "Well, I have been to Russia and the place sucks. By the way, how do you think the Russians would treat us Blackfeet?" Two-Fingers asked as Stubby reached for another donut. "Well, I bet it would be better than this racist country has treated us." That is when Two-Fingers came unglued. He stood up and went into a detailed explanation about Communism and how the people of Russia were treated under it. He explained what a totalitarian government is and how little freedom the Citizens of Russia have and how they mistreat their women and minorities. "Stubby, have you ever heard of any Russian women holding a power position in Russia? Have you ever seen a black person in Russia? How many blacks and women serve in the Politburo?" Stubby chewed on his donut awhile before he said, "What's your point?" "The point Stubby, is this is not a perfect country but it is a country of opportunity where you can be anything you want to be. Every time you start with this racist bullshit, it takes me weeks to get the young bloods to quit feeling sorry for themselves. You are an enabler Stubby, you enable the weak to find an excuse for failure. You are always crying about something that happened a hundred years ago and I am trying to govern today, you weaken all of us with your constant crying. I am trying to teach our people the meaning of personal responsibility and all you do is provide them with an excuse to fail." I remember looking over at the stenographer and she was typing like crazy, no way was she going to stop and interrupt Two-Fingers. Two-Fingers finally sat back down and added, "Besides, you do every one of our relatives who fought against Communism a terrible disservice when you speak like that. If the Russians were in control of our country, do you think they would be as altruistic towards us as the whites have been? I am not talking about the whites of a hundred and fifty years ago, I am talking about the whites of today. It is tough enough dealing with the issues of today, you do not make it any easier by always talking about the past. Finish your donut and let's get on with the business of today." Cindy Ann stood up and started cheering and before long everybody was on their feet clapping, everybody except Stubby.

That was Two-Fingers, American to the core. Once the economic situation stabilized on the Rez, he started to improve all the social services. He hired the best alcoholic counselors money could buy, he hired the best doctors and he made sure the hospital had state of the art equipment, he introduced a mentoring program that paired the young people on the Rez with responsible adults which than led to apprenticeship programs where the young people learned different trades. Soon, the Tribe had all the plumbers, electricians, machinists, painters and carpenters they needed. Apprenticeships are the best way to learn the skills necessary to do these types of jobs. Plus, you get paid while you learn, no student loans.

Two-Fingers favorite program was his program to care for the elderly Blackfeet. Unlike most of society, the Blackfeet cared for their elderly in their homes, they did not put them in old folks homes where they suffered and died. That was not the Indian way. What Two-Fingers helped to provide was in home care and there was never a shortage of nursing and assistance. The old people stayed with their loved ones and were cared for until the day they died. Two-Fingers plans took care of the young, the old and everybody in between.

The work programs he created were legendary. As I said earlier, anybody that wanted to work had a job. He enlisted his uncle Fred to create a program where young Blackfeet men and women went into the Tribal forests and cleaned them up. Fred was a task master who did not tolerate laziness and the young thrived under his leadership. The forests were cleared of all the dead trees and selectively harvested and then they were replanted to ensure future growth. Camps were set up for the young workers and they lived there all summer long doing the work and in the fall, the workers went to trade schools, apprenticeships or the Blackfeet Junior College. The program proved to be so successful that the United States Forest Service hired them to clean up the forests in Glacier National Park. Sawmills were built on the Rez and soon we were shipping lumber all across the Country. By the way, his uncle Billy got a job as an instructor at the Blackfeet Junior College where he taught Native American History classes, he was very good at it and he finally received all the respect he rightfully deserved.

During this time, Browning was cleaned up and tourism flourished, the Blackfeet were proud again and it showed in their work ethic and drive. They soon became the envy of Tribes all across America and their leaders consulted with Two-Fingers and tried to imitate his practices, the Blackfeet were happy for the first time in years and they owed a lot of that to Two-Fingers.

At another one of our Tribal Council meetings, we were approached by representatives of a Cable TV Company. They wanted to capitalize on the success of the Tribe, greed always follows money. On the Rez, we only get one TV station and it is located in Lethbridge, Alberta and the only things we can watch are curling, hockey and the occasional coronation of British Royalty. That was fine because the Tribe did not watch much TV. In fact, most of the people on the Rez did not want to own a TV.

I remember the day the suits from the Cable TV Company sat down across from Two-Fingers and the other members of the Council. They laid out their plan to wire the City of Browning in order to, "Enlighten the Blackfeet." They pitched how wonderful it would be to have a hundred plus stations to choose from and all they needed to make this happen was exclusive rights to distribution for a period of time not to exceed fifty years. Two-Fingers listened to all they had to say and occasionally he would ask a simple question and the suits would elaborate on their plans to bring the world to the doorsteps of the Blackfeet. After listening to their horseshit for about an hour, Two-Fingers stood up and stretched before he said, "So, you want us to become enlightened? You want us to sit on our asses watching other people live their lives? You want us to watch reality shows that are not

real? You want us to give up our ability to think and reason on our own? You want us to ignore one another until there is a commercial break?" The suits looked at each other and then wisely picked up their brief cases and exited stage left without saying another word. After they left, I went up to Two-Fingers and said, "I think you were a bit hasty there, I really would have liked to watch some Monday Night Football."
"Crack you, White Guy. I finally have everybody up off their asses and I am not about to have them sit back down and watch their lives pass them by." That was that. The Blackfeet lived in a time of harmony and happiness, they worked hard and they played hard. Money from gambling and the other ventures flowed in and the Tribe became less and less dependent on the Federal Government.

Chapter 39

When the reservation system was first established, Tribes only had the right to occupy their lands, they were not title holders. This communal occupancy concept changed in 1887 with the passage of the General Allotment Act which divided American Indian treaty lands into individually owned allotments that were held in trust and overseen by the Bureau of Indian Affairs(BIA). The BIA was established in 1824 and was part of the United States War Dept. The BIA has a fiduciary responsibility to oversee the collection of fees for these lands and distribute the money to the Tribes or the individual allotment owners. Over the years, some of the reservation lands were sold to individuals who were not Tribal members and Two-Fingers wanted to buy back all of the land and expand Tribal sovereignty.

So, Two-Fingers established the Blackfeet Land Company, Inc. and bought back all the land on the Rez that was owned by the whites. By doing this, that land was not subject to the rules that the BIA established decades ago and this lessened the power of the BIA on the Rez and it also lessened the power of the bureaucrat from hell, Trevor Kanowski.

Trevor Kanowski had reigned terror down on the Tribe since his arrival and he hated Two-Fingers because Two-Fingers represented change. He liked the status quo of skimming what he could from the Tribe and making them beg for what was rightfully theirs. Trevor was the modern day Indian agent of old, crooked and self serving.

Each month, Two-Fingers and I had to go to the BIA office down the street from Tribal headquarters and listen to Kanowski boast about what a great job he was doing for the Tribe. Two-Fingers had to sign off on the payments that the Tribe received from the government never knowing if the accounting was accurate or not. Everybody knew that Kanowski was living large but nobody was able to prove he was stealing from the Tribe. After each one of these meetings, Two-Fingers swore he was going to get rid of the parasite. He wrote letters to the

Department of Interior requesting that Kanowski be removed, these requests were largely ignored because Kanowski's father-in-law was still the head of the department, Two-Fingers was convinced nobody in D.C. wanted the bastard back.

One day, Two-Fingers received a call from the principal of the middle school regarding Kanowski. Evidently, Kanowski was spending a lot of time parked in front of the playground. His big Cadillac had been seen there during recess over the last two weeks and the principal was concerned about possible child abuse. Two-Fingers and I jumped in my car and went down to take a look for ourselves. Sure enough, there he sat until recess ended.

After he drove off, we went to see the principal and Two-Fingers quickly determined that Kanowski had evil intentions on his mind. Two-Fingers immediately called Smiley Heavy Runner and had him come over to his office. Smiley was the acting Chief of Police and was always on the lookout for crime, there wasn't much crime on the Rez but that didn't stop him from looking. When Two-Fingers explained the situation to him, he was all too eager to set up surveillance on Kanowski. He quickly assigned a team of his crack investigators to keep an eye on Kanowski. His team consisted of Buzzy Still Smoking and Chubby Skunk Cap, Buzzy and Chubby had recently completed a two day seminar on surveillance and they were eager to put their knowledge to work.

Chubby and Buzzy staked out the playground and tailed Kanowski during the day and after about a week of surveillance, Kanowski abruptly quit going to the playground. Chubby and Buzzy figured he was on to them and reported this development back to Smiley. Once Smiley digested the news, he decided to call off all formal surveillance until further notice.

Smiley knew better than to call Two-Fingers about his decision so he drove over to meet with him in person. I watched Smiley through my office window as he waved his arms around and paced the floor. All the while, Two-Fingers just sat there quietly listening to him tell his story. When he was finished, Smiley walked out of Two-Fingers office and bumped into Roberta Kanowski. Roberta showed up unannounced and wanted to talk with Two-Fingers. She was wearing heavy makeup and sunglasses and when she saw Smiley she started to cry hysterically. I jumped up out of my seat and helped escort her into Two-Fingers office.

There the four of us sat, Two-Fingers, Smiley, Roberta and me. We patiently waited as Roberta cried her eyes out and every time we tried to soothe her the louder she wailed. About half way through a box of tissues, she stopped crying and took off her sunglasses to reveal her swollen cheeks and black eyes that were thinly masked by makeup, she had been beaten badly.

She finally settled down enough to tell us that she had decided to come and talk to Two-Fingers in private, she did not want the whole Rez to know of her pain and shame. She asked us to keep what she was going to say between the four of us and we all readily agreed.

Actually, some of the story she told was already common knowledge. For example, we all knew that her father had helped Kanowski get his job and we all knew he was a weasel and a thief and we all suspected he was a child abuser and a wife beater. Plus, we all knew he was a nickel living in a dime world. But, what we did not know is that he really, really loved his sheep, that surprised us.

Roberta told us how she recently discovered him being affectionate with one of their sheep, a pet named Mary. They had a small ranch north of town where they had sheep, pigs, horses and cattle. She loved animals and taking care of them kept her sane. Evidently, she did not love them as much as Kanowski. When she caught him in the act, he vehemently tried to deny any wrongdoing. Typical bureaucrat, always lying when they are caught with their pants down. Evidently, they were in the barn yelling and screaming at each other as the sheep ran away. She told Kanowski she would no longer tolerate him or his abusive, sick behavior and when she tried to leave, he beat the holy hell out of her.

She had lived in shame for years and did not want to admit her mistake to her family so she suffered in silence. Kanowski's behavior sickened her and she knew she had to do something about it and she instinctively knew Two-Fingers was someone she could talk to. We all sat there in total disbelief. Two-Fingers was visibly shaking when he picked up the phone and called his sister, Cindy Ann. Roberta would stay with her until he could figure out what to do next.

After Cindy Ann arrived and took Roberta away, the three of us sat there and pondered the situation. Legally, Kanowski had broken so may laws I couldn't add them all up without a calculator. Smiley wanted to go and arrest him immediately and throw him into jail and Two-Fingers just sat there and listened to the two of us go on and on about what we should do.

Jurisdictional issues came into the discussion, we weren't sure if sheep fucking was a federal or state crime. Plus, Kanowski was a powerful federal employee and he was sure to deny everything, it would be her word against his and this thing could drag on for months without any resolution. Two-Fingers finally spoke up and said, "Well, I don't know what is worse, being a bureaucrat or being a sheep fucker but when you are both, it is time for a hanging."

Well, one thing was certain, this was not going to be a secret for long no matter how hard we tried to keep it that way. Remember, you can't fart on the Rez without everybody knowing how it smelled. Knowing that, Two-Fingers figured he would just let nature take its course. One thing the Tribe would not tolerate is the molesting of an innocent animal. So, the three of us decided to go to the Club Cafe for our lunch and let the chips fall where they may.

The Club was extra busy and there weren't any open tables. So, we just stood in the middle of the room waiting for one to open up. Smiley started up a conversation by asking Two-Fingers and I if we had any knowledge of Kanowski's interest in sheep. Smiley was not all that subtle or quiet in the way he asked that and as he spoke a deafening quiet feel over the lunch crowd, you could literally hear a pin drop. When EF Hutton speaks, everybody listens.

Two-Fingers and I looked shocked as Smiley laid out the whole crime for all to hear. We had no idea that such a thing was happening and neither did the lunch crowd, all the patrons began to raise their concerns and things got rather heated. Johnny Skunk Cap happened to be in the crowd and he yelled out, "That son of a bitch should be tarred and feathered and ran out of town." Upon hearing that, Two-Fingers eyes lit up and he knew immediately that an equitable solution to the problem had been found. The beauty of the Rez's legal system was that if a crime is committed there is no appeal, justice is swift and the punishment fit's the crime. Criminals are either banished from the Tribe, sent to jail or tarred and feathered.

Around midnight that night, Kanowski was dragged out of his barn and tarred and feathered. Then, he was placed in the back of a pickup with his hands tied securely behind his back and the pickup was slowly paraded around the Government Square as a large crowd gathered. Two-Fingers and I stood at the front door of the Tribal headquarters and watched the whole thing, another late night tending to Tribal business. Luckily, I had just purchased one of those new smart phones so I was able to record the whole thing. Shortly after the second lap around the Government Square, one of the citizens jumped onto the back of the pickup and hung a placard around the neck of Kanowski and it simply said, "So many sheep, so little time." After a couple of more laps, the driver drove to the Rez's eastern border down by Cut Bank and released Kanowski into the vast expanse of Montana.

It wasn't until months later that we heard that Kanowski was living in Hawaii. He was living high on the hog (no pun intended) on his $7,000.00 a month federal pension. Two-Fingers and I were down at the Club having lunch one day and we both were lamenting the fact that the guy still got to keep his pension. Two-Fingers looked up from his cheeseburger and said, "You know the bureaucrats and politicians would consider it cruel and unusual punishment if they had to give up their pensions. For them, tar and feathering is bad, taking them off the government teat is inhumane."

Some of the Blackfeet that were in the Club that day actually expressed sympathy for Kanowski. Not me, I felt sorry for the sheep, can you imagine the shame they had to live with? It is interesting to note that Roberta is still living on the Rez. She is happily married to a Blackfeet rancher and they only raise cattle, no sheep.

Chapter 40

Two-Fingers was the protector and benefactor for the entire Blackfeet Tribe. The progress that was made on the Rez during his years as the leader was quite remarkable, success was measured in terms of happiness and the Blackfeet were happy. Unfortunately, most of White Society was unhappy. The impending economic collapse was beginning to take its toll on America. The politicians were in complete denial and would not admit that their irrational spending had created more debt than could ever be paid off. Think about that, America is 19 trillion in debt and there is no way that debt will ever be paid off. On the contrary, it is growing exponentially and the leaders of our great nation do not have a clue on how to pay it off, they are clueless in D.C.

In 2014, Two-Fingers watched as our nation began to fall apart at the seams, America had become morally and financially bankrupt. We had become a nation of consumers with very little production, all of the good jobs were shipped overseas. The North American Free Trade Act(NAFTA) meant the loss of hundreds of thousands of good paying factory jobs, these jobs were shipped out to foreign countries and our workers suffered.

94 million working age Americans were out of work and our government was trying to convince us that things were great. If things were so great, why were we 19 trillion in debt? The gullible and ignorant actually believed this nonsense. Not Two-Fingers, he saw the writing on the wall, our Federal Government's fiscal irresponsibility would soon doom us all.

Two-Fingers had sat patiently by and hoped things would improve after the 2014 midterms. The Republicans won majorities in the House and the Senate, certainly they would hold the line on this run away spending by the Federal Government. Nope, that did not happen. They caved in and approved the spending plans of the President without so much as a whimper, We the People were betrayed once again.

So, in early 2015 he announced his candidacy for the United States Senate and he was going to run as an Independent. He would attack his opponents individual policies and the policies of the Democratic and Republican parties, he would represent Montana and do the best he could to provide the leadership that was so desperately needed.

Senator Frank Johnson was his main competition. That's right, Frank was now a Senator and had been since 1986, three terms as the Governor of Montana did not satisfy Frank's lust for power and prestige. He was the unquestioned leader of the Democrat party in Montana and what he said went. So, when he announced his run for a fifth term as a U.S. Senator, no one was surprised. Two-Fingers was actually happy about it because for the first time in Frank's political career, he was vulnerable. The policies over the last seven years were abject failures and he had voted right down the party line and obstructed any meaningful legislation that did not fit the liberal agenda. All of these policies were imploding and the financial juggling act was coming to an end.

Two-Fingers Republican opposition was an eighty year old man by the name of Pete Reynolds. Pete had been in the House of Representatives for so long he no longer called it the House, he called it Home. Pete was stepping up in class and was of the mind he could beat Frank, little did he know his real competition would turn out to be Two-Fingers. Two-Fingers did not sweat either one of them, he had faith in the Montana electorate.

When he announced, Two-Fingers was running well behind the Democrat and Republican candidates and was given little chance to win. As I had stated earlier, Frank was firmly in control of the Democrat party in Montana and he used his enormous power in his attempt at defeating Two-Fingers. He leaked information to the liberal Big Sky Reporter about Two-Fingers smoking pot and falsely accused him of being a drug addict and therefore unworthy of serving in the United States Senate.

The polling indicated that Two-Fingers was the candidate of choice for only twenty percent of all Montanans. He was caught off guard by all the negativity pointed his way because dirty politics had no place on the Rez, personal attacks were frowned upon there. So, as his campaign manager, I came up with a strategy to fight back against Frank, his principal opposition.

I got on the internet and started using all the new technology available to us to get his message across. I suggested we go on the attack against the Democrat policies of the last seven years because Frank had been a lapdog for the President and had supported every ill conceived plan he came up with, we had to take the gloves off or we would lose. Two-Fingers was resistant at first, but after experiencing attack after attack from the Democrat Frank Johnson, he finally had enough.

One day, out of the blue, I was contacted by a young female reporter/editor from the Native American Sovereignty Magazine. It is a publication out of Flagstaff, Arizona that is primarily ran by Navajo's. The Navajo Indian who wanted to interview Two-Fingers was a lady by the name of Mary Little Feather. She was curious about a Native American Indian running for the Senate and she convinced me that Native Americans across America were also interested. It made sense to me but Two-Fingers was hesitant, he did not want to make a big deal out of the fact that he was Indian, he wanted to run on his record and his record alone. After awhile, I convinced him that the more attention he got the better it would be for him, positive publicity is a good thing. Finally, he agreed when Mary said she would come to Browning for the interview and not take up much of his time. So, I reserved the bingo hall and the three of us sat down together. I had a tape recorder and recorded everything so nothing could be misconstrued. Here is an excerpt of that interview dated 7-5-2015.

Mary: "Two-Fingers, I understand your given name is Donny R. Schwartz, would you prefer that I call you Donny?"

TF: "I would prefer you call me Mr. Schwartz and then bow down and kiss my ring. After all, I am a politician."

Mary: "Are you serious?"

TF: "Of course not, you just seem a little uptight and I am trying to loosen you up. That is the name that will appear on the ballot, but all my friends call me Two-Fingers. So, please call me Two-Fingers. Should I address you as Mary or do you prefer Ms. Little Feather?"

Mary: "Mary is just fine. I would like to know your reaction to Senator Johnson's allegation that you smoked pot in your youth. Is it true and if so, do you think it should disqualify you from running for the Senate?"

TF: "You get right to the point don't you? I like that, obviously you are not a politician. I am not quite sure why Frank is so curious about my past drug use, obviously they don't make you take a piss test to be in the United States Senate. Those people must be smoking something, no one in their right minds would do what they have done to this country.

To answer your question, it is 100% true. As a young person and during my time at law school, I did partake of the bud. I never abused it but I did enjoy smoking it. By the way, I quit years ago but I am not against people smoking it. If you smoke, I believe it should be used in moderation, don't let it become a crutch. You see, I grew up in a culture of alcohol, the streets of Browning were drenched in booze and booze caused more carnage than pot ever did. I no longer drink because I saw firsthand the damage that booze does and since we are on the subject of bad choices, you may want to ask Frank if he still consumes a quart of vodka a day? Personally, I do not care. But, if you throw stones you probably shouldn't live in a glass house. I have always been honest about all of my imperfections. I do not know how anybody lives a pure life, one absent of sin or bad choices. Honesty is my virtue, unlike Frank, I have always been honest and truthful.

By the way, what is dishonest is when a politician say's he smoked pot but didn't inhale, that should raise a red flag. A politician that lies about not inhaling pot will lie about anything. No, smoking pot should not disqualify me or anyone else. Lying about not inhaling pot should result in a hanging, figuratively speaking."

Mary: "I see. Why have you decided to run for the Senate?"

TF: "Quite frankly, the country is going to hell in a hand basket. I am concerned about the very survival of our great nation. I have never seen us more divided, Republicans hate Democrats and Democrats hate Republicans. The United States of America is not United."

Mary: "Is that why you decided to run as an Independent?"

TF: "I am running as an Independent because the whole political system is broken and the two party system has failed all of us. Washington, D.C. is totally dysfunctional because we have two parties that are choking Democracy to death. I have a very good life and I have been resistant to run for any national office. But, I am willing to sacrifice my life if it helps our country. As I stated earlier, I am concerned about the very survival of our country, we are 19 trillion in debt with no answers. Remember, the best way to kill Democracy is to bankrupt it and we are bankrupt. Besides, I have always been an Independent. We do not have a party system in Tribal politics, you run on who you are not what some party say's you are."

Mary: "Speaking of Washington D.C., what do you think of the Presidential debates?"

TF: "Just another reason why I am running as an Independent. As usual, the Republicans are eating their young. Actually, their debates remind me of the wrestling cage matches I have read about. To move things along, maybe they should all get in a cage and go at it, winner take all.

Then I watched the Democrats debate and they really blew my mind. The two leading candidates were asked, "What is the difference between being a Democrat and being a Socialist?" Neither one of them could give a clear answer. So, I am going to help them with that question. As liberal as the Democratic party has become there really is no difference, both systems are built on the concept of government dependence. They are both trying to convince us we should give the government our money, property and our civil rights because they know best. For those of you out there that think Socialism is a really cool idea, you should go to an Indian reservation because that is what Socialism looks like.

Socialism is the manifestation of envy, Socialists are envious of success. Success requires freedom, hard work and dedication and that is something Socialists are adamantly opposed to. Success makes them uncomfortable because if you and I are successful, they have to take a good long look at themselves and that makes them uncomfortable. That is why they want everyone to feel comfortable with being common, they advocate commonality.

They are okay with everyone suffering because that level's the playing field for them, successful people really piss them off. They tell the uninformed that they will all be happy if none of them are achievers, they will be equal if no one has ambition or drive.

The problem they face is when the ex-believers break from the pack and strive for success, this causes discomfort because now they will have to start achieving something or they will be left farther behind. As I said before, success irritates the hell out of them. They are much more comfortable when everyone fails, it takes the pressure off of them. Again, envy drives Socialism.

Let me put it to you this way, for 150 years on the Rez we all suffered equally because there was no upward mobility, no middle class. Socialist policies kill the middle class.

Remember one thing, there will always be rich people and poor people, that is the way it has always been. The difference is there is no middle class under Socialism, no upward mobility. The reason the United States of America has prospered is because of our middle class, they pay the majority of the taxes and they are the one's hurt under Socialism. When the Socialist's tell you they are going to tax the rich and then distribute that money to the rest of us they are blowing smoke up our collective asses. The rich will either move out of the country or they will find another way out of paying, that is why they are rich. Then, the higher taxes will be the burden of the middle class because they pay the majority of the taxes, it won't be the poor paying because they are already broke and don't pay any taxes anyway. After that happens, the middle class disappears under a pile of taxes and we are all equally poor. Remember one thing, the best way to kill Democracy is to bankrupt it.

Once Democracy is dead, the question then becomes, what is the difference between Socialism and Communism? Do not wait for an answer from the Socialists because they are happily moving our country towards Communism and they do not want to answer that question until that journey is completed, at which point they will no longer have to answer any questions, our voices will be silenced.

That is what the Socialists do, they slowly take away your independence and freedom until one day you wake up and they are all gone. Democracy is a real pain in their butts because We the People still have a voice. Once that voice is silenced, they can then get rid of all of our Constitutional Rights. You know, little things like freedom of speech, freedom of religion, freedom of assembly, freedom of the press and freedom to bear arms. They certainly aren't attacking those freedoms now, are they? You never really miss those things until they are gone and then it is too late.

Again, before you all get in bed with the Democrat/Socialism concept, go to an Indian reservation and see what 150 years of government dependence has done for us. Big government is never a good idea and there is no such thing as a free lunch. Big government is bad for the economy and for the human spirit. Remember, you do not get to pick your "Easter egg" houses, they are assigned to you under Socialism.

But, if you do decide to become Socialists, the Rez would sure like to have your business. Once the Democrat/Socialist's run out of other people's money to spend, you will probably need affordable housing and I highly recommend one our handmade Teepees, they are the best money can buy and we offer very attractive financing plans. Of course, we don't want you to stay on the Rez because anyone stupid enough to get rid of Democracy and Capitalism has no place with us, we have enough problems."

Mary: "From what I have read, the economy is doing pretty good, do you disagree?"

TF "Never believe everything you read. Our National Debt has doubled over the last seven years to 19 trillion and the politicians have no idea on how to reduce the debt. We had record revenues last year of approximately 3.5 trillion and the Federal Government spent approximately 4.5 trillion, they spent approximately 1 trillion more than they took in. Add that to the debt we already have and by the time we have a new President, this country will be over 20 trillion in debt. This is what happens when you handcuff free market enterprise.

Plus, consumer debt has risen over 6 trillion dollars and student loan debt has skyrocketed. How can they say the economy is doing good when we have all this debt? We just keep charging things. Did you know that forty cents out of every dollar the Federal Government spends is on borrowed money?"

Mary: "But, things seem to be moving along pretty well."

TF: "That is because the consequences of this failed policy has not come home to roost yet. The Federal Government's credit card will be maxed out soon and all Americans will suffer, the Federal Government is fiscally irresponsible and they have no answers on how to fix it. Unless something is done soon, the economy will collapse. Leaders need to lead, I blame all of the leaders in Washington D.C. for this problem, nobody there wants to make tough choices because they are all scared they might not get re-elected. It is sad and it's not the way to govern our country, it is not the Indian way."

Mary: "Well, how does it get fixed then?"

TF: "It starts at the top. There has to be a strong leader that works with Congress to get things done. They must put their differences behind them and start working for the good of the people. As I stated earlier, I am an Independent who votes my conscience. I take voting seriously and I study the candidates and the issues before I cast my vote. That is what the Constitution allows me to do, Democracy at it's finest. Too many voters just vote the party line and never know the issues of the day, or for that matter, anything about the candidates. Voters do not realize the impact that has on society. If a party always knows you will vote for them no matter what, why would they ever change? We must have more independent thinking and less sheep, that is the Indian way."

Mary: "How do we change that? Voter apathy has run wild in this country for years, how do you engage the disinterested?"

TF: "That is the challenge and we are all guilty of it. I never told anybody this before but I voted for a candidate for President that I knew very little about. I was swept up in the moment and was excited to see a young man so passionate about the issues of the day, I voted based on my heart and not my head. That young man ended up breaking my heart and by 2010, I knew I had made a terrible mistake.

This is my personal story and I believe it is a story shared by millions of voters. We must learn all we can about our candidates because our fate is in their hands. The deciding point for me, as a fiscally responsible voter, was when the candidate addressed the growing national debt issue and stated, I have to paraphrase a little here, "The problem is, is that the way Bush(President Bush) has done it over the last eight years is to take out a credit card from the Bank of China in the name of our children, driving up our national debt from 5 trillion to 9 trillion." He went on to say that was irresponsible and unpatriotic. That was on the campaign trail back in 2007. To me, no truer words were ever spoken, runaway national debt is unpatriotic. Well, the debt sits at 19 trillion today and that is not only unpatriotic it is criminal, the American people have been robbed of their economic future. He blamed Bush, yet he takes no responsibility for his actions. That is not leadership, that is not the Indian way.

Congress is to blame as well, they did nothing to bring down the debt. We may have been able to fight the issue when we were 9 trillion in debt, at 19 trillion there is no way out other than a painful collapse that all Americans will suffer through. The two party system has failed us and they have no answers, they do not even talk about the debt to us anymore. They always say they are reducing the deficits but they never say anything about the debt. That tells me that the Federal Government can still make its minimum payment on that credit card and that is about it. Yet, they keep on charging. Someone has to be a leader and do what is right for the country, that is the Indian way."

Mary: "Hindsight is always 20/20. What could the Executive and Legislative branches have done differently?"

TF: "I could go on for days on what they should have done, are you sure you want me to do that? This interview will end up being larger than the tax code. By the way, the tax code should be 3 pages long not 10,000."

Mary: "Take as much time as you like, I think it is important for the people of Montana to know your position on these critical domestic issues. Besides, I can always cut out what I do not like. Just kidding, you are the one that seems uptight."

TF: "I know, I know, I always get that way when I talk about stupid. Back to your question, The first two years of his Presidency was wrapped up in the Affordable Care Act that was jammed down our throats. It is an absolute boondoggle that will end up costing taxpayers hundreds of billions of dollars and it will eventually collapse under its own weight. That disaster must be replaced with a state by state plan. In other words, healthcare is a state issue just as education is. Whenever the Federal Government creates a bureaucracy of this magnitude the entire country suffers. Big government is never a good idea, it is a bloated, ineffective and costly system. That is true with most Federal Government bureaucracies. State's should decide these matters and open up competition for their business across state lines. Competition and choice will bring down the costs and increase coverage, it should be handled by our free market system. Approximately 90% of those covered under the Affordable Care Act are receiving help from taxpayers. In other words, taxpayers are paying for their subsidies and those receiving the subsidies cannot afford the high deductibles. So, instead of having 20 million subscribers, we have around 9 million and the premiums continue to go up and the quality of care continues to go down.

What we need to look at is the overall health of Americans. Obesity is running rampant and being fat contributes to heart attacks, cancer and diabetes. Get Americans up off the couch and out working and our health costs will plummet. Americans have to take personal responsibility for their actions and quit depending on the Federal Government to fix every single thing. Incentivize people to get healthy, that is what we did on the Rez and we only have one fat person left and we keep him that way so he can serve as a visual aid."

Mary: "Well they also gave us Dodds-Frank, right?"

TF: "That is right, when the Democrats had the Presidency, the House of Representatives and the Senate they gave us The Affordable Care Act and Dodds-Franks. They could have passed anything they wanted and this was the best they could come up with, that is just no way to run a whorehouse.

Nationally, most people hate the Affordable Care Act and that was reflected in the 2014 Congressional election results. Republicans gained seats in an unprecedented sign of displeasure over that policy. What other issue was there? No, it is a boondoggle and it will collapse. By the way, I think it was sad that after the recent mid-term elections, the President did not come out and try to improve his relationship with Congress by congratulating the Republicans on their Congressional wins. Instead, he blamed low voter turnout for the result. Then, to further alienate the Republicans, he put his Executive Action on Immigration into play and Frank Johnson was right there with him. That is not what a leader does, that is not the Indian way.

He wasted the mandate of the people and he lost Congress, we would have followed him but he chose not to lead. Instead, he chose to divide us. I remember the night he was elected and the overwhelming feeling of hope and change. Remember that? It was a magical night. In fact, I still get a tingle up my pant leg just thinking back to that moment. We got change all right, short changed."

Mary: "You mentioned the Executive Order on Immigration, what is your position on such a complex issue?"

TF: "Well, it is not really that complex, either we are a nation of laws or we are not. Why is the United States not allowed to have secure borders? What is equally troubling to me is the sanctuary city concept. Sanctuary cities are defying federal law by not enforcing the Immigration laws that are currently on the books. They are doing this and the Federal Government is not doing anything to stop them and I think that establishes a very dangerous precedent. Our leaders, by letting this happen, are saying to all Americans that it is okay to break federal law and once Americans lose faith in their government institutions all hell will break loose. This is a slippery slope that will result in unintended consequences. What if a city decided, for whatever reason, not to enforce Civil Rights laws? Those laws are no more potent than the Immigration laws, they are both Federal laws that trace their viability to the 14th Amendment and neither one of them should be violated. When one law is allowed to be violated, how can you argue that the other should not be? Just saying, this is another example of the total failure of our Federal Government and we must elect people that are lawful and honest.

Our elected officials violate the Constitution and the criminals all hide behind it, don't these people take an oath of office to defend the U.S. Constitution? Our politicians attack the Constitution, they no longer defend it. Congress makes the laws and the President is duty bound to uphold them and not to change them because he does not like them. Should foreigners be allowed to cross our borders and take up residency in the United States illegally? Well, let me tell you a story I heard years ago, it goes something like this:

When Indian lands were first being invaded by White settlers, several Chiefs got together to decide on what to do about these invaders. So, one day they had a meeting inside a Teepee next to a roaring fire and one Chief said to all the other Chiefs, "I am worried about the strangers coming to our land. They have a strange religion and they refuse to speak our language." All the Chiefs nodded and smoked on a peace pipe for awhile before another Chief spoke up and said, "I think you are just being heartless and insensitive. Let them in, what harm can they do?" Well, that pretty much sums up my feelings on the matter. I hope the United States of America has better luck with this than us Native Americans. If our leaders continue to allow this invasion to happen, I am going back to the Rez and I am going to build a wall around it to keep all the politicians out."

Mary: "Aren't you afraid you are going to offend the politically correct crowd?"

TF: "That is what is wrong with our politicians, they are concerned about being politically correct, I prefer to just be correct. A leader has to do what is right not what is politically expedient. Political correctness is not the Indian way."

Mary: "I see. What is your stance on another hot topic this political season, gun control?"

TF: "I defend every word of the Constitution. Once the Constitution is destroyed what is left for us? America is great because of our Constitution and our rules of law. It is not just a matter of banning assault rifles, the issue is once the anti-Constitution crowd starts taking away Constitutional rights, where will it stop? There is all this terrorist activity in our country and around the world and if we take guns away from law abiding Americans we play right into the hands of the criminals and the terrorists. We have no gun zones now and where is the first place the criminals and murders go to start shooting? That's right, the gun free zones. Americans should be armed and recognize the fact that we are at war. I can tell you that on the Rez, we are armed to the teeth and we have safety lessons and classes on how to shoot.

Here is another Native American Indian lesson: When we peacefully handed over our weapons after signing all those peace treaties, we were summarily massacred throughout this land. Today, we remember what giving up our weapons meant, it meant near extinction. We value our 2nd Amendment rights because we know firsthand what happened when the government took away our weapons, we must defend the Constitution at all costs. Their political answer to these terrorists who are killing us is to take away the rights of law abiding citizens, it is not only illogical it is dangerous.

Compromises can be made but we need our elected officials to work together to solve these problems. We need a strong leader that has the interests of the majority of Americans in mind. Currently, we have no such leader. Our military must have the best weapons and the peacekeepers must have the very finest equipment to help us stay safe."

Mary: "Since you brought up the military and the peacekeepers, and I assume when you say peacekeepers you are talking about police officers, what do you think of all this anti-military and anti-police behavior? It seems to be getting worse everyday."

TF: "Well, it is not the Indian way, we respect our Warriors because we know they are the ones that fight to kept us safe. They are the ones that put their lives on the line every single day for the American people, all Americans. Can you imagine the violence and terror they see on a daily basis? I am not talking abut Iraq or Afghanistan, I am talking about Chicago, Detroit, Baltimore and practically every single major city in America. There are bad people in every profession but to indict an entire profession for the actions of a few is not right, Native Americans respect Warriors.

Mary: "You brought up a good point as to violence in our major cities, how would you, as a Senator, solve the problem with the plight of the black youth in the inner cities?"

TF: "Wow, that is an easy question, people have puzzled over that issue for over fifty years now. All I can say is that Democrats must really hate the blacks because their policies of government dependence are largely responsible for the situation. They should approach the situation much like the way we handled our dependency on the Rez, they must get rid of their Federal Government dependency.

Federal Indian Policy was in effect on our Rez at least fifty years before the 1964 Civil Rights government dependency programs went in to effect and it still amazes me to this day that they could institute laws that were so harmful to the very important concept of freedom, it never worked on the Rez and it took us years to shake off that dependency so change will not come overnight because there are too many politicians and other people that have vested interest in the current, harmful system.

Quite frankly, this system is a way to buy votes, nothing more. Each Presidential election since 1964 has resulted in blacks voting overwhelmingly in favor of Democrats and what have the Democrats done for them? If they really cared for the black youth of America like I do, they would get rid of all these harmful programs and put them to work.

Here is what we have learned as Native Americans, being constantly dependent on the Federal Government made us slaves to their policies, we had very little freedom. This resulted in us drinking ourselves to death, shooting ourselves in the head or jumping off of water towers to our death. We lost our pride, self respect and honor, that is no different than what is happening in America today.

But here is the real problem, getting the dependent to admit their dependency. No one that is dependent sees it as harmful and that is what the government counts on. Consider this, when a person chooses freedom, that is taking personal responsibility for your actions, that person needs to understand that decision is going to be met with distain by the other people in the dependency class. You will be called names, you may be injured and you certainly will be cast out. What the dependency crowd must understand, and trust me it is not just the blacks that are encumbered by it, there are plenty of whites, browns, etc. who have fallen into that trap as well, is you are slaves to the system and your freedom has been taken from you. Nothing is free, there is a price for everything.

Government dependency is evil, it saps character and strength by encouraging greed and weakness. On the Rez, we recognized this and developed programs where all our people work and take pride in working. We all took responsibility for our actions and did not fall into the trap of how bad we had it based on events that happened over 150 years ago.

Indians had their land stolen, treaties were broken, we were massacred, scalped, put into slavery and stuck on reservations where we were left to die. But, the worst thing the government did to us was to make us dependent on them, it took us years to wake up and shake free of the chains of dependency. How long before the rest of you do the same?

Believe me, it was not easy because change never is. It will require hard work, sacrifice and a strong desire to be free. But here is the good news, in America freedom and liberty are still possible, for now. That is not true in Russia, China, Iran and all the other totalitarian governments in the world. Your first step, take personal responsibility for your actions. Do not listen to the enablers who are constantly telling you how rough you have it, they want to keep you down because it raises them up. There is big money in your despair, just ask the rap music moguls."

Mary: "But what about finding them jobs?"

TF: "First of all, they, like the rest of us, have to find their own jobs. We created jobs on the Rez by cleaning up our forests for example. Every summer, we have crews thinning the trees so the whole forest is healthier. It is labor intensive and not very glamorous work but it is necessary for a healthy forest. Our national forests are burning up every summer and nobody in the Federal Government is doing anything about the health of our forests. By extension, the Federal

Government is not doing anything for the health of Americans or the economy. Instead of paying people not to work, why doesn't the Federal Government pay people that are on public assistance to clean up our forests, our lakes, our streams and our streets? The work is there, do not tell me there is no work. But, If you do not want to get your hands dirty, there really is no hope for you.

Just one other point for all Americans relying on the Federal Government for help, the Federal Government is bankrupt and when the credit is cut off to them, what programs do you think will disappear first? But, look at it this way, that may solve the illegal immigration issue because once all the money is cut off they will leave this country so fast it will make your head spin, so much for wanting to be an American."

Mary: "Since Indians are the original environmentalists, I like your idea about cleaning up our natural resources. What are your thoughts on the issue of climate change?"

TF: "I say, leave it to a politician to think they can change the weather. There has been climate change since the beginning of time. I always marvel at the rich environmentalists that want you and me to give up our cars, electricity and running water while they fly around in their private jets. They have multiple homes and leave a much larger carbon impact on the climate than you and I do. Democrats act like they are the only ones interested in a clean environment yet they do absolutely nothing to change it, they all talk a good game. I live in a log cabin and Frank has three houses yet he wants to take away my microwave oven.

They say the ocean level is rising and man has caused a severe drought in California. That may be true but what are the Democrat's solution to this? Instead of building reservoirs in the mountains to collect the water and the snow melt they let it all run off into the ocean thereby raising the ocean level and worsening the effects of the drought, they do all this so they can save smelt. They say they are worried about Mother Earth. I got news for them, Mother Earth will replenish itself after all of us are gone, we better start worrying about mankind because we are the endangered species. Democrats always have policies based on events 150 years in the future or events that happened 150 years ago. As a member of Congress, I will be working on the problems of today. People worried about the environment should consider what happens to it when nuclear war breaks out? What will that do to global warming?"

Mary: "I know, everybody is threatening to use nuclear weapons lately. I especially worry about the Russians and their immense arsenal. What are you thoughts about the Russians?"

TF: "All I can tell you is that when I traveled to Russia on behalf of the state of Montana, I never saw one black person walking the streets. Or, for that matter, one women in a position of power. I believe it is the most racist and sexist country on Earth. They have no tolerance for blacks, women or gays. I think if we have a woman President, the Russian President will disrespect her just as he has disrespected our black President. Unfortunately, we need to be able to work with them and ease the tensions but the Russians will not talk to blacks or women. That is the way it has always been, it is their culture."

Mary: "Well, I really do not have any further questions for you at this time, would you like to add anything?"

TF: "Just this, Frank and the Democrat party have attacked me since the day I announced my candidacy. That is fine, I am a big boy and I understand it. However, if you no longer understand them and think they are harming our great nation remember this, when we are stoned, we are all Democrats. It is now time to put down the pipe, clear our heads and start doing what is right for America. By the way, I want to wish everybody a belated Happy 4th of July."

It was a Sunday night on the Rez and that meant bingo. After the hour interview, the hall began to fill with eager participants, there was a $1,000.00 blackout and everybody was excited, Two-Fingers was the one who always called out the numbers.

Before the games began, we sat around talking and I noticed Two-Fingers staring at Mary as she gathered up her things. I told him she was single and it was time for him to get over being the grieving widower, he had punished himself long enough. When Mary had finished packing up, she came over and thanked us and said, "I like what you have to say. So, if you do not mind, I would like to come back for another interview." Two-Fingers mulled this over for a few seconds and then said, "If you think your readers can handle the truth, I am all in." Mary smiled at him and then walked out of the hall. "I like her, I really do. You don't find too many young people interested in politics these days." Two-Fingers said as he watched the door close behind her. "Talking about liking something, I really liked your speech. All that without any notes, wow. That was simply amazing. In fact, I got a warm feeling up my pant leg just listening to you." Two-Fingers slowly turned towards me and said, "Crack you, White Guy."

Two-Fingers never had any money and running a campaign costs money. I used a lot of our savings to help finance his trips from one small town to another, his goal was to speak to as many people as he could. When we travelled, we generally ate bologna sandwiches and slept in cheap motels.

He declared early in 2015 around the same time the other candidates had announced and everywhere he went he talked about the failure of the two party system and it worked, people were fed up with the status quo.

As I said earlier, the Republican candidate was Pete Reynolds and he wanted a shot at being a Senator before he retired, he was getting up there in age and he was starting to slow down. Pete was a nice enough fella and he ran a clean campaign but Two-Fingers and I both thought he could be beaten easily given the fact that people in Montana were fed up with career politicians and he really had nothing new to offer.

Frank was a career politician too but he was still very formidable, the Democrat Party was still in charge of politics in Montana and Frank was the Party. So, Frank was our main concern and focus, we both thought he was beatable because he was directly tied to every failed policy of the last several years. Frank had lost all of his common sense somewhere between Helena, Montana and Washington D.C. Thankfully, Montanans still had their common sense and they hated what was happening to our country. So, Two-Fingers and I kept to our plan to run against each and every one of Frank's failed policies. There were so many of them that it was like shooting fish in a barrel. Thankfully, Montanans still believe in the Constitution.

Chapter 41

We went to work and so did the Democrats propaganda machine, they poured money into smearing Two-Fingers in an unprecedented way. Never in the history of Montana politics was such a vicious attack perpetuated on an opponent. I couldn't turn on the news without seeing a negative ad about Two-Fingers and the liberal newspapers in Montana ran front page editorials calling Two-Fingers everything but a white man, they were brutal.

Fortunately, Two-Fingers was running in Montana where people took offense to such bullshit. Montanans heard of his record and many of them actually drove through the Rez and marveled at the changes that had taken place since Two-Fingers took charge. Many of them also knew of him when he was the head of the Montana International Trade Organization, his following began to grow.

The Democrats were desperate and they kept on coming with the negativity. They were spending hundreds of thousands of dollars on negative ads and between the two of us, we had about $5,000.00. Two-Fingers was always giving his money to the less fortunate and I had just finished paying off my student loans, so money was tight.

After about a week of listening to all these negative ads, Two-Fingers decided to take his gloves off and show them what he was all about. He was well received at the town meetings I had set up but the crowds were small, we needed to start running some ads and get some local press covering us but it was a slow process. Trust me when I tell you this, money goes a long way when it comes to buying elections.

We got lucky, the article that Mary wrote about Two-Fingers in the Native American Sovereignty Magazine was well received. As it turned out, it was a very popular Native American source of information and it was distributed in all 50 states. Soon after it was published, Two-Fingers began to receive hundreds of small contributions. Not much money, the largest contribution was $15.00 but there were hundreds of them coming in from Native Americans all across America. The money was very welcome but what really helped Two-Fingers confidence was the outpouring of support. He was energized and convinced he could help Montanans and Americans all across this great country.

I took some of the money he received and paid our local Blackfeet Printing Company to make thousands of bumper stickers that simply said, "That's not the Indian way." Holy shit, we had a slogan and $22,000.00 in the bank, watch out Democrats we were coming to get you.

Weeks later, we were back on the Rez tending to Tribal matters when I received a call from Mary. She asked if she could come up to the Rez the following Sunday for another interview. I did not give her an answer, I just transferred her to Two-Fingers, he needed to decompress from all the political stuff in his life and I thought he should talk to a pretty woman instead of worrying about everybody else all the time. So, I made an executive decision and transferred her call to him and they ended up talking for over two hours.

That next Sunday we sat down in the bingo hall for another interview. I had my trusty recorder with me and after everybody settled in, the interview began.

Mary: "Well, it has been almost a year since you announced your candidacy, what are your impressions so far?"

TF: "Well, I have always known that politics is not for the weak of heart, all the personal attacks are brutal and self serving and the negativity is a further illustration of how the two party system has failed us. They have the money and the power and they abuse both, they try to drown out all opposition. What are they afraid of?

Over the remaining months of my campaign, I will demonstrate how they have failed us and I will continue to talk about what qualities a person must have to be a great leader. We do not have leaders in this country, all we have are finger pointers, excuse makers and cowards. Indians are a lot of things but we are not cowards. So, if they want a fight, I will give them a fight."

Mary: "Your poll numbers since we last talked have risen quite dramatically, what do you attribute that too?"

TF: "Well, I credit most of the rise to our interview. I was not very well known and neither were my policies. I spoke with you about a few things that seemed to resonate with the voters and I have received a lot of support from people in Montana as well as from people from across the nation and I want to personally thank you for the opportunity. The one issue that every one of my supporters is concerned with is the issue of our national debt."

Mary: "Let's pick up on that issue then. What changes would you make in order to bring down that debt? None of our current leaders seem to have a clue, they seem to be hiding from the issue."

TF: "They hide because they couldn't run the country well when they were flush with cash and had surpluses. They are baffled on what to do now and they actually think they can spend their way to prosperity. Austerity will be painful but everyone must know that austerity is the only answer. To pay down debt, we must either cut costs or increase revenues and I suggest we do both.

I have heard the Democrat party say that more taxes are the answer. They never say anything about cutting big government and all the expenses affiliated with big government, they always want to tax more. They claim they are going to get the money from the wealthiest people in America and that our taxes will not be raised, yours and mine. I have a clue for them, the wealthiest people in the country know how to avoid paying taxes so the burden of their high priced big government programs will fall on the shoulders of the little guy, you and me. Besides, the wealthiest people in this country are the ones getting these people elected, do you really believe they are going after them? No, it will fall on the backs of the middle class like it always has.

If spending is not cut, they will have to keep charging the costs of the colossal big government programs on the America is Broke Credit Card until the creditors pay them a visit. Austerity and fiscally responsible programs are the only solution but that will require sacrifice and dedication to the task and that is never a popular sell to those that are dependent on the government. Just remember, the longer we put off the inevitable, the greater the pain."

Mary: "The negative ads against you suggest that the economy is doing great, unemployment is down and inflation is low, what do you say to these claims?

TF: "No inflation? I remember when you could buy a pound of hamburger for 25 cents a pound. I went into a grocery store in Great Falls the other day and paid $6.45 a pound. By the way, it tasted like crap. Nothing like the hamburger of my youth. What was the price of a pound of hamburger seven years ago? What work programs have been instituted over the last seven years? All they have done is borrow approximately 10 trillion more dollars and reduce the interest rates to almost zero. No bridges were built, no pipelines. By the way, Montanans want to know why the Keystone pipeline was not built? We were told that the 45,000 jobs created by the project would only be temporary jobs and therefore the law should be vetoed. Aren't all construction jobs by their very nature temporary? You build a house and that is a temporary job, you build a bridge and that is a temporary construction job. All temporary jobs unless the Federal Government gets involved and then it is a bridge to nowhere that takes forever to get done, lifetime employment.

My favorite argument for not building it and helping North America to achieve energy independence was it would be harmful to the environment to have that oil consumed. Well, guess what, that did not stop the consumption or production of that oil one little bit. It was shipped out of the oil fields on trains and trucks, trains and trucks pollute a lot more than pipelines.

As to the unemployment argument, we have the highest non-participation rate in the history of our country and you are telling me employment has improved? The number of people working is back to the 2007 number. The only difference is we are 10 trillion further in debt. Low paying jobs, wage stagnation and the good jobs are going overseas and nothing is being done about it. Luckily, Montanans know the truth."

Mary: "What changes to the political system would you try to make if you are elected?"

TF: "Mary, before I answer that let me just add this, Montana used to be called the Treasure State. It is rich in minerals, forests and other natural resources. At one time, Butte was the largest city between Seattle and Minneapolis. It had thousands of hard working miners employed supplying the world with copper and silver. Anaconda had a large smelter that has since been shut down and those jobs all went to the Japanese. We need to be able to produce things in this country again, the EPA has virtually shut down our economy with all of their regulations. Every time the government passes a regulation we lose jobs and we lose freedom, we need to get the government off our backs. Big government does not create wealth, if it did we would not be 19 trillion in debt. Our credit card is just about maxed out and if we do not move from a consumer economy to a producing economy soon, we are going to go bankrupt. I am going to take care of the economy so grandmother doesn't have to eat dog."

Mary: "Dog? Oh I get it, Indians were always made fun of for eating dog because we were hungry."

TF: "Exactly, if you are hungry enough you will eat anything."

Mary: "So are you investing in gold?"

TF: "No, I am investing in corn seeds."

Mary: "Corn seeds? Why corn seeds?"

TF: "Have you ever tried to eat gold? I am going to grow corn."

TF: "Back to your question about what I would change about our political system if elected, we need to have term limits and we need to pass a balanced budget Amendment to the United States Constitution. Getting the Amendment passed should be the easier of the two to get done. Term limits will be the harder issue because the professional politicians are greedy and power hungry and will oppose it. In the 1990's, there was a wave of support for term limits and the promise of limiting terms got a lot of new people elected. Once elected, they betrayed the country by not following through on their promises, most elected officials have no honor and we need to limit terms so we can limit their damage. I propose one six year term for the President and each and every member of Congress. One term and no further involvement with the government as a lobbyist or any special interest group, serve your country for six years and then go back home. Right now, our government is controlled by lobbyists and special interest groups who don't have our best interests in mind. We need our elected officials to work for Americans not for foreign interest groups that aim to do us harm.

We also need to cut the size of government by at least one half. Right now, Washington, D.C. is the new Wall Street, it is where the money is. We need to get rid of half the employees in each and every one of the bureaucracies, send them home and let's see if we even miss them. We need to shut down the Department of Energy and the Department of Education completely. If the Department of Energy is not out finding energy, why do we need them? Education should be left to the states, most matters should be under the exclusive control of states. Our huge Federal Government is ineffective and expensive and we need to get rid of all the redundancies that exist between overlapping State and Federal Government bureaucracies. In the last fifty years or so, we have moved away from state autonomy to this Federal Big Government policy and it was the wrong way to go as evidenced by the huge debt and lack of productivity."

Mary: "In light of all of the recent events regarding race relations in our country, do you believe you will be given a fair chance given the fact that you are a Native American?"

TF: "I think racism exists in all countries to some degree. So does greed, hate, conceit, envy, lust, and a lot of other human emotions. There are just certain things you can't legislate away, the folly of big government is thinking they can, human emotions can't be eradicated by a law.

I believe that the Republicans and Democrats use race as a rallying point for their interests and not for the interests of the minorities in our country. They have always exploited minorities for their political gain, another reason the Democrats get 90% of the black vote for example. They like the whole race war thing and they like the whole sexist thing. They want us at each others throats so we will vote for them based on these wedge issues and they want us distracted so we do not challenge them on the real issues of the day. Like, the destruction of our Constitutional Rights and the huge federal debt.

Our country has come a long way over the last 150 years. I am proud to live in a country that elected a black President. How many black Presidents have there been in France? England? Germany? Canada? Mexico? Italy? Russia? China? I hope you get my point. We have a long way to go to fully heal from the past sins of our great nation but we can never give up on one another and let special interests groups tear us apart. United we stand, divided we fall. If we don't get it together and become one nation again, we will all pay the price. There are plenty of our enemies betting against our ability to reconcile. If you think America is racist and sexiest, check out how Russians treat women, gays and blacks."

Mary: "So you think you will get a fair shake."

TF: "Yes I do and here is why, I voted for the President in 2008 because he told me what I wanted to hear. I did not vote for him because he was black, I voted for him because he said the national debt of 9 trillion was irresponsible and unpatriotic and he blamed Bush for it. I am not a big Bush fan and I did not support the invasion of Iraq. But, we can't let Bush's decision to invade Iraq continue to tear our country apart. Anyway, I am fiscally responsible and the number one issue for me is our fiscal strength as a nation, I know how important it is to our way of life.

Four years later, I voted against him, not because of race, but because of his fiscal irresponsibility and his anti-austerity measures. During those four years, our debt went up over 4 trillion dollars and currently sits at over 19 trillion, now who is unpatriotic? In 2012 he was no more black than he was in 2008. Yet, because of his failed policies, he lost support and blamed it on race. When the race card is pulled, you lose all credibility and I will never pull that card. I am not weak and it is not the Indian way.

Besides, if you are black and you voted for him solely because of his race, who is the real racist? I suggest his loss in popularity has more to do with his policies. Exhibit A is the Affordable Care Act. Exhibit B is his Executive Action arbitrarily changing Immigration law. Exhibit C is his Foreign Policy agenda. These are all issues that are embraced by my Democrat opponent in this race and they are all bad for America."

Mary: "As you know, I am from Arizona and his Executive Order on Immigration has really stirred things up. If elected, you will have to deal with this issue and the last time we spoke you touched on the issue briefly, is there anything you would like to add?"

TF: "Only that if the President felt so strongly on this issue why didn't he change the law through the legislative process? He had control of the House and Senate. Instead, the Democrats gave us the Affordable Care Act and did nothing regarding Immigration or, for that matter, gun control.

Executive Actions are an affront to the Constitution of the United States and he has set a very dangerous precedent. If a President can change or delete a law because he does not like it we no longer have Separation of Powers. If he can get rid of Congress, or make it ineffectual, how long will Democracy last? It is just a dangerous precedent. Once Congress is gone how long will the Supreme Court last?

Executive Orders have limits in terms of scope. We currently have three branches of government that are supposed to be co-equal. When there is only one branch, the head of that branch is known as King or Queen. Is that what you want? No, if he really cared about immigration he would have had the laws changed Constitutionally.

It shows a lack of character when you believe in something and you do not follow through with your convictions because you fear it will cost you an election. Same thing with the war on terrorism and gun control. He could have passed any law he wanted to and yet he abandoned his principles for four more years, they always want four more years.

I will do the right thing because it is the right thing to do. I will not make excuses, blame my race, blame the fact that I have one hand, blame the fact that I am ugly.... I will stand by my convictions because that is the Indian way."

Mary: "You are not that ugly. What about the terrorism issue and the response to it?"

TF: "That horse has been beat pretty good lately. All I can ask is do you feel safe? Personally, I do not think it is a good idea to release terrorists who have killed Americans. As far as overall safety, I feel safe but then again I do not live in Chicago. How long are Americans going to tolerate all of this violence in our cities? It just goes to show you how screwed up we have become when we lecture other countries on how to behave and we can't even walk down our streets without fearing for our lives. The Democrats claim that terrorists are using the internet as a recruitment tool. If so, I say to combat terrorism, we should put out a video that says: "Anybody that does a terrorist act will be caught, disarmed and sent to the South Side of Chicago on a Saturday night." They wouldn't last ten minutes, and they call us Indians savages."

Mary: "What are your thoughts on political correctness?"

TF: "Everybody is talking about political correctness. Colleges, universities and politicians are all about political correctness. Here is what I have to say about it, political correctness is another way of limiting our First Amendment Rights to Free Speech. We are chastised, humiliated and disgraced if we say words that are deemed to be wrong. You know, words like, "Merry Christmas." Political correctness is just another veiled attempt at denying people their rights. The politically correct crowd says you can have freedom of speech as long as that speech does not offend them, so much for freedom.

By the way, I commissioned a study as to what is causing global warming. I put two of my best people on it, Stogie Man and Liquid Louie. They spent months studying the phenomenon and they have concluded that every time someone is gutless and says something politically correct, the hole in the ozone grows substantially larger. They have also concluded that the only way to stop the problem is for everyone to grow a set of balls and speak their mind. They will have a full report available in 2040. Which is the time, ironically, all the new pollution policies go into effect, leave it to politicians to put off doing anything until they are all safely out of office."

Mary: "Since we are on the topic of the 1st Amendment, what do you think about the recent Federal Circuit opinion regarding the Washington Redskin copyright issue?"

TF: "Just another example of the politically correct crowd exploiting Native Americans. We have been suffering for decades under their abusive Federal Government policies and they make this the issue? Really? We were stuck on reservations and left to die and the best they can do for us is to get rid of a name? The only Indian I know of that is actually offended by this is Stubby Grant. Of course, Stubby hates everything and everybody. I guess it is nice that we are actually getting some publicity even though it is phony publicity.

Personally, I am not offended by this name. However, I am deeply offended when they violate the word Chief. In the olden days the Chief was revered and was a person of honor and integrity. What offends me is when they use the words Commander-in-Chief. In this context, it is no longer a meaningless word on a football jersey, it is a symbol of leadership, a Chief in the olden days would never abandon his Warriors, he would never eat until all the other members of the Tribe ate, he would never blame the previous Chief for the difficulties he faced, he would never lie to the people, a Chief is courageous and strong and the first one to go to battle, he is a Warrior. Chiefs in the olden days would sit in council and listen to advice, they would never be vindictive towards another member of the Tribe who had an opposing idea. Chiefs brought everybody together for the common good, they did not divide the Tribe. A Chief admits his mistakes and a Chief never rewards cowardice. But most importantly, a Chief never thinks of his legacy, he thinks of his people. So, in my opinion, until these so called "Chiefs" begin to display these qualities, they should no longer be allowed to use the word Chief. Call them Commanders, Kings, Queens or what have you, but do not dishonor the word Chief."

Mary: "Well, you are running for a national office and you will be asked to vote on a number of issues. Would you vote to close Guantanamo?"

TF: "Of all the campaign promise that were made, this is the one he is interested in fulfilling? What about the debt? All I can say is, can you imagine what would have happened to us Indians if, instead of killing Custer, we would have captured him and then released him? There wouldn't be an Indian left alive today, he would have murdered us all. Never release people that have killed innocent Americans, it's not the Indian way and I would vote against closing it."

Mary: "Have you gotten any negative blow back from our previous interview?"

TF: "Actually everything I have heard is pretty positive. I have heard a few complaints about the need to break the chains of the government dependency. But, that was expected. As I said at the time, those on the government teat never see the harm that is being done to them, government dependency is an abomination. I will add this, Native Americans were forced onto reservations, the folks dependent on the government have created their own reservations and succumbed to it without a fight, break the chains and strive for freedom and liberty while you still can."

Mary: "I really do not have any further questions for you and I can see that the people are starting to file in to play some bingo. Is there anything else you would like to say?"

TF: "Just this, I am going to be a leader for all of you just like the Chiefs in the olden days. I will bring honesty and integrity back to politics. Both political party's have betrayed our trust, they have pitted us against each other in an attempt to better themselves. Nothing is getting done in Washington, D.C. and our so called leaders act like children, they are all about vindictiveness and greed. The Republicans and Democrats in office hate each other and We the People suffer because of their hate, we are pawns in their evil game. If a good idea is proposed by the Republicans, every Democrat votes against it. If the Democrats come up with a good idea, every Republican votes against it and all the while We the People suffer, there is no leadership. The system and the players are corrupt and they are all complicate in their treason. Recently, a Presidential candidate from one party claimed the biggest enemy they face is the other party. What? How can you govern if you do not seek compromise and unity? We the People have suffered through this cowardice long enough. Montanans, if you elect me to the Senate, I will fight for right because it is the right thing to do. That is why I am running as an Independent, the two party system has failed us. With your help and the help of all Americans, we can take our country back, we just need leadership. Thank you."

Just a quick side note, Stogie Man and Liquid Louie were two of the first people in the Alcohol Treatment program that Two-Fingers was instrumental in getting established on the Rez. Two-Fingers personally went and found Stogie Man and drug him back to Browning screaming and kicking. That was over twenty years ago and he has been clean and sober ever since. After they both cleaned up, Stogie Man and Liquid Louie went off to the University of Chicago where they both received Doctorates in Applied Science, their stories are truly inspirational.

Chapter 42

It was shortly after that interview that the economic bubble finally burst, the ill conceived policies of the previous seven years started to show their disastrous effects, the shell game ended. Interest rates began to move higher, world markets collapsed and our stock market began to show the strains of the 19 trillion debt.

Our government was bankrupt, it didn't have enough money to buy a popsicle. It was an unprecedented collapse and nobody in the government had a clue on how to fix it, America is the tail that wags the dog in terms of worldwide solvency and we are bankrupt. Foreign government's begged us to fix our financial nightmare but nobody knew what to do. It got so bad, people had to give up their cable TV subscriptions and actually have conversations with their family members, it was absolutely frightening.

Then, just as Two-Fingers predicted, things got really ugly. The government was finding it hard to find anyone stupid enough to loan it money. When they did find someone to lend them money, it was at usurious interest rates. All the money they lent at less than one percent was now being borrowed back at sixteen percent, we got these loans from the very banks we helped back in 2008. In effect, the banks own America because the government lost all of its credit worthiness. Government checks stopped coming and millions of Americans were thrown out of work and the government tried to solve the problem by printing more money and the dollar quickly devalued. Inflation skyrocketed and the stock market eventually collapsed. Shortages began to take their toll and riots swept across the country.

The financial collapse was much worse than the Depression of the 1930's. Back then, the economy was terrible but the government was not 19 trillion in debt so they could finance public work programs. Socialism has failed and the only way to get out of this mess was to get private investment going, the government had to get out of the way and let Capitalism go back to work; the government's stifling economic policies had ruined the financial health of America.

Like Two-Fingers always said, the best way to kill Democracy was to bankrupt it. Private investors had to be given a reason to invest in America and that meant all of the onerous regulations and high taxes had to go. Prior to the collapse, the government received record revenues and still ran up 19 trillion dollars of debt. Big government does not create jobs it only stops economic development. Of course, all the politicians were pointing fingers and blaming the other guy as America suffered.

Montanans who had listened to Two-Fingers message over the years knew he was right and the collapse proved it. His popularity soared and his numbers in the polls skyrocketed. He was the only candidate that warned of the economic collapse and more importantly, he was the only one with solutions to the problem.

Two-Fingers had very little money and the financial collapse did not help matters. The little bit of money he had raised from individual donors did not go far and the donors eventually quit sending in money. He did not blame them, he knew they needed the money more than he did. Besides, I had discovered the internet and decided to make a political movie starring Two-Fingers and put it on YouTube. Social media was at its peak, everybody was on the internet trying to figure out what had just happened. Two-Fingers was about to tell them in no uncertain terms, reality was about to replace the fiction of the last seven years.

I was actually getting pretty good with the camera, I had filmed Kanowski's tar and feathering and I was well aware of the importance of good lighting. Two-Fingers was not the most handsome person in the world and there was no good way to light him but I tried my best.

I sat up the camera in Two-Fingers office one night and the two of us got down to business. I served as the off camera moderator and he either answered my questions or he just went off on his own tangents, mainly he just went off on tangents. I called the movie, "The World According to Two-Fingers." and it turned out to be one of the most viewed movies of 2016. Here is the unedited transcript of what was said.

TF: "My name is Donny R. Schwartz and I am a Blackfeet Indian from Browning, Montana. I am running for Senator from the great State of Montana and for the last thirty years I have been the Chairman of the Blackfeet Tribe. Do not hold this against me but I am an Attorney, I am legally trained and have spent most of my life studying the Constitution of The United States and the Supreme Court cases that impact the Constitution. As a Blackfeet Indian that was raised on a reservation, I know first hand the terrible effects of our government's dependency programs. These programs suck the very life blood out of every American that has the misfortune of living under it's spell and now all of us suffer because of failed government policies, we all in the same boat and it is sinking fast.

Our Constitution is all about freedom and liberty. The Founding Fathers tried to protect us from an abusive totalitarian big government, they knew that freedom and liberty would lift the human condition in a way that all the money in the world could not. Over the years, the Constitution has been violated by our elected officials and our liberties and freedom's have been slowly taken away from us and every time they pass a regulation or law that inhibits our freedom and liberties, they violate the principles of freedom. As a nation, we are drowning in regulations and debt.

Big corporations do not mind the regulations because they have legal staffs and accountants that help them navigate through the treacherous waters of regulation. They pass on the costs of dealing with all these regulations to the consumer, to all of us. Small businesses can't afford to deal with all the regulations and they collapse under the weight. This leaves the big corporations in charge and that is the way they like it, big corporations do not have to worry about competition because the burdensome Federal Government has buried the small entrepreneurs under a pile of regulations. The corporations then control's where all the manufacturing of their products are made. America no longer manufactures anything of importance, we have been reduced to a consumption country and that is the main reason for the financial collapse.

Our government is controlled by lobbyists and special interests groups that do not have the interests of We the People in mind. Big corporations are just as harmful to us as is our big government. But, we need corporations now more than ever because they have the money to spur economic growth, the government is broke.

The easy money of the last seven years has not evaporated, it is in the hands of the monied class. It has always been that way in every country since the beginning of time. The monied class always survives while We the People suffer. Knowing this, we have to make a pact with the devil, we must lower the corporate tax rate so the corporations invest in America.

Unlike big government, they do provide jobs and economic growth. They have taken that growth offshore and all Americans have suffered, the government policies have enabled them to do that. The government, in an attempt to fool us, say's they are going to raise the taxes on the wealthy and corporations to help finance the government. That is probably the stupidest thing they have ever said to us. Do they think we are so naive to believe the rich are going to willingly give their wealth to the government? No, the pain and the tax burden will be placed on the shoulders of the middle class. We currently have the highest corporate tax rates in the world and that has caused the loss of American jobs as the corporations go offshore. Obviously, that has not worked or we would not be broke.

Corporate profits will suffer tremendously with this recent financial collapse, nobody has money for the latest cell phone. Hopefully, the corporations will realize that when the American middle class is destroyed, so are they. We need them to invest in America again and we need to incentivize them to do so. We the People need to get rid of the government regulations that impede on our economic freedoms."

I turned off the camera and walked over to Two-Fingers and said, "Look, you are doing good but you are getting a little far out there. You are getting too windy, speak slower and loosen up. Say something funny, this will not play well in California." Two-Fingers looked at me and said, "California? I am running in Montana, I don't care about California. By the way, how do I look? They say the camera adds ten pounds and I really want to look my best." "You are the ugliest human being I know, do not worry about how you look, we have too many shallow politicians that only care about their looks. Snap out of it, we need a leader not someone who is obsessed with their looks." I said before adding, "But, just to be safe, I will turn down the lights and try to hide your face. On second thought, maybe you should wear one of those witness protection masks government informers wear when they are doing television interviews. Your viewers would probably appreciate that." "Crack you, White Guy," was all he said before we continued filming.

TF: "We the People have been violated by our elected officials and we are the ones to blame. We elected them, re-elected them and now we are morally and financially bankrupt. We must demand honesty and integrity in our elected officials or all the changes and sacrifices we make to correct things will be ineffectual, we can change things but We the People must unite. If we continue to hate each other, we will all lose. If we do not pay attention to the politicians, they will continue to destroy our country. Voter apathy is an affront to our Constitutional rights to vote and we all need to pay attention to the issues and the candidates.

My opponents policies have lead to the nightmare the country currently faces. Frank's party stood for the profound policy of, "Vote for me and I will give you free tuition. Or, vote for me and I will give you free healthcare. Or, vote for me and I will give you free food, housing and a monthly stipend." Pete's party did nothing to stop all this nonsense and voted to approve the budgets without fighting for fiscal responsibility.

Now, after the collapse, you never see either one of them. Have any of you seen your elected Representatives since the collapse? They are hiding because they have no answers on how to fix things. I did run into Frank the other day in Helena. He was in town renting space for his library. He was looking for a big place to showcase all of his achievements and I told him his achievements could be housed in a small broom closet in Havre, that is when he got in his chauffeur driven limousine and drove to the airport. By the way, Frank refuses to debate me and Pete told me he would not debate me unless Frank showed up. Just another example of how the two party system works, they each blame the other guy. We are 19 trillion in debt and they keep telling us the United States of America is in good shape. All I can tell you is this, the government is so broke the Treasury Department called me the other day and they wanted the Tribe to lend them money, I told them no way and hung up so I didn't have to hear any more of their crying. The day after they called, we started to build a wall around the Rez in an attempt to keep the stupid out."

I had to shut off the camera until I stopped laughing. Two-Fingers wasn't laughing, he took the destruction of America very seriously. Not me, I always figured I would just stay on the Rez because the Rez is the only safe place to live. Business was still pretty good on the Rez, I am constantly amazed on how broke people can find money to gamble and buy booze. The worse the economy, the more they gamble and drink. The Rez was flourishing because it was debt free and the Tribe was working. Things changed there just in time and we all had Two-Fingers to thank.

After I quit laughing I asked Two-Fingers if he wanted to add anything else and he just sat there staring at me, I imagined he was pondering the situation but I wasn't sure. Finally he said, "Do you think any of this matters? I doubt I will be able to change a thing, there are too many crooks with vested interests in charge. The deception permeates every department at every level, there is more honesty in a fair fist fight than there is in all of politics. I would gladly fight any one of the thieves but I do not know if an honest person can survive in D.C." "I know, I know. We have talked about this before and you decided to get into the race and you need to fight for change." I told him all this before he got up and paced around his office. Finally, he sat back down and told me to roll the camera.

TF: "The world is literally blowing up all around us. Frank and Pete both support the failed policies and We the People suffer, our Domestic policy and our Foreign policies are total disasters. Thanks to Pete and Frank, the Iranians, Russians and the North Koreans are threatening us with Nuclear War. We are worse off now than we were during the Cold War, their parties have ushered in a period of unrest that is unprecedented in our country's history. There is no leadership in D.C. and We the People are paying the price, not them. I believe in a clean environment but I understand the environment will disappear just like us humans if we get into a Nuclear War. Once one bomb explodes, the country's with nukes will start firing them off and we will all die. Mother Earth may regenerate itself after a few billion years, but we will all be gone. Our borders are not secure and the President hands out Executive Orders like they are candy, Pete and Frank have allowed all of this to happen."

I stopped filming and walked over to Two-Fingers and asked him if it would be okay to smoke a bowl. He just sat at his desk and stared at me with this look of disgust on his face before he finally said, "You can smoke all the pot you want on your time, right now we have to get this film finished. What the hell is the matter with you?" "Well, you are making me nervous as hell with all this nuke talk and I need something to settle my nerves." I said as I leaned against his desk. "Listen, you have to face reality like the rest of us, put the pipe down and let's get back to work. I swear, someday you may have to leave the safety of the Rez and you are going to be clueless in the real world." I returned to the camera and Two-Fingers immediately launched an attack on Executive Orders and other violations of the Constitution.

TF: "The President's recent Executive Action on immigration is overly broad and I believe it will be struck down by our Courts. Having said that, I believe the inaction regarding our Immigration laws by our Congress is totally unacceptable. For example, our politicians and the Supreme Court need to clarify who is and who is not a citizen when they are born on our soil, this inaction and lack of clarity is causing all kinds of stupid.

Right now, the way the 14th Amendment is being interpreted, a foreigner can come here and give birth to a child and that child is automatically a citizen, regardless of the citizenship of the foreigner. This liberal interpretation of the 14th Amendment means that as soon as that baby is born, it has a vested right to citizenship. Using that stupid interpretation, an alien from Mars or Pluto could come here and give birth to an alien baby and that baby would automatically be a citizen. If you do not believe this old country attorney, ask one of the Harvard educated attorneys back in D.C. if that is not right.

That is how stupid things have become. Of course, most people do not believe there is life outside our planetary system. I personally do not discount the possibility, how else do you explain Stubby Grant? That dude must have come from outer space. No way he is from Earth, E.T. phone home. The Constitution is being violated and once it is gone all the money in the world will not help us and once Americans lose faith in their institutions all hell will break loose, things are going to get a lot worse."

I stopped the camera again and walked over to Two-Fingers and said, "You are getting too complicated, I don't even know what you are talking about." Two-Fingers rarely got pissed at me but I could tell I pissed him off.

He calmly counted to ten and then he got up from his desk and found his copy of the Constitution and returned to his seat. He spread out all the pages and I could see there were notes in the columns and it had been heavily highlighted, there were even copies of case law in his stack. Once he had his papers arranged in front of him he calmly looked up at me and said, "Did you spend any time studying the law in law school or were you there just to chase after my sister?" I always knew he was mad when he prefaced his remarks with, "my sister." I thought oh shit, here comes the lecture, so I sat down across from him and braced myself for what was to come.

"People are furious about the current state of our Immigration laws and I am trying to highlight the stupidity and the inaction of our elected officials like Frank and Pete. Am I the only guy on the Rez that reads a newspaper? Americans are mad as hell and it is getting worse everyday and one of the main points of contention is our giving citizenship to babies that have no connection to the United States other than the fact they were born here.

Citizens have a right to be concerned because the 14th Amendment, in my opinion, is being misinterpreted." He pulled out the 14th

Amendment that he had enlarged and laid it out in front of me, he was very careful with it as he gently smoothed out all the wrinkles. Then he asked me to read out loud the first sentence in Section 1. I nodded my head, cleared my throat and said, "All persons born or naturalized in the United States, and subject to the jurisdiction thereof, are citizens of the United States and of the State wherein they reside." I read it a couple of more times and then said, "Well, it seems pretty straightforward, however, I am just not sure what they meant by "subject to the jurisdiction thereof." Two-Fingers nodded his head and said, "Exactly, that is the key part of the 14th that is conveniently overlooked. So, let's just focus on the born in the United States aspect of this, naturalization is a completely different issue."

Two-Fingers leaned back in his chair and took a long drink of water. I wanted to take a piss but was not about to endure his wrath by mentioning it, when the professor talked Constitutional Law and History nobody moved, I just sat there hoping he did not go through every frigging Amendment. "As you know from law school, you can't look at the Constitution and the case law that followed in a vacuum. You must educate yourself on the intent of the lawmakers and the times and circumstance that existed when the Amendment was passed." Two-Fingers took another long drink of water before continuing. "The 14th Amendment was passed in 1868 in an attempt to strengthen the Civil Rights Act of 1866. You do know that an Amendment to the Constitution has more weight than an Act, don't you?" He did not wait for my answer he just kept right on going. "Both of these measures were designed to help blacks. They were enacted after the Civil War and our lawmakers intent was to give blacks more rights. Think about it, back then, there were whites, blacks and Indians populating America. These laws went a long way in helping the plight of the blacks."

He then shuffled through his papers and pulled out a copy of the Civil Rights Act of 1866 and laid it out in front of me and said, "You know the drill." I stared at him and shifted uncomfortably in my chair before I began to read the 1866 Act, "That all persons born in the United States and not subject to any foreign power, excluding Indians not taxed, are hereby declared to be citizens of the United States." I had to read this section a couple of times and when I finished Two-Fingers asked me if I noticed any difference. "Well, other than the obvious that Indians were not granted citizenship if they were not taxed, I do not see any difference." That is when Two-Fingers came completely unglued. He stood up and yelled, "How in the hell did you ever graduate from law school? I swear White Guy you drive me nuts. Did you ever go to a Constitutional Law class?" I sat there rather sheepishly and finally said, "Yeah, I went and I would have spoken in class more but you were always talking." That did not seem to sit well with him and he kept pacing around before he sat down and said, "Concentrate on the words, "not subject to any foreign power." How do you interpret that, remember it all comes down to interpretation." I read it again before I said, "Well, it seems to me the passage is intended for the parents of that child, and if the parents are citizens of another country they owe their allegiance to that country and that country's power. So, unless the parents are in the United States legally and under its jurisdiction, any baby born here is not automatically a citizen." "Bingo!!" Two-Fingers exclaimed before he slapped me on the back. He was overjoyed, I was suddenly his star pupil. "There must be more of a connection to the United States than just coming here and having a baby."

Two-Fingers was really enjoying himself and my kidneys were about to explode but I did not interrupt him. "There must be another connection and that is evidenced by all the hoops Native American Indians had to go through to become citizens. Did you know that Native American Indians were not granted birth citizenship automatically even after the 14th Amendment was passed? Native American Indians who lived their whole lives on American soil, their children were not granted citizenship at birth. That tells me that the lawmakers intended there be more to gaining birth citizenship than just being born here. Illegals and foreigners can't automatically claim citizenship for their child, it is illogical. Remember back to who occupied America in 1868, white adults and their children, black adults and their children and Native Americans and their children. White and black babies were granted citizenship at birth because the whites and blacks had a connection to the United States, they lived here, were domiciled here and were subject to the laws of the United States of America. Indians were viewed as having allegiances to their Tribes and not to the United States and therefor they excluded newly born Native American Indian babies from citizenship.

This was true all the way up until 1924 when Congress passed the Indian Citizenship Act. So, if Native American Indians who lived, died and were born on American soil were denied birth right citizenship because Congress and the judges and the other lawmakers who took up the issue determined that we, when born, owed our allegiance to our Tribes and not the United States of America, how can they claim that foreigners who are citizens of another country do not owe that other country their allegiance?

Their babies, born here, have the same allegiance as the parents. Both passages in the Civil Rights Act and the 14th Amendment must be read in present tense, future allegiance is not the issue, allegiance at the time of the birth is. No infant has allegiance to anything other than it's mommy's teat. So, it must mean what is the allegiance of the parents? That is what was said about Native American Indians and it must apply to the situation at hand. There must be more of a connection to the United States of America and if there isn't, the Pluto and Mars analogy is right on point. Earth is such a mess I am not sure any right thinking alien would want to live here but if they did, under the current interpretation of the 14th Amendment, their babies would become citizens automatically upon their birth on American soil. Think about it, if a Martian gave birth to a baby in the United States of America, under the interpretation that is in effect now, that Martian baby would automatically become a citizen.

The 14th Amendment is more restrictive as to who can become a citizen by birth then the Civil Rights Act of 1866 as evidenced by the omission of, "excluding Indians not taxed." They made it more restrictive because they were not going to grant birth citizenship to us even if we paid taxes because they were always concerned about allegiance to the United States of America and any statute passed into law to the contrary is unconstitutional." Two-Fingers finally took a breath and I bolted for the john.

After returning from the restroom, I engaged Two-Fingers in more conversation regarding the Constitution, I figured he had worn himself out and I could take advantage. "So, do you lay awake at night and count Constitutional Amendments before you fall asleep?" Two-Fingers smiled at me and said, "Actually, I do. America is 19 trillion dollars in debt and foreigners are pouring into this country and taking advantage of our welfare system, billions of dollars are being spent on people that have no allegiance to this country. That system is an example of the idiocy that is so prevalent in Washington, D.C. The Supreme Court has the power to clarify the law so it is not misinterpreted, somebody needs to bring a case and get the issue before them, something has to be done for the Citizens of America.

Clearly, the 14th amendment and the Civil Rights laws were intended to help the blacks and Native American Indians were just an afterthought, my people have always been just an afterthought. I get that and I do not blame anybody for that, if Native American Indians were held to such high standards regarding birth citizenship, how can foreigners be held to a less stringent test? No, the intent seems clear to me that there has to be more to getting birth citizenship then the mere fact you flew over, or swam over here and had a baby. I know I am belaboring the point, but if we continue down this road of stupid, I am seriously going to have a wall built around the Rez. By the way, you need to look into getting a dome built over us as well, have Liquid Louie and Stogie Man get on that."

I sat there looking at my watch thinking it was late and he would probably want to go home and get some sleep, I was wrong. "Start up your camera I want to get something off my chest." Two-Fingers said as he stood up and started doing jumping jacks, I was worn out and the guy was doing jumping jacks. "What is bothering you?" I asked from behind the camera. "As you know, I am concerned about the minorities in this country and I have a message for them that needs to be said, it may not be politically correct but it is my hard won opinion. Now, start the camera and get comfortable, this could take awhile." I started the camera and went over to his cowhide covered sofa and laid down.

TF: "Well, we have a Presidential election coming soon and the Democrats are out pandering for our votes. They are telling all of us minorities how bad we have it in America, they want us to know that everybody is out to get us and they are there to protect us. They really care about us and they need our vote. Of course, after the elections are over we won't see them again until the next election.

As a Native American whose ancestors were used as slaves, whose ancestors were scalped and massacred, whose ancestors were raped and maimed, whose ancestors had their land stolen from them when the treaties we entered into were violated, I say this: Nobody can turn back time and change things for any of us. Many of us have been given free education, free housing, free food and free money and now the country we all live in is broke. We must break the chains of dependency, not embrace them. It is time we all start acting like Americans, we need to quit rocking the boat and start rowing together or we are all going to sink, we need to ignore the professional politicians that only care about getting re-elected.

That is the message I have delivered to my Tribe and it is a message I think needs to be heard by all Americans. Everybody must take personal responsibility for their actions and quit blaming the other guy. If you think your pain is anywhere near the pain of a Native American, think again. I say this to help you and it needs to be said, you are being played by the politicians and you are willingly letting them do it to you.

Welfare is an abomination and it has ruined more lives than it has ever helped, poverty levels are higher now than when they passed the idiotic laws. The politicians are using us as pawns in their evil game, all they care about is getting elected and re-elected. Our leaders in this country should be helping you by investing that welfare money into job creation. Be a plumber, an electrician or a machinist, get a trade because that is where the money is and there is little or no competition for those jobs, nobody wants to get their hands dirty anymore.

Every time I need an electrician it costs me a minimum of $500.00 and the women spends less than an hour at my cabin. She does great work and all but as the Chairman of the Tribe, I only get $20.00 per hour. Other than not asking you to take personal responsibility for your actions, what are your leaders doing for you? If you want to work, the deck is stacked in your favor. We need to get off the white man's back, they are starting to crumble.

I have heard a lot of complaining going on about the lack of civil rights, where were all the civil rights seekers when Native Americans occupied Wounded Knee back in 1973? We were bringing attention to our plight and I never saw another minority there, nobody else had our backs. I guess civil rights are only important when they are your civil rights. As I said, I did not see one minority other than Native Americans at the occupation but I did see a white guy. Come over here White Guy, let the folks see what a true Warrior looks like." I was dozing off when he startled me awake, I didn't even have time to comb my hair before I was pushed in front of the camera. I sat at his desk and stared blankly into the lens as Two-Fingers continued, "You talk about a minority, here is a true minority. For a long time, this dude had nobody to hang out with other than a bunch of Indians. He had his ass whipped, teased, chased and ridiculed from the day he moved to the Rez until now and I never heard him cry about it. Think about that, we are all minorities at one time or another. The difference is he did not get free college, job preference or welfare of any kind. He does get to sleep with my sister but that is an entirely different issue.

On the Rez, it took us awhile to change because change is never easy and it requires hard work. If you do not want to work then there is no hope for you. But when you do not work, do not blame anybody else for your failure. Here on the Rez, we do not have to lock our doors, our children can now walk safely to school because we all share the same values and we respect each other. If you do not know right from wrong, no one can help you. Color is not the issue, being an asshole is the issue. Quit blaming others, it's not the Indian way."

I turned off the camera and laid back down on his sofa. It was quiet for quite awhile before I said, "$20.00 an hour? I can't believe we pay you that much money." Two-Fingers finally quit choking on the apple he was eating when I continued, "You do know that Washington, D.C. has some of the highest crime rates in the country, right?" Two-Fingers thought on that a second and then said, "Screw it, I am going to get me bodyguards like the rest of the public servants." I laughed at that and said, "What is the first thing you are going to do when you get to Washington?" Two-Fingers quickly replied, "I am going to find the Black and Hispanic Caucuses and ask every member this question: "Why do you hate your constituents so much?"

Two-Fingers finally went home and I posted the film on the internet. It was unedited because I do not know how to edit anything, I was lucky to figure out how to get it posted. If you really want to know, I am not a very technical person.

Early the next morning, Two-Fingers and I met at the Club Cafe for breakfast, he was already seated when I walked in. Spread out in front of him was the liberal Big Sky Reporter, he was reading through it and he barely acknowledged by presence. I ordered a cup of coffee and was looking over the one page menu when he looked up from what he was reading and said, "Say's here that a Supreme Court judge down in Alabama is refusing to enforce the gay marriage thing, I knew something like this was going to happen. You can not allow sanctuary cities to operate in open defiance of Federal laws without causing dissension among the ranks, I have told you that a hundred times. People are losing faith in their institutions. Politicians, rich people and celebrities have one set of rules and the rest of us have another. Sanctuary cities that are allowed to break the law without any repercussions are going to cause nationwide anarchy, sure as hell. Has it come down to obeying only the laws you agree with?" I looked up at him from my menu and said, "Is that a rhetorical question or are you asking my opinion?" "I am opening up the floor for conversation and I am interested in your opinion, I know you would rather read the comic section but I am interested in your opinion regarding all this lawlessness." Two-Fingers said as he closed the paper and stared at me. "Personally, I think the world is so screwed up there is no saving it. That is why I am staying on the Rez when you go off to Washington, D.C." "Bullshit, you are going with me, I am going to make you my Chief of Staff." Two-Fingers motioned for more coffee before continuing, "I am not going to pay you anything but you will have a nice title." I thought on that a moment and decided to move on to a different subject. "I have a question for you, if women have it so bad in the United States of America, how come Bruce Jenner wants to become one of them?" Probably wasn't the best question to ask him when he had a mouth full of coffee, he spewed it all down my nicely ironed $10.00 shirt.

It was another EF Hutton moment in the Club, everybody was listening. Liquid Louie piped up with his opinion that Bruce should be forced to return his gold medal from the 1976 Olympics. "Well, hell if the dude is really a women than he should have to return the medal." Louie said as he hovered over Two-Fingers and me. Soon there was a crowd standing around us voicing their opinions. Finally, an issue that galvanized the electorate. "Think about it," Louie continued, "If he is a women that was competing in a men's event, he should have to give the medal back." It was quickly pointed out that being a woman and winning a men's event was quite an accomplishment. Louie thought about that for awhile before he said, "Well, all I know is that if a man won a women's event they would make him give back the gold and if he doesn't have to give his back, I think it is sexist." I sat there with my head spinning off of my neck thinking the world had come to an end, Liquid Louie had actually used the word "sexist." I actually blacked out for a moment and my entire life flashed in front of me.

When I regained consciousness, I sat there thinking there was no place to hide from the insanity that was sweeping across our country. The Rez, my little cocoon, was being swept up in the tornado of political correctness that was swirling across the land.

Two-Fingers was concerned that I passed out but that didn't stop him from launching another attack, "Well, since you are talking about sexism and all that, I have been reading up on the Democrat party's demands for more money to pay for abortions. I know this is a touchy subject but you got me thinking." Two-Fingers said as the room quit spinning around me. "Hey, don't start this with me, I had a vasectomy and I have paid the ultimate price for birth control, leave me out of it." That was all I could say. Then, from way over in the corner somewhere, someone yelled, "So, you got your nuts cut off, White Guy?" It was as if we were on a speaker system or something, you can't say a word in the Club without everybody knowing what you are talking about and I really resented that.

"The feminist crowd wasn't satisfied with the Roe V. Wade holding that women have a right to a safe and legal abortion. Oh no, that is not good enough for them." Two-Fingers continued unabated. "Now they want us to pay for it all. Where in the Constitution does it say we have to pay for their abortions, where? It was a stretch for a bunch of old white men on the Supreme Court in 1973 to come up with the privacy argument, but where does it say that taxpayers have to pay for it all? When you ask that question, you are labeled a sexist. Just another attempt by the Democrat party to divide us as a nation. They know that millions of Americans can never morally accept abortion but they keep pushing them." Two-Fingers ordered a stack of pancakes before continuing, "Push, push, push and take, take, take and they wonder why the United States is about to explode. Roe is the law of the land but they want more, just another example of why the Constitution is becoming unrecognizable. They start with little things like gun rights, or freedom of the press, or freedom of religion, or freedom of speech and they take it all away slowly. Our leaders are always telling us it does not have any effect on our rights, bullshit." I kept looking at the door and seriously thought about running away and hiding. Please, no more Constitution talk.

Two-Fingers was getting tired but that didn't keep him from talking, "The Democrat party died in Dallas in 1963. Remember JFK? He was the last great leader of the Democrat Party. At his inauguration in 1961 he said, "Ask not what your country can do for you, rather ask what you can do for your country." 55 years later and the answer seems to be, "We are going to suck the life blood out of America and piss on the Constitution. That is no way to govern and it is not the Indian way." That was the moment when I called for the check.

Later that day, after I returned to my office, I noticed Two-Fingers movie had already gotten over a million views. Since there are only 800,000 Montanans, I figured his message had gone mainstream.

Chapter 43

In the days that followed, Two-Fingers started to receive a lot of attention throughout the state and the entire country. He rose in the polls and was dominating the race for the Senate seat and the reality of being elected began to sink in and that caused him real anxiety because he was overly concerned that no one would listen to him once he got to the Senate, he would be walking among the snakes and he knew it.

Two-Fingers pure motives for running would be drowned out by the hypocrisy that is Washington, D.C. Everyday the economy got worse as interest rates moved even higher, unemployment continued to increase and the only thing moving downward was the spirit of America. The policies of the last several years were beginning to become all too real and nobody had any answers.

The promise to raise people up was not possible with the Socialistic polices that were in effect. Rather than raising people up, people were all brought down to a level of mediocrity never seen in this country before. What was really weird to Two-Fingers was the fact that a lot of the citizens were okay with the change as long as they were not directly affected, it wasn't their ox being gored. Two-Fingers always asked this question, "How can you call yourself a Progressive when you have never had an original thought in your whole life?" On this issue I agree with him. I admit I don't know a lot about Constitutional law but I do know a lot about Business law and all I have to say is Capitalism works and Socialism doesn't. All the policies being tried now have failed in the past. What is so Progressive about Bankruptcy?

Two-Fingers worried most about the vanishing middle class because they are the ones that do most of the living, dying and spending in America and they were being swept away by the burdensome economic policies that the political class had placed on their backs. He was worried that his basic core values regarding hard work and fiscal responsibility would be attacked and minimized. America was drowning in debt and he knew that, 19 trillion in debt and they had no answers. He always said the demise was inevitable when cowardice was favored over bravery, deceit over honesty and treachery over patriotism. When these are the new values of a country, the end is near. Given all that, he was heartened by the positive response he received, there were still a few patriots out there.

He was not able to do much campaigning off the Rez and was glad to use the new technology to get his message out. He did not know how it all worked but he was glad we used it. He never owned a cell phone, home computer, television or any of the other "distractions" as he called them.

He was scheduled to go to Washington, D.C. and testify regarding a lawsuit the Tribe filed against the Bureau of Indian Affairs. The lawsuit was filed because the Tribe believed the government was negligent in the management of their lands. The Tribe asked for a lot of money for damages and as Chairman of the Tribe, Two-Fingers was summoned to speak to a group of Senators who presumably wanted to settle the case out of Court. Normally, as the Tribal Attorney, I would have gone with him. But, he did not want us both to go and since he had to go, I was to stay behind and keep things going.

Before he left for D.C., Two-Fingers received a call from one of Frank Johnson's aides. Frank wanted to meet up with Two-Fingers to see if they could bury the hatchet, Two-Fingers agreed knowing full well the only place Frank wanted to bury the hatchet was between Two-Finger's shoulder blades. The only condition Two-Fingers made was that Frank had to come to the Rez for the sit down.

I clearly remember the day Frank came into town in his chauffeur driven limousine with it's tinted windows and wet bar. It was Frank's first visit to the Rez, he did not associate with the Blackfeet because he never needed them to win an election. When he arrived at the Tribal complex, he had his door opened and he departed the limo like a King, ever so careful not to step in the mud puddles that adorned the parking lot. He had the look of a guy that lived in the lap of luxury, he was bloated by fat and power. He shuffled about like he was totally inconvenienced, he had come down from the Mountain and was meeting with a mortal man. His wife Ann had died years ago and she, according to Two-Fingers, was the only human being in the marriage. After she died, Frank lost whatever morals and ethics he had. He was once a human being but the political life stripped him of all that was real. He was a complete phony and Two-Fingers hated phony, he tolerated a lot of things but he would not tolerate a phony.

So, after a very clumsy greeting, Two-Fingers, Frank and I sat down in the conference room down the hall from our offices. Frank's security team stood guard in the hallway and after I closed the door and sat down, the meeting began. First thing out of Frank's mouth was his demand to meet with Two-Fingers in private. Evidently, what he had to say was for Two-Fingers ears only. Two-Fingers thought about this for awhile before he said, "White Guy is here for protection." "Protection, you do not need protection, I have brought all the protection you will need." Frank said as he gasped for air. "I am not talking about my protection, Frank. I am talking about yours, I'm not sure I will be able to control myself once you start spouting your bullshit and White Guy is the only person I will listen to. All the security in the world will not prevent the ass kicking you deserve and the only person that can stop me is White Guy so I suggest you agree to his staying."

I was always amazed by Two-Fingers brass, he was 62 years old and could hardly beat an egg but he kept on talking.

Anyway, Frank needed to talk to Two-Fingers a lot more than Two-Fingers needed to talk to him, so he moved on to what he was there for. "Listen, I came to make you an offer. I know you are rising in the polls and things are looking pretty good for you right now. But, if the economy hadn't collapsed you wouldn't have a chance." Frank said as he tried to catch his breath. "I would like to propose that you drop out of the race and if you do, I will see to it personally that you will be my Party's nominee in six years, you will be a shoe in. I have a lot of unfinished business and I need to be re-elected to get things done. You have my word that my party will support you 100% in 2022." Two-Fingers sat there patiently listening as Frank pleaded with him to step down. He made promise after promise and was on the verge of tears when Two-Fingers finally interrupted him, "You want six more years? This country can't take six more weeks of your insanity. We are

19 trillion in debt and you have no answers on how to get us out, you and your crew are the ones that got us in this mess, it wasn't White Guy or me. You have shipped our jobs overseas and increased government dependency and you want six more years? Why is it that you career politicians always want six more years? We are a divided nation and you have Americans at each others throats and you want six more years? Americans are not safe to move around their own country and you want six more years?" I glanced over at Frank who was physically shrinking as Two-Fingers continued, "You have offended and abandoned our Allies and you want six more years?" At that point Frank looked stunned, obviously he had only been reading the liberal press and was unaware of the damage that he had done to the country. Reality began to take hold when he abruptly stood up and said, "I am finished here, I will see you next week and then you will be on my turf. You will no longer have the safety of your reservation to hide on." With that, he stood up and shuffled his way off the Rez.

Two-Fingers and I sat there for a while before I said, "You know, I think that went pretty well, what do you think?" Two-Fingers thought on that before he said, "I think I had better win the election or there will not be a wall high enough to help any of us."

The days leading up to his trip to Washington, D.C. were extremely busy, last minute details had to be attended to. He was leading by double digits in all the recent polls and his Senate victory appeared inevitable.

We were working in his office the morning he was to leave for D.C. when an announcement came on over the radio that Associate Supreme Court Justice Scalia had died in his sleep. Within an hour of that announcement spokespeople for both the Republican and Democrat parties came on and announced the importance of selecting a Judge that shared their views politically. Two-Fingers sat down at his desk after all this noise and said to me, "Just another attack on our Constitution, the Supreme Court per the Constitution is supposed to be apolitical." I correctly sensed another lecture on Constitutional law so I made myself comfortable on his cowhide sofa and tried to stay awake.

"Just another attack on the Constitution and a knife in the back of Democracy. The Constitution is being violated and both political parties are guilty, they only appoint someone to the Court that shares their political views and the Constitution is an afterthought. Just another reason why I am running as an Independent. When I get back from D.C. we are going to make another movie with this topic as our platform." I got up and turned on my tape recorder as he continued, "We are supposed to have three branches of government with equal powers. If the Supreme Court rules based on political philosophy and not what the Constitution says we no longer have Separation of Powers. Their primary duty is to interpret the law not make it. Now you know why American's are losing faith in our institutions, we are being played. Think about it, what is the point of having a Constitution if it is misinterpreted? Individual political views should never enter into the equation." "You are right but you know they are not going to take responsibility for their actions." I was sitting up straight as I fueled his oratory. "You know that is going to happen." Two-Fingers said as he paced around his office. "The Republican controlled Senate will wait until the next President is in office to confirm a nominee, that is their Constitutional right. The President has the Constitutional right to nominate and given the fact that he has never worked with the Republican party, that nomination will likely pass away into the darkness of time. But until then, they will argue and fuss and make a big deal out of it while We the People continue to suffer. It is the political shell game that occurs all too frequently. They avoid the real pressing issues of the day like the national debt and they zero in on subjects that divide us all. They do that because they have no idea how to pay down the 19 trillion in debt and they are comfortable bad mouthing each other on secondary issues because trying to fix the debt problem is over their collective heads. So, they will debate this issue all the way through the elections and hope nobody notices all the depravation." Whenever he talked debt I got nervous as hell but I saw his point, his concerns regarding the destruction of our Democratic and free market system was finally beginning to sink into my thick skull.

"Doesn't the President have a conflict of interest issue in reference to appointing anyone? I mean, isn't he and his Administration being sued and isn't that case before the Supreme Court right now?" I asked.

"Seems to me that may in and of itself preclude him from nominating anyone, that person would hear his case, right?" That is when Two-Fingers collapsed in the middle of his office. He laid there shaking like an epileptic and I was scared I may have to call for paramedics. Finally, after dousing him with a bucket of water, he came to.

We sat on the floor in the middle of his office as Two-Fingers gathered himself. Finally he said, "That is the most legal thing I have ever heard you say and I am so proud of you I may give you a raise. In law school parlance, that is the A question. Does he have a conflict of interest? Great question, his administration is a party to a case before the Supreme Court and he is going to nominate a judge to hear his case, I am going to research that very question when I am in D.C., well done." He sat up and drank some water before continuing, "Seems like a conflict of interest to me, at the very least it will be a case of first impression because I am sure this issue has never been raised before and I bet the Harvard boys have never even thought of that and if they have, they will go to their graves with it. You know, them being Constitutional lawyers and all." I felt good about that I really did, I would have felt even better about it but the raise never materialized.

I drove him to Great Falls to catch his flight and on the way we reminisced about our youth and how far in life we had both come. He was settled in his belief that he could help the country to become united again and he was willing to make the sacrifices required to make that happen, he was going to leave his ego in Montana and go to work for the entire country. In short, he was feeling very good and was optimistic about the future.

We sat in front of the airport while he gave me a few last minute instructions on what he wanted done while he was away and then he grabbed his small bag out of the back seat of my car and disappeared into the busy lobby of the airport. He never looked back and after a few minutes I drove back home to the Rez, that was the last time I saw him.

Chapter 44

He usually called from his hotel when he travelled to let me know he had arrived safely, that call never came. With the time difference and his late arrival, I was not overly concerned that I had not heard from him that night. But, when I didn't hear from him the next morning, I began to worry.

It was around noon our time the next day when I finally called the Ambassador Hotel and tried to reach him, he always stayed at the Ambassador and he had a reservation to stay there. The problem was, he never checked in and no one had seen him. That was when I began to get an uneasy feeling that something terrible had happened to him.

I called the airline to make sure the flight had arrived. They said it arrived on schedule but they could not say whether or not he had gotten off in Washington, D.C. They were able to confirm he had checked in at Great Falls without checking a bag and that made sense because he did not take anything other than his small bag. I called the airline security people at the airport in D.C. and they could not help me. I called the D.C. city police department and they had no information for me. Finally, I called the FBI and reported Two-Fingers missing. It became apparent from my discussion with their agent, John Dixon, that I needed to get to D.C. as soon as possible. When I decided to go, I did not tell Two-Fingers parents or his sisters that he was missing, I didn't want a panic to sweep the Rez. I just told everybody I needed to get to D.C. because the settlement of the lawsuit was imminent.

On my flight to D.C., I desperately tried to piece together all the events that had taken place over the last few months. I became more and more anxious about things as I flew across the country, it was just not like Two-Fingers to not report in. He always let me know where he was when he traveled, always. Inevitably, he would have something for me to do, he never shut down, he was always thinking about Tribal business. As I looked down on the lights of D.C. that night, a feeling of loss descended upon me, where was Two-Fingers?

The next morning I met with John Dixon, he had an office in one of those large, white granite buildings the government is so proud of. His office was on the fifth floor and when the elevator doors opened, I was overwhelmed with all the activity that was going on. Agents were running back and forth, telephones were ringing incessantly and every male agent had their ties loosened around their neck. They were fighting hard and trying not to lose ground to the upsurge of criminal activity that was sweeping the nation.

John Dixon is a very intense agent. He was on the job for approximately five years and he looked like a guy that needed a vacation, he was in his early thirties and he had black rings under his eyes and wrinkles on his forehead. His office was out in the middle of the room and it looked like one of those kiosks you see at the mall. When we sat down to talk, I noticed he did not have any pictures of family, a dog or a cat, no pictures at all. He seemed to me to be a guy who was stranded on an island without any lifeline. Finally, someone who seemed to give a shit about national security, Two-Fingers would like him.

As soon as we were both seated, John got right down to business. He asked to see the pictures I brought of Two-Fingers and as he examined them he told me he had called the D.C. Police Dept. and they discussed jurisdiction and the fact that Two-Fingers had been missing for less than 48 hours. I was told the D.C. Police Dept. had to give Two-Fingers disappearance the requisite amount of time before they started a full blown investigation.

Dixon told me he wasn't waiting because Two-Fingers was running for the United States Senate and he believed that ultimately the FBI would have jurisdiction. But for the time being, he was working with the local authorities and not stepping on their toes.

I was interviewed for quite awhile and I laid out exactly what had happened over the last several days. I told him about dropping Two-Fingers off at the Great Falls Airport and then not hearing anything from him. He was looking at Two-Fingers photograph and making notes. He kept repeating, "So, you were the last person to see him?" I kept saying, "I hope I am not the last person to see him." After he finished the interview he said there was nothing more I needed to do but he suggested I stay in town for awhile. What did he think I was going to do, run off to Bermuda or something?

I was staying at the Ambassador and as soon as I got back there, I started asking questions. I talked to virtually every employee on duty and, even though he had not checked in, I insisted on being shown to the room he had reserved. The bellman took me up and waited for me as I inspected the room. The bed was made and there were no signs that anyone had slept there. I stopped and spoke to the lady who cleaned the rooms and asked if she had cleaned that room recently and she said that she hadn't. Nobody in the hotel had seen him and most of the people I talked to knew him from when he had stayed there over the years. It was clear that he had not made it to the hotel.

I went across the street to a deli and decided that, after I ate, I would go to the airport and look around. To be honest, I really wasn't sure what to do. I read about things like this happening to people but I never thought in a million years I would be faced with such a nightmare. I spent the rest of the afternoon at the airport asking questions and making a fool out of myself and on the taxi drive back to the Ambassador, I decided to rent a car the next morning and go visit my folks up in Cherry Hill, the hell with John Dixon.

My folks are doing well, they get around pretty good for being in their eighties. Over the years, Paula and I flew out to visit them several times. In fact, we flew them out to visit us on a number of occasions and each time they came to the Rez they paced around and seemed eager to get back home, maybe if we had children they would have wanted to stay longer. Paula and I even tried to have them move in with us and they always came up with a reason not too.

As I drove the 150 miles from D.C. to Cherry Hill, I kept wondering how I was going to tell Paula that her brother may be dead. I knew I had to tell her but I just couldn't bear the thought of it. It was a Friday afternoon and I was going to talk it over with my father and see what he thought. So, I decided to give it the weekend and then I would let her know.

My folks had sold their greenhouse and nursery business years ago. They now live in a small house in a nice neighborhood not far from mom's favorite church. They were surprised but very happy to see me when I came in unannounced, they were both watching TV when I made my grand entrance. We sat and talked late into the night and the next morning I took dad out for breakfast at his favorite diner.

After we were seated, I came clean as to why I was really in the area. As he drank his coffee, he listened intently to me as I described the events leading up to Two-Fingers disappearance. He is still very sharp and seemed to be both saddened and excited at the same time. He always liked Sherlock Holmes and now he had a chance to aid in the solving of a mystery, he grilled me hard about every little detail. Finally, he sat back and said definitively, "Frank Johnson had him killed, no doubt about it. Who else had the motive to do him in?" He was excitedly awaiting my response. Actually, I thought that he may be on to something. Frank was livid with Two-Fingers at our recent meeting and he would gain the most if something happened to Two-Fingers. I was trying to wrap my head around the possibility of a sitting United States Senator being involved in Two-Fingers disappearance, the implications of such a thing were huge. True, he had a lot to gain but he also had a lot to lose, right? Two-Fingers was winning the Senate race and Frank was way behind. Pete Reynolds, the old worn out Republican, was so far back in the polling he thought he was ahead. No, the winner would either be Two-Fingers or Frank, no doubt about it.

I sat there with my head spinning as my dad kept on with the grilling. "Who else would do it? Two-Fingers did not have any enemies, did he?"

I thought long and hard on that. I could honestly say that he was beloved by the entire Tribe and I could not think of anyone that thought badly of him. Of course, there was always the possibility of an accident or amnesia, you know something that wasn't so sinister. Murder? I wasn't convinced.

I decided to only spend Saturday night there and drive to D.C. the next morning. Before I left, dad suggested I call Paula as soon as possible and let her know what was going on.

On the way back to D.C., I decided to take the old man's advice and call her as soon as I got back to the Ambassador. I was too late, about an hour before I called, she received a call from John Dixon. She was sobbing when I called and in no mood to talk to me, when she gets mad, she gets mad all over. When I tried to explain she just sobbed so I finally told her I would call back in a half hour and hung up. I was sitting on the bed staring at my cell phone thinking I must be the dumbest S.O.B. in the world. Of course the FBI was going to start investigating and of course they were going to call the Rez. Just my luck, a Federal agency actually doing it's job.

I was stretched out on the bed looking up at the ceiling when my cell phone rang, it was Paula, we spoke for a long time before she forgave me. She alternated between being angry, sad, fearful and really, really pissed off. She told me to come home, obviously I wasn't doing any good there. After she got done talking at me, I hung up and called Agent Dixon's office. The phone rang twice before he answered. "Hello, Agent Dixon here." I explained to him that I had to leave immediately and go home and all he said was, "So, you were the last one to see Two-Fingers alive... let me know when you get home and do not leave the country." Then he hung up on me and I just sat there staring at the phone, I stared at the phone a lot that day.

I caught the red eye to Great Falls and it was mid-day Monday when I arrived at the Rez. When I got to the Tribal office it was jammed with Tribal members and newspeople asking about Two-Fingers. There was a line of people that stretched from the Tribal headquarters lobby all the way out to the parking lot, the whole place was buzzing with activity.

As I squeezed through the front door of the Tribal headquarters, the Tribe started to yell, "What did you do with him, White Guy?" The Tribe was anxious and they were striking out at the last person to see Two-Fingers alive. That was what the headline of the liberal Big Sky Reporter stated in big bold letters. As I made my way through the lobby, people were shaking the paper in my face and yelling at me.

I finally got into my office and shut the door behind me. There, spread on my desk, was a copy of the paper with my picture on it, someone had highlighted the entire article and left it on my desk. I sat there reading it as members of the Tribe paced back and forth staring coldly at me through my office windows, it reminded me of my first day of school on the Rez. Only now I was all grown up and without my best friend.

I sat there and tried to concentrate on the article with my picture plastered on the front page, the headline read: "This is the last person to see Two-Fingers alive." The story was filled with rumors and conjecture, it kept referring to unnamed sources and an on going investigation. Anybody who read it would think I was guilty of Murder One. Of course, at the end of the article they concluded by saying, "As always, when more information becomes available, we will report it to you in a timely and thorough manner."

After reading the article, I stood up and opened the door and tried to explain things to anyone willing to hear my side of the story. They listened but I could tell by the look of hurt in their eyes, they weren't buying it.

Thankfully, the crowd began to disperse when Max, Pam, Cindy Ann and Paula made their way to my office. Once they were in my office, Max sat in his wheel chair and the ladies sat in leather office chairs staring at me. Max and Pam looked like they had aged ten years since I last saw them five days earlier. I cleared my throat and told them everything I knew, I talked and talked and didn't leave anything out, I was as concerned and confused as everybody else.

Finally, Max picked up the newspaper from my desk and said, "I have read this article several times and my conclusion is it is a hit piece. If what you say is true about Frank, they are covering for him. They have protected him for years, unnamed sources my ass." We all shook our heads in agreement as he continued. "The liberal press has had their collective noses up Frank's ass for so long, he could never be held accountable because it would make the paper look bad."

"You know, I am not sure we will find Two-Fingers unless we hire our own private detective." I said. After a few seconds, Cindy Ann, Paula and Max agreed, Pam still had a hard time believing the government couldn't be trusted. "Two-Fingers has attacked the government's policies for years, I am not sure they are behind this, but I am sure they will not break their backs finding out what happened to him." I sat back in my seat and told them again about the argument that

Two-Fingers and Frank had a few days before and my dad's conclusion. Finally, Cindy Ann said, "I think you are right about getting a private detective. Someone will need to go to D.C. and that someone is going to be me. Besides, I need to find out where we are on our settlement talks and while I am there, I will hire a private detective." Paula looked directly at me and said, "You need to stay here and take care of Tribal business, there are a lot of angry Blackfeet and you need to stay and answer their questions. There are so many of them that are just not thinking rationally right now."

The next morning I went down to the Club Cafe like I did virtually every morning and as soon as I entered, I was bombarded with questions. The place was packed and everybody was grumpy. I was answering questions as quickly as I could when Johnny Skunk Cap pushed his way towards me and yelled, "What did you do to him White Guy?" That was the moment all hell broke loose in the Club, Johnny and I went at it like we were teenagers. I finally got the better of him and was beating the hell out of him when I was dragged off the top of him. I looked around the room and then slowly walked out the door.

It took me a couple of weeks to heal up from my fight, at 62 you just don't bounce back as fast. I was totally pissed off about the whole situation and the reaction I got from the Blackfeet. Shortly after the fight, a lot of Blackfeet came up to me and apologized for doubting me, they were just looking for answers and I was an easy target to strike out at. Still, it left a bad taste in my mouth and in Paula's.

Chapter 45

It has always amazed me on how Two-Fingers could just drop off the face of the Earth without a trace. How was that even possible? The private detective we hired did not turn up anything. After awhile, the FBI ignored us and when they did talk to us all they said was the investigation was "ongoing."

The 2016 elections were just a weeks away and Frank was way ahead in the polling, everybody assumed Two-Fingers was dead. Then something very strange happened, Frank Johnson was found dead in his Georgetown Mansion. There was no mystery surrounding his death, it was suicide. He was found in his living room dressed in his pajama's and robe with a suicide note in his hand. The note read, "Two-Fingers was right." That was all it said. "Two-Fingers was right."

I think about Frank's death and his suicide note a lot and it just doesn't make any sense to me. He was a shoe in to win re-election once Two-Fingers was out of the picture so it made no sense to kill himself. Over the years, Two-Fingers and I talked about what was worse, a person with no conscience or one with a guilty conscience? Two-Fingers always argued that it was the person with no conscious that was the most evil. For too many years to count, Frank acted like a person with no conscience. He did things in a sneaky and evil way without any outward signs of remorse. I think Frank finally found that voice, his conscious, buried deep under all of the excuses he made to himself as to why doing evil was okay. He found his conscience and when he did, the reality of his actions were more than he could handle.

Shortly after Frank's death, the liberal Big Sky Reporter ran a front page story about Frank's passing and his many accomplishments. The article was very long and at the end of it they said, "As always, when more information becomes available, we will report it to you in a timely and thorough manner."

When the elections were held, Pete Reynolds, who ran unopposed, barely won.

Results of the Tribal elections strengthened Two-Fingers legacy. Cindy Ann campaigned on his policies and won by a landslide and because she received more votes than any other candidate, she is the new Tribal Chairman. Stubby Grant and his Socialist/government dependency policies was swept from office. In the days leading up to the elections, he promised everybody a new cell phone, free satellite TV and extra commodity cheese, he was truly desperate. Thankfully, the Tribe didn't buy into his bullshit and he no longer sits on the Council.

Paula and I have been "honeymooning" lately and all is well on the home front. She is busy with me and work and seems to be getting back to normal but she still cries herself to sleep every night. I am not sure if that is because we are having sex again or if she is missing her brother.

For me, I find myself driving aimlessly around the Rez looking for Two-Fingers. I drive and drive hoping he is just wandering around lost, I suppose. My search continues and it will probably never end. Recently, after one of my drives, I came to the conclusion that I probably knew Two-Fingers better than anybody else in the entire world. But, as it turns out, I really didn't know him at all.

The End

Printed in the United States
By Bookmasters